continued . . .

ATLANTIS RISING

THE WARRIORS OF POSEIDON SERIES
BY ALYSSA DAY

Atlantis Rising
High Prince Conlan's Story

Atlantis Awakening
Lord Vengeance's Story

Atlantis Unleashed
Lord Justice's Story

Atlantis Unmasked
Alexios's Story

Atlantis Redeemed
Brennan's Story

Atlantis Betrayed
Christophe's Story

Vampire in Atlantis
Daniel's Story

Heart of Atlantis
High Priest Alaric's Story

SPECIALS
"Wild Hearts in Atlantis" from *Wild Thing*
Bastien's Story

"Shifter's Lady" from *Shifter*
Ethan's Story

HEART OF ATLANTIS

A Warriors of Poseidon Novel

ALYSSA DAY

BERKLEY SENSATION, NEW YORK

THE BERKLEY PUBLISHING GROUP
Published by the Penguin Group
Penguin Group (USA) Inc.
375 Hudson Street, New York, New York 10014, USA

Penguin Group (Canada), 90 Eglinton Avenue East, Suite 700, Toronto, Ontario M4P 2Y3, Canada (a division of Pearson Penguin Canada Inc.) • Penguin Books Ltd., 80 Strand, London WC2R 0RL, England • Penguin Group Ireland, 25 St. Stephen's Green, Dublin 2, Ireland (a division of Penguin Books Ltd.) • Penguin Group (Australia), 250 Camberwell Road, Camberwell, Victoria 3124, Australia (a division of Pearson Australia Group Pty. Ltd.) • Penguin Books India Pvt. Ltd., 11 Community Centre, Panchsheel Park, New Delhi—110 017, India • Penguin Group (NZ), 67 Apollo Drive, Rosedale, Auckland 0632, New Zealand (a division of Pearson New Zealand Ltd.) • Penguin Books (South Africa) (Pty.) Ltd., 24 Sturdee Avenue, Rosebank, Johannesburg 2196, South Africa

Penguin Books Ltd., Registered Offices: 80 Strand, London WC2R 0RL, England

HEART OF ATLANTIS

A Berkley Sensation Book / published by arrangement with the author

ISBN: 978-1-61793-659-3

BERKLEY SENSATION®
Berkley Sensation Books are published by The Berkley Publishing Group,
a division of Penguin Group (USA) Inc.,
375 Hudson Street, New York, New York 10014.
BERKLEY SENSATION® is a registered trademark of Penguin Group (USA) Inc.
The "B" design is a trademark of Penguin Group (USA) Inc.

PRINTED IN THE UNITED STATES OF AMERICA

This one is for my wonderful readers,
who have been asking me
for Alaric's story since you first read about him
in Atlantis Rising,
the book that started this whole fantastic journey for me.
I can never express
how much I have appreciated your support over
the years as we followed the
Warriors of Poseidon on their incredible adventures.
Thank you all from the bottom of my heart.

Dear Readers:

For those of you who have been with me and my hunky alpha male Warriors of Poseidon from the beginning, yes, this is it! You finally hold in your hot little hands the long-awaited story of Alaric, high priest of Poseidon, and his one true love, Quinn Dawson, the rebel leader and empath whose dark and tortured past may even rival Alaric's. All of you can go ahead and skip straight to the prologue, with my heartfelt thanks for making this series such a resounding success.

For those who are new to Atlantis, never fear! Each of my books stands alone and this one is no different. However, some of my readers told me that it might be more fun for those new to the series to know a little bit about the history of Atlantis and High Priest Alaric, in order to enjoy this book even more. So here is a touch of what you may have missed:

Eleven thousand years ago, during a battle between the gods of many different pantheons for control of the world, Atlantis escaped beneath the sea to avoid destruction. The sea god Poseidon, who has an affinity for humans and their boisterous, charming, lovable ways, created an elite group of warriors sworn to his service, each of whom takes an oath to protect humanity from evil.

Today, the world is in a precarious place. Vampires, rogue shape-shifters, and other dark creatures once thought to be only legend have declared their existence and are beginning to take over, treating humans as little more than cattle. The Warriors of Atlantis are needed more than ever to help hold back the attack. Now, finally, Atlantis must rise.

In order to do so, the seven missing jewels from Poseidon's Trident, scattered to the far reaches of the globe, must be found and restored. So far the warriors have located and retrieved all but one of the gems—and have found the loves of their lives along the way.

Now, all that remains is to find Poseidon's Pride, the final jewel, and only Alaric can accomplish this dangerous mission . . . if he chooses to do so. But he has vowed to remain at the side of the woman he loves and never leave her again, the fates of Atlantis and the entire world be damned.

Thanks for coming along on this amazing journey.

Alyssa

Research note for the fact junkies like me: As you know by now, I love to use historical fact and actual archaeological discoveries in my books. I was delighted to read that archaeologists at Gobekli Tepe in Turkey discovered what is believed to be the world's oldest temple, dated at approximately eleven thousand years old. Since that is exactly when Atlantis sank beneath the waves in my books, this fit in with the history of my Warriors of Poseidon perfectly. The Smithsonian Magazine reported:

Six miles from Urfa, an ancient city in southeastern Turkey, Klaus Schmidt has made one of the most startling archaeological discoveries of our time: massive carved stones about 11,000 years old, crafted and arranged by prehistoric people who had not yet developed metal tools or even pottery. The megaliths predate Stonehenge by some 6,000 years. The place is called Gobekli Tepe, and Schmidt, a German archaeologist who has been working here more than a decade, is convinced it's the site of the world's oldest temple. Read more at http:// www.smithsonianmag.com/history-archaeology/ gobekli-tepe.html.

The Warrior's Creed

We will wait. And watch. And protect.
And serve as first warning on the eve of humanity's
   destruction.
Then, and only then, Atlantis will rise.
For we are the Warriors of Poseidon, and the mark
   of the Trident we bear serves as witness to our
   sacred duty to safeguard mankind.

Prologue

The wilderness near Sedona, Arizona, just past twilight

Alaric, sword at the ready, stepped into the path of the oncoming vampire and struck its head from its body before it had a chance to get anywhere near Quinn.

"Stay down," he shouted at her, another futile plea disguised as a command. She wouldn't listen. She never listened.

Quinn, all smoldering heat and explosive fury wrapped up in a small, dark-haired package, smiled at him, and he nearly lost his balance.

"A gentleman wouldn't keep yelling at me," she said, firing one of the many guns she kept on her at all times. Then firing another. "Why are they attacking now? How did they find us? I'm sick to death of battling vampires and shifters, and it's bad enough when we know *why* they're after us. This? This is just crazy."

"I never claimed to be a gentleman, and most vampires are, by their very nature, insane," he said, launching himself into the air toward a pair of wolf shifters that clearly intended to claim either a rebel leader or a high priest of Atlantis—or both—for a late-night snack. The moonlight glinted blue streaks in Quinn's untidy mop of hair, and he had a fraction of a second to wonder why he was noticing her hair in the midst of a heated battle. Why the scent of her skin and curve of her lips formed the puzzle pieces of his greatest obsession.

He refused to admit the truth of it, even to himself. Battle now. The rest of it later.

Alaric released the energy sword and conjured ice daggers as he flew up and over the shifters, and then hurled both of them down at precisely the exact time and angle needed to simultaneously pierce both of their hearts. They fell, thudding to the ground together in a shapeless mass of unrealized rage and thwarted ambition.

Enemies were here to deal death tonight, and Alaric, who'd been Atlantean warrior and high priest to Poseidon for centuries, had no intention of allowing even one of them to succeed. Not if he could help it.

"Beware," he called out, but a tiger's scream drew his attention from Quinn after she shot an attacking wolf shifter.

Jack, one of fewer than a dozen tiger shifters still in existence, fought like a berserker from old, only a dozen paces from where Alaric and Quinn stood. A vampire's head rolled from its body seconds after Jack struck. Serai, the Atlantean princess Jack protected, trembled and backed away.

"Help Serai," Quinn shouted at Alaric. "She's just out of stasis after eleven thousand years. It's not like she knows how to protect herself from this."

But seconds later Serai transformed into a beast that had been extinct for millennia, using ancient magic long forgotten. A shimmer of brilliant silver power surrounded her, and then a saber-toothed tiger roared where an Atlantean princess had shivered in the cool night air.

The cacophony of battle, rude and loud and clashing, stilled for a frozen moment in time as attackers and defenders alike swung toward the sound of an ancient, deadly predator. The forest itself froze as nature's darkest memories conjured up long-forgotten fears.

Quinn's small guns barked out a warning—once, twice, thrice—and Alaric whirled to find a dead vampire slamming into the ground at his feet. He looked up to meet Quinn's gaze, all smoke and mystery in the moonlight.

"I may not have any magic, but I do okay," she said, shrugging her slender shoulders.

Before she'd finished speaking, Alaric was leaping toward her, calling power to himself and forming energy spheres in both hands. The trio of bloodsuckers rushed at Quinn with deadly intent, and Alaric knew that whoever had masterminded this attack had painted a target on her. Kill the North American rebel leader, and maybe the entire human rebellion falls apart.

He almost laughed at the thought. Maybe not the rebellion, but a single man—both warrior and priest—yes, that man would fall apart. And the world would be lucky to survive it.

Quinn saw him coming and swung around in a half circle so he could stand at her back. She fired her guns, and he hurled energy spheres with both hands, dealing oblivion and the true death to vampires and shape-shifters both.

When the wave of attackers subsided, either dead or regrouping, Alaric heard the single vampire who was actually on their side shout Serai's name.

"That's Daniel," Quinn said. "What happened?"

"Serai has fallen," Alaric said grimly. "Whether from wounds or from too-ambitious use of her magic after eleven millennia of stasis sleep, I cannot tell from here."

Daniel flew through the air toward Serai and landed with one foot on each side of her waist, standing over her prone body. He snarled something at her and then slashed his crossed daggers at an attacking vampire with such preternatural speed that even Alaric almost didn't see him do it.

He saw the vamp's head roll across the ground, though.

"We have to help them," Quinn said, and she started to run.

Alaric did not waste a single breath arguing with her. He simply followed her.

Protected her.

Until someone else screamed, and Quinn skidded to a halt so abruptly that he nearly knocked her over.

"The tiger is down," someone cried out, anguish raw in her voice.

"Jack? Jack!" Quinn shouted his name and changed course. Alaric knew that if Jack were killed, Quinn might not survive it. The shifter and Quinn had fought the rebellion together for long years, as close friends and powerful allies.

But they'd never been lovers. Or so Alaric hoped, but doubts stalked him some days with caustic thoughts. Thoughts he only wrestled with in the deepest reaches of the dark, when nightmares donned their garments and walked the surfaces of mortal minds.

He knew that *Jack* loved *her*. That was hard enough to accept.

He shook his mind free of mental meanderings as they reached Jack, and Quinn collapsed down to her knees on the cold, rocky ground and fell on top of the blood-soaked tiger.

"Jack!" she screamed, over and over and over, like a hammer beating at the fragile bulwarks of Alaric's sanity. "Save him. You have to save him."

Alaric called to Poseidon to lend him the magic he would need to heal the dying tiger. He threw his head back, closed his eyes, and strained every muscle and tendon as he forced his body to hold power beyond measure. He turned to Jack and thrust the power into the tiger's body, only to have it slam back into him in a vicious backlash that knocked him off his feet and smashed him to the ground.

Alaric could heal nearly any wound, but even he, high priest of the sea god himself, could not retrieve those who had gone past the gates of death. Now it only remained to destroy the woman he loved. He drew in a deep breath, in spite of the acrid scents of battle, bile, and blood that infused the air.

"I'm sorry, Quinn. He's dead."

As the rebel fighters who were still capable of walking drew near, Quinn screamed her denial and threw her body over Jack, as if to protect him from the Reaper's merciless gaze. But death came to all mortals—even Atlanteans—and Alaric's only thought now was to remove her from this place before their enemies returned. He met Daniel's gaze and realized that the vampire was experiencing Quinn's anguish through the blood bond, even as Daniel held a semiconscious Serai in his arms.

"I cannot help her," Daniel said quietly, his face grim.

"We must leave before they return. We've lost more than half of our fighters, and I have no idea what reserves of soldiers they can call upon."

Alaric crouched down next to Quinn. "You can't stay here. You know Jack wouldn't have wanted it," he said, touching her arm.

"No, leave me alone!" She wrenched away from him, but then grabbed his hand and pulled it toward Jack's prone form.

"Wait. You can heal him," she said imploringly. "You healed me before. I've seen you heal lots of people. You can do it. Fix him."

"He's gone, Quinn. I can heal grievous wounds, it is true, and you know I would do anything for you, but I cannot heal death. Only the gods can do that."

Quinn screamed again, tears rolling, unheeded, down her face; sorrow pouring forth from a wellspring too deep to be denied.

Serai, conscious now but still in Daniel's arms, suddenly spoke. "He's not gone," she said, and icy chills chased each other down Alaric's spine at the sound of her magic-drenched voice. "He's almost gone, but a small part of him remains."

Alaric stared at her and raised his hands as if to block any attack Serai might try. She made a dismissing motion and ignored him, focused entirely on Quinn and Jack.

"Put me down. There next to Jack," Serai said to Daniel, who obeyed instantly.

Alaric's eyes narrowed. Ally Daniel might be, but a primal wariness in Alaric warned him against allowing a vampire so near to an Atlantean princess. It was, however, a problem for another time.

Serai gently nudged Quinn to one side and lay across Jack's body, but Quinn shoved her away.

"No! What are you doing? Get off him!"

Serai turned to Alaric and spoke to him through the Atlantean mental pathway.

She must let me try to reach him—I believe a tendril of his essence remains on this side of death's gate.

It took only a moment for Alaric to recognize the deep magic in Serai's aura, and he gently pulled Quinn back and away from Jack.

"Give her a chance, Quinn. The ancients had magic we have long forgotten."

Quinn trembled in his arms as Serai ran gentle hands across the tiger's bloody fur. The princess began to sing wordlessly before turning to Quinn.

"Part of him lives, but only his animal side is still— barely—on this side of the river of death. I can call to the tiger that is Jack and help him come back, but his human side is almost certainly lost forever."

Quinn's suspicion all but radiated out from her body. "What *are* you?"

"I am Serai of Atlantis, and the Emperor gifted me with ancient magic not seen on this world since before my continent dove beneath the oceans," Serai responded, silvery light shimmering around her. "I gift you his choice, as another once gifted me the choice of life or death for one I loved. Shall I let him seek out his ancestors in the afterlife or do you wish him to live, though it be perhaps only a half life?"

"I choose life," Quinn said fiercely. "You make him live, do you hear me? No matter what it takes. Make at least part of him live, and I can find the rest of him somehow. Someday. You *make him live*."

Serai began to sing, and currents of magic danced around her in a ballet of delicate power so intricate and complex that Alaric doubted anyone still walking the earth had seen its like. Mere seconds passed before Jack's body arched up off the ground, and he coughed harshly.

"Does he know who he is?" Alaric demanded.

"Honestly, I don't know what he knows," Serai said. "Or

who he knows. If he has reverted fully to tiger and only tiger, he's not safe to be around."

"Thank you. No matter what else, you brought him back from death. We'll figure the rest out. I owe him that much," Quinn said.

Alaric healed the tiger's bloody wounds and tried to feel for a shred of humanity, but he could not. "I can't tell. I just don't know. Shape-shifters are too different from Atlanteans, and Poseidon's power recoils from trying to analyze the mind of a tiger."

"Your magic is unbalanced without the soul-meld," Serai said, rocking Alaric back on his heels.

The soul-meld? When he was sworn to an eternity of celibacy and isolation?

"What do you mean? I am the most powerful—"

"Yes, yes, I've heard it," Serai interrupted. "Most powerful high priest in the history of Atlantis. But it's not true, you know. I've been around for all of them since Atlantis dove beneath the sea. Your power is not even close to what Nereus wielded. At least, before his wife died and he almost drowned the world."

"What—"

Quinn cut him off. "I don't care. I don't care about any of it right now. Not the bankers, or the rebellion, or any damn part of it. I sure as hell don't care about Atlantean ancient history. I'm leaving, and I'm taking Jack with me. Somewhere he can be safe, until we figure this out. I owe him that. I owe him my life, several times over."

"Of course. I know just the place." Alaric drew in a deep breath and called to power, and he swore a new and different oath—one that he had no intention of ever breaking. "I'll take you there now, and I'll never, ever leave your side again."

He called to the portal, wondering if the capricious gateway magic would bother to answer him. As the familiar silvery ovoid shape formed, he remembered his duty and turned to Serai.

"You should come with us, princess," Alaric said. "We can help you."

"You need *my* help, priest. I have protection beyond your knowledge in the presence of the mage beside me." She moved closer to Daniel, who snapped his head up and stared at Alaric.

"I can help, possibly. Let me try to reach Jack," the vampire said.

"What can you do? Try to blood bond a tiger?" Quinn shook her head. "Go away, Daniel, there's no need for your special skills here."

"I have forgotten more magic than most of your human witches ever possess, Quinn, and one of my talents as senior mage of the Nightwalker Guild was to teach others to call out to the souls of dying mortals," Daniel said. "Let me try. It can't hurt him, not now. Maybe I can help."

Quinn nodded, and Alaric, in spite of serious misgivings, allowed it. He felt the brush of powerful magic, so very foreign to his own that he couldn't begin to comprehend it, and then the feeling passed as swiftly as a bird seeking prey in the cool night air.

The tiger shivered and then lay still. Daniel shook his head.

"I don't know if he'll ever return. All I know is that he's somewhere in there. Deep inside, or maybe even not inside the tiger, but very nearby. But he won't come back because we push him. He warned me quite specifically that if we try, he'll choose never to come back."

"If he thinks he's more stubborn that I am, he's sadly mistaken. Let's go, Alaric. Take us away, and give me time to let this tiger heal and find himself again," Quinn said, finally rising from her knees.

Alaric took her hand and called to his magic to lift Jack on a wave of power. He took a step toward the portal and then hesitated.

Duty, again. Somehow, after centuries thinking of nothing else, it was suddenly so hard to remember. He looked to Reisen, the warrior who had first betrayed Atlantis and now worked so hard to redeem himself. Or so Quinn said. Alaric had his doubts. One never trusted a traitor a second time. But Reisen wasn't his concern. Healing the injured was.

"Do others here need healing? I forget my duties."

Reisen shook his head. "No, we have only minor injuries in those still alive. You . . . you go to Atlantis?"

"You can return home," Alaric said reluctantly. "Your exile was self-imposed. Conlan offered forgiveness and healing."

Reisen didn't move. "I have one final mission to perform for Quinn."

The small human from Quinn's group moved closer to Reisen and offered her thanks for his help as tears streamed down her pale face. She said something to Quinn; something about taking care of Jack, but Alaric didn't listen. Didn't care.

Everything he cared about in the world was wrapped up in Quinn's happiness, and he'd failed her. He'd been unable to bring Jack back to himself. He started to follow her as she headed toward the portal, head bent, gaze on the ground. Her shoulders hunched around her neck, as if awaiting another blow.

Alaric issued a final warning to Daniel, whose quest with Serai must succeed, and then he and Jack, who still rested on his cushion of magic, followed Quinn into the shimmer of light, which would hopefully take them to the one place he doubted any would think to look for them.

Not even the sea god himself.

"Take us to Mount Fuji."

Chapter 1

A hidden cave inside of Mount Fuji, Japan

The portal opened and Alaric, warrior and high priest of Atlantis, stepped through, followed by a shell-shocked rebel leader and a five-hundred-pound tiger shape-shifter who might have permanently lost his humanity.

"Oh, Alaric," said the ancient man who stood waiting for them, sighing and shaking his head. "You do get into the most fascinating trouble."

"Interesting you should say that, Archelaus," Alaric said. "I need a place to hide for a time, while Quinn tries to help Jack remember that he's human, too, and not just a tiger."

Quinn barely glanced at him, her eyes dull with pain and exhaustion, but she never let go of his hand. It was more physical contact than he'd allowed himself to have with her in a very long time.

Archelaus took them all in with his sharp gaze. The old man, long since retired as mentor to the Atlantean warrior training academy, never missed anything.

"And Atlantis? Are the Seven Isles still in jeopardy?"

"Aren't they always?" Alaric sliced a hand through the air

in dismissal of the topic. "We need a place to rest. Food. A refuge—we need to hide a tiger."

Archelaus pointed at something behind them. "Who is that?"

Alaric whirled around, shocked to see a stranger—a delicate, dark-haired woman—step out of the portal.

"Who are you?" he demanded, pushing Quinn behind him. None but Atlanteans could call the portal, and this woman clearly was not Atlantean, but of Asian descent.

She blinked in apparent confusion. "*Konnichiwa*," she began, offering a basic greeting in Japanese, but then she continued in ancient Atlantean as she slowly collapsed until she lay curled up on the ground next to the tiger, who ignored her completely. "I am the spirit of the portal, and I am this woman, who came to Mount Fuji to die."

"*You* came here to die. *We* came here to force Jack to live," Quinn said, and then she started laughing, a terrible, almost hysterical laugh. "Lucky we have Poseidon's high priest with us, isn't it?"

Alaric stared down at Quinn and fought the tidal wave of unfamiliar, unwanted emotion threatening to swamp him. "Yes. I will do what I can for him, as I promised."

Archelaus sighed again. "You have amazingly bad timing, my friend."

"Timing has nothing to do with need," Alaric snapped, finally out of patience with the day, the situation, and the centuries of standing alone as priest to a capricious god.

"Timing has everything to do with danger," the older man returned calmly, as he draped his sweater over the unconscious woman who'd claimed to be what she couldn't possibly be. "The vampire goddess Anubisa is back from her sojourn in the land of Chaos, and this time she swears to destroy Atlantis and every member of the Atlantean royal family. You have never been more needed by your people in your entire life, I would imagine."

"I am needed here," Alaric said, staring at Quinn. "Atlantis can burn in the nine hells for all I care. I have sacrificed enough to Poseidon. My days as high priest are done."

Quinn collapsed onto a low bench against one wall of the room or cave or wherever they'd ended up. Strange that she'd spent more time in caves since becoming the leader of the North American human rebel contingent than she'd ever dreamed possible. Straight from caves in Sedona, where she'd battled vampires and evil bankers, to Japan. A wave of grief and exhaustion, fought back and repressed for far too long, swept through her and threatened to drown her in futility and despair.

Jack. Her comrade; her partner in the rebellion. Her friend. She could finally admit she loved him with some small part of her stony, blackened heart, although it wasn't the kind of love he might want. She loved him like a brother; the one she'd never had and had never known she wanted. Her big, scary, wounded warrior of a brother, who just happened to shift into a quarter ton of tiger sometimes. They'd fought together for years—years of trying to fight back the tide of darkness after the vampires announced to the world that they were real and then promptly proceeded to try to take it over. No matter how hard they pretended otherwise, vampires viewed humans as sheep for the slaughter. Unfortunately, most people were easily fooled or else too apathetic to care that the town's new mayor or sheriff just happened to be a bloodsucker making a power grab.

Easy enough to make people disappear from behind the authority of a badge. Even the FBI's P-Ops division had discovered that, when they'd found traitors in their midst. The president fired the director of Paranormal Operations and half of his staff when that inconvenient truth had surfaced.

Quinn sighed, fully aware that her brain was jumping from thought to thought in a futile effort to quit thinking about Jack. If they couldn't help him . . . but they would. *Alaric* would. She refused to question her unshakable belief in Alaric or even to peer more closely at the reasons for it. She didn't have time to get involved with *any* man—and certainly not with a man who was bound by both sworn oath and magic to Poseidon. The sea god himself, swimming out of the page of legends and into the middle of her pain-wracked, screwed-up life.

She stared at the floor, unable to muster even a spark of interest as Alaric conferred with the older man. Archelaus. Although *older* might not apply. Just because the man looked to be at least a century old, appearances were deceiving with Atlanteans. A casual glance would put Alaric in his early thirties or even late twenties, until the one doing the glancing looked into the dark caverns of those emerald-green eyes.

Ancient eyes. Centuries of brutal knowledge, blood, and death had passed before them—those eyes that were always faintly glowing with the overspill of magical power he couldn't quite contain. He was at least five hundred years old. Strong enough to be the most powerful high priest Atlantis had ever known, or so some said.

Differences of opinion on that subject had been emerging, however. Politics. Like she gave a flying crap about politics. Bottom line: he didn't look like a man who'd lived half a thousand years . . . until you looked into his eyes.

He was nearly six and a half feet of pure, primal warrior. His black hair had grown past his shoulders; it had been a few inches shorter when she'd first met him. Not much time for haircuts when a man was saving the world, probably.

She laughed to herself. He'd saved her life and broken her heart. Strange that healing one bullet wound could accomplish all of that.

She closed her eyes but could still see his face, as if it had imprinted on her mind with the strength of a hammer into molten brass. A face too strong—too male—to be called beautiful, but too perfect to be called anything else. All hard lines and sculpted angles. The face of a man who commanded absolute obedience, unqualified respect, and . . . something else. Something he'd never wanted.

Terror.

Vampires and rogue shape-shifters alike were terrified of the rumors and the reality. Quinn had heard men call him the high priest of death—but they never called him that to his face, or even very loudly. That, by itself, was no bad thing in a warrior priest, to be feared by his enemies.

But it was more than that. Even Alaric's allies sometimes feared him, and Quinn had seen how brutal a blow that was to him. Poseidon's high priest would be called a wizard of the highest level if he practiced his magic in the human hierarchy. Hell, he blew the hierarchy out of the water.

Ha. Water. Atlantis. She'd made a funny.

Alaric shifted to capture her in his hot green gaze, and she wondered if he knew she'd been thinking about him. Archelaus said something, and Alaric turned his head back toward the man, giving Quinn the chance to study him unobserved. Even in ripped and bloodstained clothes from the battle they'd just fought, his body was a seductive delight, worthy of starring in any woman's fantasies. All hard muscle and perfect proportion. Even she, who'd spent the past decade or so surrounded by warriors and soldiers in her rebel army, had to admit that Alaric was in a class all by himself.

And he could never, ever be hers. Even now, devastated and destroyed by what had happened to Jack, she felt a dull pang at that.

He turned toward her again, and this time he stared a blazing path down her body. Probably looking for any injury he could heal with his magic. She herself wasn't much to look at. It never failed to surprise her that an Atlantean god of a man would be interested in a scruffy, skinny freedom fighter who dressed in other people's castoffs and hadn't worn makeup since she was sixteen years old. Back when the world was innocent of all the dark and twisted things that did far worse than merely go bump in the night.

Alaric headed toward her with that nearly vampire-fast speed of his, and he was kneeling before her almost before she'd seen him take his first step.

"Are you injured?" It was command more than question. The *Tell Me Now* was implied.

"No." She lifted her chin, knowing he'd read her defiance. Not caring much.

His eyes narrowed, and he gently grasped her jaw in one strong hand, tilting her chin to the side.

"You lie. Blood is seeping from this scrape on your neck."

A pulse of blue-green light shimmered briefly, and she knew from the accompanying warmth that he'd healed her.

She attempted a smile. Failed. Settled for truth. "Your manners could use some work. 'You lie.' Really?"

He released her chin but rested his hand against her now-healed skin, as if unwilling to break the contact. "How is stating fact a breach of manners?"

This time, she did smile, although it was a mere quirk of her lips. He was untamed and always would be, like the other feral man in her life.

"Jack," she said, her voice anguished. "Alaric, will we ever find a way to restore his humanity?"

Her warrior priest turned his powerful gaze to the tiger, lying so still on the ground.

"I will do all in my power, Quinn, but I cannot lie to you. The chances are not good."

Chapter 2

Six weeks later

Quinn sat in her claustrophobic room and stared at nothing, trying to ignore the quarter ton of tiger leaning up against her. She wondered if she should take another shower, wander back to the garden, or simply bash her head against the wall to alleviate the unmitigated disappointment and sense of failure. As always, the idea of showers in a cave vaguely amused her. She hadn't bothered to ask how Archelaus had installed showers and other modern amenities in a cave. She'd seen enough of Atlantean power over the element of water to take it for granted. Of course, in a world where vampires, shape-shifters, and even the Fae had walked out of fairy tales and into reality a little more than a decade ago, there were many, many things that nobody bothered to disbelieve anymore.

The crystal clear water in her cup was from a mountain stream right here on Mount Fuji—no magic involved except that of Mother Nature herself. It tasted better than any water she'd ever had before. She stared down at it as if answers to her multitude of problems might be hidden at the bottom of the cup.

Whiskey would have been better. She could usually find

an answer or two at the bottom of a whiskey bottle. Even if they were the wrong answers, at least she had a place to start. The one thing she'd never, ever been good at was feeling helpless, and now she'd lived through six entire weeks of being completely and utterly unable to help Jack.

They'd rested. He'd healed from his physical injuries and eaten enough to clear out half of Japan's livestock, probably. But human Jack—*her* Jack—still hadn't put in an appearance, and it was looking less and less likely every day.

Jack looked briefly around the room and then dropped his head back down on her leg. The low bed sagged from the weight of five hundred pounds of tiger, but she wasn't about to tell him to sleep on the floor. He'd voluntarily followed her into the room and up onto the bed, after ignoring her for the past week. She was glad and—maybe, just maybe—a little bit hopeful that he'd followed her at all.

She hesitantly put a hand on his head, and his eyes snapped open. Another mystery of the shape-shift: his eyes were green in human form and pure amber fire as a tiger. She stared into their depths, thinking of that saying about eyes being the windows to the soul. If it were true, then there was nobody home in Jack's soul.

Nobody human.

Only a disturbingly feral intelligence peered out at her from behind that glowing amber. She steeled herself against the shudder trying to shake its way through her body and rubbed one silky ear between her fingers. Jack closed his eyes, and they sat there, two wounded warriors, heart-sore and silent, for several long minutes. Jack's rumbling snore was hypnotic, and Quinn's eyes started to close. Jack tensed and lifted his massive head a few seconds before she heard Alaric's voice.

He'd been there for her, staying in the background and giving her the time and space she'd needed to rest and heal; the time she'd needed to try to help Jack recover his humanity. But during every minute of those long weeks, no matter how her heart filled with despair over Jack, Alaric had remained in her awareness. A solitary presence, brooding and watchful. He'd told her when Serai and Daniel had succeeded in their quest; he'd let her know that Riley and the baby were doing well. Other than that, he'd honored her request for time alone, but she could tell from the intensity of his emotion that his patience was coming to an end.

"Are you ready to talk to me yet?" he asked quietly, dividing his attention between her face and the tiger at her side.

"Where is that woman, or portal spirit, or whatever she is?" Quinn asked. She hadn't had the energy to be curious about anything before now.

"Archelaus and his people are tending to her. As you know, this place is a sanctuary, for those with the most dire need. They are well prepared to care for lost souls."

"Is that what we are? Is that why you brought us here?" She heard the bitterness in her voice but was too tired to try to disguise it. The fight had been too long. The losses too high. More than a decade of her life fighting for human independence from the vampires and shape-shifters who were taking over the country and the world, and she was no further along now than she'd been as a desperate teenager. Even with the Atlanteans on her side, it never felt like enough. Never felt like the rebels could win. Now there were even some humans joining Team Evil—black magic practitioners and, horribly, non-magical human collaborators who willingly served the bad guys, like sheep volunteering for the slaughter.

She shook her head. "Let them do it. Why do we even care? It's social Darwinism."

"What are you talking about?" Alaric crossed the room to her side and pulled her to her feet, and she caught her breath at the electricity that surged between their clasped hands. Even the lightest touch from him was like a roundhouse punch to her emotions. She didn't need to be an emotional empath to know what he was feeling right now.

Burning need. Intense desire. A furnace of wanting seared between them, and she fought to maintain her balance. She put a hand on his chest to hold him at a distance, but the feel of his heartbeat under her fingers only made it worse.

"I need for you to put a damper on all the strong emotion,

please," she whispered. "I don't have the reserves of strength right now to handle it. I've spent so much energy trying to convince Jack to come back—"

He brushed a kiss on her forehead, and her knees nearly gave out from the tidal wave of longing she felt from just that brief caress. But after that—nothing. It was as if a metal shield had slammed down between them. Suddenly, she couldn't feel even a hint of his emotions.

Perversely, she hated the loss of them. She looked a question at him.

"I've had hundreds of years to learn to block my feelings, *mi amara*. Even a powerful *aknasha* such as yourself cannot penetrate my defenses," he said calmly. Or at least he *sounded* calm. For all she could tell, he might have been boiling with suppressed emotion, but not an ounce of it leaked out.

His words finally registered in her tired mind, and she pulled away from him. "Don't call me your beloved, when you know we can never be together, okay? *Aknasha* is fine; we all know I'm an empath. But I can't be your *amara*."

She turned away and whispered, almost to herself, "Even if I want to be."

Jack, as if sensing the tension in the room, lifted his lips away from his fangs and growled at Alaric.

"I'd almost rather he had enough fight in him to attack you," she said.

"Thank you," Alaric replied dryly. "Your concern for my safety is touching."

She rolled her eyes. "I'm not worried about *you*. I've seen you in action, remember?"

Jack turned those huge golden eyes to her and growled again, almost as if he understood her. He and Alaric had thrown enough testosterone at each other since they'd met that the Jack she knew—*human* Jack—would never have put up with her comment. The fact that tiger Jack didn't seem to like it either gave her another moment of hope.

Archelaus appeared in the doorway and nodded to her. "My lady, you want your privacy, I know, but our guest wishes to speak with the two of you."

Quinn had to think for a second or two before she remembered what guest he was talking about. By then, Alaric had caught her arm in a firm grasp, as if to prevent her from moving. She pointedly looked down at his hand and then up at him.

"No. I don't trust her," he commanded.

"Of course you're not talking to me, are you? You would know better than to try to give me orders, Your Royal Priestliness, wouldn't you?" she asked in a voice so sweet it made Alaric blink.

"You—"

She cut him off. "Stop it. As far as I know, I'm still the leader of the North American rebel alliance, even after this hiatus. I'm not a helpless woman who needs the big, strong Atlantean to tell her what to do. Let's go see this woman."

"But—"

"The sooner we see her, the sooner we can find out who she really is," Quinn explained, in her most reasonable tone. She figured reasonableness was better than pulling out her Glock and shooting him in the foot. He'd just heal himself, anyway, so it wasn't like he'd learn a lesson in Not Being Bossy.

She yanked her arm out of his grasp and strode across the chamber toward Archelaus, surprised to find the older man grinning like a delighted child.

"Oh, Alaric, you are in so much trouble, aren't you?" Archelaus said, shaking his head.

Alaric snarled something in a language that might have been ancient Atlantean, but whatever he'd said, it only made Archelaus laugh out loud. "Good luck with that, youngling."

Quinn, who knew Alaric was at least five hundred years past being called a youngling, shot a suspicious look at Archelaus but decided she was too tired to care about the relative ages of Atlantean warriors. "Just take us to her. Jack, are you coming?"

Jack slouched down off the bed and padded after her as she followed Archelaus down the stone corridor toward a kind of courtyard. The area was enclosed by the walls of the cave, but high up on one side an opening allowed sunshine to stream into the space. The surprise at first had been the garden flourishing in the heart of a cavern, filled with fantastical flowers that she'd never seen before. She noticed a trace of a smile cross Alaric's face and wondered at the source. She realized they'd never both been in the garden at the same time before.

She raised an eyebrow. "You like flowers?"

"It's a miniature replica of the main palace courtyard in Atlantis, even to the tiny fountain burbling in the corner," he said.

Archelaus nodded. "Yes. A bit of home I couldn't resist bringing with me. My friends are always asking for cuttings and seedlings, so I fear I have introduced Atlantean life to the surface before Conlan was quite ready."

"I doubt the high prince is concerned about this kind of population," Alaric said dryly.

Quinn tilted her head and stared up at the jagged edges of the window, which was actually not much more than a cleft torn in the ground above. "Had any hikers fallen in recently?"

Archelaus smiled. "As you know, there is a powerful repellent spell in the area above. I may not have mentioned this before, but no hiker has come near the spot since the last shogun, Tokugawa Yoshinobu, came on a pilgrimage to the sacred Fuji-san in 1867."

"The mountain is sacred to the Japanese?"

The Atlantean elder nodded. "Yes. Certainly more at that time than now, as so many of our gods and sacred places have lost their meaning in this modern age."

"But not to you," she pointed out, slanting a long look at Alaric. "Your god, Poseidon, is as real to you today as he ever was."

Jack, who was prowling around the edges of the room, lifted his shaggy head and aimed his amber gaze at Alaric, growling softly.

Alaric ignored the tiger. He crossed his arms on his chest and stared right back at Quinn. "As real, and even more demanding. Yet not all of us will continue to dance to his tune forever."

"You are his sworn high priest, my son," Archelaus said, his face troubled. "What you speak is worse than blasphemy; it is akin to breaking an oath."

Alaric turned away from the man, as if dismissing the topic, and pointed at the dark-haired woman sitting silently on a bench in the middle of the space. Her back was toward them, but Quinn recognized the cut of her hair and her slight figure.

"Yes, that is our visitor. Her name is Noriko, and it is also Gailea, as far as we can understand. She speaks in an odd language—a confusion of ancient Atlantean mixed with Japanese. Between my friend Mizuki and myself, we've managed to cobble together what we think she means, but she mostly has sat silent, as you see her, since she arrived, refusing to talk much at all. She was very ill when she arrived and now she appears to be somewhat better, but she will not allow us to examine her, nor will she allow Alaric near enough to attempt a healing." Archelaus frowned. "I confess I do not know how to proceed with her. I am merely an old warrior, not wise enough in the ways of women or lost souls."

The woman turned her head and pinned her dark gaze on Archelaus. "You are quite wise, and your heart is evident, Old One," she said in perfect, lightly accented English.

Alaric stepped forward slightly so that he stood between Quinn and the woman. Probably thought he was being subtle about his protectiveness. Quinn rolled her eyes as she dodged around him.

"Now that you have deigned to speak to me, state your name and how you appeared in our portal," Alaric demanded.

The woman rose gracefully to her feet and bowed, dark eyes flashing with a hint of defiance. "I needed time to discover the shape of my current reality. I am Gailea, the one you know as the spirit of the portal, and you, Alaric, are as arrogant as ever, I see."

"The shape of your reality. Yeah, because that makes

sense," Quinn said, studying Gailea's delicate Japanese features and raising an eyebrow, not caring that the other woman recognized her skepticism. "You look so much like the other ancient Atlantean woman I know. You and Serai could practically be sisters."

Gailea bowed again, this time toward Quinn. "And I am also Noriko, the woman you see before you. She came to Mount Fuji to die. She recently discovered that she had an advanced stage of cancer, and having lost her family to the tsunami, she believed she had no reason to live."

Shame flushed Quinn's cheeks with heat, but she knew better, after years of dealing with traitors, spies, and villains, to take anything that anyone said at face value. "And we should believe you why, exactly?"

Noriko/Gailea calmly said quite a long paragraph of . . . something.

Alaric snapped to attention, whatever it was that she'd said. His body tensed and he clenched his hands into fists at his sides.

"Poseidon's long-term plans and schemes can no longer rule my life," he snapped. "I don't want to know what you think."

Before Gailea could respond, Jack snarled viciously and leapt through the air toward her, knocking the woman/portal spirit to one side. As Noriko backed away toward the cave wall, Quinn automatically drew her gun and dropped into a battle-ready crouch; years of fighting with Jack at her side had trained her responses to his actions to be instantaneous. She followed Jack's gaze up and up. The light in the chamber suddenly dimmed, and everyone else looked up at the opening in the top of the room, too, just in time to see the first of a wave of wild creatures with bared fangs and outstretched claws leap down through the air.

Quinn's mouth dropped open. "Monkeys? Now we're being attacked by flying monkeys?"

Chapter 3

Alaric didn't even blink at the sight of a dozen or more man-sized brutish apes leaping down upon them. Their red faces contorted into feral grimaces as they shrieked and roared. After hundreds of years as a warrior and Poseidon's high priest, veteran of thousands of battles and survivor of nearly as many deadly schemes, Alaric was surprised by nothing anymore. Especially when Quinn was around.

Not even flying monkeys.

"Quinn, get out of here," he barked, as he called to his magic. First, he wove a powerful protection spell over the barrier to prevent further intruders from dropping down on their heads. Then he formed twin spheres of blue-green electricity in his outstretched palms, and he hurled the first with fatal accuracy at the lead ape. For an instant its brown fur shone with a luminous blue light, like a bizarre mammalian form of deep-sea creature. The light abruptly vanished as the ape collapsed and died.

The harsh bark of gunfire reverberated through the room, and the second ape dropped to the ground, dead, directly in front of Gailea. Alaric whipped his head around to glare at Quinn, who glared right back at him.

"Run from danger?" she called out, taking fresh aim at another attacker. "Have you *met* me?"

Alaric snarled out an Atlantean oath and whirled to protect Gailea, but she'd already thrown up a protective shield around herself in the form of a miniature dome of transparent energy. Two of the apes thudded against it as he watched, but it held firm.

Alaric spared a glance for his other companions, and discovered Archelaus wielding a sword he'd produced from somewhere, slashing and stabbing at the creatures in a whirlwind frenzy. Across the room, Jack tore into two more of them with the primal fury of an apex predator.

"Behind you," Quinn shouted, and Alaric formed a sword of pure, flashing magic and spun around, slicing through the air and sending three of them to the nine hells. The echoing report of Quinn's gun barked again and again, and only the sure knowledge that none of the creatures came even close to approaching her kept Alaric sane.

One of the apes jumped on Alaric's back and dug its sharp claws deep into muscle and flesh. Alaric roared out in wordless denial, twisted his body enough to grab the large furry head, and wrenched it to one side. The thick neck snapped with an audible crack, and the ape fell heavily to the ground. After that, it was fur and fangs and blood for several long minutes until the final ape crashed into the cave and met Alaric's grim brand of justice.

Alaric scanned the room and glanced up at the skylight entrance, but no new creatures appeared. The room was filled with dead and dying apes, but as far as he could tell, none of his companions were injured. He knew Quinn, at least, was unharmed. He could always feel everything she felt. Every single scratch. Even the tiniest bruise.

It was enough to drive a man mad.

"Jack, hold!" Archelaus ran across the room toward the snarling tiger far faster than his age seemed to allow. "We need one of them alive to talk."

It was a futile attempt. Jack never even hesitated as he leapt up and bit down on the shoulder and neck of the final ape still attempting to fight. The tiger shook the ape in his mouth in a grim parody of a house cat with a rat, and then he hurled the dead ape across the room and roared; whether in triumph or defiance, Alaric was unsure.

"Damn it, Jack," Quinn said, but her voice was filled with exhaustion, not anger. "What if they were shifters? They must have been. It would have helped if we could have coaxed one of the monkeys back to human shape long enough to tell us what is going on here."

Jack bared his fangs in Quinn's general direction but didn't return to human form to argue with her, unfortunately. He might never again regain human form. But that was another problem, for another time.

The floor was covered with the bloody shapes of the current problem.

"They're definitely shape-shifters, but they invaded the sanctuary," Archelaus said. His face was drawn and pale, as though he'd aged a hundred years in an hour.

"The *sanctuary*," he repeated. "We have had agreement here with the shifters and vampires alike for more than a century. What possibly could have caused them to break it?"

"What were those?" Quinn asked, shoving her guns into their hidden holsters under her shapeless shirt. "I've never seen apes that looked like that, outside of a horror movie."

"They were a grossly distorted version of a Japanese macaque. The real thing has the same brownish fur and red face but runs about twenty-five pounds," Archelaus said. He was breathing hard, and Alaric sent a silent, questing tendril of magic to discern the extent of his injury, if any.

Archelaus raised an eyebrow, and Alaric realized he'd been caught. "I'm just old, Alaric. Nothing you can do about that, unless you've suddenly learned how to turn back time."

"I'm feeling rather old myself, Wise One," Noriko said, finally emerging from behind her shield, which she let disperse slowly. The woman's face was as pale as a snow-dusted grave. "I never had to deal with attacking apes in the portal.

I must apologize for my cowardice. All of you fought the attackers, but I have no weapons, nor do I have knowledge of how to do battle."

Alaric shook his head. "No one expected you to fight. You did well to protect yourself so we did not need to expend resources to defend you."

Noriko bowed. *"Arigato gozaimasu."*

Quinn abruptly sat down on the floor next to Jack and started laughing. "Don't make me get my flying monkeys," she said, shaking her head.

Everyone stared blankly at her, except Jack, who tilted his shaggy head, his tongue lolling out, as if sharing an inside joke.

Quinn looked up and saw them all looking puzzled. "Never mind. It's *The Wizard of Oz*. It's—never mind. So, what now? Attack by flying monkeys doesn't strike me as a random act. Who's after you, Archelaus? Or do they know we're here, and it's an attack against me or Alaric? Or even Jack? Plenty of targets to choose from in this room."

Noriko collapsed down on a bench. "I thought the opportunity to be mortal again would be a precious gift. Instead, I find I desperately miss the power to be anywhere I want to be and nearly omniscient. What can I see—where can I go—trapped in this body?"

"Welcome to my life," Quinn said, with only a trace of bitterness. "I'm surrounded by vampires, Atlantean warriors, and powerful shape-shifters, and all I've got is a gun or two and whatever street smarts I've picked up over the years. It's like fighting the Spartan army armed with a toothpick."

"I would challenge the Spartan army for you, Quinn," Alaric said quietly. "You don't always have to take it all on by yourself."

"I didn't," she said simply. "I had Jack. And then, if only for a little while, I had you and your prince and his warriors. Now I'm not sure I want any of it. I'm tired. Ten years of fighting the good fight should be enough for anybody."

Jack sneezed and rolled over on his back, all the while keeping those orange eyes trained on Quinn.

She almost smiled. "No, I'm not giving up and showing the bad guys my belly, fur face. And if you want to give me crap about my decisions, you're going to have to change back into a human and do it out loud."

The tiger deliberately turned his head away, and a shimmer formed in Quinn's eyes before she dragged one sleeve across her face.

Several white-robed people appeared at the entrance to the courtyard, wearing expressions of horror, disbelief, and even shock. Alaric attempted to view the scene through their eyes and realized it was, in fact, worthy of horror and shock. Dead, bloody bodies lay in crumpled heaps all over the floor. The peace of the sanctuary had been brutally invaded.

He was too tired, too jaded, or too hardened to feel horror, though. Just a grim resignation that now, yet again, the battle was on. Even when he tried to escape the fight, it followed him. As did skepticism, cynicism, and suspicion. Why were these people only arriving now? Had they been part of a larger betrayal?

One of them started babbling. "Archelaus, what happened? You— We heard— The portal—"

"I'd like to know that, too." A calm voice interrupted the man's broken words.

"Ven," Alaric said. "I should have guessed."

"Somebody needed to save you from yourself," Ven said, striding into the room. "I figured it oughta be me."

∿〰〰⌒

Quinn's lips quirked into a grin as another six and a half feet of Atlantean warrior—this one a prince—joined the party. "Ven. Always a pleasure to see you. Do we need somebody beat up and I forgot?"

Ven laughed and scooped her up off the ground and into a bear hug. "Hello, little sister. Glad to see you in one place. What in the nine hells happened here?"

"Flying monkeys."

He roared with laughter. "So does that make kitten over there Toto?"

Quinn noticed Alaric's face darkening as he watched her in his friend's arms, and she didn't have to be an emotional empath to know what he was feeling. She tactfully stepped away from Ven and glanced at Jack, who was snarling at them all.

"Don't flash those fangs at me, Meow Mix," Ven advised, but she could see the concern underneath the banter. He and Jack had developed a friendship over the course of time they'd known each other. Of course, it was hard not to like Ven. He was gorgeous and didn't know it; a funny, direct, "let's grab a beer and watch some bad movies" kind of guy, who just happened to be hell on wheels with a sword, a gun, and pretty much every other kind of weapon. He was the high prince's brother and guardian—which made him Quinn's sister Riley's brother-in-law—he was known as the King's Vengeance, and he was pure adrenaline in a battle.

And his girlfriend Erin was the most powerful witch Quinn had ever met.

Right now, though, there was no trace of amusement on Ven's face as he scanned the destruction. "Do you want to explain this?"

Alaric scowled but said nothing, so Quinn filled Ven in on what had happened.

"That's it? No reason? No evil villain monologuing on why he's attacking you, blah blah blah?" Ven whistled. "This stinks of something bigger than a random monkey attack."

"Not to mention, they're not random monkeys," Archelaus said, from where he'd been sitting in the shadows.

"Greetings, old friend," Ven said, bowing. "What have you gotten us into this time?"

Archelaus smiled and shook his head. "This, from the most unrepentant troublemaker the warrior training grounds have ever seen."

"I did what I could," Ven said, ducking his head modestly.

In spite of everything, Quinn laughed out loud. Ven would be Ven, no matter the situation. It was oddly refreshing to a woman who dealt in death and despair.

"The King's Vengeance," Noriko said, smiling a little. "You have long been one of my favorites."

Quinn's eyes narrowed. Another thing this woman shouldn't have been able to know—Ven's title.

"Ven, meet Noriko, who claims to be the spirit of your magic doorway," she said, before turning to pin Noriko with a suspicious glare. "What exactly did you want to talk to us about that was so important? You weren't luring us here for the attack, were you? Six weeks later, and suddenly you want to talk to us at exactly the moment shifters arrive?"

Alaric called up his energy spheres again, and Noriko took a step back and away from them all, turning even paler, if possible.

"I had nothing to do with that," she protested. "My need to see you was to convey very dire news to Poseidon's high priest."

Alaric's face hardened. "What is it?" he demanded.

"The final gem has been found," Noriko said, twisting her hands together. "Everything in your world is in danger."

"How could you know that?" Quinn asked. "You've been here, not talking to anybody, for weeks."

"I was the portal spirit for millennia," Noriko said, raising her chin. "Do you think that kind of magic simply vanishes? I can feel much that goes on in this world, especially that which is connected to Atlantis."

Ven tensed, all traces of humor gone from his expressive face. "What kind of danger?"

"Atlantis itself could be destroyed," Noriko said. "I don't . . . I don't . . ."

Ven rushed forward to catch the woman when her eyelids fluttered shut and she collapsed.

"If she is truly what she claims, then she is probably in shock from expending so much power," Archelaus said. He motioned to his followers. "Or Noriko's illness might be causing this. Please bring her with us."

Alaric stepped closer to the woman Ven held, passed a hand over her head, and then shook his head. "She has been improving, you said, and I can detect no remaining trace of illness. This is probably simple exhaustion and shock."

"We will move to another space, so my friends can remove the bodies and reinforce the spells protecting this area," Archelaus said. "Thank you for your assistance in that regard, Alaric."

"Yeah, your monkey-repelling spells didn't work all that great, did they?" Quinn said dryly. "Maybe a nice electric fence next time."

As they moved away from the courtyard, Archelaus led them down a corridor. Archelaus's people took Noriko away to get some rest. Which was just as well, since Quinn was far too cynical after all of her years in the rebellion to buy her story all that easily. She didn't trust Noriko. She didn't trust anyone. The less the woman heard, the better.

Ven looked a question at her, and she explained the portal spirit/dying Japanese woman problem.

"You couldn't stay out of trouble if you tried, could you?" he asked her, but then he grinned. "On the other hand, who could make this stuff up? This would be a great Syfy Saturday night movie. *Sharktopus* has nothin' on us."

Quinn didn't know whether to laugh or punch him. She narrowed her eyes and was about to blast him with a snappy comeback when she realized he was right. Her shoulders slumped. Jack padded up behind her and nudged her hip with his shoulder, as if in moral support. Or maybe she was ascribing human motives to him as a kind of wishful thinking, when he was becoming more and more tiger by the moment.

At the entrance to the cave, a wall of air shimmered in waves of pearlescent opal, as if magic protected this opening, too. Which, of course, it did, Quinn reflected, as she walked through a barrier that had the consistency of a soap bubble. It snapped shut behind her, hopefully offering better protection than the monkey doorway.

She took a deep breath of the fresh mountain air and allowed her gaze to sweep the view from an upper slope of Mount Fuji. "It's so beautiful here. So high above battles and blood and death, or so you'd think. Almost like a waking dream—but of someone else's life."

"We're above the clouds," Ven said. "The exact opposite of my home so far beneath the ocean's surface. It kind of takes your breath away, doesn't it?"

"More than eleven thousand feet elevation here," Archelaus said, joining them. "Over twelve thousand at the summit. Fuji is one of three sacred mountains—"

"Perhaps we could save the ancient history for later and discuss the current problem?" Alaric's voice cut through the air like a sword through silk.

Quinn could sense—just barely, though, even with her empath senses flaring to high—the tension boiling beneath his icy demeanor. She wondered if she'd be around when he finally erupted. An interesting thought: Alaric and Mount Fuji, both dormant volcanoes; both with majestic exteriors hiding barely leashed danger. She grinned at the idea of telling Alaric he was exactly like a lava-filled mountain, and he slanted a look at her, clearly wondering where her mind was.

"Nice of you to give a damn, after weeks of being mostly incommunicado," Ven said dryly. "Anyway, that's just it—the current problem *is* ancient history. Noriko was telling the truth. Archaeologists at Göbekli Tepe in Turkey have found Poseidon's Pride."

Alaric and Archelaus simultaneously inhaled. In anyone *not* an Atlantean warrior, Quinn would have called it gasping.

"Poseidon lost his pride?" Quinn glanced from face to face. "Did he also lose his gluttony, avarice, and lust? Is this some weird seven deadly sins kind of thing?"

Alaric was shaking his head before she'd finished her admittedly lame joke.

"Poseidon's Pride is the final missing jewel from his Trident. It's a tourmaline that gives immense, possibly immeasurable power to its wielder. We've been searching for it for centuries."

"Göbekli Tepe sounds familiar," Archelaus said. "Why is that?"

"Human archaeologists recently discovered the site. It's an Atlantean temple built around eleven thousand, six hundred years ago, and they're calling it the oldest known example of *human* monumental architecture, which is kind of surprising, now that they know about supernatural creatures and magic, but whatever. It's the first known building bigger than a hut, basically," Ven said. He shook his head. "They've all got their panties in a twist over how a bunch of people who were still nomads foraging for food could have transported sixteen-ton stones."

"Ridiculous concept," Alaric said dryly. "Of course Atlanteans built it. The Elders at the time sent our people to all corners of the earth to perpetuate our race before Atlantis descended beneath the seas at the time of the Cataclysm. Certainly many of them would have built temples."

"Atlantean magic," Quinn said, finding it easy to imagine, given what she knew of their powers. "Serai could probably move a boulder without smudging her lip gloss."

Alaric shrugged. On him, even a shrug looked elegant. "Serai is an eleven-thousand-year-old Atlantean princess. Her magic is more powerful than mine in some ways."

"Not many ways," Ven said. "Not in *battle* ways."

Alaric's eyes glowed a hot green. "No. But that vampire she's in love with isn't likely to let her anywhere near a battle again."

"Daniel knows better than to try to tell Serai to do anything," Ven said. "She turned into a saber-toothed tiger, dude."

"Never, *ever* call me dude."

Quinn sighed. "So the *point* is . . ." She made a "move along" gesture with her hand.

"The point is that nobody but Alaric can touch that gemstone without dying horribly. So far, seven people associated with the dig have spontaneously combusted." Ven shuddered. "Bad way to go."

"So Alaric must go retrieve it," Archelaus said.

"I'm going nowhere," Alaric said. He leaned against the rock face on the side of the mountain and almost casually drew

Quinn back against him, wrapping his arms around her waist. She felt his breath in her hair as she stared out at the clouds, and for a moment she tried to pretend they were the kind of people who could go sightseeing together.

The kind of people who could say *no*. No to duty. No to honor.

It didn't work.

She let herself lean against his powerfully muscled chest for just a few seconds longer, and then she forced herself to move away, trying to ignore the pain that pierced her chest. Even a rebel leader could fall in love, after all. It's just that nobody could ever know.

Ever.

Not even Alaric.

"Christophe can go. Or even Serai. They both wield sufficient magic," he said grimly. "It doesn't always have to be me. Look what Serai did with the Emperor. She's an expert in retrieving lost gems."

Jack snarled at him and bared his fangs again.

"I agree with the tiger, Temple Rat," Ven said. "It's not like you don't have reason to be fed up, but we need you, and it's your duty."

"To the nine hells with duty," Alaric growled. He raised his arms and shouted up to the sky. "Did you hear that, Poseidon? I'm done with you."

An explosive boom of thunder cracked through the sky, shaking the ground under their feet.

Quinn mentioned the fact she'd just been considering. "Mount Fuji is a volcano."

"It is," Archelaus agreed. "But it's dormant."

"Sure, that's what they all say, just before the lava starts spewing," Quinn muttered. "Let's not make the nice sea god angry."

Ven shoved his hands in his pockets and stared silently out at the panoramic vista, until she elbowed him.

"Hey, I'm not arguing," Ven said. "Cataclysm? Doom of the gods? Atlantis sinking beneath the ocean? Any of that ring a bell? I never laugh in the face of potential disaster."

Alaric's look of disbelief was priceless. "You *always* laugh in the face of potential disaster."

"Always," Quinn agreed.

"Oh. Right." Ven shrugged, grinning. "What can I say? It's a gift."

"Regardless of all that, I think your answer is clear, youngling," Archelaus said to Alaric. "You may be done with Poseidon, but he's not done with you."

Alaric's stare was a nearly tangible thing, burning into Quinn with the heat of living flame—strange, that, since fire was the one element forbidden to Atlanteans. But the high priest had his own form of wild magic, she knew. One that whispered to her of silken seductions in the middle of the night, during the fractured hours of sleep when she found herself consumed by impossible dreams of a dangerous warrior.

He had always worn his duty and honor like a shield, one that matched her own shield of shame, remorse, and regret. Between the two of them lay a vast chasm of dark and bloody acts sacrificed at the altar of good intention. Not even a world-bending kind of passion could bridge that canyon, regardless of what Alaric, in his temporary insanity, might believe.

"Poseidon," Alaric said slowly, catching Quinn's gaze with his own, "is no longer my priority. Both he and you will come to believe me soon enough."

The pressure—of the moment, of the day, even of the decade—built up inside her until her lungs seemed unable to push air into and out of her body. Pain—physical, emotional, even spiritual—swept through her, burning its way through determination and resolve. Quinn finally did the one thing she hadn't done in a very long time. She ran from danger, instead of facing it. She turned and strode back into the cave, blindly seeking refuge from the man who'd just staked his claim on her future. At her side, the man who'd been so essential a part of her past stalked down the corridor on all fours, leaving his humanity further and further behind with each swish of his silken tiger's tail.

Future and past were both too much to contemplate for

Quinn's exhausted mind, so she focused on the present. She found an empty room with beds in it, and she collapsed onto the nearest one, silently apologizing to the bed's owner for the tears she could no longer contain.

She'd solve it after she slept. All of it.

Before exhaustion pulled her under, she thought she saw an Alaric-shaped shadow appear in her doorway, but when she tried to stir, a gentle glow of silvery blue light surrounded her and she found herself drifting further into sleep.

Jack snarled and then began to snore, a low, rumbling noise, and she thought she heard Alaric's laughter.

"You may be sure, *mi amara*, that we will discuss this habit you have of allowing another man into your bed."

Her lips almost curved into a smile, and then the world curled around her into the warmth and safety of darkness.

Chapter 4

Quinn woke up from a dream of walking through fire toward a dragon with glowing emerald eyes, and found herself alone on a bed in a room she didn't recognize. She automatically checked her knives and guns; all were in place, so she took her first full breath since opening her eyes.

"Always the warrior first."

She snapped her head toward the darkest corner of the room, where Alaric leaned against the wall, blending in with the shadows as if the darkness within him had become tangible while she slept.

"Interesting comment, coming from the warrior priest," she countered. "Which comes first with you?"

"*You* come first with me," he said harshly, as if he despised her for it. Or hated that she'd asked; that he'd been forced to voice taboo desires. An Atlantean priest sworn to celibacy wanted a rebel sworn to redemption. All of his gods must be laughing.

"Always you, since the moment I first lay my hands on you to heal that bullet wound. Since I fell inside your soul. Don't you know that by now, Quinn?"

She caught her breath at the stark pain in his voice, but steeled herself against it. Warriors and rebels had no business falling prey to emotion.

"You can't protect me from the monsters, Alaric," she said quietly.

His laughter was dark and somehow terrifying, even to Quinn, who lived her life pretending to fear nothing.

"Protect you? I would drown the entire world for you, and laugh as every single living being on it died. *I'm* the monster, Quinn. Better you find a way to protect yourself from me, because I am the high priest of blood and battle, and the lord of death and destruction. I will never, ever let you go."

Before she could begin to form a response to that, he was across the room and yanking her up off the cot and into his arms. "Never, do you hear me? I will give up my friends, my country, my duty, and even my honor—but never you."

He swallowed her protest with his lips, as he captured her mouth in a searing kiss that devoured her, claimed her, branded her as his. She felt herself falling, melting, burning, and she had no chance to deny him or even her own feelings. The walls between them shattered and—for one glorious moment—they stood together, locked in a tempest of need and want and a far more powerful emotion.

One she didn't dare name.

She tangled her hands in his silky hair and kissed him back with every ounce of longing she'd been suppressing for so very long, and the feel of rightness—of *home*—that unfurled within her was so intense that she almost didn't hear the shouting.

Almost. But so many years of training couldn't be denied for the illusory dream of a moment. Not to mention that Jack had shown up and was snarling and baring his teeth at Alaric. She spared a moment's embarrassment that he'd seen her kiss Alaric but dismissed it as the unimportant detail it was.

Flying monkeys, attacking vampires, Atlantean portals come to life? Check.

One kiss? Not such a huge deal in the scale of things. She

almost involuntarily raised her fingers to her swollen lips, though. Alaric's eyes darkened as he watched, and he bent down as if to kiss her again.

"Alaric, get your priestly ass out here, or I'll kick it for you," Ven roared from somewhere in the maze of caves and corridors. "We have an emergency."

Alaric tightened his arms around her for a moment, but then he sighed and leaned his forehead against hers. "When is it ever *not* an emergency?"

"It never stops for people like us," she told him. "You know it, and I know it. World-bending kisses don't change reality."

He lifted her into the air until they were at eye level to each other, and the slow smile that spread across his face was nothing but pure masculine satisfaction. "World-bending?"

"Yeah, don't let it go to your head," she muttered. "And put me down."

He lowered her to her feet and then kissed her again, hard and fast, before turning toward the bellowing sound of one seriously outraged Atlantean prince.

"World-bending," he repeated. "Those may be the best two words I've heard in five hundred years."

With that, he strode out of the room, leaving her to follow on still-shaky legs. She consoled herself for her weakness with the excellent view of his very fine ass.

Jack, still in tiger form, slouched into the corridor and head-butted her, grumbling some kind of cat complaint.

"Eye candy," she told the tiger formerly known as her best friend and co–rebel leader. "Pure eye candy, in the form of an absolutely delicious backside, wasted on a man who doesn't even realize he's beautiful. Stupid Atlantean."

He snarled, and she decided to take it for agreement.

Ven rounded the corner, saw them, and belted out a string of what she was sure were the choicest Atlantean swear words. "Finally," he said, breaking into English. "Where in the nine hells have you been?"

Then he glanced behind Alaric at Quinn, and stopped short. "Oh. Ah, yeah. You two were . . . uh . . ."

"No, we were not," Alaric snapped. "Though not for want of trying, not that it's any of your damn business."

Quinn felt her face flush with heat, but she clamped her mouth shut against the retort trying to bubble up.

Ven's mouth fell open. "Did you just say— But you— Ah, okay. I don't have time to go all Oprah with you. We've got a big problem."

"When do we not?" Alaric sliced a hand through the air. "What is it, already?"

"We're too late to retrieve Poseidon's Pride. Some lunatic who calls himself Ptolemy Reborn has taken it, Alaric."

"That's impossible. No human, even a powerful wizard, would have the magic to be able to touch that gem," Alaric said.

"What about a vampire?" Quinn asked. "Or shape-shifter? Their magic is different from yours. Maybe—"

"Impossible," Alaric repeated. "Only an extremely powerful Atlantean could touch the tourmaline. It's the crown jewel, so to speak, of Poseidon's Trident."

"That's just it," Ven said, his face grim. "Old Ptolemy is claiming to be the king of Atlantis."

Alaric's face hardened, and his eyes flashed so hot that Quinn was surprised that twin laser beams of emerald light didn't incinerate Ven where he stood. "He claims *what*?"

"Ooh, boy, Conlan and Riley do not need to deal with this," Quinn said, her own anger rising at the thought of more trouble for her sister, who'd almost died at the hands of vampires and then nearly lost her baby during a particularly difficult pregnancy and childbirth.

Riley would be queen of Atlantis, but at what cost? Quinn glanced at Alaric and wondered if she could ever be as brave as her sister and risk everything for love. A hot wave of shame washed over her, leaving bitterness and bile in its wake. Not that Alaric could ever love her, when he knew what she'd done. What she'd become.

Ven threw his hands in the air in disgust. "Are we going to stand here and talk about it, or do you want to come back with me and see the impostor son of a bitch?"

"He's here?" Alaric's energy spheres were already swirling into shape in the air surrounding him when Ven shook his head impatiently.

"No, he's having a press conference, believe it or not. Old Ptolemy is a media whore apparently."

They swiftly followed Ven down a few turns and twists, to find Archelaus already watching the news conference on television when they arrived in his chambers. Quinn knew from a quick study of his body language that the news was all bad.

"He's speaking in front of the United Nations building in New York, and he's claiming to be descended from Atlantean royalty. It's not good. He just told the reporters that Atlantis exists, claimed to have any number of witnesses who have met High Prince Conlan or, as Ptolemy calls him, 'the pretender to the throne,' and said that Atlantis is positioned to rise to the surface of the ocean any day now."

Ven shook his head. "We knew we couldn't keep the secret forever, not with the way we run around protecting humanity, kicking vampire ass, and generally making a nuisance of ourselves with the big, bad, and uglies that go bump in the dark."

"But this isn't anything expected, is it?" Quinn asked. "Is it possible he really is who he claims he is? I mean, he is holding your jewel in his hand, isn't he?"

"It must be a fake," Alaric said. He stared at the television screen so hard she was surprised the heat in his eyes didn't burn a hole in the screen. "Can you make the device speak louder?"

"Turn up the volume," Ven said.

"As I said," Alaric snapped.

Quinn shook her head at the two of them.

Archelaus pressed a button on the remote and the voice of the wannabe Atlantean king filled the room.

"I have documented proof that I am the direct lineal descendant of Alexander the Great, conquerer and Atlantean, and I will take my rightful place upon the throne as soon as Atlantis rises from its watery grave," he intoned.

Ven snorted. "Watery grave? Seriously?"

Quinn was stuck on a different part of the man's statement. "Alexander the Great was Atlantean?"

Alaric shrugged. "Narcissist. Lust for power. Amazing while it lasted, though."

Quinn studied the man standing at the bank of microphones. He definitely looked regal. He was tall and imposing, with a TV politician kind of look to him. All toothpaste-commercial teeth and good hair. Even a tan, whether real or spray-on. But under the made-for-prime-time charisma, she could just see the jagged edges of something with real teeth. Something that would chew up enemies and vomit up their remains before calmly flossing.

She shuddered. "There's power there. Dark power. I've seen enough *wrong* in the past decade to recognize it. He's just . . . not right."

Alaric slanted a measuring glance at her. "I tend to agree, even without the added incentive of his ludicrous claim."

"He does kind of look like you," she pointed out. "The collective you. Atlanteans. Same dark hair, same height and bone structure, but with an added layer of smarm. Are you sure there's no chance he could be a descendant, like he claims?"

"Impossible to tell from here," Alaric said.

Reporters surrounding the man shouted questions at him, but he stood calmly in the center of the firestorm of attention, smiling slightly as if he were mildly amused. Finally, he held up his hands, and the questions slowly died down as the reporters began to fall silent in order to hear what else he would say.

"I will answer all of your questions eventually, but what I have to say now is of the most urgent nature." He drew a sheet of paper out of a large envelope and held it tightly, making eye contact with each reporter in turn.

"We Atlanteans have long been on a mission to protect humanity. Our goal has been, and always will be, to work with you to secure your lives and safety against the vampire menace that threatens to destroy you. To that end, I must speak with this woman. If any of you know how to contact her, please have her call me at the Plaza Hotel. It is quite literally a matter of life and death."

He slowly turned the paper around, and revealed that it was actually an eight-by-ten-inch photograph.

Of Quinn.

Alaric swore so viciously in a mixture of English and Atlantean that even Quinn, who was well accustomed to being surrounded by people who used colorful language, flinched.

"This is Quinn Dawson, the leader of the North American rebel alliance. I understand that by revealing her secret identity on national and international TV, I have placed her in extreme danger."

The camera zeroed its focus in on the photograph, which was grainy in the blurry picture but unmistakably Quinn.

"My cover is blown," she said numbly. "I'm a dead woman."

Alaric's face was a study in icy rage. "No, *mi amara*. It is he who is a dead man."

"Call me, Quinn Dawson," Ptolemy continued. "Together, we will take back the planet. Human and Atlantean together. This I swear."

The reporters, all swooning over the double scoop, shouted questions so fast and furiously that they were unintelligible, but the man simply bowed and held up his right hand with the enormous gemstone in it, and a flash of sickly orange-red light enveloped him. When the light was gone, so was he.

"A cheap trick," Ven said dismissively. "Any five-dollar magician can do that."

"But a five-dollar magician could not touch Poseidon's Pride, let alone wield it," Alaric said slowly. "If that truly is the missing gem, there is something to this man's claim, at least of being Atlantean, perhaps."

Quinn started laughing, and it was high and wild. "Well. Think they're hiring at McDonald's? Because that, my friends, just put me out of a job."

Alaric stared at her in disbelief. "Out of a *job*? Are you insane? What he did, *mi amara*, was to paint a giant target on your forehead. Every faction in the vampire conspiracy, every rogue shape-shifter, and even the many humans you've crossed over the years—they will all be after you. I will have to kill every one of them after I kill Ptolemy."

"I'll be right there to help," Ven said.

Jack, who'd been so silent Alaric had almost forgotten about him, roared so loudly the walls seemed to vibrate with the sound.

"That's too many to kill, you idiots," Quinn said wearily. "I may as well stay here and start a flying monkey ranch. Life as I knew it is over. Will you teach me how to speak Japanese, Archelaus?"

Alaric made a horrible snarling noise, deep in his throat, so primal that it rivaled Jack at his tiger worst. He raised his hands and hurled an intense whiplash of power so massive that the entire room flashed as bright and hot as if they huddled inside a lightning bolt, praying for the storm to end. The television shattered into a thousand pieces, as did the table beneath it, the chair next to it, and a significant part of the cavern wall.

The world itself seemed to hold its breath in the aftermath of the violence, until finally Alaric's voice broke the silence.

"Remember what I said, Quinn," Alaric said calmly. He turned those deadly eyes on her, but she forced herself not to flinch. "I will kill them all."

Chapter 5

Alaric watched Quinn follow Archelaus out of the room. She'd grown quieter and quieter while they argued over what to do next, and then she'd finally said she was going to find some food.

"Not much else to do, now that I'm unemployed," she'd said, contorting her face in what she may have intended to be a smile, but which came out as a death's head grimace.

Jack followed, her silent, deadly shadow. Alaric realized yet again that in another world—another timeline—she could have loved Jack and, perhaps, been happy. The realization added yet another layer of tarnish to the rusted remains of his conscience, but did not in the least tempt him to give her up.

At least Alaric had stopped casually plotting ways to kill Jack whenever he thought of Jack with Quinn. That was progress, of a sort.

"That is one scary expression on your face, my friend," Ven said. The prince folded his arms over his chest. "Do I even want to know what's on your mind?"

"Your wants are of no concern to me. My mind is my own. I leave now to confront this fake Ptolemy. Once he's dead, and I retrieve the gem, our problems will diminish."

Ven shook his head. "Not by much. The world still knows that Quinn is a rebel leader. That bell can't be unrung. She's done being safe—or, for that matter, going undercover—forever. And we should check in with Conlan and the rest of the Seven and find out if they even know what's going on. It's not like they get CNN in Atlantis."

"Fine. You check in. I'm going to New York." Alaric called to the portal, belatedly wondering if it would even answer, if Noriko truly was the portal spirit or presence who had directed its magic.

A shimmering oval of light answered his question, but before entering he stopped and addressed it, feeling a fool.

"You. Spirit of the portal. Can you speak in that form?"

Silence was his only answer, which was no answer at all.

"Fine. Take me to the Plaza Hotel in New York," he commanded, as he stepped into the swirling magic.

As the vortex took him, Ven followed.

"Somebody needs to save your ass," the prince said.

"Whatever you say, Your Highness."

"Call me that again, and I'll *kick* your ass instead."

The portal deposited them in what appeared to be a garden or park, in a stand of trees. The rich scent of plants, flowers, and trees, with an underlying touch of metal and machine, infused the night air, and stars twinkled overhead.

"Night here, day in Japan. The time zone change is messing with my brain," Ven said.

"Where are we?" Alaric demanded.

"This is Central Park. See that overgrown mansion of a building? That's the Plaza. Finest hotel in New York." Ven grinned. "I met this brunette in the Champagne Bar once—"

"Yes, I'll be sure to tell Erin all about that." Alaric had even less patience than usual with the prince's banter. Quinn's *life* was in danger. Rage thrummed through his bones and his blood like the war cry of ancient tribal drums.

A look of pure horror crossed Ven's face. "You wouldn't do that. Erin knows she's the only woman for me. I was just— Never mind. Let's find this Ptolemy."

Alaric headed out of the trees and toward the hotel, not

caring whether Ven followed or not. This bastard of a pretender had put Quinn in danger.

Ptolemy had to die.

"Did you tell Quinn you were leaving?"

"She won't even notice I'm gone before I return with the news of Ptolemy's defeat," Alaric said grimly, acknowledging, if only to himself, how quickly he'd been forced to break his vow never to leave her. But her life itself was at stake—he'd had no choice.

The portals to the nine hells were built with good intentions, too, or so the old stories went. Good intent or avid self-interest? At times the barrier between the two was as thin as a coward's resolve.

Ven caught up with him, whistling under his breath. "Mistake. Big mistake."

Probably. Every step Alaric took with Quinn was a mistake. But he had many long years to work on doing better. For now he'd do what he did best—battle his enemies.

Kill them all.

He stared up at the luxe hotel, wishing he could see through the walls. But he had the next best ability—he could sense Atlantean magic. And, like it or not, at least that much of the pretender's claim must be true, unless there were another Atlantean inside the building wielding control over the elements. He could feel the pounding pulse of incredibly strong power coming from one of the upper floors of the building.

"He's experimenting with Poseidon's Pride," he told Ven from between clenched teeth, as every fiber of his being protested the very thought of it.

"I can feel it. Or at least feel something. The hair on my arms is trying to climb off my skin. Quinn nailed it, though. It feels wrong," Ven said.

"His magic isn't pure. It certainly isn't ancient," Alaric said, closing his eyes to concentrate more intently. "It's tainted with something that feels oily and perverted."

"Perverted magic? What does that even mean?"

Alaric opened his eyes and scanned the busy street they'd approached. "Most magic comes from a wholesome place.

Water, earth, air, and even fire, which, though forbidden to Atlanteans, is pure and untainted. This . . . this is something different. Twisted. Demonic, perhaps."

Ven whistled. "I have no desire to run into another demon. One per half a millennium is plenty for me."

"Demon or no, he dies tonight."

"So you keep saying, but don't you think we should get him to answer a few questions first?"

A group of pedestrians approached, weaving drunkenly and singing. Alaric flashed them a single look, and they abruptly turned and started walking very quickly in the opposite direction.

"Humans annoy me," he growled.

"Not all humans," Ven said, making Alaric want to blast the prince with an energy sphere right there on the street.

"Almost all humans," he amended, instead. "Yes, you may be right. If he is drawing on demonic magic, I'd like to know how an Atlantean or Atlantean descendant with that kind of power escaped our attention all this time. You know I've scanned for any of our line with magic every time we come to the surface."

"Less talk, more action?" Ven suggested.

Alaric scowled, and a woman who'd been tentatively approaching them, holding out a camera, screamed and ran across the street, barely escaping being hit by a car.

"That, my friend, is one terrifying face," Ven said.

"Less talk, more action," Alaric replied.

Together, the two Atlanteans crossed the street to the Plaza Hotel, where one pretender to the Atlantean throne was going to die a long, slow, horrible death.

❧～❧

Japan

Quinn sat at the deserted table, her untouched plate in front of her, and stared into space, arms clutched around her waist, trying to contain the empty hole that used to be her insides. She'd known the day might come; she'd crossed too many powerful people for it to be otherwise. But she hadn't expected it to come so soon, and in spite of what she'd said about being tired, there was no part of her that was ready to give up the fight.

"Now I might have no choice," she told Jack, who kept right on snoring at her side.

Damn tigers were worse than house cats. All he did in this form was sleep. Although he was probably going to need to eat again soon, and she hoped that didn't present a problem. Tigers ate a lot.

A *lot*.

Sushi and noodles wouldn't cut it. Archelaus had told her there was an actual safari-style zoo at the base of Mount Fuji somewhere, and it had been supplying him with tiger chow. One problem solved, seven million to go.

A shadow blocked the entryway from the corridor, and she looked up to see the woman who called herself Noriko standing there. The Japanese woman, or Atlantean portal, or whatever she was, bowed slightly before entering the room.

"Are you aware that your companions have gone?" Noriko asked.

Quinn nodded. "Yeah, I'm surprised you didn't hear the shouting when Archelaus told me."

A fresh stab of pain sliced through her. Alaric had *left her* without so much as a "see you later," after promising never to leave her side. When he came back, she was going to point that out to him.

If he came back.

"I'm just going to call you Noriko, because the rest of it is too unwieldy," Quinn said abruptly. "Or, what did you say your Atlantean name was? Galillee?"

"Gailea. I have not heard that name in so long that I am as unused to it as I am to Noriko, although the one whose body this is reacts to her name, of course."

"That's just creepy, you know, right? Doesn't she mind that you hijacked her body? Not that I'm sure I believe any of it."

Noriko dropped gracefully down to kneel beside Jack. She tentatively placed a hand on his head and began to stroke his fur, and Jack's snore changed to a rumbling purr.

"Well, at least Jack thinks you're okay, but he once had a drinking buddy who belched the national anthem for fun, so he's not exactly the best judge of character." Quinn knew she sounded unwelcoming at best, and openly hostile at worst, but she didn't have room for one more problem in what was left of her life. Her mind already felt like it was cracking a little around the edges; her future fracturing into a shattered fun house mirror of thwarted hopes and doomed plans. She tried not to wonder if Alaric had been any part of any one of her futures.

Too little, too late. If even half of her enemies had seen that broadcast, she'd be dead soon. Better to focus on Noriko's bizarre story, rather than her own probable early death.

Noriko, unaware of Quinn's dark thoughts, smiled, which transformed her skeletal face into something approaching loveliness. "Tigers are very wise. I'm sure his friend had a good heart, beneath his churlish ways. And, no, Noriko is at peace that she will not die from the cancer."

"Yeah. Maybe. And you? What kind of heart do you have?"

"One that wishes to assist you in any way that I can, Quinn Dawson," Noriko said, staring at Quinn with eyes both old and sad. "I have watched you and your sister during the past few years, and I have come to know the strength and goodness in your own hearts. Riley is truly fit to be queen of Atlantis."

"Why did you quit being the portal?" Quinn asked, ready to change the subject. Sure, Noriko knew things she shouldn't know, but that still didn't mean her story was true.

"Poseidon plays his games. This is one of them. I must prove that I am worthy to be mortal again—a woman instead of an untouchable spirit." Noriko dropped her head so her hair covered her eyes, but Quinn didn't miss the single tear that escaped and made its way down the other woman's cheek.

Either Noriko was telling the truth, or she was an Academy

Award–worthy actress. Quinn still wasn't betting on which one it was. She decided abruptly that she didn't have time right now to care.

"Help me, then, if your heart is so true," she challenged. "Noriko must speak Japanese, right? If she's in there, too, help me find a way to the airport. I need to get to New York. Ptolemy wants me? Okay, then, he's going to get me."

Noriko's eyes widened. "But your companions meant for you to stay here . . ."

Quinn rolled her eyes. "If you're going to live in this century, Gailea, you need to learn something. Women do whatever they want to do these days."

Noriko nodded and drew a slim phone from her pocket. "I will find out the fastest way to Narita International Airport in Tokyo and book you a flight. We have something called a Visa platinum card, evidently."

"JFK Airport, please," Quinn said. "If you have access to unlimited funds, by the way, instead of worrying about dying or Poseidon's games, you might want to consider joining the rebel alliance and helping out. We're humanity's best hope."

"Are you recruiting me?"

Quinn shrugged. "Once a rebel leader . . . If you'll excuse me for a minute, I need to say good-bye to a hungry tiger."

Noriko rose and bowed again, and then left the room, tapping away at her phone. Quinn looked down at Jack and wondered how to say what would probably be her final good-bye to the best friend she'd ever had.

Jack opened one eye, probably some tiger sixth sense or something at work. Quinn dug her hands into the fur on the sides of his face and pulled his shaggy head up closer to her own.

"I have to go, fur face. I have to find out what that nut ball Ptolemy wants from me and what he's up to. If the jewel really is what Alaric thinks it is, and it really has that much power—well, who knows how much damage it can cause. Somebody has to stop him, and I seem to be out of any other kind of job, so I guess it needs to be me."

Jack pulled away from her and snarled, placing one heavy paw on her leg as if to hold her down.

"Look," she said, almost desperately, fighting the tears threatening to close her throat and run down her face. "I can't do this without you. I don't *want* to do this without you. Can't you please come back? Please be human again, just for a while?"

She stared into his eyes, searching for any trace of his humanity, but saw nothing to reassure her. Nothing but wildness and ferocity. Maybe Alaric was right. Maybe Jack really was gone—permanently gone—and only a faint memory of their friendship kept him from mauling her or worse.

She stopped fighting the tears. Nobody was around to see them anyway, and Jack deserved at least her tears.

"You saved my life so many times I can't even count that high," she whispered. "You loved me when I didn't deserve it. You stood by me when I took us into trouble, and battles, and worse. You even stood by me when I fell in love with an Atlantean priest who has sworn a vow of celibacy to a god."

He snarled again, more quietly, and gently butted her shoulder with his head.

"I never deserved you, Jack. Not your love or your friendship. Not even your amazing ability to always have my back," she continued, openly crying now. "I never did, and now I can never hope to. I love you, you know? Not the way you want, but I love you. If you really love me, try to come back. For me. Please."

She gave up at that point, since further words would be meaningless. Jack—her Jack—knew what was in her heart. Instead, she put her arms around him as best as she could and she cried into his soft, silky fur until it was soaked, while her heart shattered into tiny, tiger-shaped pieces.

Finally she stood up and scrubbed at her eyes with her hands. "Good-bye, my friend."

In the most painful blow of all, he didn't even try to stop her from leaving. He just sat there and silently watched her walk away.

Chapter 6

The Plaza Hotel, New York City

"Pretty fancy, isn't it?" Ven looked around and whistled. "Whoever he is, he has money. This place doesn't run cheap, and he's in one of the best suites, from what you tell me of where you feel that magic."

Alaric shrugged. He didn't care about money or hotels with gold and gilt fixtures. He cared about Quinn. Her life was in danger. Nothing else mattered.

"It's probably a private elevator to get there," Ven said. "This could be a problem, if you want to be subtle."

Alaric raised an eyebrow. "Elevator? Subtle? Really? Has domestic bliss befuddled your mind?"

Whirling around, he headed back out to the street, leapt on the edge of the fountain, and then shot straight up into the air, transforming his body into mist on the way. What did he care for subterfuge or hiding his powers from humans now? Ptolemy had announced the existence of Atlantis to the world, so what did it matter if a few New Yorkers saw Alaric as he claimed Atlantean water magic?

Below, he saw Ven stare up at him, cursing, and then take a less dramatic approach to achieve the same end, ducking behind one of the ubiquitous yellow taxis before he, too, transformed. Alaric felt a moment's grim amusement at the idea that practical jokester Ven had acted with more caution than he had. He soared up until he felt the source of the magic as it pulsed and pounded in front of him, coming from behind a wall of glass.

Nice view these bad guys have, Ven sent to him on the shared Atlantean mental pathway.

Let them view this, Alaric returned, just before he blasted a hole in the window and soared through.

Ven changed back from mist to his body mere seconds after Alaric did, and the first thing he did was punch Alaric in the arm.

"Way to go. Seriously, nice stealth move."

Alaric ignored him, concentrating on the group of green-robed humans cowering on their knees in the room. "It's them again. The Platoist Society. Remember, with Reisen? They worship anything they think is Atlantean."

"They don't have to wonder if I'm Atlantean. I have already told them, and the world, that it is so," Ptolemy said, stepping out from behind a teenage boy who was the only human standing.

The boy was trying desperately to look brave, but sweat stood out on his dark skin and his eyes were wild. Ptolemy still carried the enormous tourmaline, but he'd fastened it to the end of a gaudy gold-gilt scepter. It glowed faintly, and Alaric could feel pure Atlantean magic course through every nerve ending in his body. From underneath and around the shimmer of power, however, the tainted pulse of demonic magic bit into him with jagged teeth.

"What are you, really?" Alaric demanded. "Tell me now, and I may at least make your death quicker."

"Ah, such a generous offer," Ptolemy said. He laughed mockingly. "Who exactly are you that you dare to make it when I hold the most powerful jewel of Atlantis in my hand?"

"How do you know that jewel is Atlantean?" Ven asked, edging closer to Ptolemy's right, to flank him.

Ptolemy pointed the scepter at him. "You must be one

of the false princes. I recognize the stench of undeserved arrogance."

"I am the King's Vengeance, and you are going to die if you don't start answering questions right now." Ven pulled his daggers from their sheaths and dropped into a battle-ready stance.

Ptolemy aimed the scepter at Ven and fired off a blast of sickly reddish-orange power that slammed Ven into the wall. When Alaric called to his own magic and drew back his arm to hurl an energy sphere at the pretender, the man yanked the teen boy in front of him.

"I think not," Ptolemy taunted Alaric. "Not unless you want to kill this boy, and you don't do that, do you? You think you're the good guys. Humanity's heroes from legend—what a joke. Which one are you, anyway?"

"I am Alaric, high priest to Poseidon, friend to the true ruler of Atlantis, and I am the one who is going to rip your intestines out by way of your throat," Alaric told the impostor. His teeth ached from the residue of tainted magic, and he still couldn't figure out exactly *what* Ptolemy was. Demon or human? Not vampire, that much was clear.

If demon, he was the most skilled demon Alaric had ever encountered. Most of them couldn't hide their true forms for longer than a few seconds, or a minute at most. This one had done the press conference, and still now he stood before them in human form.

As Ven struggled to his feet, swearing a blue streak, Alaric decided simply to ask, "What makes you think you're Atlantean, demon?"

Genuine surprise crossed Ptolemy's face. "Demon? Oh, no, you have me mistaken for something far less powerful, priest. I am the king of Atlantis. I am the wizard who will destroy your house, enslave your women, and make your false princes my pets. Watch me and learn."

Ven lunged for the man, trying to create a distraction so Alaric could strike him down, but Ptolemy must have been anticipating just such a move. He leapt to the side, dragging the boy with him.

"Choose now," he taunted. "Save the boy or catch me. His name is Faust, by the way. Don't you find that deliciously ironic?"

With that, he lifted the boy and threw him out through the shattered window in one powerful heave, slammed the scepter against his chest, and disappeared in another flash of light. Alaric had a split second to decide whether to save the boy or try to follow the emanations of residual magic from the scepter.

It wasn't really even a choice.

He caught the boy five feet from the sidewalk below, and Ven was right behind him.

The upper floors of the hotel exploded into a ball of fire over their heads.

~⌒⌒~

Tokyo, Japan, in a car on the way to Narita International Airport

Quinn stared out the window at the passing scenery, not really seeing any of it. She listened with a fraction of her attention as the elderly Japanese man driving her to the airport tried to give her a history lesson on the area. He was gracious and kind, and she was in the mood for neither. She'd left her only real friend trapped in a tiger's body, with no hope of ever seeing him again, and she had no idea where Alaric was. Not to mention that she'd never yet met her only nephew, who just happened to be the heir to the throne of Atlantis, and now she probably never would.

Life was just peachy.

She'd left Archelaus with only a hasty good-bye, as he worked the phone and his contacts to try to discover what the monkey-shifter attack had been about. Hello, more chaos. She had a feeling that there was more than enough on her plate at the moment, though, so she decided to stop worrying about flying monkeys—shape-shifters or otherwise. The two-hour hike to the parking lot at Fifth Station, midway down the mountain, had provided more than enough time for every worst-case scenario—many involving her own torture and death—to circle through her mind like wastewater through a gutter.

"I don't understand this," her driver suddenly said in an entirely different tone from the tour guide voice he'd been using. "We have no bad weather forecasted for this area today."

Quinn sat up in her seat and stared forward, into a sky that had gone suddenly dark and sullen. Clouds whipped in a frenzy of storm formation, and apple-sized hailstones began to pummel the car and the road around them. The car just in front of them in the long line of crazy Tokyo traffic swerved and almost hit the car next to it, and a domino effect of near-collisions began all around them.

Quinn's driver slammed on the brakes, throwing Quinn forward and almost into the dash, and then he made a weird yelping noise and pointed to his left. Quinn stared out at what he was indicating, and recoiled in horror. She hadn't seen anything like that outside of a bad movie.

It was a funnel cloud, and it was heading right at them. The car behind them stopped too late and almost rear-ended them, throwing Quinn forward again. Score one for excellent seat belts. The air bag didn't deploy, though, and she almost had time to wonder about that before the funnel cloud touched down in the single open spot of road in front of them, and a dark shape walked out of its heart.

Alaric.

He raised his arms as he walked, and the tornado flew up and away from the road at his command. He kept walking, never looking back or to the side, all of his grim focus on Quinn.

"Apparently this is my ride," she said apologetically to her terrified driver. "Thank you, and I am so sorry for your fright."

She unbuckled her seat belt, climbed out, and then stood, fists on hips, as Alaric approached.

"You don't get to hurt innocent people, Alaric. That puts you on the wrong side of the equation, and I won't stand for it." She was proud that she stood her ground while a whirlwind of fury and magic in the shape of a man stalked toward her, caught her around the waist, and leapt into the air.

"No human is injured," he told her. "Not even their machines."

"You frightened them—"

"You will never leave me again," he said into her hair, and his voice was agonized; crazed. The voice of a man driven to the brink of madness. "If Ptolemy captures you, or *any* of your enemies find you, now that your face is plastered across the news all around the globe . . . Quinn, you would not want the world to try to survive my insanity if I lose you."

Quinn drew upon reserves deep within herself to remain calm as she found herself swirling counterclockwise in the heart of a tornado, somehow protected by Alaric's strength and magic.

"You can't do this, ever again. You cannot hold innocent lives hostage against my cooperation. That makes you no better than the murderers—human, shifter, or vampire—who kill people every day. The ones I've spent ten years fighting," she said, her mouth close to his ear so the wind didn't snatch her words away.

He shuddered against her, as if fighting a tidal wave of emotion. "I know. Don't you think I know? I, who pride myself on my logical, rational state of existence? I don't know what to do, Quinn. You must help me."

"I'd be better able to cope if we weren't flying around inside a freaking tornado," she shouted, finally losing the edges of calm. "Get me out of here!"

He nodded, and the glimmering oval of the portal appeared underneath them just before he dropped her. She screamed all the way down.

Chapter 7

An island in the Bermuda Triangle

After Alaric had calmed the storm and dispersed the tornado so none of the humans would be harmed, he followed Quinn through the portal to the beach on the other side, but prudently walked ten or so paces away, to give her a moment to recover from the fall. Now that he had time to consider the matter, it seemed that dropping her the five or six feet to the beach like that had perhaps not been the wisest course of action. After all, the woman was armed and definitely dangerous.

Dawn was breaking, and Quinn was so fierce and beautiful in the golden light of morning that he found himself almost unable to breathe at the sight of her, until she looked up and scowled at him. She sat, face like one of Poseidon's darkest thunderstorms, in about six inches of water. Waves broke against her and splashed on the glistening white sand around her, and she was completely drenched.

"You are a total slime ball, you know that? A . . . a scumbucket, useless pile of—"

"Perhaps you should carefully consider your words," he said, cutting her off before she had the opportunity to more fully demonstrate her command of insults. "I didn't have a lot of time to control the portal, since you wanted me to protect your humans from the storm."

"The storm *you* created," she snapped.

He couldn't help it. He started laughing. She resembled nothing more than a kitten caught in a rainstorm, snarling and spitting her dismay.

She narrowed her eyes, scrambled to her feet, and started toward him, moving fast. He watched, expecting her to stop before she reached him.

She did not.

Instead, she hit him at a full-on run, and knocked him backward so hard that he fell flat on his ass in the surf and sat there, sputtering seawater out of his mouth and staring up at her in total shock.

Quinn's narrowed-eye stare all but dared him to stand up again. "Do not ever, *ever* laugh at me after you throw a tornado at me, drop me from way too high up in the sky—*without* a parachute, I might add—and scare me half to death. Do you hear me?"

"The situation has little likelihood of coming up again," he said cautiously.

"You are so frustrating," she shouted at him, kicking more water on him. "Why couldn't you find some other tough rebel chick to drive out of her mind? Why did it have to be me?"

He shoved his dripping wet hair out of his face and, relief finally overwhelming him, grinned up at her. "World-bending kisses," he smugly reminded her.

Her mouth fell open, and she stood there gaping at him for several long moments before she shook her head and started laughing. "You are insane, you know that, right? Totally, entirely insane."

"The thought has often occurred to me," he admitted. "May I stand now, or do you plan to knock me over again?"

She tilted her head, as if considering her options. "Just stay there," she advised. Then she turned and walked away from him until she was about twenty feet from the surf line, where she sat down and stared out at the waves.

He waited another few minutes before he stood up. Just in case.

Clearly, he wasn't the only one on the beach who was balancing on the crumbling edge of sanity. He'd gone mad when he'd believed her to have been kidnapped or worse. Now that he knew she was safe, she could kick water on him all day long. He smiled again, and sent a fervent prayer to whatever gods were listening—although quite pointedly *not* to Poseidon—that he could continue to keep her safe.

No matter what the cost.

∽───∾

As the sun rose over the horizon, Quinn stared out at the waves and tried to let the beauty and serenity of the island sweep through her. The pure, salty scent of the ocean surrounded her as the breeze of the water played with the damp ends of her hair. The gentle roar of the tide all but demanded that she relax and let nature's peace calm her raging thoughts. She could pretend she was on a vacation. Tourists would pay a fortune to visit this unspoiled beach, and it was all hers.

Well. All hers, if she didn't count *him*.

She was trying to ignore him. *That* would teach him. Probably nobody ever ignored Alaric, Mr. High Priest Arrogant Son of a . . . Actually, she didn't know whose son he was. She didn't know anything about his family. Did Atlantean high priests even have mothers? Did they spring, full-grown, from some kind of whale egg?

It would never work between them. Yes, they had some insane animal attraction between them, but what did they even know about each other? She glanced at him out of the corner of her eye, and then almost laughed as the most terrifying warrior and most powerful magic-wielder she'd ever known sat in the water, waiting for her permission to stand up. She counted down under her breath, ". . . three, two—"

He stood up before she got to one, as expected, and it ticked her off even more that he rose up out of the water with his usual elegance. Alaric moved with the grace of a predator stalking prey, and too often lately she'd felt like the bunny rabbit to his wolf. His natural arrogance and belief he was in charge of every situation and every person he encountered wouldn't allow him to understand her: her fear of losing herself to his dominating nature; her fear that if she gave in, even once, to passion with him, she'd never be able to resist him again.

As he walked out of the water and onto dry sand, a brief shimmer of blue-green magic glowed around him. When the light dissipated, his clothes were completely dry. She wished she knew how to perform that handy trick, since her jeans were soaked and sand was sticking to them.

Alaric waved a hand in her direction, and her clothes also dried in a shimmer of light, as if he'd been reading her mind again. She didn't like it. Not one bit.

She pitched her voice to carry over the crashing surf. "Can you read my mind?"

He raised one dark eyebrow and smiled. "No, I have told you I cannot. It does not take thought-mining to anticipate that you would wish to be dry, however."

"Right. Can you guess what I'm thinking now?" she asked sweetly, as he approached. *What lovely broad shoulders you have*, she thought, and then felt her face burning.

He studied her face, and his smile slowly faded. "Ah. I cannot imagine it is anything complimentary."

She forced her mind back to the issue at hand, and away from how well his hard-muscled body filled out his clothes. "Let's talk about how you might have gotten some of those people in the cars back there killed."

"I would rather discuss kissing you," he said solemnly, and she nearly laughed but fought it down.

"This isn't funny."

"No, it isn't funny." He shoved a hand through his hair. "You are right. I could have caused people to die. This displeases you, so I will not allow it to happen again. It's a simple solution."

She blinked. "Alaric, we're the good guys. We wear the white hats. It should *matter* to us that people don't die just because they get in our way."

He made a complicated gesture with one hand, and a dolphin shot up out of the air in a graceful pirouette, rising to at least twenty feet in the air, before wafting back down to the waves at a gentle pace that clearly was not governed by the laws of gravity. It was a beautiful and terrifying display of restraint and power.

So he was frustrated with her. Most people rolled their eyes when they got frustrated. Alaric made dolphins do ballet. The symbolism of the differences between them wasn't lost on her.

"I have spent hundreds of years protecting these innocents you care so much about, *mi amara*. You judge me so harshly?" His face was all hard angles and lines, as if he waited for her to condemn him. She found, ultimately, that she couldn't.

"Nobody was hurt?"

"None that I saw," he replied. "I must be truthful with you, however. Every person on that road could have died if that had been what it took to protect you. See me for the heartless monster that I am, Quinn, and make no mistake that your safety is my only priority."

"It's not a burden I want," she said. "I can't say the same—you can't be my only priority. I need to get to New York and confront this Ptolemy and see what he wants. Maybe I can stop him, if he needs to be stopped."

"Oh, he needs to be stopped," Alaric said grimly. He sat down next to her on the white sand and told her what had happened at the Plaza. She listened in silence until the end, when he confessed his "idiocy" in saving the boy instead of following Ptolemy.

When he finished, she placed her hand on his arm. "You just can't help it, can you? You're a hero even when it's in spite of yourself."

"You weren't there," he reminded her with brutal honesty. "If you had been in danger, the results would have been far different. The boy would have died."

She shook her head. "No, you would have found a way to save us both. Or I would have saved him and you would have saved me, or we would have saved each other *and* the boy. We would have figured it out together, Alaric. We're a team. We have to be, or the bad guys win. It's as simple as that."

He shrugged. He'd been doing a lot of that lately, and she didn't like it. It was almost as if he'd given up the fight, just as surely as Jack had done.

She decided to change the subject. "Well. Enough of that. Where exactly are we? This isn't Mount Fuji anymore, that's for sure."

She scanned the pristine length of beach and its beautiful palm tree–covered border. The ocean was so brilliantly blue it almost hurt her eyes, and the rising sun shone on the water as brightly as if the entire vista had escaped from a traveler's favorite postcard. Seabirds played diving games with the sparkling waves, and a trio of dolphins chose that moment to leap into the air in synchronized splendor. The only sounds were the gentle pounding of the surf in front of them and the calls of birdsong from behind them.

Alaric pulled her against him, and she leaned her head on his shoulder, trying to soak in a rare moment of peace. Not quite sure how to achieve it.

"This is an unnamed island in the Bermuda Triangle, Quinn. Atlantis is in a deep-sea trench directly underneath us, about five and a half miles down."

Quinn couldn't believe what she was hearing. "Really? Did you just tell me the real location of Atlantis after thousands of years of every explorer and crackpot in history searching for it?"

"I did. Does that buy me back into your good graces?"

"Maybe a little. Wow. But, wait. Bermuda Triangle? Really? Is something freaky about to happen? Also, I thought Atlantis would be somewhere off the coast of Greece."

She could feel his body begin to shake silently, and it took a moment for Quinn to realize he was laughing.

"What now? Don't make me shove you in the surf again," she threatened.

"It's the way you said 'something freaky' as if that didn't describe most of your life. Caught me off guard."

She had to admit he had a point.

"Yes, we were originally located near Greece, when Atlantis rode the surface of the waves, but in the Cataclysm the gods created, Atlantis was transported here inside a tremendous magical vortex. None of our Elders or our records can say how. Since then, this area has been the center of a powerful magical fluctuation that often causes havoc with weather patterns."

"Are there sunken ships, airplanes, and spaceships littering the seafloor near Atlantis?" Quinn was fascinated and willing to continue the conversation for a while. She deserved a moment or two without worries about death, danger, or deceit.

Surely she'd earned that much over the past ten years.

"No spaceships that I know of, but I wouldn't discount the notion," he said without a trace of humor. "We did the best we could to assist any of your ships floundering in various massive storms, especially ones Poseidon caused when he was in a petulant mood, but we are limited in how much we can help, according to how many of us can travel by portal at any time. We can't exactly swim up from the dome."

"The pressure would crush you."

"Not to mention our best swimmers can only hold their breath for six or eight minutes. Five miles is a long way down."

"This may be the most bizarre conversation I've ever had, and that's saying a lot," she said. "Let's at least walk and see if we can find something to drink and some fruit."

He held up one hand, and a swirling ribbon of water spiraled playfully through the air from the trees until it stopped and hovered in front of Quinn.

"It's perfectly safe to drink."

Quinn took him at his word and drank deeply from the magical water fountain. "It's delicious," she said, surprised. "As pure as the water at Fuji."

"You're unlikely to find any purer. Nobody ever comes here but me, as far as I know. The island doesn't show up on your radar, or tracking devices, or whatever instruments your people use to chart the planet."

Alaric drank, too, and then released the swirling water, and it retreated back through the trees.

"You don't always have to take it all on, either, you know," she said quietly, making a sharp detour in the conversation. Even when she was frustrated and angry with him, even though he'd blocked his emotions from her, the crushing weight of his loneliness hovered at the edges of her awareness. "The weight of the world. The responsibility for everyone else's problems. Sometimes it's okay to let somebody else worry about *you*."

His eyes darkened, and a glimmer of something almost too powerful to be faced head-on looked out at her from behind that emerald glow. But a bird broke through the trees nearby, and the sound broke through the moment.

He held out his hand to her. "Let's explore, if you like."

She stared at him, afraid that she would be accepting so much more than just his hand.

"It's your choice, Quinn," he said, his eyes shuttered against her—against the possibility of rejection.

In the end, it wasn't a choice at all. She put her hand in his and simply waited, breathing slowly in and out so as not to react, as the electric sense of connection settled into place between them. They could deal with the issue of their attraction later. For once, she simply wanted to be Quinn. Not rebel leader, not forbidden love of an Atlantean high priest—just Quinn.

He said nothing, as if recognizing and granting her wish. They started walking, and she pretended, if only to herself, that they were normal tourists, sightseeing in paradise.

For once—just this once—pretending would be enough.

Chapter 8

Alaric watched Quinn as she walked along the beach, head down, eyes fixed on the sand or on a place he could not see; perhaps her own dark past. He'd long found that the solitude of the island setting was a balm to his own soul. A place where no demands would be placed on him—where no legions of enemies lined up to be battled, defeated, and killed.

They visited him, though, those legions. The faces of everyone he'd ever defeated, in the never-ending battle to protect humanity from its own folly; they haunted him in his sleep and, at times, visited him in his waking hours, as well. The ones he'd lost through his failure to protect fast enough, hard enough, or with sufficient scope—those ghosts accused him, too. A parade of death that had long caused him to believe his future would be a rapidly narrowing tunnel of madness and despair.

But then he'd met Quinn. Strong, courageous, and compassionate. A small human female who dressed like a homeless teen, fought like a hardened battle veteran, and plotted like a master strategist. It was she who should be claiming to be descended from Alexander the Great. None would have the slightest doubt.

Quinn glanced up at him, her brows drawn together in concern. For *him*. The experience was so novel that it sent another shock wave pounding through his body. Someone worrying about him—the monstrous high priest of terror. The one Atlantean women warned their children about, as if he were the bogeyman of their nightmares. *"Be good, or High Priest Alaric will take you away to the temple."*

They thought he didn't know. He'd trained himself to ignore it.

They thought he didn't care. He'd forced himself not to.

"What are you thinking about? You have a death grip on my hand," Quinn said, stopping and turning to look up into his face. "It's Ptolemy, isn't it? We should go. As long as he has Poseidon's Pride, everybody is in danger."

Alaric loosened his grip on her hand and then raised it to his lips. "Yes, Ptolemy. And other things, thoughts of little merit. This place has that effect on me, I'm afraid. Too much time and space for darker thoughts to intrude on common sense."

A shadow crossed her face, and she pulled her hand away from him and hugged herself as if cold, in spite of the warmth of sand-reflected sun. "I don't have the centuries of this battle behind me like you do, but believe me, I know about darker thoughts. I sometimes wish I could have been the sweetly ignorant person I pretended to be for my cover identity. It's amazing what a pink dress and a little lipstick can do for a woman's perceived IQ."

He knelt to retrieve a perfectly intact shell, pearly white with creamy brown striations, and shook off the sand before presenting it to her.

"I do not know what this IQ is, but I believe I understand your meaning. Perhaps we should buy Ven a pink dress, so he fools the enemy the next time we go into battle?"

Quinn laughed. "Oh, boy. Can you imagine? No, wait. How about Lord Justice? With that crazy blue hair and the ever-present sword? Actually, though, that might be even scarier."

She ran a finger along the edge of the shell before closing her hand around it. "Thank you. This is beautiful."

"A reminder that life is not all blood and death," he said, wishing he believed it.

He could see in her eyes that she did not believe it, either.

"Ours have been."

"So that the lives of others would not," he returned. He found another shell, a broken one, and hurled it far out into the waves. "It has always seemed a fair trade. Until now."

"Until now," she repeated slowly. "Alaric, I can never be what you might want me to be. I have forgotten anything I ever knew about any emotions but rage and pain and vengeance."

"Emotions can be relearned, Quinn. Brennan taught us that."

"Brennan was a warrior under a horrible curse from Poseidon not to feel any emotion until he met his one true love and then she died. How cruel and twisted is *that*? Your god isn't exactly what I'd call loving and benevolent."

"But Brennan found Tiernan, and she saved him from both the curse and himself. Don't you think we're all looking for exactly that?"

Quinn started walking again. "I don't know. I don't have time to care. I have to find Ptolemy and discover what he wants with me, before one of the many enemies I've made in the past tracks me down to put a final end to my adventures in rebellion."

"I have a bargain to propose," Alaric offered. "We spend the day here, not thinking or talking about enemies, or pretenders, or death. Then tomorrow we can return to our normal lives and kill all the 'bad guys,' as you so eloquently put it, that you might want."

Quinn's eyes were enormous as she weighed his words, and finally she nodded. "I agree. But Alaric, I never *wanted* to kill anybody. I just so rarely seem to have a choice. When nobody else is there to stand up for what's right . . ."

As her voice trailed off, he finished the sentence for her.

". . . somebody has to do it. Far too often, that somebody has been you, hasn't it?"

Their gazes met in perfect understanding, but Quinn shook her head slightly and looked away. "Let's explore and find out what's beyond these trees, okay?"

So much courage. Too much. His admiration for her increased each time they talked, until he could no longer untangle respect from desire from need—all of it centered on one small human.

One small, *sexy* human. She headed for the tree line, and Alaric watched her go, forcing his mind and libido off the instant raging want caused by the sight of her tight little ass walking away from him. It was almost funny, this sexual desire. After centuries of celibacy, he'd thought himself immune to it, and then Quinn had hit him with the force of a tsunami.

His mind, always trained to cold logic and objectivity, could now turn in a split second from thought of battle and enemies to considering what he would like to do with her naked body.

She turned to call back to him and he stopped, stunned by the simple curve of her cheek. She didn't possess the classical beauty of the women of his race. She had something more. A purity of spirit and a hidden sensuality that all but begged him to release it.

Just as soon as he figured out how to release his own. Hundreds of years of celibacy. That would be . . . *interesting* . . . to overcome.

His body tightened to an almost painful hardness as he swept his gaze over Quinn's curves, almost but not quite hidden by the ragged clothes she wore. So. At least certain parts of him had no concerns at all about how to proceed.

He followed her into the trees, smiling his first unqualified smile in many years.

~⁓⁓∾

Quinn watched Alaric reach up to pluck a bunch of bananas, unable to take her eyes off the play of muscles in his lovely chest and arms. He'd removed his shirt, a concession to the heat, and she found herself looking for excuses to touch him.

To put her hands all over that hot, slightly sweaty male skin. He was bronzed a golden tan, which surprised her, considering that she'd always pictured him doing, well, priestly things in Poseidon's temple. Lighting incense or whatever. Her dim memories of attending Catholic mass with a childhood friend seemed to have informed her impression of what Poseidon's high priest would do.

"So, do you conduct services in Atlantean?"

He tossed her a banana. "Do I what?"

"Church services. Do you all get together and sing songs and pray to Poseidon or whatever?"

He looked genuinely perplexed. "What are you talking about? Also, do I seem like the kind of man who gathers with a group to sing?"

She peeled her banana and started laughing. "Not exactly. Unless it was some kind of battle cry. I was just thinking about what exactly it is that you do as high priest to the sea god."

"Ah. That." He devoured the fruit in three quick bites and tossed the peel into the grass, to become fertilizer for the next generation of plants.

"No. It is not a temple like your churches. As high priest, I am the bearer of Poseidon's most powerful magic, protector of Atlantis, keeper of the scrolls, mentor to the acolytes, and chief counselor to those who need intercession with the gods."

"Chief counselor?" She didn't quite buy that one. "Really?"

He grinned so wickedly that she wondered if her clothes would spontaneously disappear.

"I'm not much of the counselor type. My chief acolyte handles those requests. He says I am more likely to tell them that life is meant to be difficult, and the gods do not reward those who moan and complain."

"So, in other words, the 'suck it up, buttercup' style of priestly counsel," Quinn said, forcing the words out through her laughter. "I can see why he doesn't let you talk to people."

Alaric raised his eyebrows. "I believe you just insulted me. I am perfectly capable of talking to people. I just don't like it."

"Really? I never would have guessed."

"People are annoying," he announced, folding his arms, which did delightful things to the muscles in his arms and chest. Her throat suddenly went dry. She felt like she'd been celibate almost as long as he had, and surely that was the reason her body trembled and her breath caught in her lungs whenever he was nearby. It was a good thing he wasn't allowed to have sex, or they'd either set the island on fire with their passion or set a world record for clumsy fumbling.

"Poor baby," she finally answered him, with an utter lack of sympathy. Then she finished peeling her banana and took a huge bite, closing her eyes in bliss as she chewed and swallowed.

"This is delicious—" She forgot what she was saying when she glanced up and met his gaze. He was staring at her mouth, and his eyes were a blazing emerald green.

"Delicious," he repeated, his voice strained. "Quinn, you tempt me beyond reason. I have spent the past several hours waging a private war against myself to keep from touching you, and I find I am losing the battle."

He took a deep breath. "I need to kiss you now. Will you allow this?" He'd lowered his arms to his sides, and she saw that his hands were clenched into fists.

"I don't think it's a very good idea." She realized her hands were shaking, and she dropped the fruit so she could hide them behind her back. Never show weakness to an enemy.

Or a potential lover.

She considered various responses and finally settled on the simple truth. "If you kiss me, how will we ever stop? I'm not sure I can be strong enough for both of us. Not with you."

His smile sharpened and grew predatory. "Quinn, I don't want to ever stop." He took a step toward her and then another. "I could kiss you for an eternity, and it wouldn't be enough."

She knew from their very few, very brief encounters that he was telling the truth—truth enough for both of them. She was helpless in the face of it.

"Then kiss me already," she said, surrendering to the inevitable.

He flew across the space separating them, and she barely had time to draw in a breath of the deeply scented tropical air before he was on her, wrapping his arms around her and lifting her nearly off her feet.

"I have waited all of my life for you," he said roughly, and the stark honesty in his face humbled her.

"I feel the same way," she whispered, knowing she should deny it. Knowing it was wrong. She'd done such horrible things in the name of the rebellion. Dark and deadly things. Twisted and awful things. She could never deserve Alaric, this warrior priest who'd stepped right out of the pages of mythology and into her heart.

"Stop thinking so hard," he murmured, and then he took her mouth with his, and she found herself incapable of thinking anything at all.

His kisses burned her skin—her mouth, her face, her neck. He kissed her as a dying man might beg for grace or benediction; desperately and without reserve. She felt herself falling, drowning, sinking into an abyss of wanting and *feeling* and needing, and she realized her arms were twined tightly around his neck and she was pressed against his body so close that not even a breath separated them.

It wasn't close enough.

She sank into a whirlwind of feeling; a storm of longing that made the tornado he'd created in Tokyo seem like nothing more than a soft breeze. Nerves long untouched signaled bright flares to the pleasure center in her brain, until she felt herself incandesce with the sharp, almost painful brilliance of pure desire.

She moaned, or he did, and he lifted her higher in his arms, and she wrapped her legs around his waist and pressed even closer, feeling from the large, hard bulge of his erection that although rules may have stopped him in the past, he certainly wasn't unwilling or unable now.

He wanted her, and the knowledge drove her further and

further over the edge, past sense and reason, and into an abyss filled with need and want and hunger.

He pulled back a little and stared down at her, his eyes burning in a face gone stark and hard with desire.

"Quinn, I need you. Now. I need you naked and underneath me or on top of me or however you want, but I need you to be naked. Right. Now."

Chapter 9

Alaric had never been more in danger of losing his sanity than he was right at this moment with this woman he held so tightly in his arms. If she stopped kissing him, he was sure he would die from the loss of her touch. Everything he was and ever had been was centered on the burning waves of need and hunger rushing through him. He wanted Quinn like he'd never wanted any woman before in all the long, lonely centuries of his life.

He needed her. To the nine hells with the repercussions.

"Alaric? Your emotions just changed. What are you thinking about?" Her eyes were dark and dazed, but trying to focus.

"Nothing important," he said firmly and kissed her again.

"No," she said, struggling to put a bit of space between them. "That's not true. What is going on in your brilliant but dark and twisty mind?"

He shook his head and leaned toward her again, but she put a hand up between them and pushed.

"Tell me."

He gave in, knowing she would persevere until he did so.

"All of my life, I have been told that the vow of celibacy is the key to my power. The Elders strongly impressed upon me the need to protect myself from the desires of the flesh or the call to softer emotions."

She squeezed his arm and then backed away a step so she could look up into his face as he continued.

He had no choice now. He had to tell her, and there was no way to pretty up the stark truth, so he just said it. "There's a good chance that if I break my vow of celibacy, I'll lose my magic."

The bald statement hung in the air between them for several long moments, and then Quinn backed away from him so fast she stumbled and fell on the ground. He moved to help her, but she shook her head, scrambling backward on all fours.

"Don't touch me! How can you possibly say that to me and then try to touch me?" Her voice held a tinge of hysteria, and her eyes were wild. "I can't bear that burden, Alaric. Don't ask me to."

"No, you don't understand. This is only what the Elders told me. Keely, the scientist who has soul-melded with Justice—she's an object reader. She told me that the Elders lied or at least were wrong. That in truth the most powerful high priest in the history of Atlantis was not only not celibate, but he was actually married. Nereus was married to Zelia, and from what Keely said, they were extremely happy and in love."

She kept shaking her head, back and forth, over and over. "Keely said. She's human, right?"

He nodded the affirmative.

"So a human who claims to be picking up psychic woo-woo emanations from *objects* tells you that, okay, sure, Alaric, it's okay to break your sacred vow, it will all be fine, no worries, and you think that's good enough?"

"Serai confirmed as much," he said, a little desperately.

"Right. And there couldn't be anything wrong with *her* memory, after eleven thousand years of stasis, right?" Quinn shook her head. "We can't take that chance. Maybe this

Nereus never had to swear the same vow you did. Maybe his powers worked differently. Or maybe she's just wrong."

"When you say it in those terms, of course—"

"And what happened to this Nereus? Happy ever after? Many fat babies?"

He paused. This was where the story broke down. "Actually, Zelia died, and Nereus tried to drown the world. He nearly destroyed the dome and everyone in Atlantis with it."

"So he went *nuts*, is that what you're saying?" Quinn scrambled to her feet and continued backing away from him. "Bat-shit crazy, insane, loony tunes, rubber room material? Nearly destroyed your *entire civilization*, but hey, let's get naked?" Her voice had risen and she was shaking.

"The two are probably unrelated," he began cautiously. He had no idea how to fix this, but he was desperate to find a way to do so—to fix everything—so that the terror and disbelief he heard in her voice would disappear.

His body, rebelling after so many years of denial, ached with frustration and the desolate certainty that his chances of remaining celibate for the foreseeable future were increasing with every word out of his mouth.

"Probably. Unrelated. Sacred vow, insanity, destroy Atlantis, but it's okay, probably unrelated," she muttered, stalking off toward the beach. "Get me out of here, Alaric."

"We don't have to leave now. I refuse to take you anywhere until we talk this out," he commanded, following her.

Unfortunately, the irritating woman didn't respond at all well to commands.

"Get. Me. Out. Of. Here," she said, enunciating each word as if slicing it with a dagger. "Also, don't touch me again. Not now, not ever. Or at least not until your people don't need you anymore, and you're old and gray and retired."

He strode ahead of her to hold a low-hanging palm frond out of her way before she marched right into it, and she stopped and poked a finger into his chest.

"Except that won't happen. You won't get old and gray. I'll get old and gray, if I live that long, which I probably won't, and you'll still be young and beautiful and hot and sexy, and

I can never kiss you again, and you made me want what I can't have, and right now I kind of hate you for it." She finally stopped to draw breath. "And—and—put your shirt on!"

He watched her stalk off down the beach, completely unable to think of a thing to say that would fix everything and get them back to the part where she was kissing him. The faint tingle of magic behind him alerted him to the portal, and he whirled around to see the high prince himself step out onto the sand.

Conlan looked at Alaric and then at Quinn's departing figure, and then he whistled. "What did you do to my sister-in-law? Riley only stomps off like that when she'd rather be punching me."

"I only wish she would strike me," Alaric said glumly. "I fear this problem is far too big for that."

"How bad can it be? At least you didn't threaten to abdicate the throne for her," joked Conlan, who had done just that for Riley, Quinn's sister.

"Worse. I threatened to break my vows to Poseidon."

Conlan's eyes widened. "You're willing to trust that Keely is right about your magic?"

"What choice do I have? I petitioned Poseidon, over and over, and he refuses to answer. I petitioned the Elders, and they tell me exactly what they always have: if I 'succumb to fleshly evils,' I will lose all of my power. I can believe them and spend the rest of my life alone, or I can believe Keely and Serai are right and claim Quinn for mine." Alaric smashed an extra-large energy sphere into the sand in front of him out of pure frustration.

"Serai?" Conlan raised an eyebrow.

Alaric filled him in on what Serai had told him.

"Quinn doesn't seem to be in the mood to risk your future," Conlan observed, as Quinn flopped down on the sand, with her back pointedly toward them.

"Quinn needs to be convinced," Alaric growled. "I can best do that in Atlantis."

"I can't influence you on this, I know, without the utmost hypocrisy, but I'm worried about the repercussions, too. I can't imagine you as anything other than the high priest of Atlantis, and there's the little matter of how in the nine hells we're going to retrieve Poseidon's Pride if you can no longer touch it," Conlan said, his face somber.

"That, as always, is the ultimate truth," Alaric said, clenching his hands into fists. "My duty must always come before anything else."

"Now that we've figured out your love life, or lack thereof," Conlan said, smiling ruefully as if to let Alaric know he shared his dismay, "what else is new?"

Alaric smacked himself in the forehead, and Conlan's mouth fell open.

"I don't believe I've ever seen you do anything so uncontrolled in your life," the prince said.

"My life is so far out of my control right now, I don't even recognize it." Alaric smashed another energy ball into the sand next to the intricate glass sculpture the first had formed. "The most important thing of all, and I'm only now mentioning it. My apologies."

"Mentioning what?" Conlan said with elaborate patience.

"There is a pretender to the throne. He calls himself Ptolemy Reborn and claims to be descended from Alexander the Great. He stole Poseidon's Pride, and he plans to crown himself king of Atlantis."

Conlan blinked once and then bared his teeth in a grim parody of a smile. "This? This I think we'd better sit down for."

~~~~~

Quinn didn't need much persuading to go to Atlantis. She'd been anticipating this moment since she first learned her sister was in love with the Atlantean high prince. Plus, she had a tiny nephew she was dying to meet. She'd ignore the insane high priest and his magic-giving-up lunacy for as long as necessary, and then she'd escape and make her way to New York, hope Ptolemy was still there, and confront him. Or else find a way to go get him. It was a plan.

Not a *good* plan, or even much of a plan at all, but it was a start. If her heart would only stop aching so much at the thought of it.

She stepped into the portal again, wondering how many trips through a magic doorway it took before a person became blasé about it. Whatever that number was, she hadn't reached it yet. Maybe she never would. She certainly didn't anticipate traveling to Atlantis very often, in what was left of her sure-to-be short life.

The magic doorway deposited her on a grassy space, and remembering Noriko, she turned around to face the shining oval. "Thank you for the transportation, and for not dropping me to my death in that tornado. I appreciate it."

The armed guards standing in a loose semicircle around the space stared at her with varying expressions of amusement, until the portal flashed with a brilliant blue light and a deep male voice emanating from the center replied.

"You're welcome."

Then the guards' expressions changed to astonishment, and it was Quinn's turn to be amused.

"It never hurts to be polite," she said loftily to the one who looked like he was in charge.

He bowed, a grin quirking at the edges of his lips. "Yes, my lady."

"I wondered about that," Alaric said, but he tightened his lips against saying anything further when she deliberately turned away from him and toward Conlan, who was staring at the portal with slightly widened eyes.

"So is this it? Is this the famous . . . oh. Oh, holy cow." She stopped talking; she almost stopped breathing, as she looked up and up at the crystalline structure curving gently above her head. The dome. It was really true.

A scattering of twinkling lights swam past the outside of the surface of the dome nearest her, and she walked closer, fascinated, until she was close enough to realize they had done just that—*swum* by—because it was a school of some kind of tiny iridescent fish whose bellies lit up like Christmas lights. It was beautiful and breathtaking, and Quinn finally allowed herself to calm down and simply enjoy the moment.

When she slowly turned away from the fish, and looked up, she realized that the twilit sky inside the dome sparkled with starlight, but in patterns she didn't recognize.

"Are they representations of constellations you saw before? Back when Atlantis was still on the surface like the rest of the continents?"

Conlan nodded. "Yes. It's a self-perpetuating magic, created more than eleven thousand years ago. We understand the stars have shifted since then."

"And of course you're here in the Bermuda Triangle, which might affect any stars you see, too, right?"

"Yes, but we hope that changes when we rise and take our place on the surface again. We believe the magic required to sustain and hide us so far beneath the waves is what causes the temporal disturbances above."

She didn't even want to tackle that. Sounded like physics or science fiction, and she was too tired for either. In the meantime, she'd noticed something else.

"There's no moon."

Alaric shook his head. "No. Never a moon. An oversight or deliberate, we don't know."

She turned to look at him and was nearly undone by the sadness in his eyes. He was caught on the horns of a terrible dilemma, and she didn't want to be part of his downfall. *Couldn't* be. Couldn't watch him turn bitter with despair, as his inability to help his people ate at his soul.

She knew that kind of despair, up close and personal. She would never willingly cause it in another. Especially not Alaric. Never him.

So instead she pasted a happy smile on her face. "Now I think it's time I meet my nephew, don't you?"

Conlan grinned. "He will steal your heart and drool all over your shoulder. I'm just warning you in advance. This teething thing is a barnacle."

She laughed. "A barnacle? We say something difficult is a bear."

"I know, but it doesn't make any sense. Bears are fluffy things that roam. Barnacles are hateful creatures that stubbornly stick around for far longer than you want them." The prince ran a hand through his hair, and she was suddenly struck by his resemblance to his brother Ven.

Her nephew would look like these men, tall and dark and classically gorgeous, and look like a Dawson, too. She wondered if he had Riley's deep ocean blue eyes or her own dark ones, maybe. If he had golden curls like his mom, or Conlan's dark beauty.

She quickened her pace. "You have a point about barnacles. I think I'll use that expression from now on. But can we hurry, um, Your Highness? I haven't seen Riley in far too long."

Conlan laughed again and slung a companionable arm around her shoulder. "Hey, none of that. We're family now."

Family. Atlantis. The myths just kept coming and coming.

Chapter 10

As they walked through fantastical gardens whose flowers shone and sparkled in the magical starlight, Quinn stared around like a country bumpkin gone to visit her city cousins. The scents of the flowers jumbled together in a delicious blend of aromas so wonderful she almost wished she were a perfume maker.

"That—is that a cousin to a daisy?" She pointed at a blossom fully three feet across, with a deep purple center and fuchsia petals. "It's like I've walked into a Dr. Seuss book."

"Riley said exactly that," Conlan said. "She bought the entire collection for Aidan, so I could see what she meant. You'd almost think the author had been Atlantean."

"If I see any talking elephants, I'm running for cover," she warned, and he laughed.

Alaric, walking silently beside her, said nothing, but his face grew darker and darker, as if he had little or no patience for light chatter about flowers and books. Considering the sword that had been hanging over his head for centuries, it wasn't surprising.

She had to put it out of her mind, at least for a while,

though, or she'd go crazy. She focused on the incredible garden, pretending she was just an ordinary woman enjoying the beauty of the night-drenched view.

When they walked out from beneath the canopy of a bower of silver-leaved trees, she looked up and actually gasped. "Wow. Just wow. Cinderella's castle has nothing on this place."

The delicate marble and crystal spires and towers of the palace shone like a jewel box. It was a dream from a fairy tale, and she was walking up to the perfect fantasy of every five-year-old girl on the planet. And with Prince Charming, no less.

She started laughing. Really, what else was a girl do to?

The heavy wooden front doors swung open, and her sister ran out of the palace and flew at Quinn, embracing her in a huge bear hug.

"You came, you finally came," Riley said, both laughing and crying.

Quinn found her own eyes tearing up while she hugged her sister. It had been far too long. Too many duties had kept her from the only family she had left in the world.

"I missed you so much," she whispered.

Riley sniffled. "Too much for too long, crazy girl. Enough of this Quinn the Terminator crap. Get in here and be Auntie Quinn for a while."

Quinn shot a look at Alaric over her sister's shoulder, and the grim understanding in his face almost undid her. She might have nothing left to her *except* to be Auntie Quinn.

Could she live with that?

She might have to find out.

"We have a lot to tell you," she said, the full weight of Ptolemy's claims and actions settling back down on her shoulders. "None of it good. But first, let me meet my gorgeous nephew."

They left the men behind, to Quinn's relief, and Riley led her through rooms and hallways and past people dressed in flowing clothes that seemed to belong in a fairy tale. Riley kept up a running commentary, but Quinn gave up trying to remember it all after the third or fourth "this is the way to the breakfast kitchen" or "this is the warriors' wing" or "the household staff lives down this way."

"You have become somebody who has household staff," Quinn marveled. "Who would have thought?"

Riley stopped short and turned around, an embarrassed smile on her face. Her dark blue eyes flashed with amusement, and she sent a powerful blast of embarrassed resignation through their shared emotional connection. "I know, it's ridiculous, right? But what was I going to do? It came with Conlan, kind of a package deal."

"Prince Charming," Quinn drawled. "Does that make you Sleeping Beauty?"

"No, that was Serai. I think more like Cinderella. Not that we lived in ashes, but you know what I mean. It's a long way from the life of a struggling social worker to life in a palace on a mythological lost continent."

"Mom would have loved it. Remember all those stories she told us?"

They shared a moment of sad fondness for the woman they'd lost too early, and then Riley took off again, her cloud of red-gold hair flashing. "Come on. Aidan should be awake by now."

"Isn't it bedtime? Not that I know anything about babies."

"No, he has an after-dinner nap, and then he's awake for a while and goes back to sleep around ten," Riley said, racing down a hallway lined with tapestry-covered walls.

Quinn was no expert, but she thought the tapestries looked old and intricate enough to belong in a museum. Which was funny, considering that the entire place belonged in a museum of antiquities. Every archaeologist and anthropologist on the planet was going to wet his or her pants when word got out about this place.

Up one final staircase, and Riley flung open two ornately carved doors to an enormous room that looked like it belonged in a magazine. Gorgeous carved woods, silver and crystal accessories, and rich, lush fabrics combined to make the room a showplace.

A thin wail coming from a round white wicker bassinet in the center of the room alerted them to the occupant's state of mind.

"He's up, and he's mad. I'm supposed to be right there when he wakes up," Riley said, smiling. "His 'prince of the manor' arrogance showing up early, I guess."

Quinn eagerly followed her and was rewarded by an armload of warm, squirmy, angry baby being thrust into her arms.

"Meet your auntie Quinn while I get a diaper, kid," Riley advised her son, before disappearing into another room.

Baby and rebel leader stared at each other with matching expressions of total surprise. The baby's emotions pulsed strongly, wrapping themselves around her in a cocoon of love and contentment. This child was loved, and he knew it. His innocence and purity shone like a beacon, and underneath both there was something else—something *more*. A strength and self-possession that was unbelievably powerful in such a tiny baby.

"Oh, boy," Quinn whispered. "Welcome to the world, Aidan. You are destined for great things, my sweet nephew."

He grinned up at her, gums flashing, and Quinn realized she'd just fallen hopelessly in love for the second time in one day.

❦

Conlan and Alaric headed for the war room, bypassing Conlan's fancy and rarely used throne room on the way.

"Do you want me to tell you now or wait till everyone is gathered?"

"Most of them aren't even here," Conlan said. "Ven returned several hours ago, but Erin was in some kind of trouble in Seattle with her witch's coven, so he portaled out of here after telling me cryptically, 'We've got big trouble, bro.'"

"He's not wrong," Alaric said grimly.

"Justice is here. I'll call him." Conlan didn't even pause, but Alaric knew he'd sent out a call on the Atlantean shared mental pathway to his half brother, the only Atlantean in the royal family who was also descended from the ancient race of Nereids.

Complicated family tree in the Atlantean royal house.

Justice arrived at the war room seconds before them, and he held open the door. His long blue braid reached his waist and almost covered the broad battle sword sheathed on his back. He was wearing fighting leathers, as usual.

"No more guards?" Alaric said, surprised to see the change.

Conlan's face hardened. "It was a waste of resources. Anybody who infiltrates the palace will go for Riley or the baby, not a stuffy roomful of old scrolls and maps."

Justice snarled out an Atlantean curse. "If any should try to harm the prince or your lady, we will personally deliver him to you. In several trips."

At the sound of the plural *we*, Alaric sent out a subtle mental touch, to discover if Justice were still walking on stable mental ground. He was relieved to find that all was well.

Justice grinned at him. "I was talking about we, the warriors, not we, the two halves of my dual soul, priest, but thank you for your concern for my welfare."

Alaric couldn't get over the change in the man since he'd found Keely and their adopted Guatemalan daughter, Eleni. Justice had always been hard, vicious, and almost terrifying. He was still all of those things, when battle called for it, but he had somehow found the ability to laugh, too.

Conlan led the way to the scarred wooden table that had seen countless war councils for thousands of years. He pulled out a chair and sat heavily.

"Here we go again," Conlan said wearily. "I'm more and more tired of being high prince some days."

Alaric took the chair opposite the prince, and Justice leaned against a wall.

Alaric glanced at them both in turn. "Well, then, you will be delighted to hear that there is a man on the surface who has just declared to the world that *he* is the rightful king of Atlantis."

He leaned back in his chair and waited for the explosion.

It didn't take long.

Conlan smashed his fist on the table. "You need to explain this now. It took everything I had to wait this long to hear the story behind what you told me on the beach, but I did not wish to ruin my wife's sister's first visit to Atlantis so soon. I also wonder why my brother didn't tell me this. Did he know?"

"He knew, but you said Erin was in danger. He had to go to her. None of us would have done differently, and you know it," Alaric pointed out. "Also, Quinn is in the middle of all of this, and she will not appreciate being treated as a helpless female who needs to be shielded from plans."

Conlan blew out a deep breath but then nodded.

"She knows this, though, and I don't. Tell me. Everything."

The door slammed open, and Ven ran into the room. "Sorry I'm late. Got held up. Erin is going to put me in an early grave."

Erin, walking in behind him, rolled her eyes. "I'm the most powerful witch in my coven. If I can't handle a little uprising from black magic wannabes, I deserve to be stripped of my wand."

"I thought you said wands were for Harry Potter," Justice said, tilting his head.

She grinned at him. "Figure of speech. 'Stripped of my wand' just sounds cooler than 'stripped of my elemental magic and the Wilding,' right?"

Conlan glared at all of them. "Can we focus? Now? Please? Consider this a royal decree, if that helps." He pointed at Ven. "You and I will discuss your lack of communication skills later."

Ven snorted and flung himself into an upholstered chair near the table, one long leg draped over the arm. Alaric told them everything. Everything about Ptolemy Reborn, the attack in Japan—all of it. Except for what had occurred between him and Quinn on the island, of course. Some things were meant to be private.

Conlan sat back in his chair, stunned, when Alaric finished his recitation. "The portal is alive? We guessed it had some form of sentience, but this is . . . surprising, to say the least. And now apparently the portal spirit is male, not female, if the voice we heard when Quinn spoke to it is an indicator."

"I think we have no time to concern ourselves with the portal just now," Alaric said.

"Yeah. It's worse than even you know. That blast, Alaric? The one Ptolemy blew up the hotel with? News reports are saying that the king of Atlantis announced his presence in the world by killing seventeen people," Ven said grimly. "Those Platoists and a few of the hotel staff."

Conlan's face turned to stone. "I have been preparing the way for Atlantis's arrival on the surface for months. Foreign dignitaries, heads of state, all of it ruined by this impostor."

Alaric's fury rose up inside him with the force of a typhoon over open ocean. "Yes," he snarled. "We wouldn't want the deaths of a few innocent humans to get in the way of *politics*."

"You know I don't mean that," Conlan shouted at him. "How long have you battled beside me? Has anything ever gotten in my way when it comes to protecting humanity? I take my oath as a Warrior of Poseidon very seriously and you should know that."

"He has Poseidon's Pride, Conlan," Alaric said quietly. "He's able to use it. And it gets even worse. I think he might be demon kin."

"Yeah, demon kin, whatever," Ven threw in. "You want worse? Anubisa is back. Archelaus wasn't just slinging rumors. She walked into the Primus today and destroyed every vampire member of Congress in one fell swoop. Told the humans who happened to be there to pass along the word that no vampire in the world was safe until they delivered the heads of the Atlantean royal family to her on a plate."

"She has always had a flair for drama," Alaric observed, mostly to give Conlan a chance to regain his composure. Anubisa, the vampire goddess, had held Conlan captive and tortured him for seven long years before he' escaped. Alaric thought that a bit of madness still lurked in Conlan's mind from the ordeal. How could it not?

"Good. Maybe she'll kill Ptolemy for us," Ven said.

"Why would she go after the vampires, though, is what I don't understand," Erin said. "They're her progeny, right? Why not threaten to kill humans instead?"

"Humans don't have the juice to find us," Conlan answered. "She knows every blood pride in the world will be after us now. One of them is bound to get lucky."

"Yeah, and we have an answer to your flying monkeys, too," Ven said. "Shape-shifter communities are going wild all over the world. Losing any vestige of civilization and turning feral. Interestingly enough, all of this started within a day of when those scientists in Turkey found Poseidon's Pride. The jewel must be driving them nuts somehow."

"The Trident may act as a stabilizing influence on its raw power," Alaric said.

"Which is why you need to go find it," Conlan said. "Take Ven, take everybody you need. I'd go, but I'm going to have to do a lot of damage control right now. When you find the bastard, call me, though. I'd love to face this man who would be king."

Alaric defied his prince only rarely.

This would be one of those times.

"I will not leave Quinn. Didn't you hear what I told you? He announced her identity to the world. Every vampire, rogue shifter, and any of a dozen other shapes and sizes of big and bad will be after her." Alaric called to his magic until his body glowed bright blue-green from head to toe and he held so much power inside him that one simple flick of his fingers could have leveled the palace. "I will never leave her side, or allow her to be in danger again."

"She's safe in Atlantis, and you know it. No vampire or shifter can enter through the portal," Conlan said calmly. "And turn down the lights, my friend. We get that you're scary. We get that you have an insanely overprotective need to make sure Quinn is safe. We'll find a way, but we have to stop this man, or demon, or whatever in the nine hells he is. Now."

A quiet voice came from the doorway, and they all turned

to see Quinn standing at the open door, sheer rage stamped on her delicate features. "Perhaps the next time you decide to discuss my future, you might remember to include me in the discussion. Especially when the future of the whole damned world is at stake."

Chapter 11

Abandoned subway tunnel, New York City

The one now known to the entire world as Ptolemy Reborn slouched insolently in a chair while Anubisa, goddess of Chaos and Night, matriarch to all vampires, supreme ruler of the dark, vibrated with fury as she hung floating in midair, halfway to the ceiling.

Frankly, she was boring the shit out of him.

"Yeah, yeah, I get it." He finally interrupted her tirade. "You'll help me in my quest to take the throne of Atlantis, and I'll deliver the current royal family to you. Do you just want the two and a half princes, or do you want the women and the baby, too?"

She froze, mid-rant, and stared at him, then levitated back down until her silk slipper–clad feet touched the floor. "Baby? Did I know there was a baby?"

She flung her arms out and did her best impression of a mad ballerina as she capered and twirled around the room, her hip-length black hair floating around her like a cloak of spider silk. "Oh, I don't remember, my time in the Void was so long and so dark and twisted, with lovely, broken creatures. Did I know there was a baby? Did I?"

"Whether you did or not, there is one. Conlan's kid. Heir to the throne. Do you want him?"

She smiled at him in a grim parody of happiness, and her fangs sliced into her lips and chin, gouging flesh and blood that ran down her face.

"Oh, yes, I want the baby," she whispered. "I must have the baby, I will count his little fingers and his little toes, and then I will bite them off and drink every drop of blood in his fat little body, and finally, *finally*, that will be the end of those hideous Atlanteans."

Ptolemy was a little skeptical about her calling anybody else hideous, seeing as how she was a few dozen bricks short of a load, but as they liked to say in his world, "*Evil plans make a bad day joyous.*"

He planned to have a *very* joyous day.

"I'll deliver them to you, and you'll hold up your end of the bargain. The vampires will recognize me as the true king of Atlantis and uphold my sovereignty."

She levitated again, cackling, still chanting about the baby, but then a look of sly calculation swept over her face. In spite of the gore and madness, it was still the most stunning face he'd ever seen; she had a deadly dark beauty that would cut and bleed any who dared come close.

Good enough. He had no plans to get close to this crazy bitch. Soon he'd have Quinn. He thought about all that would entail, and he finally smiled. Anubisa mistook his smile for appreciation of her wonderfulness, apparently, because she glared haughtily down at him from a few feet up.

"The likes of you will never have me, demon," she hissed.

He yawned. "I am no demon of your realm to be cowed by you, vampire," he said. "My Atlantean mother bore me to the Higher Demon who stole her from her home, and their blood, combined, will make me the most powerful ruler Atlantis or this world has ever seen. Join in or be left behind. It matters little to me now, and will mean even less when I use the power of Poseidon's Trident to open the doors between worlds and allow my brethren access to this garden paradise of a planet."

The vampire started laughing, chanting a nonsensical song, and Ptolemy laughed right along with her. It was going to be a very, *very* joyous day.

Chapter 12

The war room, Atlantis

Quinn sat in the chair the farthest away from anybody who'd recently pissed her off, which included everyone except her sister, so the logistics were tricky unless she wanted to move out into the hall. She put her empty plate down on the table next to her and considered going back for more roast chicken. She might be angry, but long years of fighting and hardship had taught her that you ate when there was food, slept when there was a bed, and felt grateful for either or both.

Riley leaned over and handed Quinn a chocolate cookie. "Are you going to even look at him? Poor man is dying over there. He's the scariest guy in the world, and yet I think he's a little bit afraid of you."

Quinn scoffed. "I don't know what you're talking about. He's not afraid of anything, although you'd think the size of his over-inflated head would be terrifying as it crashes into walls."

She crammed the cookie in her mouth and tried not to bliss out too obviously as the melted chocolate and spices exploded on her tongue.

"He's worried about you," Riley murmured. "And he

doesn't know how to worry about anyone. His life has been all about power and command; balancing the demands of a capricious god with the bleak reality of his loneliness. For Pete's sake, Quinn, you should have seen him when I was pregnant. He practically set a peacock on fire for daring to walk across my path in the garden one day."

Riley screwed up her face into a fierce scowl. "It might have tripped you and damaged your womb or the heir to the throne, Princess," she said gruffly, clearly imitating Alaric.

Quinn started laughing. "Damaged your *womb*? Oh, no, he did not!"

Riley handed her another cookie and sat back in her chair. "Oh, yes, he did, and I could tell you worse stories. Let's just leave it at this: Alaric has never been in love in his life and he's head over heels for you. He has been since that first day we found you on the ground, with a bullet in your shoulder, and now he thinks he might be able to do something about it, thanks to Keely. Can you blame the poor man for losing his mind?"

Quinn shook her head. "I can't quite wrap *my* mind around the idea of centuries of celibacy," she whispered. "Even if Keely is right—and that's far too big of a chance to take— what if he doesn't remember how?"

Riley rolled her eyes. "I imagine it's like riding a bike."

The sisters both froze and then looked at each other and cracked up.

"Riding a bike," Quinn gasped out. "Can you imagine?"

"Doing—doing wheelies," Riley said, which set them off again.

By the time they caught their breath, every other person in the room was staring at them.

"Care to share the joke with the class?" Erin said, grinning.

And that started them off again. They were both gasping for air by the time they could regain control and stop laughing.

"Dinner at your house must have been very interesting," Ven said.

"You have no idea. Two emotional empaths during puberty? It was hell," Quinn said.

The men winced, and Erin laughed.

Just then the door opened and a tall, athletic redhead walked in. Justice jumped up and pulled her into his arms, so it must be Keely.

"We have been alone for too long today," Justice said firmly, but Keely just laughed.

"Hey, relax. I'm starving after a long, dusty day translating scrolls from the library of Alexandria. Thank goodness Eleni is having a sleepover with one of her many friends tonight."

"It is good she finally has friends, after what she endured," Justice said grimly.

Their gazes met in a glance of shared understanding, and then Keely leaned down to grab a slice of bread from a basket on the table, tore a piece off, and ate it.

"Now I need a plate full of whatever smells so delicious, and a hot bath, and, oh, hey, we have company," she said, as she finally saw Quinn in the corner.

"That is not company, that is family," Justice said. "Keely, my love, meet Quinn Dawson."

Keely whistled, her gaze quickly snapping to Alaric and then back to Quinn. She dropped the rest of her bread on a plate and quickly crossed the room, hand outstretched. Quinn stood to shake her hand, but at the last minute, Keely pulled her into a hug.

"Family, right? Hey, I am a big admirer of yours," she said seriously after she released Quinn. "It takes a lot of courage to do what you do every day, without special powers or magic. Thank you for making the world safer for the rest of us."

Quinn shuffled her feet, uncomfortable with the expression and even more so with the honest sincerity of emotion the woman projected. "Yeah, it's nothing. I mean, I'm just one of many, and we all do our part."

"Untrue," Alaric said. "You are first among many, and you do far more than your part."

"Jack was first," she fired back at him. "And I left him, trapped as a tiger forever for all I know."

Riley took her sister's hand and squeezed it. "We were all so sorry to learn about Jack. We've been praying that he finds his way back."

Quinn couldn't bear to take comfort she knew she didn't deserve, so she snatched her hand away. "Praying to which god? Because from what I've seen of Poseidon, he isn't much of a bargain."

"I still believe the same things and pray to the same god," Riley said softly. "My worldview has expanded, that's all."

Keely headed back to the table and quietly began arranging a plate of food. While she ate, Conlan and Ven ran through everything that had been discussed, but Alaric sat silent and brooding. When she, Quinn, and Riley were up to speed, Keely nodded and put her fork down.

"I don't know if this is a good time for this, then, with the impostor and the danger to Quinn and Anubisa and everything else. But I have confirmation about Zelia and Nereus, Alaric. They were definitely married. I know why the ruling king at the time and the Elders implemented the new rules about celibacy, too."

She looked at Quinn and then returned her gaze to Alaric. "It's absolutely definite. Nereus went insane when Zelia died, and he almost blew up the entire dome."

～～～

Alaric sat back in his chair, a mask of implacable calm on his features, his emotions shut down behind an impenetrable steel wall. Everyone was staring at him—everyone but Quinn, who looked anywhere else *but* at him. He felt like someone had torn out his guts and put them on display for everyone in the room to pick over and examine.

"I have no interest in this story at this time," he lied.

"Oh, no, buddy, you can bet we're going to hear this," Quinn said, addressing him for the first time since walking into the room more than an hour earlier. "After what happened on that island today? You bet your sweet ass we're going to listen."

"On the island?" Ven said, looking back and forth between Quinn and Alaric as if he were at a sporting match.

"Sweet ass," Justice repeated, grinning like a fool. "Oh, this is going to be good. We knew we liked her."

"I will strike both of your personalities dead," Alaric told him in an ice-drenched voice.

"Not with me in the room," Keely said cheerfully. "I'm pretty good with a shotgun, and I always get my man, big boy, so why don't you hush and I'll tell this and get it over with?"

"What is your source?" Quinn demanded. "Anything beyond your so-called touchy-feely crap?"

"Quinn," Riley chided her, but Keely just smiled. "It's okay, I'm used to that. Although someone who is a verified *aknasha* shouldn't be the first to throw the touchy-feely stone, but whatever. Yes, there is more. I read about it in a hidden set of scrolls, which somebody shoved deep into a niche in a wall behind a thousand-pound statue a very long time ago."

"Hidden scrolls?" Alaric was interested in spite of himself. "Behind which statue?"

"The one of Poseidon, ah, enjoying himself. With himself," Keely said, blushing scarlet.

Alaric nodded. "Ah, yes. The Elders must have had a sense of humor, back then."

"Or the statue was later moved in front of the niche, who cares, get on with it," Ven urged.

"It was actually a narrative history sealed inside a case with a copy of a proclamation," Keely said. "The librarians verified my translation, and they're making a copy for you, Alaric, and another for the Elders and—"

"What did it say?" Quinn cut in, unable to bear it for one moment longer.

Keely blinked and then grinned. "Sorry. Scientist's curse, we blather on. Anyway, here's the headline: after Nereus almost destroyed Atlantis and everyone in it, the Elders proclaimed, on behalf of Poseidon, that every high priest from that time on must swear a vow of celibacy, in order to decrease their power. That way, nobody could ever be as powerful as Nereus again and thereby endanger Atlantis."

Everybody in the room started talking at once, but Alaric ignored them all and stared steadily at Quinn. She looked back at him, and she didn't look happy, either.

"So it's all a lie," Conlan said. "You don't need to keep to that stupid vow."

"I feel like we should not be discussing such personal matters about Alaric," Riley said, and Alaric nodded at the princess, appreciating that at least one person respected his privacy.

Quinn's voice cut through the general chatter. "It doesn't matter. What a few scrolls might say, what Keely might have felt—none of it matters. This was how long ago?"

"Nereus was high priest around eight thousand years ago, give or take," Conlan said.

"Exactly. Even if that's true, your insane dictator of a sea god has had thousands of years to turn it into a real rule. There is every likelihood—and a pretty damn good probability, I'd say—that breaking the vow today does *exactly* what the Elders say it does. Alaric would lose his magic and his ability to protect you just when you need him most."

Alaric sat silent as the woman he loved stated his own innermost thoughts. Until Poseidon said otherwise, he was forced to believe the truth as the Elders had told it. And Poseidon—his "insane dictator of a sea god"—wasn't talking.

"Thank you all for your impassioned analysis of my sex life," he finally said, ice coating every syllable. "Now I would ask that we get back to discussing how to capture or kill this Ptolemy impostor and retrieve Poseidon's Pride before, all the gods forbid, Anubisa gets her undead hands on it."

The room subsided into silence and general noises of agreement.

Riley stood up and took her sister's hand. "No. Not tonight. Quinn has been through too much in too short of a time, and she needs a good night's sleep. We can discuss battle plans, and which of us are off to put our lives in danger this time, in the morning over a good breakfast."

Alaric rose and bowed to Riley, but he felt the wildness growing within him at the thought that anyone, even her sister, would take Quinn away from him.

"With all due respect, Princess, Quinn will stay with me tonight."

Quinn's eyes flashed. "Here we are, full circle, at the point where people are making decisions for me. Guess what? Quinn will do whatever Quinn damn well pleases, or Quinn will shoot somebody."

She pulled out her Glock and pointed it at the floor, an edge of violence in her eyes.

Riley held up her hands, palms out, and grinned. "It's not like I could ever tell you what to do. Why would I start now? What do *you* want, my darling sister?"

She glanced at Alaric. Considered. Decided. "I'll visit Poseidon's temple with Alaric. I've wanted to see it for a long time, and I'm too wound up to sleep now."

She whirled around and snapped at Alaric when he dared to smile. "And then you'll take me back to Riley, so I can get some uninterrupted sleep, without flying monkeys or tornados or anything else attacking me. Plus, I want to cuddle my nephew some more. He may be the only male I've ever met who isn't an arrogant ass."

"Give him time," Conlan advised, grinning. "It runs in the genes, or so my lovely wife tells me."

Riley just laughed. "Okay—temple, bath, bed, baby, breakfast, in that order. All discussions of impostors and danger are hereby officially on hold."

She hugged Quinn. "When you run with this crowd, you learn to take respite where you can find it. There's always another crisis."

Quinn blinked rapidly against the tears Alaric could tell she was battling, and he clenched his fists as he fought his powerful need to go to her and offer comfort. She wouldn't welcome it; she'd hate being made to feel weak in front of so many. But he could help in another way.

He took her hand before she could stop him, and the electricity that shot between them just at the touch of his fingers on hers reminded him of their kisses on that beach. His body clenched, hardening just from that slight touch, and she gasped. It was a tiny sound and probably none but he heard it, but it was enough to set his pulse racing. The uncharacteristically vulnerable look in her eyes called to every protective instinct he possessed, and he leaned down toward her.

"At least we know there won't be flying monkeys," he said softly.

She started laughing. "Lead on. Let's see this temple and get to the group singing, already."

This time, it was Alaric who laughed out loud. As he led the way out of the room, he glanced back over his shoulder and realized that every single person in the room was staring at him, mouth hanging open in shock.

"He laughed," Ven said. "Did you hear that? He actually laughed."

Alaric all but dragged Quinn down the hall to get away from them.

"I laugh," he muttered defensively.

"The occasional evil *mwah ha ha* doesn't count," Quinn said, grinning up at him.

He couldn't help it. He laughed again.

Damn it.

Chapter 13

Quinn climbed the steps and entered the imposing but some-how delicate building, all graceful arches and curves, and reflected that it was entirely unexpected.

"From everything I hear about Poseidon, I picture him as a self-indulgent thug. Seems odd that his temple is so graceful."

Alaric laughed, but a white-robed man with a face like a bulldog's gave her a scandalized look as he scurried by, muttering something in that liquid language that had to be Atlantean.

Quinn stared after him, bemused. "What was that? 'Blas-phemy, you blasphemer' kind of thing?"

"He's sure Poseidon will strike you dead at any moment and wants to be out of the line of fire." Alaric's deep voice was rich with amusement, and a shiver tingled its way up her spine from the sound.

"Man up," she told bulldog guy, making sure that the flee-ing coward didn't hear her. Her mother would have had her guts for garters for disrespecting someone else's religion. Of course, it wasn't the religion she didn't respect. It was the selfish god at its heart.

They walked from the foyer into a giant, high-ceilinged room bathed in soft light. The walls were marble, inset with jade, amethysts, and other precious stones that Quinn didn't recognize. She wasn't exactly a jewelry kind of girl, though, so it wasn't surprising.

Tall green plants flourished in every corner, and long, low upholstered benches were scattered about the space, beckoning the occupants to rest, reflect, or simply *be*. She looked around the room for a long time in silence, enjoying the peace and tranquility almost in spite of herself.

"Well, it seems like a place where you could commune with the gods quite happily," she finally said diplomatically.

"Poseidon is not a peaceful, communing kind of god," Alaric replied. "When he wants me, it is usually for something involving gaining power, jockeying for power, negotiating for power, or—"

"Yeah, I get it," she cut in. "Those old gods are still bloodthirsty and power-hungry?"

"Some things never change. He does his best to protect his children."

"Children?"

"We of Atlantis are his children," Alaric said. "Since you are *aknasha*, you're clearly descended from Atlantean ancestors, so technically you're his to protect, too."

"No thanks," she said firmly. "I've seen what he calls protection. Letting Riley die, branding her, the way he treats you—I don't want anything to do with any of it."

"If you accept me, you will have no choice," he said, taking her shoulders in his hands and turning her to face him. "Even if I were to leave the temple, I could never completely escape Poseidon. Would it be so bad a bargain?"

She shook her head, helpless to know how to answer. Her heart cried out for her to answer no, but her head urged caution.

"I need to kiss you again," he said.

She backed away, shaking her head. "I can't. Not now. Please. Just . . . just take me on the tour."

His face hardened from her rejection, but he nodded and took her hand again, as if he needed to feel her touch. As they left the room and entered a corridor, he gestured to a dull black wooden door.

"Through that door and down those stairs is where I faced the Rite of Oblivion. I eventually survived it and became high priest," he said with an obviously false nonchalance.

Whatever lurked down those stairs carried bleak and painful memories for him that were so powerful she caught faint traces of the emotions from around the edges of his mental shield. She knew she should ask—they needed honesty and acceptance between them—but she could not.

Would not.

She had her own secrets to keep. And after she'd miscalculated so badly and spent more than a year imprisoned by the vampire she'd targeted, a ritual named for blessed forgetfulness had a certain appeal.

In any event, she had no reserves of strength left. Not enough to face entering a room where something called the Rite of Oblivion took place. Not tonight.

His eyes darkened, and her throat tightened at the realization that she was failing him through her silence. She had to ask at least one question; discover the answer she most needed to know.

"What would have happened if you'd failed the test?"

"I would be dead. You never would have met me. Perhaps an entire set of problems would have been avoided," he said bleakly.

"Never say that. *Never.* No matter what happens between us, now or in the future, the world has been a better place for having you in it, Alaric." Her throat felt raw from allowing the starkly sincere words to escape. Emotion, raw and vulnerable, burned inside her until she had to fight tears yet again. Twice in one night. She was falling apart. Maybe it was better for everyone that her days as a rebel were over.

He pulled her into his arms and rested his cheek on the top

of her head. "You honor and humble me with your honesty, *mi amara*. I can do no other than return it. You must know by now that you are everything in the world to me. Please stay with me tonight. Just for a little while longer. Please."

And, for all of her defiance earlier, she couldn't refuse him. Not then, maybe not ever. She'd stay strong and stay out of his bed, but she couldn't refuse to hold him, even just for a little while.

❧～～❧

As Quinn showered, Alaric paced through his austere suite of rooms, seeing the place with new eyes. With *her* eyes. Everything was gray and hard-edged and bleak. No softness, no color. It was like a portrait of the inside of his soul. No wonder she'd flinched when she first walked in. He vowed to change everything. He'd add color. Texture. Sensual fabrics. Art on the walls.

Maybe she wanted jewels or baubles or presents. He didn't think so, but Ven always told them women loved trinkets, and Erin certainly wore enough jewelry. All those rings. But wait, those were tools and symbols of her magic. Did that count?

He stopped dead on the edge of the floor and banged his head against the wall. He, Alaric, high priest to Poseidon, most feared man in Atlantis, had turned into a blithering idiot. All because there was a naked woman in his bathroom.

No, not *a* naked woman. *The* naked woman. The *perfect* woman. The one he wanted to spend the rest of his life with.

When the door finally opened, he was pretending to read a book, which he promptly dropped on his foot as soon as he saw her. Her short, dark hair was wet and combed back and away from her perfect face, and she was wrapped in his white silk robe. It was far too big for her, even with the sleeves rolled up, but she looked like a fallen angel; all porcelain skin and huge, dark eyes.

He wanted to run.

He wanted to shout.

He wanted to worship at her feet.

"I hope you don't mind that I borrowed this," she said nervously. "I washed my clothes out in the sink, so as soon as they dry out—"

"Keep it," he said hoarsely, fighting hard to keep from leaping across the room and pouncing on her like a lust-crazed youngling. "It looks far better on you than it ever did on me."

She plucked at a sleeve. "I feel like this is a huge mistake, being here, and wearing this, and—"

"Nothing could be further from the truth. Everything in my life that doesn't have you in it is a mistake," he replied with total sincerity. "I am willing to spend eternity telling you that."

He couldn't bear being apart from her for one more second, so he slowly crossed the room, giving her time to say no. "I need to touch you, Quinn. I need to taste you and feel your skin against mine. I need to know that this conflagration inside me isn't only one-sided."

She lifted her chin defiantly, but she didn't back away.

She didn't back away.

He sent a quick prayer of thanks to any and all gods who may have ever existed, simply because she didn't back away.

"It's not only one-sided, and you know it," she said softly, and she may have said something else, at least her beautiful lips formed words, but then he was kissing her and didn't hear anything but the rush of desire beating underneath his skin.

He devoured her lips and caught her tongue with his and kissed her so deeply he was unsure where he ended and she began. He was clumsy and frantic, and he was afraid that she would reject him for either or both of those things, but she gently touched his face and slowed down the kiss before breaking away and taking a deep breath.

"I'm right here," she whispered. "You don't have to make up for hundreds of years in the next five minutes."

His laughter held the edge of madness. "Do you promise? You won't disappear? Because I can't imagine how I'd ever survive if you did."

She took his face in her hands. "No sex. Not yet, maybe not ever, until we figure this out. But for heaven's sake, kiss me, already."

She didn't need to ask him again. He held her as tightly as he could and kissed her as if the world would end if he ever stopped. The earth could have cracked open and devoured them, and he wouldn't have cared, because he was finally kissing her. In fact, the room felt like it was shaking underneath his feet from the sheer rush of hunger desperate to be fulfilled. By all the gods, she was *his*, and he'd be damned to the lowest of the nine hells if he'd ever, *ever* let her go.

Quinn trembled in his arms, and suddenly his hand was under the silk of the robe and touching the silk of her breast. His body shook with the force of his need, and he feared he'd go off like an untried boy, right there in his pants, simply from the touch of her skin.

"Please touch me," she moaned. "Oh, this is dangerous, but I don't even care."

He didn't care, either, not about rules or oaths or consequences. His heart raced, and his blood burned like liquid electricity in his veins, and the sound of pounding battered at him until he realized it was *actual* pounding . . . on the door.

On the *godsdamned door*.

"Go away, or I will destroy you where you stand," he roared.

His chief acolyte, voice shaky but determined, answered him through the door.

"My lord, the Trident is malfunctioning. It's shooting blasts of pure magic throughout the temple. Two of our people are injured and one barely escaped with his life. My lord? You must help us."

Alaric's dazed mind took a few seconds to register that the floor probably *had* been shaking, after all. He snapped his focus to his surroundings and suddenly the erratic blasts of power emanating from Poseidon's Trident stuttered through his consciousness.

How in the nine hells had he been oblivious to that?

But even as his mind asked the question, he looked at

Quinn and his gaze snagged on her lips, swollen from his kisses, and he knew the answer.

"Put me down, Alaric," Quinn said. She trembled like a leaf caught in a thunderstorm, but her expression firmed into resolve. "We have people to save, magical objects to fix, and a world to save. No time for kissing."

He groaned, but then nodded and released her. "When this is over, if it's ever over," he ground out from between clenched teeth, "I am taking you so far away from duty and responsibility and civilization that it would take months for anybody to find us."

"Maybe Fiji," she called out, laughing a little, as she ran for the bathroom.

She dropped the robe, and he saw the delicate line of her back and the curve of her lovely ass before she moved behind the door to dress, and he groaned again. "I might have to kill something for this."

"Count me in," she said, walking back out, checking her knives and guns. "I'm very handy when there are things to be killed."

He waved a hand at her damp clothes and sent the water from them, and she smiled her thanks. When they opened the door, they were both laughing, and the man standing there raising his hand to knock again looked at them as if they were insane.

He wasn't wrong, Alaric reflected. Not even a little.

Chapter 14

Quinn held out her hand, determined to make a fresh start with bulldog guy, in spite of the way he was staring at her flushed cheeks. "Quinn Dawson. Nice to meet you."

The man looked at her hand, and then back at her face.

"It's human custom to shake hands in greeting," Alaric said, already heading down the hall. "Myrken, this is the woman I'm going to spend the rest of my life with. Be nice."

Myrken, already pale, wobbled a little, as if he were going to fall over right there in front of the ancient tapestry on the wall behind him. Silvery green dragons soared over an island kingdom of perfect, tiny stitches.

"He does that now," Quinn confided to Myrken. "Smiles. It's almost frightening, isn't it?"

"There you go again, making unfounded declarations about my future without consulting me," she called after Alaric's retreating back.

"Sorry, I have a crisis to solve." He flashed an unrepentant grin over his shoulder, and Myrken made a weird noise that sounded like a cross between a gulp and a yelp.

"Did he . . . Did Lord Alaric just smile again?"

Quinn shrugged. "I know. It's kind of freaking me out, too."

Leaving Myrken to his shock, she ran down the hall after Alaric. "Wait for me. Team, remember?"

They descended stairs and flew down hallways at top speed, arriving at a room Quinn had definitely not seen in the tour Alaric had given her on the way in. The entire room, maybe twenty-five by twenty-five square feet, was completely empty. No benches, no plants, no art on the walls. Nothing at all in the room except for a pedestal, topped with a cushion, where she guessed the Trident had previously been on display. Currently it was floating in the air, twisting and turning like it was alive, sending out brilliant flashes of white, blue, and green light.

She skidded to a stop, almost running into Alaric's muscular back.

"Is it supposed to do that?"

He shot her a look.

"I'll take that as a no. Do you think this has something to do with Ptolemy playing magic games with Poseidon's Pride?"

"Almost certainly. The Trident has never, in all of recorded history, acted like this."

She watched it as it whirled in a surprisingly elegant manner for what was, basically, an overgrown fork with jewels in it. She counted six jewels of various colors, plus one empty setting that was clearly waiting to be filled with the missing gem.

"Did you have to find all the others, too?"

"Yes, it has been an interesting time. The final gem must be safely in place in the Trident before Atlantis can rise."

Alaric bodily lifted her and leapt to the side as one particularly bright flash of white light blasted the spot where they'd been standing and smashed a hole in the wall.

"This thing isn't kidding around," she said. "Is there an off switch?"

"Unfortunately, no. If I approach it, I may be able to put

it in stasis, but getting that close to it may be challenging," Alaric said. His hands glowed with blue-green light as he called to his magic, in preparation for whatever suicidal trick he was planning.

The problem was, she didn't know how to stop him, or if she should even try. It didn't seem like a job anybody else could handle.

"What can I do?" She scanned the room for ideas of any way she might be able to help, but came up empty. The only variance from the blank palette of bare walls and floor was a series of niches that may have been designed originally to hold plants or art, high up on the walls, above and out of the Trident's current firing range pattern.

"What if I find a way to get up there above the line of fire and drop down on top of it? Do you have a rope—"

"If I had a *rope*, I would tie you up with it," Alaric growled. He whirled to face her, and his eyes were flaring with heat and magic. "Do you ever, even once, not immediately decide to throw yourself in the middle of the most dangerous situations possible?"

She pretended to think about it for a second or two, and then grabbed his arm and yanked him out of the path of a blast of green light that blew a hole in the door behind them.

"Nope," she said. "Lucky for you, since *you're* the most dangerous man I've ever met. A sane woman would run *away* from you, not toward you."

He cast his gaze up, as if asking for divine intervention, then grabbed her and kissed her so fast she almost didn't realize it was happening. Then he stepped between her and the Trident and hurled a barrage of energy spheres at it as fast as he could form them.

These weren't the destructive kind, though. Quinn watched as the spheres joined together to form a large bubble around the Trident. The bubble at first dispersed the force of the magic blasts, and then contained them altogether.

Quinn started clapping. "Great job. Now what?"

Alaric didn't answer, and when she turned to look at him,

she discovered why. His face was taut with strain, and he held his hands out in front of him as if physically holding the force field or energy bubble or whatever it was in place.

"Can't hold this alone for long," he gritted out. "Go get help."

She paused to pat him on the back. "Hey, it's the magical symbol of a god. It's got big juju. I'm impressed you managed to stop it at all."

He raised an eyebrow. "Big juju?"

"I'll explain later."

She ran out of the room, shouting for help, and almost collided with Myrken, who was wringing his hands right outside the door.

"Get all your most powerful people in there to help Alaric contain that Trident," she told him. She paused, remembering what Alaric had told Ven back in Japan. "I'm going to the palace to find Christophe and Serai. He mentioned them as the most magically powerful, right?"

Myrken just stared at her, and she started to get mad. "Look, if this is some kind of 'we don't take orders from women' thing—"

"Humans," he muttered. "Your gender is immaterial."

She rolled her eyes. "Even worse, you . . . you . . . species racist. Get your ass in there and help Alaric, or I'll make sure you don't live to regret it," she snapped out in her best rebel leader voice.

The man all but saluted and headed inside, shouting for the other acolytes as he did. Quinn didn't wait to see what happened, but ran for the door so she could go find the castle.

~~~~~

Alaric fought with the brutal power of the Trident for what felt like years, until Myrken and several of the strongest acolytes arrived to help. He ruthlessly drew on their power to help contain the Trident from unleashing any more of those unstable blasts of magic. It wasn't the physical damage to the room that concerned him. The Trident's magic had been an integral part of the infrastructure of Atlantis since the continent first sank below the waves. Without its underpinning, he didn't know how long everything else would hold together.

Conlan entered the room, followed closely by Quinn, Ven, and Erin.

"Christophe and Serai aren't on Atlantis, but I got Erin," Quinn said.

Erin was already calling to the Wilding, and Alaric felt the cool breeze of her human magic swirling around him, its eddies whispering dark promises of mayhem and madness.

"Erin, *stop*," he said. "We can't know how the Wilding would interact with the Trident's current unstable magic, and we already know it doesn't respond well to your control here in Atlantis. You might help, or you might make everything far worse."

The Wilding faded, and Erin nodded. "You're right. I'm sorry; it was an instinctive reaction. I wish I could be of more help, but I'm afraid you're probably right. We heard reports yesterday that magic has been misbehaving all over the world, and it started right around the time your gem was found in Turkey. I'm wondering if all of this is related."

Myrken flashed a reproachful glance at Alaric, took a deep breath, and bowed to Conlan. "Your Highness. You are welcome in the temple, as always."

Alaric groaned as he dug deeper for enough power to reinforce the containment field. "I think we can dispense with the courtly manners this once."

Myrken gasped. "My lord, it's the *high prince*."

"Whose ass will be drowning right along with the rest of us if we don't contain the Trident," Alaric snapped.

Conlan nodded. "Thank you, Myrken, but Alaric is right."

Alaric knew in a brief flash of regret that Myrken had been embarrassed by the conversation, and then he realized that it wasn't his regret. He was feeling Quinn's emotion.

"Myrken, I want to apologize for my comments before," Quinn said, her cheeks flushing a dull red. "I was very concerned for Alaric."

Myrken bowed deeply, but not before Alaric saw a kind of wonder in his eyes. "It is an honor to take commands from one who so obviously cares so deeply for my lord."

"Well, let's not get carried away," Quinn muttered.

Alaric didn't know what to say or think or even feel, as the realization hit him that, yet again, Quinn had been trying to protect him. He didn't even mind the grin Conlan aimed at him, but apparently Quinn did.

"What is this, junior high? Don't we have better things to do than stand around smiling at each other like idiots?" she snapped.

Myrken gasped, and the other acolytes in the room nearly fainted. The *human* had just spoken disrespectfully to the high prince *and* the high priest. Alaric had to fight to keep from laughing out loud, in spite of the dire situation. That was his woman. Defiant to the bitter end.

Conlan's smile vanished, though, and he nodded sharply. "Yes, we do, and I need answers, now. What in the nine hells is going on and how much damage to Atlantean infrastructure will this cause? And where is Poseidon?"

Alaric frowned, having wondered the same thing. Poseidon was perfectly content to show up whenever he wasn't wanted, so why didn't he show up when he was desperately needed? Only he could truly contain the Trident's power.

"Poseidon, I petition you for your assistance," he called out, in a thunderous voice supported by magic. "Please come to our aid and to the aid of Atlantis."

They all waited, almost holding their breath, for several long moments, but silence was the only response. Poseidon either wasn't listening or didn't care. They were on their own.

"Huh," Quinn said. "I don't suppose he has an iPhone? BlackBerry? Skype?"

Myrken glared at her, but Alaric just shook his head.

"No, although it would be easier, wouldn't it? If he'd ever answer his phone, that is."

"Yeah, he seems more like the 'press 1 for godly intervention, press 2 for unwanted interference with your love life' kind of guy," Erin said.

Ven snorted, but then looked nervously around. "Let's not mock the god in his own temple, okay, Erin?"

"What can we do?" Conlan asked, directing the question at Alaric. "Is there enough power here among your people to sustain this? We need for you to go after Poseidon's Pride, and even you can't be in two places at once."

"It should hold," Alaric said, gingerly testing the perimeter of the containment field with his magic.

"It *will* hold," Myrken said firmly. "I will make sure of it."

A commotion at the door heralded the arrival of Justice, who strode quickly into the room, his long blue hair flying unbraided around his shoulders.

"We're in big trouble," he gasped out, winded. "Huge. Whatever was going on here has damaged more than just the walls in the temple. Lights are out, power is fluctuating, and worse. Much worse."

He paused to suck in a deep breath. "I ran all the way to and from the dome. We're in big trouble, everyone. The blast somehow damaged the dome itself. Tiny cracks, no bigger than a hair, have formed all over the surface."

Justice took another breath and stared straight at Alaric. "The dome is going to fail, and we're five and a half miles underwater. Everyone on Atlantis will die."

Chapter 15

**At the portal landing area, next to one
section of the dome, an hour later**

A single drop of water.

Only one.

Quinn and the rest of the group stared at that single drop
of water as if it held the answers to all the questions of the
universe. It was impossible, or so they'd told her, but the
impossible drop beaded along the edge of one of the thousands of cracks and then trickled down the side of the dome
to the grass.

And Quinn's latent claustrophobia flared into excruciating
existence.

"It's really true," she whispered, as if any sound could
send the whole structure crashing down around their ears. Of
all the ways she'd imagined her demise over the years, death
by suffocation and drowning, while being crushed by water
pressure, had not even once been among them.

Figured.

"What are we going to do?"

Alaric put an arm around her and pulled her close to his
side, as if he could protect her from anything, even a collapsing dome over a soon-to-be-lost-for-real continent.

"We shore up the dome's magical barrier, continue to stabilize the Trident, kill Ptolemy the pretender, retrieve Poseidon's Pride, restore it to the Trident, force Atlantis to rise, and save, as you would say, the day," Alaric said calmly.

But she was *aknasha*, and even as fiercely as he was shielding, she could feel that some very strong emotion was going on under that veneer of control. Not quite yet "oh, god, oh, god, we're all gonna die" emotion; not Alaric, maybe not ever that, but certainly "oh, holy whale shit, how am I going to pull this out of my ass" emotion.

She was feeling kind of "oh, holy whale shit" herself.

So it was more than a little surreal when one swam by. An actual whale. She stared into its massive eye as it looked back at her, and she wondered hysterically if they could hitch a ride.

"How can a whale survive down here at this pressure?"

"There are many species of marine life who have adapted to a deep, deep sea environment," Alaric said.

She knew it wasn't important, given the situation, but it was still interesting.

"We will also start evacuating everyone we can through the portal, but it takes no more than several at a time, so it would be an impossibility to save everyone that way," Conlan said, lines of strain clear on his face.

"Riley and the baby must go," Quinn said immediately. "Are they even awake?"

"Yes, I sent to her to grab whatever she needed for the baby, and Marcus, my captain of the guard, will escort them here in a few minutes," Conlan said.

"You will go with them," Alaric told Quinn. "If I have to throw you into the portal myself."

"I'm not leaving if there is anything here I can do," she said. "I can help organize the evacuation. I've had a lot of experience with large groups over the past ten years."

Alaric's eyes glowed such a hot green she was almost distracted from their argument. "Don't your eyes get hot when they get all glowy like that? I'd think it would fry your eyeballs. You're going to get cataracts or something. Also, haven't you learned by now that you can't order me around?"

Alaric snarled—actually snarled, like a feral animal—and she was only saved from whatever he'd been about to say when the portal suddenly flared into existence.

"What is this?" Conlan took a step back.

"Did you call?" Alaric asked.

Conlan shook his head. "No. Riley's not here yet."

That same deep, resonant voice she'd heard before spoke from the heart of the portal. "You have need, Quinn Dawson?"

Quinn's mouth fell open. "What? No, I don't need you. Thanks, but I'm going to stay and help out—"

The rest of her words were cut off as the portal swept Quinn into its center. The last thing she saw was Alaric leaping after her, reaching for her, before he crashed to the ground as both she and the portal vanished in a vortex of swirling light.

All she had time to think was *Oh, he's going to be so pissed off*, before the portal abruptly dumped her onto a street that looked vaguely familiar.

"Oh, how did she do that? Is she part of your act?"

Quinn blinked in the early light of what she realized was dawn. They'd somehow spent the entire night dealing with the Trident, at least if she'd stayed in the same time zone this time. The elderly woman who'd asked the question about an act was dressed in pink from the hat perched on top of her blue-tinted white curls to the tips of her neon-pink tennis shoes.

"What act? Where am I?" Quinn looked around, but her tired brain hadn't yet caught up with the rest of her.

"Tied one on last night, I bet," a man said. He was not wearing pink, but a very large blue sports jersey that said TEAM BEER and strained against his oversized belly. "Doesn't even recognize the Naked Cowboy."

Quinn whipped her head to the side, and sure enough, there he was in all of his not-so-glorious reality. The Naked Cowboy. She looked up, and up, and up, and confirmed she was standing in the middle of Times Square, New York.

The portal certainly did have a sense of humor.

She suspected the members of the NYPD approaching the group, however, did not, and she was carrying three knives and two guns. Two *unregistered* guns for which she did not hold a concealed carry permit.

She smiled at the tourists and bowed with a flourish, as if she were indeed part of the act, ducking her head to avoid photographs, and let out a relieved breath when the police kept moving on by. Then she started walking, slowly and nonchalantly, as if she had all the time in the world, in the opposite direction. She was exhausted, starving, and worried sick about her sister, her nephew, Alaric, and everyone else in Atlantis. One problem at a time, though, and the only one she could solve in the middle of Times Square was breakfast.

After purchasing a bagel and coffee from a sidewalk vendor with some of the small amount of cash in her pocket, she headed down a side street, away from the tourist heart of the city, to eat, caffeinate, and think. She spent a few more of her precious dollars on a pair of sunglasses and a ball cap, since her face had been plastered all over the news by Ptolemy and his stunt. As she approached an electronics store, she noticed a crowd gathering in front of its banks of screens.

"What's going on?" she asked a man wearing a couple of weeks' worth of straggly beard, a ragged flannel shirt, and jeans at least three sizes too large for him. He smelled like he lived in a doorway and, unfortunately for him, he probably did. The vampires in Congress weren't big on spending money on social programs for homeless humans.

They preferred to just eat them.

She schooled herself not to flinch at the stench, though. She didn't want to insult a potential source of information any more than she wanted to hurt his feelings, and anyway, there had been times in her life when she hadn't had a roof over her head, either.

"They're talking about that Atlantis fella again. Says he's going to unite with the vampires, since the United Nations won't listen to him." The man looked at her out of the corner of his eye. "Nice-looking bagel."

She broke off half and handed it to him. She'd been hungry, too, more times than she could count. "Another press conference? Dude's a glory hound, isn't he?"

"Yeah, but not till eight A.M. Wants prime coverage, I guess."

The news reporter on the screen arranged her too-perfect features into a smile. "So there you have it. Ptolemy Reborn, who claims to be the rightful king of Atlantis, will be holding a joint press conference with the mayor and Senator Hengell at nine. Back to you, Ann!"

Quinn ventured one more question before she moved on. "Where is that, do you know? That building she's standing in front of?"

The man rolled his eyes. "Didn't take you for a tourist. That's City Hall."

Quinn thanked him and headed off, careful to amble like she didn't have a care in the world, as she heard the news anchor on the TVs behind her make a reference to Ptolemy's message for "alleged rebel leader Quinn Dawson."

"Hey! Hey, lady!"

She ignored the shouting and kept walking, only hurrying her pace a tiny bit. Nothing too suspicious to any observer.

"Hey, thanks for the bagel!"

Her shoulders slumped in relief, and without slowing, she raised a hand in acknowledgment and kept right on going. She didn't take a full breath, though, until she'd reached the end of the block and rounded the corner.

That was too close. Any one of those people could have recognized her through her pitiful disguise, and then what? She didn't have time to be detained. She needed to find Ptolemy, retrieve the gem, and return it to Alaric before he blew some kind of magical gasket trying to keep the Trident from blowing up the dome.

Alaric was probably furious by now. She couldn't help it; she grinned.

"You won't like me when I'm angry," she growled in true Bruce Banner fashion, and then she started laughing when a woman passing by gave her the finger.

"Oh, yeah. I'm in New York."

She finished the coffee, dumped the cup in a handy trash can, and headed for a souvenir shop to find a map of the city. She needed to be at City Hall by eight.

~~~~~~~~~

Alaric paced and ranted and swore and raved until Conlan threatened to hit him over the head with the nonpointed end of a spear.

"She's gone. Unprotected. Every single murderer and thug on the planet will have seen her face by now, and she's up there all alone because the portal has decided, for the first time in all of recorded history, to do whatever in the nine hells it feels like doing!" Alaric was shouting by the end of it, and Conlan narrowed his eyes and picked up the spear.

"I'm not kidding. I will hand your ass to you on a plate, and you are too busy keeping the Trident from nuclear melt-down, and the dome from collapsing, to zap me with magic, so for once it would be a fair fight," the pain-in-the-ass high prince of Atlantis said.

Alaric forced himself to take a deep breath. "Fine. I will calm down. I will pretend that the entire continent is not about to be destroyed. I will pretend that the sea god is not ignoring us. I will pretend that I can do this on my own, even though the Trident grows more unstable with every second that passes, and I am nearly at the limits of my strength already."

He bared his teeth at Conlan. "Don't we all feel better already?"

His entire body pulsed with the strain of pushing more magic than he'd ever channeled, and the Trident kept increasing its erratic instability. He knew he didn't have much longer, if something didn't happen to shore up the balance on his side of the equation.

"We need one for the good guys, as Quinn would say," he said, flinching as a sharp pain stabbed him in the temple.

Conlan's eyes widened a fraction, and he reached over to touch Alaric's ear. His finger came back red with blood.

"Just how much power are you having to expend to keep the dome from shattering?"

Alaric grimly shook his head. "Trust me, you don't want to know."

A shout heralded Marcus's arrival at the head of an armed contingent of half a dozen warriors surrounding Riley and the baby, Erin, and Keely with Eleni.

Erin and Keely were both furious, and they immediately started letting Conlan know it.

"We are not about to scuttle through the portal like rats abandoning a sinking ship, when we can stay here and help," Erin said.

"I'm surprised Marcus managed to drag you out here," Alaric said, before wincing as another sharp pain in his head nearly blinded him. At this rate, he'd be dead before the dome collapsed, anyway.

"He threatened to stab us," Keely said dryly. "When we didn't believe him, he threatened to stab that guy." She pointed to a youngling barely old enough to hold his sword.

Marcus nodded grimly. "And they knew damn well I'd do that."

The young warrior gulped audibly, but stood tall and tried to look brave. Conlan laughed a little before he pulled Riley and Aidan into a fierce embrace. Alaric tried not to envy Conlan those last moments with his family, even as every fiber of his being demanded that he abandon the battle to contain the Trident and go after Quinn.

"You know, he would have done it. He stabbed me once, in training," he told the young man, whose eyes grew huge.

Keely took in the situation with her scientist's keen grasp of a problem, and then turned to Alaric. "Right. Where's Quinn? You two need to reach the soul-meld, right here and now, or Atlantis isn't going to survive."

Chapter 16

Alaric glared at the damnable woman. "What in the nine hells are you talking about?"

"I tried to tell you last night, but nobody wanted to listen. What happened to Nereus was his power increased exponentially when he achieved the soul-meld with Zelia. He became the most powerful priest in the history of Atlantis," she said. "That's why the Elders decreed celibacy for the high priest. They decided nobody should have that kind of magic. They were afraid he could gain enough power even to challenge Poseidon, if it came to it."

"So you just want them to throw down right here?" Riley's face turned hot pink. "I know this is a crisis, but after all those years of celibacy, I doubt Alaric wants to strip down in the middle of a field and—"

"No," Alaric shouted. "No, no, no. We are not having this discussion. Quinn is gone, in any event. The portal abducted her, but even if she were here, we *would not be having this discussion.*"

Ven made a choking noise, like he was strangling on his own tongue, and Alaric whipped an ice ball right at his head, then immediately regretted it, as calling to even that tiny bit of water magic increased the strain on his overtaxed powers.

"Where is my sister?" Riley demanded, and little Prince Aidan started crying.

Alaric closed his eyes and tried to pray for patience, but he realized that he was done with praying to any gods. Poseidon could have his damn temple, just as soon as Alaric saved the people of Atlantis from this current disaster. Atlantis would rise, and he and Quinn would head to a beach. Or maybe mountains, far, far from any ocean.

Maybe the Alps.

"Alaric? Did you hear me?"

Alaric opened his eyes to find Keely staring up at him. He didn't have the strength to be angry at her.

"He can't risk it," Conlan said. "Even if Quinn were here. The Elders say the loss of celibacy is the end of power. If there's even a chance that they're right—the Trident would destabilize and we'd lose the dome and everyone in Atlantis. It's not a chance we can take."

Alaric closed his eyes again, as rage and humiliation battled for supremacy inside him. He'd be better off if he just let the damn dome collapse.

A piercing whistle interrupted his misery, and when he opened his eyes, everyone was staring at Erin.

"Alaric, you don't have to have sex to reach the soul-meld. If we can find Quinn, and she agrees, you can soul-meld and expand your power without risking the anti-celibacy oath-breaking thing," she said, her cheeks flaming red.

"I cannot believe everyone in Atlantis is discussing my sex life," Alaric said from between clenched teeth.

"Actually, we're discussing your lack of sex life, dude," Ven pointed out.

"If you call me dude again, I will drop the dome on your empty head."

"Can he do that?" the young warrior asked.

"Silence," Marcus said, staring at the dome, where the warm light of magically created dawn highlighted the water trickling down, now in a small but steady stream.

Alaric tuned them all out and searched for the still, cold center of his being, where he retreated when there was no choice but blood, battle, or death. He reached a conclusion so devastating that it pushed everything else out of his mind.

"Here's the situation," Alaric finally said, pretending to be calm, as if the lives of all of his people were not at stake. "Even drawing upon the magical reserves of everyone in Atlantis, I am not quite powerful enough to hold the increasingly unstable Trident and also support the dome. We need Poseidon's Pride, we need to return it to the Trident, and Atlantis must rise. However, there is no one else who is strong enough to retrieve the gem without being burned to ash by its power. So, as I see it, we have two choices. First, I can do nothing but what I'm currently able to do, and Atlantis will slowly be destroyed as the leaks increase and my magic is depleted. Everyone dies."

He took a breath and continued. "Second option: I can somehow find Quinn and attempt the soul-meld, if she agrees, and hope that the story of Nereus is true and it gives me enough power to solve these problems. The issue there is that I'll be channeling my magic at a very long distance, if the portal even takes me to her, which will further weaken me. And if the story of Nereus is false, everyone dies."

He looked around at the people he could finally admit he loved. His family. He would willingly die for them. And he probably would. Soon.

"Bye-bye, Alaric," Eleni said, smiling a sweet, gap-toothed smile.

Everyone stared at her. The child had the ability to see a short distance into the future, so of course she must see that she would be leaving through the portal. He wondered, though, why she'd named him in particular.

The portal flashed into existence before anyone could venture an opinion, and again that deep male voice called out to them. "You need?"

"Wait," Conlan shouted, but the light flashed a brilliant sapphire blue, and two things occurred simultaneously: Riley, Aidan, Keely, Eleni, and Erin all disappeared, and Christophe and his soul-melded mate, Lady Fiona, flew out of the portal and landed on their asses on the ground.

Then the portal winked out of existence again.

"I have had enough of this," Conlan said.

Alaric could only nod, as he stumbled forward, the pressure in his skull reaching an unbearable level. "Christophe, I'm going to need some help," he said, and then he fell forward into the relentless dark.

~⸺⸺∾

When the world snapped back into focus, Alaric realized that his subconscious had somehow maintained his magical hold on all the dangerous balls he was juggling, and the dome had not collapsed.

He somehow wasn't even shocked to see Christophe sitting across from him on the grass, grinning.

"Please tell me this is all part of the nightmare," Alaric said wearily.

"Got your back, my friend," Christophe said smugly. "Feel free to say thank you at any time."

Alaric took stock and realized that the warrior was indeed carrying some of the magical load. Quite a bit, in fact. He leaned back and took his first full breath since the crisis began.

"Thank you," he said, and then enjoyed watching Christophe's shock. Alaric didn't have a history of expressing appreciation or gratitude.

"We were a bit worried for a moment," Lady Fiona said in her crisp British accent. "Lovely to see you up and about. Now what do we do?"

Alaric stood up and nodded to her. "Welcome. Now that Christophe has taken more than his fair share of the magical burden, I can leave to find Poseidon's Pride. All we need is for the portal to—"

"You need?" came the voice and flash of light, and Alaric went spinning through the vortex.

"I know you're sentient. I met Gailea," he shouted. "What in the nine hells do you think you're up to?"

"Ask your sea god," came the cryptic response, and then Alaric plummeted down through an early-morning sky. Before he had time to transform into mist, he crashed through a skylight made of blacked-out glass, and he landed on his feet in the middle of at least a dozen vampires.

"This," Alaric said, looking around for who he'd have to kill first, "I did not need."

The room was high-ceilinged and lit only by a couple of bare lightbulbs hanging drunkenly from frayed cords. Stark black-and-red graffiti, both words and images, crawled across the walls like the spreading stain of blood from a wound. The stench of vampire permeated the room, making him think the abandoned building must have long been their lair.

"You've interrupted lunch," one of the bloodsuckers hissed. "That means you become part of it."

"Always with the cheesy dialogue, as Ven would say." Alaric shook his head and got ready to turn into mist and escape, until he saw exactly what they were preparing to eat for lunch.

Whom they were preparing to eat for lunch.

Damn.

It was kids.

"You again?" The kid in the red shirt looked familiar, and Alaric realized it was the same boy he'd saved from Ptolemy.

"That is far too large a coincidence. What are you doing here?"

The vamp who thought he was the leader snarled at Alaric. "You can address me if you have something to say."

"Shut up. You were saying, kid?"

The kid jerked his chin at the group of five smaller children who were huddled and crying in the middle of the group of bloodsuckers. "I take care of them."

"Not very well, apparently."

The kid lunged at Alaric, trying to get away from the vamp who held him, but bloodsuckers had unnatural strength, so it was a futile struggle.

"You're angry at the wrong person, Faust," Alaric advised, forming a sword out of pure energy and slicing off the kid's captor's head before anybody could move. "I'm not the one trying to eat you and your friends for lunch. What do you say we take care of this and get out of here?"

Faust dropped to the floor, pulling a gun out from underneath his shirt in one quick motion and firing on the nearest vamp before Alaric had come to the end of his sentence.

"Guns don't work on—"

"Silver to the brain stem does," Faust interrupted, surprising Alaric. Not many humans knew that. "Help me get these kids out of here?"

The vampires started shrieking, hissing, biting, and clawing—all the things vamps usually did—but Alaric had endured too damn much to put up with any of it. He set to work with the shining sword, with Faust at his back taking aim with his gun.

Within minutes every vamp in the room was dead and dissolving in a pile of acidic slime, and only one of the children was badly injured: a girl with a nasty bite on her neck bleeding out on the floor. Alaric could feel her life force ebbing as he watched, and she was a tiny bit of a thing, probably no older than five.

"I need to get her to a doctor, man," Faust said, panicking.

"There's no time," Alaric said, as gently as he knew how.

The boy ignored him and carefully gathered the girl in his arms, and in the space of those few moments, Alaric considered his options. He was teetering on the edge of overuse of magic as it was; would the energy to heal one human child who was already so close to dying send him over the edge? Could he risk it, when the result might be to condemn thousands of Atlantean children to death?

The girl cried out, and he realized he didn't actually have a decision to make at all. He couldn't do nothing and watch this child die.

He stopped Faust and placed his hand over the site of the wound. Blue-green light flared as Alaric's healing energy swept through him and into the child. She stiffened in the boy's arms and then sat up, grinning.

"Do it again!"

The bite on her neck was gone as if it had never happened.

"But—" Faust looked wildly from Alaric to the child. "How did you—"

"The bite is healed and any vampire venom is completely destroyed, so she is not at risk from the blood bond, either," Alaric told him. "I have to go now. Try to stay out of trouble, won't you? I don't have time to keep rescuing you. I have to go kill that impostor who calls himself Ptolemy."

Faust called out to him before Alaric reached the doorway. "I can take you to him. He's getting ready to have a press conference at City Hall at eight o'clock."

Alaric paused and then swung back. "We're in New York?"

The little girl he'd healed giggled up at him. "Mister, you're not very smart, are you?"

He shook his head. "No, sweetling. I'm not very smart at all."

Chapter 17

Outside City Hall, New York

Quinn stood on the sidewalk in City Hall Park, staring up at the grand limestone façade of the beautiful building, and considered her options. She'd been thinking subtle: steal her way into the building and find Ptolemy; confront him privately. See what he had in mind for Atlantis. For Poseidon's Pride.

For *her*.

No dice, though. The public hadn't been allowed into City Hall since a horde of drunken wolf-shifters had eaten all the tour guides one day a few years back, or so her laminated map said.

She was running out of choices, and Atlantis was running out of time.

Well, as Jack always said, the best defense was a good offense. She squared her shoulders and swallowed the lump of pain and regret that formed in her throat at the thought of him. Later. She could think about Jack later. For now, she'd walk right up to the front door and show them her best credential.

Her face.

The guard just inside the door didn't look up. She was seated at an old wooden table that may have dated from as far back as the building itself and was oddly incongruous next to the modern doorway-shaped metal detector. "Next."

Quinn was doing enough looking up for both of them, though. The soaring rotunda and magnificent staircase that winged to each side transported her to a world of nineteenth-century New York aristocracy, glittering with sparkling jewels and even more sparkling conversation. Oddly enough, it reminded her a little of the Atlantean palace, if not on nearly as grand a scale.

"Next," the guard said again, louder. The woman was built like a warrior: sturdy muscle packed into a small, stout body. Her tightly curled gray hair was cut close to her head, and her face, like Quinn's, was devoid of makeup. Quinn might have smiled, recognizing a kindred spirit, under other circumstances.

"I'm Quinn Dawson."

"Key card."

"I'm Quinn Dawson," she repeated slowly. "Ptolemy is looking for me."

"I don't care if you're Elvis, you're not getting in here without a . . . Oh. My. God," the woman said, finally looking up at Quinn. "You're her? The rebel leader?"

Quinn drew a deep breath and admitted it. Out loud. "Yes."

The sturdy woman practically hurled herself out of her chair and around the metal detector to grab Quinn in a crushing embrace. "My Johnny wouldn't be alive without you people. You got him out of a gang before he could make the ultimate bad decision and go vampire. I can't thank you enough, young lady."

Quinn was finding it hard to breathe by the time the woman finally released her—a combination of overpowering emotion, boiling up from the woman's genuine gratitude, and the sheer force of her hug—but she did take ruthless advantage of the moment to edge around, instead of through, the metal detector.

"I'm so happy to hear that, Ms. Rutkowsky," she said,

reading the guard's name tag. "I really do need to see Ptolemy as quickly as possible, if you could . . ."

"I'll take you right up there myself. Personally," the flustered woman promised. "Frank! Get over here and watch the door."

So within minutes of entering the building, Quinn found herself in a stately, elegant conference room, staring down the length of an enormous, shiny table at the man she'd seen so recently on television, destroying her life. She ignored the seat he gestured for her to take.

"I'm Quinn Dawson. I hear you want to meet me."

Ptolemy was even more imposing in person. He exuded a dark, menacing charisma, like most of the best con men, vampires, and criminals. He was a thug dressed up like a politician, but he remained just unpolished enough for anyone meeting him to know that here was a man who would do his own dirty work, and—what's worse—he'd enjoy it. She scanned for his emotions, but what she found was so alien she had no way to read it. It was twisted and oily and viciously gleeful, like nothing she'd ever encountered before, and suddenly she had to work hard not to show that she'd noticed.

Right now he was smiling at her like she was Santa and the Easter Bunny all wrapped up in one pint-sized package, and the reek of his perverted glee, which wafted across the room, made her nauseous. He headed down the room toward her, arms outstretched, and she backed away, circling to the other side of the table.

"Surely the renowned and feared leader of all North American rebels isn't afraid of me," he said, smiling a snake-oil smile.

"I'm afraid of everything until I kill it," she said flatly. "That's what keeps me alive. So what is it you want with me?"

She studied him as he stilled, watching her with the hooded expression of a cobra preparing to strike. The smile never left his face, though.

"I didn't think you'd come," he said, ignoring her question.

"You have something that belongs to a friend of mine."

He glanced at a small wooden box sitting on one end of the table. "Oh, did the big, bad Atlanteans send a weak, little human to do their dirty work?"

"I thought I was feared and renowned. Make up your mind." She scanned the room for possible exits, threats, or allies. The windows were thick glass that was way too strong for her to break; the second door led to other offices, not the hallway; and not a single soul had dared to step into the room since she got there.

"It's almost eight, Ptolemy. Don't you have a press conference to get to? I won't delay you. Just give me the gem, and I'll be on my way." Bluffing wouldn't work with him, but it was second nature for her to at least try, and it worked as a good stalling technique while she figured out her plan of attack.

"I do, now that you mention it," he said, his dark eyes measuring her. Finding her wanting. "You need new clothes. I can hardly present my future consort to the world dressed in rags."

Quinn's knees tried to buckle, and ice snaked down her spine. She grabbed the back of the chair in front of her to steady herself and then she pulled out one of her guns and pointed it at him. "What exactly did you say?"

"I said you need new clothes," he said calmly, completely ignoring the gun. "Did I offend you? I haven't even mentioned the hair or makeup yet."

"Consort. You said *consort*," she said, clenching her jaw shut to keep her from chattering. Not *again*. Not another one. She couldn't be trapped that way again.

He laughed, and tendrils of terror swept through the air around her, enticing her to give in. To surrender to the roiling fear and madness he gave off like dark emanations from his twisted soul. She'd never been so afraid in her life.

Which, of course, only pissed her off.

"In your dreams, buster. Now, give me the gem before I turn you into a girl." She very deliberately pointed the gun at his crotch.

He laughed. Not the usual reaction a man had when confronted with the loss of the family jewels.

"I think your gun won't work," he said, and she flinched and cried out as the metal flashed to searing hot. She dropped it, fast, and watched in horror as her Glock melted into a puddle of shiny liquid metal, ate a hole through the table, and pooled on the floor.

"If you have any knives or more guns on you, I'll give you a moment before I melt them, too," he said. "I wouldn't want you to suffer any burns in inconvenient places."

The knives and her backup gun were seared to molten heat so quickly that she rushed to remove them and tossed them on the table before her clothes caught on fire.

"Is that all you've got?" she challenged him.

"Oh, no, I have much more," he said, taunting her. "You'll discover just how much when I impregnate you with the new heir to Atlantis."

Reality tilted on its axis for a moment as her brain tried to process what he'd said, and her skin tried to crawl off her bones and run away from the overwhelming revulsion and terror of his words.

No. Not again.

She almost hadn't survived the last time.

∽⸻⸺

Alaric followed Faust out of the building into the dirty gray street, and the immediate problem became apparent. The children.

Alaric pointed to two women on the other side of the street who were dressed in the law enforcement uniform of the city. "They will care for the children."

Faust shook his head. "No. No way. They'll put them in foster homes. I take care of them, man."

Alaric raised one eyebrow, but didn't state the obvious again. They were out of time for debate. "Then point me toward City Hall and remove yourselves from this place."

Faust gave him quick directions, and then he and the children disappeared around a corner so fast it was as if they'd never been there at all. Alaric watched them go and then headed off toward City Hall, transforming into mist to travel so he could avoid any more nasty surprises. He spared a moment to wonder why the portal would send him to Faust, but then dismissed it as unimportant to the mission at hand as he sped past broken and boarded-up windows of abandoned and decrepit buildings.

Quinn, Quinn, Quinn, Quinn. Her name beat though his mind like a command.

She could be anywhere in the world—probably was so far from him he'd never find her—but his senses automatically scanned for her in a wide pattern to try to catch any hint of her presence. Just as he did, a wave of Quinn's emotion— pure, unadulterated terror—slammed into him so hard it sent him crashing down through the air, out of his mist form, and smashed him into a parked car.

She was here in New York. *Here.* He struggled to climb out of the dent his body had made in the hood of the car, and another blast of her emotion knocked him down again. Wherever she was, she was so scared she could hardly think. A renewed flare of white-hot power surged through him, and he shot into the air again, ignoring the crowd of humans that had formed around the car. Whoever had scared Quinn was about to learn exactly what the high priest of Atlantis was capable of—and it was going to be a very, very painful lesson.

He followed Quinn's fear and rage across the city to find, to his utter lack of surprise, that it was coming from City Hall. The coincidences were just piling up, and none of them were good. He didn't bother to knock, just headed straight for the window closest to where he could sense Quinn and arrowed straight for it, planning to smash it open on the way.

Instead, he crashed into an invisible shield of magic and bounced back through the air. The force of his collision with the shield pushed him out of his mist shape again and smashed him down to the ground. He lay there for a minute or so, shaking his head at the offers of hands up or any other help, simply trying to force air back into his abused body and snarling at the humans until they all gave up and left him alone. Ptolemy's press conference was bigger news than a man falling from midair, evidently. As he climbed to his feet, a sharp ache alerted him to the presence of at least one cracked or broken rib.

"This day just keeps getting better and better," he growled, and a woman standing nearby pulled her child closer to her.

He almost laughed. Even the humans he'd spent hundreds of years protecting thought he was a monster. So be it. He'd be monster enough for any of them.

He spared a moment and the smallest touch of energy to heal his ribs so he'd be ready to fight, and headed for the stairs to the ornate building, but a truck with antennas bristling all over it drove up and parked, blocking his way.

"Move, man, don't get in the way of the TV crew," somebody said, and shoved him.

If he'd had the energy to spare, Alaric would have blasted the fool with an energy sphere just on the principle of the thing. Luckily for the human, Quinn's welfare was far more important than minor annoyances, so today he got to live. Alaric took another few steps before he realized he had yet another big problem. The magical wards shielding the building were far too powerful for him to take down without draining himself of the reserves he needed to continue to shield Atlantis. He'd either have to trust Quinn to take care of herself for a little while, or sacrifice all of his people to save her.

Today was turning out to be his day for bad fucking options.

Chapter 18

Quinn stared at herself in the mirror. Ptolemy had handed her a red dress and heels and the choice to either wear them or watch him tear the head off one of the office workers. Like so much in her life lately, it wasn't really much of a choice.

Now the image looking back at her in the mirror was a caricature of herself. Pale, with styled hair and skillfully applied makeup that seemed to float above the surface of her face. The TV people had done it. She didn't even know how to put on eyeliner, let alone all the other goop. One overly zealous woman had tried to spray her with perfume, but Quinn's expression had stopped *that* in its tracks, at least.

She looked like a little porcelain doll, they'd told her. As if that were a *good* thing. Didn't they understand that porcelain was fragile and easily shattered?

The door opened on silent hinges, and Ptolemy walked into the ladies' room. Quinn didn't bother to act surprised. She could already tell the man was a control freak.

"You're as beautiful as I knew you would be, underneath that scruff and grime," he said, and she suddenly, *desperately,* wanted her guns.

"You're a bullying piece of shit who needs to be put down like a rabid dog," she said, smiling sweetly. "Who are you, and what is this about?"

"I'm not going to fill you in on all my plans just yet. I'm not some comic book villain with a need to impress," he said, walking closer.

The stench of evil nearly suffocated her as he drew near, and she started choking on the intangible emotion that nobody else would be able to perceive. "What *are* you? The only thing I can think of is demon, but it's not exactly that, either. Unseelie Court Fae?"

He sneered. "As if I'd associate with them. No, my darling queen-to-be, you have never encountered anyone like me. Or, rather, you've encountered many like my dear, dead mother, but my father? No. He was in a class by himself."

He bowed and motioned to the door. "Shall we do this? We have a press conference to give."

She headed for the door, bracing her shoulders against attack from behind, but he only sniffed her hair as she passed. She didn't manage to contain her shiver of revulsion, and he started laughing. His laughter was rich and deep as it surrounded her—invaded her—tasting like burning acid in the back of her throat. She fought her gag reflex. She *would not* let them see her be weak.

At the end of the hall, a man wearing headphones ushered them into another large room, and this one was set up for the press conference. Huge cameras, large, square light boxes on poles, and more wires and electrical apparatuses than she'd ever seen in one place fought for space. Two men she pegged immediately as vampires stood at the back of the room, near the podium, and another she thought was human hovered ten feet or so away from them. A flurry of people with press passes hanging around their necks swarmed everywhere, and Quinn's fingers itched for her knives.

She took a small step toward the door, but Ptolemy grabbed her arm. He shook his head slowly, mocking her, and she wrenched her arm away from him and tried not to vomit. Whatever dark magic he had, the sensation of it had intensified a hundredfold when he touched her, even through the sleeve of her dress. If he ever touched her bare skin, she thought she would go mad.

"Everyone who isn't absolutely essential, get out," Ptolemy said, never raising his voice.

Instantly, the swarm thinned to only a manageable few, as most of the people in the room all but fell over themselves trying to escape. Now that she could get a better look at the men near the podium, she realized something highly troubling. One of them was the first vampire mayor of New York, and the other was the first vampire secretary-general of the United Nations. The man lurking a distance away she didn't recognize.

"What's the plan?" she asked, sure that Ptolemy wouldn't tell her anything, but unwilling to meekly become a part of whatever evil strategy he had in motion.

"The secretary-general will either officially recognize me as the king of Atlantis, right here and now, or I will kill him on international TV," he said, as casually as if he were discussing what to have for lunch.

Her hand was partway to her gun before she remembered it was gone. Ptolemy dragged her to the front of the room, and the surge of nausea she'd been fighting burned through her. She was barely able to contain her stomach's urgent need to empty its contents all over him.

"Your magic and I are definitely not compatible," she said, taking in shallow breaths. "What makes you think I'd let you close enough to me to . . . to . . ."

"To have my baby?" He leaned closer and whispered. "You won't have a choice. Nobody said you had to be conscious during the begetting."

Ptolemy took advantage of her shock-induced paralysis to drag her in front of the cameras.

"This is my consort, Quinn Dawson, the only human worthy to be queen of Atlantis," he said, smiling for the international audience. "We are here this morning to accept Secretary-General Filberson's acknowledgment of our sovereignty."

The secretary-general was made of sterner stuff than she was, Quinn thought, or else he didn't have the ability to sense Ptolemy's twisted magic at all, because he stepped right up, displaying no hint of fear or revulsion.

"Since the secret is out, we do acknowledge that Atlantis exists and has been preparing to rise from the bottom of the ocean and rejoin the international community. However, I have been dealing with High Prince Conlan for more than a year now. This man is a pretender, and the United Nations does not recognize or support him."

The mayor backed away from Filberson, clearly anticipating the worst. It didn't take very long for him to get it. Ptolemy reached out a hand that had transformed into that of a beast. His fingers now terminated in five-inch-long claws, and he slashed Filberson in the face. Then, before the secretary-general even hit the floor, Ptolemy kicked him so hard it caved in the side of his head.

Quinn gasped as the secretary-general's emotions swung violently from calm determination to pain, rage, and terror, and then she slammed her mental shield into place. She knew from previous experience that she couldn't feel all of his emotions as he died and still remain conscious, and if she passed out she might wake up dead.

"This is unfortunate," Ptolemy said calmly, wiping his bloody hand on the side of Quinn's dress.

She silently vowed to kill him. Slowly. She wanted him to suffer for what he'd done to Filberson. For what he'd done to her.

Ptolemy pointed to the mayor with his hand, which was still smeared with blood despite his use of Quinn's dress. "Do you have something to say?"

The mayor stepped over the moaning secretary-general and faced the cameras. "Yes, we agree," he said hastily. "The city of New York recognizes you as King Ptolemy of Atlantis. No problem. No problem at all."

"And you?" Ptolemy pointed again, this time to the man who still lurked a dozen or so paces away.

Quinn didn't know who he was, but he looked familiar. He

walked slowly to the podium and stepped carefully around the dying vampire on the floor before facing the cameras.

"I will absolutely recognize you as king of Atlantis or any other damn continent you want to rule," he said slowly. "I have a family and grandchildren, so I don't want to die. And this will be my last official act as governor of New York."

The governor walked carefully away, down the long conference room and out of the door, undeterred by anyone in the room. Quinn looked at Ptolemy, surprised that he'd let the man escape, but he shocked her by laughing.

"And so it begins," he said. "Now, my beautiful wife-to-be, to prove your loyalty I only have one request. I need for you to end what's left of the life of this miserable worm on the floor. If you disobey me, I will kill every human in this building, slowly and painfully—"

"Done," Quinn snapped. She whirled around to grab a rather flimsy-looking wooden side table and snapped one leg off over her knee. Then she knelt down next to the secretary-general.

"I'm sorry," she whispered, before she plunged the makeshift stake into his heart.

She'd just committed murder on live TV. Another act for which she could never, ever forgive herself. She opened her mental shield, just a crack, for just a moment.

Good-bye, Alaric.

~~~~

The blast of Quinn's pain and remorse swept through Alaric with the force of a tidal wave, before she shut it down hard. She was trying to tell him good-bye.

Alaric needed to kill something.

Bad.

"Oh, my god, she really did it," shouted the man with the portable viewing device. It had been Alaric's only window to Quinn and Ptolemy for the past several minutes.

She'd had no choice. Yet again he had the thought that they were all ultimately helpless pawns in a chess game played by gods. Another stain on her soul, and Quinn had already been sure that she could never atone for the dark deeds she'd performed in her short life.

He, of all people, knew what it had cost her to kill that man. Even though the secretary-general had been a vampire, he also had been a man working for good in the world, not trying to conquer and enslave humanity. Even though she'd been forced to it—even though she'd clearly given him a quick end when his alternative was a long and agonizing death—and in spite of the threat that Ptolemy would kill humans if she did not comply.

It didn't matter. She'd killed, again, and this time not in direct self-defense, or at least so she would believe. Alaric's skin heated up as his very bones vibrated with fury. If he did not find an outlet for his rage, he might very well set off an explosion. The humans closest to him backed away as Alaric's body began to glow with hot, silver-blue energy.

"Ah, hey, man, are you all right?" one of them, braver than the others, dared to ask.

"No," he managed to say. "No, I am very far from all right. You should leave now. Leave and take all of your friends. This area is about to become very dangerous."

"Oh, wow," the man with the viewing device yelled. "The king of Atlantis is getting ready to do something bad, again. He has that woman he called his consort by the hair—"

"Move, fool." Alaric snatched the device from the man, just in time to see Ptolemy pull Quinn up into his arms.

"Now I'll be a little busy for a while," Ptolemy said, smirking directly into the camera. Quinn's eyes were wide and blank, staring at nothing, like she'd reached and then moved past the end of her endurance. Alaric's mind stuttered at the thought of what else Ptolemy might have done to her in that building.

He wondered how long he could make it take for Ptolemy to die.

Ptolemy's next words smashed through Alaric's plans of blood and death.

"I have to impregnate my future queen." Then, in a flash of light, he pulled another of his vanishing tricks, and this time he took Quinn with him. When the ugly smoke cleared, there was nobody left in view on the small screen but the mayor, who picked up a chair and smashed it into the camera that was transmitting the scene. The news feed went black.

"Give me my iPad, man," the human whined, grabbing for it, and Alaric hit him in the face with his precious toy.

Alaric tried for several seconds—that lasted for an eternity—to sense Quinn anywhere within the range of his power. *Nothing.* She was gone. She'd disappeared as surely as if she'd died. Alaric stood silently as the prospect of his future without Quinn washed through him in waves of bleak, desolate despair.

Then he called to his power and began to destroy the world.

He destroyed the news vehicle in front of him with a single blow, and it disintegrated in a satisfying explosion that blew pieces of shrapnel thirty feet in the air. The columns in front of the building went next, one by one. He smashed every one of them into rubble.

Humans ran wildly in every direction away from him, and Alaric laughed. Madness and murder and death swirled through him, and he laughed as he hurled it outward, destroying everything in sight. He shot ropes of pure magic at a car, lifted it into the air, and threw it against the side of a building, taking out half of the wall. He levitated into the air, dimly sensing Christophe calling to him, trying to stop him, demanding to know what in the nine hells was going on. Alaric slammed shut the door to their mental communication and shot a blast of energy at the park, taking out six trees at once and leaving a giant fireball in their place.

It wasn't enough. It would never be enough. If that monster touched one hair on Quinn's head, Alaric would drown the entire world and laugh as every human on the planet died. He froze, mid-thought, his hands encircled by glowing spheres of destructive power.

Drowning.

That was it.

He'd drown them all, city by city, nation by nation, until

he found Quinn. If that didn't give them incentive to cooperate, nothing would. He centered himself and reached deep into the reservoir of his power for every last ounce of magical reserves he might have, and then he ruthlessly stripped power from every human witch in a hundred-mile radius. All sorcerers, wizards, and magic practitioners of every kind suddenly found themselves bereft of power, as one of the most powerful high priests Atlantis had ever known tore their magic from them.

It was fast, dirty, and painful—and he didn't care.

It left some of them screaming and some of them in comas—and he didn't care.

He threw all of it into the ocean, where he drove the power with a towering fury, twisting and turning, breaking and battering, until he got exactly the result he wanted. A tsunami larger than any ever seen on the surface of the planet formed in the Atlantic Ocean and headed straight for New York City.

It was two thousand feet high and still growing when it was a mile out from shore, and nothing—*nothing*—on the eastern seaboard would survive it.

He stared down at the fools with news cameras who'd been stupid enough to remain in the area, filming his actions.

"If he harms Quinn Dawson, you will all die."

Chapter 19

Quinn lay on her side on a couch, its rough fabric scratching her face and the smell of years of dust and mildew clogging her nose. Ptolemy had bound her hands behind her back and tied a rag over her eyes. She didn't bother to struggle. She had nothing left to fight for. She'd failed to retrieve Poseidon's Pride in time, so Atlantis was probably lost by now, with everyone she loved in it, except for Jack, who had been lost to her for days. And Riley . . . Quinn's heart shattered into tiny, broken pieces at the thought of her sister and nephew. She'd wanted to save them all, and now she couldn't even save herself.

Even if she wanted to continue the fight—even if she could find some way to care enough to keep on keeping on—she'd been outed as the rebel leader and shown to be a cold-blooded murderer on international TV.

There was nothing left. She'd find a way to kill herself and take Ptolemy down with her. That was her one final mission. Her one final goal.

She'd tried to reach out to find Alaric with her mind, the way he always seemed to be able to find her, but the obstacle there was that he was a powerful magic-wielding Atlantean and she was a human with only a single talent. Even that was useless; Ptolemy's tainted, foul magic clouded her senses so badly that she was sure she'd go insane if she didn't keep her shields up, so even if Alaric were trying to reach her, she wouldn't hear him.

Anyway, what good was a final good-bye? Alaric knew how she felt.

Maybe.

Probably.

She didn't bother to try to nudge the mask from over her eyes, because she could see enough to know the room was pitch-black. Ptolemy had dumped her there after they'd gone through a vortex not unlike a fun house–mirror version of the portal. He'd quickly and expertly bound her and tossed her on the couch, with orders not to move. Apparently they were someplace where he didn't have to worry about her screaming for help. She'd tried for a while, but nobody had come running to her assistance.

She'd waited for a long time but then finally, in spite of everything, she'd dozed off. Her body had been exhausted, and her mind had shut down to protect her from the hopeless despair of knowing she was all alone in the world. Always before, she'd had someone to fight for. She'd known she was making the world safe for her sister and her sister's children to come. But now? The world could take care of itself.

She passed some time in fitful sleep, waking and then dozing again, she didn't know for how long, before she heard voices. Ptolemy and someone else, a woman, but the voice was familiar in a horrible way. She hadn't heard it in a long time, but it wasn't another rebel, it was too . . .

Oh.

Oh, *no*.

She curled her legs into her chest, praying desperately for a wooden stake, a gun loaded with silver bullets, or divine intervention from God or, in fact, any of the gods. Unfortunately, she didn't exactly believe in any of them. What kind of supreme beings would allow so much pain and suffering in the world?

Her mind was set to full-on babble now, as the one creature alive that she feared even more than Ptolemy and his demonic raping agenda entered the room where Quinn lay helpless, blind, and bound.

Anubisa. The vampire goddess.

This was going to be bad. She'd been ready to die, but her mind rebelled at the thought of meeting her end by slow torture.

"What do you have for me, my ally?" Anubisa crooned in her sickeningly sweet lilt. Her voice carried the tone and feel of rusty daggers and bashed-in skulls. Quinn winced in real pain, her eardrums aching from the sound.

"She is not for you," Ptolemy said harshly. "Quinn Dawson is mine."

"Quinn? I know that name," Anubisa hissed. "She is mine. I must have my revenge against this one."

Quinn rolled over onto her stomach with her legs underneath her, ready to piston her way back and hopefully smash somebody's face with her head before she died. It wasn't much, but it was all she had for a plan. Bound human versus demon and vampire goddess didn't bode well for the human.

She heard tentative footsteps, and a new voice entered the mix. This one sounded like a girl, so Quinn put a pause on her head-bashing plan, as gentle hands lifted her and removed the scarf from her eyes. A scared-looking girl, probably in her late teens, stood in front of her, holding the cloth in shaking hands.

"Don't fight him," the girl whispered. "It's even worse when you fight."

Quinn studied the bruises that covered one side of the girl's face, and any trace of fear in her own heart seeped away, to be replaced with cold, hard, welcome rage. Not the berserker kind of rage; no, not Quinn. She fueled her spirit with the kind of anger that knew how to plot, and scheme, and bide its time until she could find the best way to kill anyone and everyone who had hurt the innocents Quinn considered to be under her protection.

Like this girl.

"I'll help you," Quinn said. "Don't be afraid."

The girl clearly didn't believe her, but Quinn couldn't blame her for that. The circumstances didn't really support her claim.

"Get out of the way," Anubisa said, backhanding the girl with one small, slender white hand. The girl flew at least ten feet through the room and landed in a crumpled heap on the floor, where she lay still, quietly sobbing.

Quinn looked up at Anubisa and smiled, careful not to look into the vampire's eyes. "That's one," she said calmly.

"One what, stupid human?" Anubisa drew her hand back to strike Quinn, too, but Ptolemy stopped her by the simple virtue of pointing a stick at her and blasting. Anubisa fell to the floor, apparently unconscious or dead. She didn't breathe, so Quinn couldn't tell.

Quinn stared at Ptolemy and his stick of death, wondering if she were next. On closer examination, however, she realized it wasn't a stick at all but the scepter with Poseidon's Pride inset at the tip.

"You're pretty brave, using one god's possession to kill another," she said, hoping to taunt him into making a mistake. Petty tyrants could often be trapped by the gilded ropes of their own vanity.

"She's not dead, more's the pity," he said. "But, yes, it was rather fun. I wonder what I'll do next. Maybe destroy your White House and turn the area into a parking lot for my new fleet of automobiles. Wonderful things, your cars. You actually pay money to move from place to place in vehicles that destroy your environment while you use them."

He shook his head in apparent wonder, and she realized something she'd only guessed at before.

"You're not from around here, are you?"

He tilted his head, and for one brief second, his eyes flickered and changed from normal, dark brown human eyes to something different. Alien. There were no pupils at all; only swirling traces of color on a pitch-black background. No whites at all. His eyes weren't the demon red she'd been halfway expecting. They were far worse.

They were nothing she'd ever seen before, or heard about, or read about, which meant only one thing. He *really* wasn't from around here.

"You're a Martian?" She started laughing. "I expected green skin and little antennas poking out of your head."

He smiled, and for the first time, it wasn't polished. It was nasty, which meant she was getting to him, so she smiled right back.

"Mars, no. Another dimension, far away and far different from this one? Yes. Not so far that my demon kin father couldn't steal my Atlantean mother around twelve millennia ago. Not so different that he couldn't force her to bear son after son for him until she killed herself after I was born," he snarled, and the veneer of polished politician was chipping away fast. It was doing more than that; it was peeling off in sheets like ancient paint stripped from rotten wood, and suddenly Quinn wasn't sure she wanted to be around to see what was underneath.

Anubisa stirred, and Ptolemy stepped back and pointed the scepter at her again.

The vampire came awake and up off the floor like a freight train, headed right at Ptolemy, but the threat of the raised scepter stopped her at the last minute. Anubisa flew up to the ceiling and floated there in the corner, staring down at them both and hissing.

"I am a goddess," she screeched.

"A few more screws loose since the last time I saw you," Quinn mused, and Ptolemy nodded in agreement, which made her flinch. She didn't want to do or say *anything* that he agreed with.

"Yes, she has evidently been somewhere called the Void for a long time, and it made her a bit crazy, I'm guessing," Ptolemy said, his terrible gaze trained on Quinn.

He hadn't bothered to disguise his eyes again, and Quinn found herself falling into them. So he could subjugate a human mind in the same way a vampire could. She filed that away for future reference as she wrenched her gaze free. She wouldn't look into the eyes of either of the monsters in the room again. Suddenly, she wanted to live long enough to kill them both. Not slowly, not by torture—she had no fancy or grand plans. She just wanted them dead.

Dead, dead, dead.

"Kill her," Anubisa screamed. "Kill her, and I will allow you to be my consort."

"Wow, there's an incentive," Quinn said, rolling her eyes and feeling stronger for it. Defiance suited her far better than fear.

Ptolemy laughed, and Anubisa screamed.

"I will eat your intestines," she shrieked at Quinn. But she didn't move from her corner. Apparently fear of what the scepter could do to her stopped her.

"I will, I will," Ptolemy said to Anubisa in a soothing voice. "Later, after she has served out her usefulness. Why don't you leave now and continue your hunt for the Atlantean false princes, so we can move ahead with our plans?"

Anubisa shrieked at Quinn one last time and then turned into a spiral of oily-looking smoke and flew out of the room. Quinn's shoulders loosened, in spite of the fact that the monster who remained in the room with her was clearly the more deadly of the two.

"Where are we?" She looked around but recognized nothing that gave her a clue. She didn't even know if they were still in New York. Magic portals being magic portals, they could be anywhere. She was guessing they were still on Earth, because it seemed unlikely that a separate demon dimension had bothered to invent ratty polyester couches.

"This is a room in an abandoned subway tunnel far down under the streets of Manhattan. We will move soon, but I knew Anubisa wanted to speak to me, and I have no intention of letting her know where my real lodgings are."

He closed his eyes briefly, and when he opened them again they'd transformed back to human shape and color. For some reason, that unsettled her even more, but all she had to do to firm up her courage was glance at the girl still cowering on the floor.

"Let the child go, already. You have the rebel leader as hostage, you don't need some weak child," she said, putting as much scorn into her voice as possible.

"Done." He motioned to the girl. "You. Get up, get out. My future queen demands it. Remember that you have Quinn Dawson to thank."

"Right," Quinn said. "I know this trick. Your minions catch her right outside the door."

"I don't need minions," he said gently, and it was more terrifying than if he'd shouted. Quiet confidence meant that he really *was* exactly as powerful as he claimed to be, in which case Quinn had no chance.

None at all.

The girl ran out of the room, and Ptolemy approached Quinn.

"You'll have to tolerate the transport once more, and then you can rest." He waved his hand, and a spiral of orange light enveloped them both. Quinn experienced another moment of gut-roiling nausea, and then they were somewhere else.

Somewhere far fancier, where polyester had probably never been allowed to rear its ugly head. It looked like a deluxe suite in a fancy hotel, not that Quinn had much experience with those, but she'd watched the occasional TV show.

"Are you planning to untie my hands before I lose all circulation and they fall off? And when are you going to tell me what you want with me? If you think I can convince the rebellion to work with you, you're out of luck," she said, sneering. Why bother with politeness? She had nothing left to lose.

He said nothing, merely turned her so he could reach her hands, and as his fingers unfastened the knots in the rope, Quinn scanned the room and stopped, frozen in shock, when her gaze reached the far wall. The entire wall was plastered with hundreds of photographs.

And every single one of them was a picture of her.

Chapter 20

Alaric slowly rotated in the air fifty feet up above City Hall, his arms thrown wide to the sky, glowing with so much power that he wondered briefly if he would go supernova and shatter into a thousand miniature suns. Even in death, he could rain destruction down on the humans who had allowed his woman to be captured and harmed.

Kidnapped.

He couldn't survive if he focused the blame on where it really belonged—himself—so he closed off that part of his mind. He could indulge in self-hatred after he'd found her.

The gods alone knew what that monster might be doing to her. A fresh burst of wrath infused his power with a further wave of deadly rage—enough to build up the leading edge of the tsunami bearing down on the city to even more towering heights. He'd kill them all. Drown the city, drown the state, drown the world.

He called to the portal, but silence was his only answer. Silence from the portal—silence from Atlantis. Poseidon's Pride was gone; there was no chance to save Atlantis. Perhaps it was already lost. Quinn was gone; so the world must die. He spared a thought for Nereus, his kindred spirit. No wonder he'd nearly destroyed Atlantis when Zelia died. It must have seemed a minor price to pay.

A small voice somewhere deep inside him—a voice that sounded suspiciously like Quinn's—yelled at him to *cut it out*. But he had no time for auditory hallucinations, so he shut it down, shut out the phantom Quinn, and continued to channel all of his pain and fury into the storm.

For a moment he thought he heard another voice telling him to stop, this one coming from far below him, but it was easy to ignore. It didn't sound *at all* like Quinn. But then a bolt of searing flame shot through the air toward him and sliced through the leg of his pants, blazing a path of pain across his right knee.

Now he paid attention. He hurled down toward whichever stupid human dared to shoot at him, and found himself on a collision course with the only man idiotic enough to be still standing in range. But it wasn't even a man—it was a mere boy.

It was Faust.

Alaric managed to keep from slamming into the boy, but only barely. He landed on the rubble of destroyed pavement next to Faust, grabbed the kid by the throat, lifted him off his feet, and spoke very, very softly.

"What exactly do you think you're doing, you stupid boy? Do you have a death wish? Did I save you for no discernible reason?"

Faust made a choking sound, and Alaric realized he had to loosen his grip so the boy could talk. He dropped him on his ass, and Faust rubbed his throat while he glared up at Alaric.

"You can't do this, man," the boy finally choked out. "I saw the news. That wave is going to kill millions of people."

Alaric shrugged. "This means nothing to me. Leave if you want to live."

"It's too late," the boy shouted. "Nobody can get out in time. You're going to kill us all. Children and babies and old people—what have we ever done to you?"

"You let Quinn be taken," Alaric said implacably, barely

managing to keep the rage boiling inside him from overflowing and incinerating the youngling. "You will all die. Get out if you can. Take the children."

"With what? I can't do it, man," Faust said, all but crying. "I don't have a helicopter. Only the rich people are getting out, and some of them are being beat to death for their choppers. You gotta stop it, man. This just isn't right."

"Find Quinn. Then I'll stop it," Alaric responded. He turned away and leapt back into the air, ignoring the boy's shouts, until another bolt of flame hit him in the other leg. This one was a direct hit, not a graze, and he had to waste energy healing himself. He flew back down at Faust and yanked him up into the air by the front of his shirt.

"Where is the gun you are shooting at me? Do you want to die right here and now?"

The boy's bravado was betrayed by the slight quaver in his lips, but Alaric had to respect his courage.

Faust held up empty hands. "I'm not shooting a gun, you lunatic. I'm a flame starter. It's a curse or a gift or a talent, I don't know what, but if you don't make that tsunami go away, I'm going to set your damn ass on fire."

Alaric nearly dropped the boy. A flame starter? He hadn't heard of that gift since before Atlantis sank beneath the waves. All the old abilities really *were* coming back, just in time for Atlantis to be destroyed. The irony was not lost on him.

Which meant nothing, since Atlantis was surely drowned by now, and Quinn was gone.

"Give it your best shot, kid," he advised. Ven would be proud of him for using slang.

If Ven and Erin weren't dead.

He dropped the boy, who fell the half dozen feet to the pavement, but this time he landed on his feet.

"Try to burn me again, and I'll kill you now, so those children you care for will die alone," he told Faust, and then a voice he hadn't heard in far too long crashed through the air and buffeted him, nearly knocking him out of the sky.

YOU MORTALS ALL DIE ALONE. IT IS SAD THAT MY HIGH PRIEST HAS BECOME A DERANGED FOOL.

The sea god, Poseidon himself, appeared in the clouds above Alaric's head.

"I don't think you have much room to talk about deranged fools," Alaric shouted, committing blasphemy, idiocy, and possibly suicide all in one sentence.

Shockingly, Poseidon bellowed a booming thunder strike of a laugh.

WHY DO YOU DO THIS? YOU MAY NOT TAMPER WITH MY SEAS IN THIS MANNER. YOU WOULD DESTROY MILLIONS OF LIVES, AND YOU ARE NOT A GOD TO CHOOSE BETWEEN LIFE AND DEATH FOR SO MANY.

"I am tired of gods choosing between life and death. Why aren't you helping in Atlantis when the dome is in danger of failing? All of your children will die. Why didn't you answer my call about the Trident? What good is a god who doesn't even answer his own high priest in the times of dire need?"

I HAVE BEEN BUSY. THE SECOND DOOM OF THE GODS—A NEW RAGNAROK—IS UPON US, AND I HAVE BEEN LOCKED IN BATTLE WITH ARES AND A FEW OF THE NORSE AND EGYPTIAN GODS OVER HOW TO SAVE MY ATLANTEANS AND AS MANY OF THE HUMANS AS POSSIBLE FROM ANOTHER CATACLYSM.

"Well guess what? You're too late!" Alaric threw even more power toward his tsunami, only to find that Poseidon was in the process of dispersing it into gentle swells of manageable waves.

Alaric's grief, rage, and helplessness overpowered him, and he gathered everything he had and poured every ounce of that energy into the blast—and he aimed it at Poseidon.

"You're going down," he shouted, knowing it would mean his own death, but not caring.

I said, cut it out, *you idiot,* Quinn screamed inside his head, and this time he knew it wasn't an illusion, because she proceeded to call him every inventive name she could think of, and his own subconscious wasn't nearly that creative.

The shock drove him down out of the sky, and he almost fell on top of Faust, who was staring up at Poseidon with his mouth hanging open.

"Now would be a good time to get out of here," Alaric told the boy. "You're safe. The tsunami is gone. You don't want to be caught up in whatever punishment Poseidon metes out to me."

"No thanks to you," Faust said, still eyeing the sea god. "Hey, you don't deserve it, but I'm going to put the call out to my contacts and see if we can find your girl. If, you know, Poseidon doesn't crush us both."

Alaric stared at the boy, unable to understand why he'd do such a thing for the man who'd nearly killed him.

Poseidon had to make his opinion known, of course:

ONE OF ARES'S BRATS, I SEE. STAY AWAY FROM THAT ONE, ALARIC, HE'S PROBABLY AS TRICKY AS HIS FATHER.

Faust actually winked at Alaric, before he turned and ran away.

One of Ares's brats? But Poseidon didn't give Alaric time to think about Faust any further.

ATLANTIS IS SAFE, FOR NOW, BUT IT WILL NOT HOLD FOR LONG. I MUST RETURN TO MY BATTLE. FIND MY GEM AND RESTORE MY TRIDENT. ITS CALL WILL BRING ME BACK TO ASSIST IN ATLANTIS'S RISING.

Alaric bowed. "Yes, I will find Poseidon's Pride and save Atlantis. But when I have succeeded, I am done. You will have to find another high priest."

FUNNY. I WAS GOING TO SAY, SUCCEED OR DIE HORRIBLY. I LIKE MINE BETTER.

With that, the sea god vanished, and the last of Alaric's strength drained out of him. Christophe's message on the Atlantean mental pathway rang into Alaric's mind, loud and clear.

Thanks for whatever you just did. We probably have around forty-eight hours now before the dome collapses, so use it well and find what we need. And don't block me again, or I'll kick your ass when you get back.

Alaric realized that his own rage and pain must have blocked Quinn and Atlantis from contacting him before. In his desperation, he'd actually caused his own suicidal idiocy and despair. He groaned once, but then pushed it out of his mind and distilled burning fury to icy calm as he reinforced Atlantis with all of the power he could send such a long distance.

Forty-eight hours. Quinn was alive, and Atlantis still had a chance. He called out to Quinn.

Where are you?

She sent him a visual impression of the images out her window, so he knew she was in a building overlooking Central Park, and he could follow his senses to find her.

It's warded by pretty strong magic, so be careful, Alaric. It's demon magic—from another dimension.

Oddly enough, he was relieved to hear it. At least it took a monster from another dimension to create something strong enough to have kept him away from Quinn.

It wouldn't happen again.

He transformed into mist and arrowed toward the park. Toward Quinn.

Toward a future he suddenly wanted to live in, again.

⌒〜〜⌒

Quinn walked around the palatial bedroom, which was dressed in rich blues and tawny golds, silk and fine linens. Whatever hotel this was, they'd spared no expense in the décor. Even the air smelled like money—cool and crisp. She didn't have time to appreciate luxury, though—she needed to find a way out. The windows were impossible without tools she didn't have, the air vents were too small, the doors were bolted from the outside with unpickable locks, and the phones had been ripped out of the walls. Ptolemy had abruptly told her he needed to go out for a while, locked her in this room, and left.

At least he'd given her food. Before he'd gone, he'd had room service deliver a cart full of various delicious meals for her to sample, and she'd done her best to devour as much as she could. It was much easier to plot and scheme on a full stomach, even though now that she'd been fed, her exhaustion was pulling her down, trying to suck her into sleep.

The moment she felt Ptolemy's demonic presence disappear into a wave of creepiness that felt like that portal again, she tried to contact Alaric. She didn't know how to call out to him, exactly, so she opened her senses as far as she could and shouted his name. An image flashed into her mind: Alaric in the air, rage burning through him, as he went entirely nuts trying to find her.

He was—oh no, oh holy crap, no—he was trying to destroy the world. Flashing impressions of a giant tsunami and of Poseidon roaring at Alaric punched into her mind, and she yelled at Alaric to cut it out, but he either didn't hear her or he was too far gone to care.

She took a deep breath and put every ounce of energy she had into trying one more time, before he did something so horribly destructive it could never be fixed, and she yelled at him—out loud and in her mind.

I said, cut it out, *you idiot.*

This time, somehow, she was sure he heard her, but the momentary connection between them faded. To distract herself she decided, in typical rebel fashion, to eat while there was food. By the time she'd eaten two more plates of dinner and worked her way to the chocolate mousse, she couldn't keep her worry at bay any longer. What if Poseidon had killed Alaric? Or smited him, or whatever gods did to misbehaving high priests?

Alaric's voice sounded in her head, and she nearly fell off the chair in relief.

I am on my way to you now.

He was alive. He was *alive.* She scrubbed at the tears running down her face with one sleeve and tried to send a message back to Alaric.

The staff here is either not allowed on this floor or has been paid well to ignore shouting. You'll have to find a way to get a key, and—

The window shattered, and Alaric blew in before she could finish the thought. Right. Who needed a key when you had an Atlantean?

He hit the floor running, caught her up in his arms, and took possession of her lips with deliberate, possessive intent; branding her body and heart with his fire. Searing her soul with his passion.

"Never, never, never leave me again," he murmured, over and over, as he kissed her, but he didn't allow her breath to respond before he captured her mouth again .

She'd never been kissed with such single-minded intent as this man brought to it—her skin flashed hot, and her entire being rose up to meet him, as though gravity lost its claim on her when Alaric touched her. He kissed her so completely— so deeply and thoroughly—that it was almost hard to remember they were surrounded by shards of glass in what had briefly been her very well-decorated prison.

But she finally did remember, and she reluctantly pulled away.

"We have to get out of here, Alaric," she whispered, her voice trembling from the aftershocks of intensity.

If they ever made love, she didn't know how either of them would survive it. Just from his kisses, she was weak at the knees. And hot in places north of the knees, which made her face flush to realize.

"Where is he? I need to kill him and get that jewel," Alaric said when he finally raised his head. His eyes were pure green fire, and she never, ever wanted him to let her go.

"Your cheeks are quite charmingly pink," he said slowly, a smile spreading across his gorgeous face.

Of course, that only made her blush harder.

"Forget my cheeks. Focus. Ptolemy left, I don't know where he went, and he took Poseidon's Pride, I'm sure of it. He always has it on his person or very close to him," she told him. "I felt a blast of that creepy magic, only a thousand times worse than usual, just after he locked me in here. I think he might have temporarily returned to his demon dimension to get backup."

"Then we will leave now and develop a plan, and I will return to confront him once you are safe. We have maybe forty-eight hours, I'm thinking forty to be safe, and then Atlantis collapses. There is no time for Ptolemy to disappear into another dimension. If he doesn't return soon—"

She interrupted him. "Oh, I don't think he'll leave me alone for long," she said dryly. "Take a look in the other room."

Alaric gestured with one hand, and the door flew open, smashing into the wall behind it. He stalked out into the other room, keeping Quinn behind him until he could check for danger, and then he stopped dead, just as she had earlier, and she knew he'd seen the Wall of Creepy.

"He has been after you for a long time," Alaric finally said, his voice so coated with ice she was surprised a snowstorm didn't spontaneously form in the room.

"I know. Don't you think I know?" Her teeth started chattering from delayed reaction. "Some of these pictures are from years ago. He wants— He said he wants—"

Alaric swept her into his arms. "I don't care what he wants. He's not going to get it. We're leaving, now, and you'll never have to see him again."

With that, he blasted the glass out of the windows, picked her up, and flew out of the building with her in his arms. She closed her eyes, held on to him with all her might, and offered up a sincere wish that he was right. Also, that he wouldn't drop her.

They were due a little good luck, weren't they?

Even as she thought it, she realized she'd probably jinxed them, because that was how the life of Quinn Dawson, ex–rebel leader, was going these days. Would it be fire, hail, or a plague of flying cockroaches?

They rounded the corner of the hotel, heading for the park, and nearly ran into a police helicopter and the officer hanging out the side with a loudspeaker.

"Stop flying now, land on the nearest surface, and put your hands up," he commanded, and Quinn started to laugh. She couldn't help it.

"Here we go again."

Chapter 21

Alaric raised a hand to blast the annoying metallic monster out of the sky, but Quinn stopped him.

"No. Those are the good guys. Can't we just make a quick getaway?"

So he swooped underneath the helicopter, darted right, and was halfway across the city before the machine had time to turn around. There were advantages to his method of flight.

She directed him to a large building near the water, and he landed in the alley next to it, managing not to draw any more unwanted attention.

After a brief battle where her desire to walk fought his need to hold her, he finally, reluctantly, released her. She led the way up three flights of stairs to an industrial loft with a state-of-the-art security keypad next to its massive steel door. She punched in a long string of numbers and then held her thumb over a small square of glass. It scanned her, and the door opened.

"Welcome, Quinn," an electronic voice said, as they entered the space.

"She's an artist, but she also does something for the northeast region of P-Ops," Quinn explained.

Alaric didn't know what to expect, given the location and security, but it turned out to be an artist's studio. Finished and unfinished paintings and sculptures filled the enormous space. The tools of an artist's trade littered every flat surface, paints and brushes crowding mallets, knives, chisels, and tools he did not recognize.

Quinn walked over to a large canvas propped against the far wall, near a bank of enormous windows, as the door automatically swung shut behind them and a metallic click announced that the security system was again engaged.

"This is amazing," she said, her voice hushed. "Almost makes me believe in hope again."

Alaric had no time for art, especially now. His first impulse was to blast a hole in the painting so his woman would turn around and look at *him*, instead of at a lifeless bit of canvas and paint. He took a steadying breath and shook his head.

Bad enough to be insane. He wouldn't add childish to his list of flaws.

He walked over to join her, and she reached for his hand. The gesture went a long way toward calming the beast that had been raging inside him since he'd watched her be taken.

It was a deceptively simple canvas. A child and an old woman sitting companionably on a park bench, feeding the birds. But the details shone through to provide a spectacular sort of wonder to the mundane scene.

"The puppy chewing on her shoe. I don't know why, I'm not really a puppies and kittens kind of girl, but there's a hopefulness there, that a woman so old would get a puppy and believe she'd live to see it grow into a dog," Quinn said softly, her face pale and strained with the weight of the horrors she kept imprisoned in her mind.

"You're going to have to tell me," he said gently, when what he wanted to do was rage and storm and break things. "What happened with Ptolemy, and what happened with that vampire? I need to know, and I think, even more than that, you need to tell it."

She inhaled deeply, blew it out, and then finally turned to face him. "That's just it. Nothing happened. I mean, plenty happened—he made me kill someone, Alaric. He made me kill the secretary-general of the United Nations on live TV."

Tears shimmered in her lovely dark eyes, but she impatiently scrubbed them away with the back of her hands. "This dress—I need to get out of it. Now. Let me go take a long hot shower and find some of Lauren's clothes, and I'll tell you all about it."

She ran up the metal spiral staircase as if she couldn't bear to wear the offending garment a moment longer, and Alaric followed right behind her, because the last thing he planned to do for the foreseeable future was let her out of his sight. He slowed, however, as he realized that the shower itself posed a problem, because the gods themselves knew he had no idea where he'd get the control to keep from following her in.

By the time he reached the top of the stairs, the dress was wadded up in a metal trash receptacle and he could hear the sound of running water from behind a closed door. He scanned the high-ceilinged, clearly feminine room for obvious dangers, sent his magic searching for any that weren't obvious, and then settled down on the floor in front of the door to wait for her, energy spheres in hand against any possible threat.

He finally took a moment to try to communicate again with Christophe and Atlantis, as much as a means of distracting himself from the image of Quinn's wet, soapy, naked body as anything else.

We are well, but I don't know for how long. Conlan is losing his mind, since we don't know where the portal took the women and children, and it won't answer our call. We cannot evacuate anyone. But the magic is holding, and somehow Serai realized what was happening, from wherever in the world she and Daniel are, and she's reinforcing our magic, too. Between that and what you did, we are holding strong for now, but you need to find that gem and get it back here.

Alaric told him some of what had been happening, but left out anything to do with Quinn. There was no need for sharing that information. Or the news of the tsunami he'd almost used to destroy the eastern seaboard of the United States.

Poseidon helped shore up our defenses, Christophe. He said he's locked in a battle with the gods of other pantheons to determine the fate of the world, but we don't have time to worry about that until the current crisis is resolved.

Well, fix it, Christophe returned. *That's what you do, right? I'm just here temporarily, so don't get any ideas about leaving the priesthood to me. No how, no way.*

Alaric cut off the conversation without responding. He had no patience with Christophe's carefree ways. Not now, when every fiber of his being was demanding he cut ties to his own responsibilities and flee with Quinn before anything worse could happen. Or perhaps his lack of patience was a mask for an emotion far darker—a manifestation of his own bitter envy.

He could never do it—doom his people to extinction without even trying to save them. Not even for Quinn. But it was surprising how enticing the idea was to him; he, who hadn't been tempted to swerve in his duty even once in so many centuries, suddenly wished fervently to throw it all over and live a simple life with the woman he could finally admit he loved.

Tempting brought him back to thoughts of Quinn in the shower, and his pants suddenly no longer fit properly. Yes, the body knew what it wanted to do, and the parts definitely worked, so there were two concerns alleviated about the possibility of ending hundreds of years of celibacy. The sound of the running water stopped, and he groaned at the lovely mental image of Quinn drying off her body. Driven by a primal hunger that was far older than Atlantis itself, he climbed to his feet, shoved his dagger in its sheath, and put his hand on the doorknob.

There were some things a man—even a warrior—should not have to endure.

∼⌒⌒⌒⌒∞

Quinn dressed in an old pair of jeans and a sweater of Lauren's and opened the door to find Alaric on the other side, hand on the doorknob, an expression of such intent hunger on his face that she almost backed up a step.

"I cannot bear to be apart from you a moment longer," he said, his voice rough.

She nodded, feeling the exact same way, but suddenly apprehensive about what would happen next. None of their problems had gone away; Alaric was still bound to a terrible promise to a cruel god. And yet here they were in another bedroom, and she had the feeling there would be no malfunctioning Trident to save them this time.

She wrapped her arms around his waist, leaned her head against his muscular chest, and stood there, content to feel his arms around her. Content with the silence.

"I never get *this*," she finally said. "To allow myself to depend on someone else's strength. I had Jack, of course, but we didn't lean on each other like this."

"I'm glad to hear it," Alaric said, a tinge of a growl in his voice.

"I've been in charge for so long I've forgotten how to let someone else be strong, just for a moment's respite. A break in the action." She wanted to do what she'd never done before—*surrender*. To Alaric's strength and protection. A purely feminine impulse that was so shocking to her, she who'd lived her life as a fighter. He made her want to love and protect and be cherished in return.

Forbidden longings teased the surface of her skin, and something hard and cold in her heart unfurled like one of the fantastical Atlantean flowers. It was too much, too quick, and her emotions threatened to sweep her under like a bit of driftwood caught in a storm-tossed ocean.

That her mind presented her with metaphors of the sea made her smile, press her face into his shirt, and breathe deeply of the scent of sea and salt and sun that was so uniquely Alaric.

"And yet you are so quick to defend me and so fierce about it," Alaric murmured, stroking her back. "The warriors and I fight together, but never in all the years of my existence has someone tried to protect me the way you have. I do not deserve it, and I am humbled by it."

She pressed even closer to him and suddenly noticed the very hard bulge pressing against her abdomen. Her cheeks flamed hot, and she tried to move back, but he tightened his arms.

"No. Not yet. I cannot bear to let you go until I can truly believe you are safe."

He lifted her into his arms and moved to the bed, where he sat carefully on the edge with her in his lap and told her everything that had happened with Poseidon and also what Christophe had reported.

She gave him a reproachful look when he told her about the tsunami, but she didn't say a word. Perhaps she was beyond words. He needed to know, though. She owed him that.

"Now it's your turn. I want to know everything, Quinn. Can you bear to tell it?"

She shook her head. "Not yet. I need a few minutes."

After warding the room with his strongest magics, Alaric left Quinn to gather her thoughts. He only went as far as the bathroom, where he sped through a quick shower, but every instinct he had urged him to *hurry, hurry, hurry*.

After he cleaned and dried his clothes with Atlantean water magic in the space of a few seconds, he returned to sit silently next to her on the bed. When she raised her tearstained face to him, he asked her again.

"Can you bear to tell it?"

She nodded and fisted her hands in the fabric of her sweater. As she told him all of it, from the press conference to the murder, he grew more and more furious, but at her first mention of Anubisa, he glowed nearly incandescent with rage.

Literally.

She had to shield her eyes.

"Hey, you're going to need to tone it down for the human," she said gently.

He instantly dimmed the energy so she could bear to look at him again.

"My apologies. I am holding so much power, channeling it to support Christophe and Serai in stabilizing the dome and the Trident, that it takes little to push me over the edge."

"I understand, but if you want to hear all of it, you're going to need to calm down a little. I don't want to cause your brain to explode."

He nodded, but she could tell from the way the muscles in his jaw clenched that he was gritting his teeth very hard. She told him the rest of it, right up to the point where he'd arrived to rescue her.

"He told you he wanted to impregnate you," Alaric said.

She could tell from the way he so carefully enunciated that he was on the verge of going berserk.

"He said it, but he didn't touch me. Not like last time," she said softly, almost too softly to be heard.

His entire body tensed beneath her, as if steeling for a blow. "Last time?"

She bowed her head and told him something she never, ever talked about anymore. "Six years ago. When that murderous bastard of a vampire kept me as his plaything and—worst of all—I let him. Alaric, I know you think you want me, but you'd be far better off without me."

Silence. Utter, complete silence. It took a while for her to gather the courage to look up at him, but when she did, the revulsion and rejection she'd expected were nowhere in sight. Instead, a far more powerful emotion blazed forth from those beautiful emerald eyes, and he kissed her so thoroughly that she'd nearly forgotten her own name by the time he lifted his head.

"There is nothing you could ever do that would make me think less of you, *mi amara*," he said. "There is no deed, no matter how horrific you may have found it, in your past that could compete with the grace and courage of your soul. Tell me, if you will, or do not tell me, if you would rather never speak of it. Know this, though: I will fight everyone on this planet—even *you*, if it must be—who attempts to make me give you up."

Chapter 22

Alaric watched Quinn carefully as a yawning chasm of insanity beckoned at the edges of his consciousness. He fought it back in the toughest battle he'd ever waged. This was absolutely, in no way, about him.

His rage for what some monster had done to her.

His anguish that she had been violated.

None of it—not *any* of it—was about him. If he didn't control his emotions and contain his fury, he would lose her trust forever.

He locked down, hard, on all of it and simply rested his cheek on the top of her head and held her. Said nothing, did nothing; just held her for a very long time and focused on the scent of her still-damp hair. She smelled like flowers and some kind of fruit.

She smelled like home.

Finally, she stirred a little and looked up at him, and he could tell she'd been crying.

"Thank you," she said huskily. "That's exactly what I needed."

"I hope I can always do whatever you need, especially

when my every instinct is crying out for the opposite," he confessed.

"You want to protect me. You want to go back and find that vampire, whom I killed myself by the way, and kill him all over again. Piece by piece, so he suffers for hours."

"Suffers for days. *Months*, perhaps," he growled. "But instead, I will ask you if you are willing to tell me what happened."

"I don't talk about this," she said, her eyes dark pools of painful memory. "Not in casual conversation, not ever, really. Riley doesn't even know, but Jack does. He helped me find Moira."

Alaric watched as she clenched her hands into fists and then relaxed them, over and over. He wondered if she even realized she was doing it.

"Moira was my therapist. She helped me to be able to talk about it and, after a long while, to be able to heal and move on." She shrugged. "Pretty stupid, a big, tough rebel leader needing a shrink, right?"

"You're not that big," he said lightly. "More like a pocket-sized rebel leader."

She elbowed him, but she did smile a little, which was what he'd intended.

"No matter how tough you are, nobody survives pain, or torture, or violation without needing some help to get through it, *mi amara*. Even Conlan would not have survived the aftermath of captivity without support from your sister." He was amazed that he'd kept his voice so steady. No wound he'd ever suffered in battle had pierced him deeper than the agony of being unable to undo her past.

"And you. Riley told me how you helped Conlan get through that and cope with everything that happened when she and he met. You're kind of a hero, aren't you?"

"I prefer rock star," he said loftily, wondering a little wildly when the gods had given him the ability to banter while the walls he'd built so carefully around his heart over the centuries, stone by stone, shattered into rubble inside him.

It was almost a miracle. *She* was the miracle.

Quinn stared down at her clasped hands and drew in a shallow, fractured breath. "It was a terrible plan," she began, her voice so quiet he could hardly hear her.

"A terrible plan. Since then, I've come up with a hundred ways—a *thousand* ways—we could have done better, but we thought it was a great idea. We'd sneak into his lair, stake him as he slept, and save our little corner of the world. He was a ruthless, murdering animal, and somebody needed to take him down."

"And somebody was you," he said, hating it. Understanding it.

"Somebody was me," she agreed. "Except, he didn't stake so easily. We didn't know, back then, the full extent of the powers of the old ones. We didn't realize they could wake up and suck a human into their minds during the daylight hours."

He clenched his jaw against the questions burning in his throat for release, giving her time to tell him the story in her own way.

"He caught us, and he killed everyone else with me. He . . . he took a liking to me. Thought I was the girlfriend of one of the shifters or something. Didn't realize I was one of the fighters. So he decided that he'd keep the whore for himself. Spoils of battle," she said, bitterness dripping like acid from each word.

"I'm glad you killed him," he said fiercely; the only comment he'd allow himself.

"I didn't." She lifted her face to look him in the eyes. "I couldn't—not for a while. For far too long. I had no opportunity and no weapons. He was way too strong for me. Instead, I came up with horrible plan, part B: I pretended to *like* him. I thought if I could get him to trust me, I could find out more about his plots and conspiracies, and . . . and . . ."

She broke down and started to take deep, calming breaths. "Breathing exercises. Moira taught me to use them, you know? For a while, they were all I had to fight back the nightmares."

Alaric tried to take her hand, but she flinched away.

"No. Let me tell it all, first. You see, he didn't rape me. I let him . . . I *let* him. I became his toy. I pretended to like it. I became the whore he thought I was, just to survive. Just to find a way to kill him." Tears streamed down her face, unchecked, and he wondered if she even noticed them.

He swung around and dropped to his knees in front of her; not touching her, not crowding her, but facing her so he could tell her the most important truth he knew.

"No. Never that. Never a toy, never a whore. What you were—and are—is a survivor. You survived, under impossible, unbearable circumstances. You survived, and you made sure that he did not. Your strength humbles me, *mi amara*. I am in awe of your courage."

Slowly, tentatively, she reached for him and touched his face with one delicate hand. "You really mean that, don't you?"

"I have never meant anything more in my life," he said, leaning into her touch. "You are a survivor, and you have protected so many because you had the courage to endure the unendurable."

A ghost of a smile traced her lips. "Moira said the same thing. Maybe you're not so hopeless at this counseling thing, after all. I'll have to tell Myrken."

"He will be elated," he said dryly.

She laughed a little, and he knew he'd never heard any sound so sweet.

"Will you hold me now?"

"Always," he said, and he gently pulled her into his embrace, as careful as if he touched the most fragile of cherished treasures; realizing even as the thought crossed his mind that, in fact, he did.

"I've, ah, recovered a great deal since then," she whispered. "Moira helped, and Jack helped, but mostly just the passage of time and throwing myself into my work helped me to heal. I'm not . . . I'm not *fragile* anymore."

He stilled. "Quinn, what are you saying to me?"

She blushed a hot pink all the way to the tips of her delicate ears. "I'm saying that I'm not afraid to be intimate. I— well. I had a sort of casual, sort of not casual encounter . . .

well. Enough of that. I'm not afraid of physical closeness, Alaric. I just never found anyone worth trying to have it with, before now."

"I am honored that you would trust me with this gift," he said, humbled yet again by her bravery. Wondering if his own could match hers.

She suddenly laughed. "It's a lot of pressure, isn't it? All those years of celibacy, and now you have to throw in my background trauma. I'm surprised you're not flying out of that window."

He knew, by the sincerity of her laughter, that she'd told him the truth. She'd overcome her past and was ready to move forward. Now it fell to him to deserve her. He had to tell the truth and let her see his flaws. Chief among them, at the moment, was a searing jealousy.

"If we are to have honesty between us, I must admit that I would kill *him*, too, this casual encounter, if I could," he said, a wave of fierce possessiveness surging through him. "You should know that if you ever give yourself to me, there will be no more casual or not casual encounters in your life, ever. You will be mine, utterly and completely, as I will be yours."

She blinked. "You know, these days, people have amicable breakups all the time."

He narrowed his eyes. "No. Not for us. I will keep you forever. Everything in Atlantean culture dictates free will, Quinn. Even the soul-meld does not take away choice, but I must be entirely candid with you. I know my own nature, and I will never, ever let you go if you say yes to me. You must factor that into any decision."

She grinned. "So, no casual sex, is that what you're saying?"

He laughed then and kissed her thoroughly, not stopping until she was breathless. "And yes, I will always want to kill anyone who ever even *thinks* about harming you. That, too, is in my nature."

She laughed a little, but her eyes were shining with unshed tears. "You can't protect me from my past, Alaric, but I confess I love you for wanting to."

He stilled, every inch of his body turning motionless. She'd said she loved him.

She *loved* him.

She loved *him*.

"Say it again," he demanded.

She tilted her head. "Say what?"

"No. No, you do not get to say those words to me and pretend you don't remember saying them." He stood up, still holding her, and tossed her on the bed, then pounced and landed just above her, careful not to press her down or make her feel trapped.

"You said you love me," he told her. "Say it again."

Her eyes widened. "Oh, I said . . . No, I meant—"

"Do not. Do not begin to pretend that you don't love me, *aknasha*," he whispered. "I have seen inside your heart, remember? When all of Atlantis might be destroyed in the next forty-eight hours, do not deprive me of the truth of your feelings during this brief moment before duty calls me away from you."

She suddenly shoved him, hard, and he fell over next to her. She rolled over to face him, and her expression was far too serious. Or maybe not serious enough. Alaric found himself wishing he could take back his impulsive words.

"I do love you," she whispered. "I didn't want to admit it, because if ever there were a textbook version of a doomed relationship, we're pretty much it. But I can't help myself, no matter how hard I've tried. I've seen inside your heart, too, remember? And there you were, shining in the darkness. Honor, courage, duty, and a heaping helping of iron will. How could I not love you?"

He rolled onto his back and shouted a wordless cry of triumph to the world, and then he paused and looked at her. "And?"

"And what?"

"And world-bending kisses," he said, and he pulled her on top of his chest. "Let me demonstrate."

So he did. He kissed her until he no longer knew where

they were or what their names were. There was no Alaric; no Quinn. Only the passion that burned so brightly between them he could hardly countenance that it did not set the room on fire. The silken feel of her lips against his breathed hope and laughter into his soul, and hunger turned to an emotion far deeper—far more powerful—far more life-sustaining.

Fire and warmth and *home*. She was and forever would be home to him, no matter what foes or battles he faced. The realization blazed through him like the summer sun breaking through the clouds after a tropical thunderstorm, and the kind of peace he'd never known suffused his mind, his heart, and his soul.

His body hardened past the point of endurance, until need and hunger drove him toward madness. He had to touch her—touch her *now*—touch her everywhere. He stroked the silky skin of her arms and shoulders, and even dared to press kisses along the elegant line of her collarbone. She was so thin—too thin—but far more beautiful than any woman he'd ever known.

More beautiful than any woman in the history of the world.

He abruptly stopped kissing her when a concern surfaced. "You need food."

"No, I had room service, remember?" She pulled his head back to kiss him some more and then she raised her head. "Do you need food?"

"I'm interested in dessert. You," he said, his voice straining to sound even a little calm. "Quinn, I think we have to make a decision right now, because I'm going to tear your clothes off in approximately seven seconds if we keep this up."

She grinned. "Oh, are we keeping you up?"

She put her hand on his erection, and he nearly jumped out of his skin.

"I cannot believe you did that," he said, trying not to go off in his pants like an untried youngling. Or, more to the point, like a man who had been celibate for most of his five centuries of existence.

"I don't actually believe it, either," she said, looking a little stunned.

"Five seconds," he ground out. "Four, three—"

"Wait!" She jumped up and off the bed and backed away, panic written on her delicate features. "Nothing has changed. You can't—we can't—"

"Apparently I can," he said dryly, adjusting his pants to try to find a comfortable fit.

"But Poseidon—"

"He can get his own woman."

Alaric climbed off the bed and started stalking her across the room, step by step.

"We can't," she blurted out. "Not with Atlantis hanging in the balance."

Maddeningly, that was the ultimate truth. No matter how hard he'd tried not to think about it, just for these few stolen moments, everyone in his world depended upon him. He had to find Poseidon's Pride and return to Atlantis, no matter how tempting this interlude with Quinn had been.

It was as if the cold light of reality had suddenly pierced through the web of self-delusion he'd been hiding in for the past hour or so. His exhilaration at finding Quinn had left him stupid—almost punch-drunk—and now he must face his responsibilities and save his people.

"You're right," he said flatly. "But there is one thing we can do. If you agree, however, it must be solely for your own reasons, or for what is between us, and not from any misplaced feeling of altruism. You have given enough, done enough, and suffered enough for one hundred lifetimes."

"What are you asking me?"

He stared at the perfect face that had haunted his dreams since he'd first met her and asked the question driven by need; the question that should have been posed only through love:

"Quinn Dawson, will you agree to attempt the soul-meld with me?"

Chapter 23

Quinn forced herself to pause before shouting *yes*. Everything about Alaric made her crazy: crazy impulsive, crazy passionate, just . . . crazy. She wanted that feeling of belonging to him forever and ever, didn't she?

Doubts and fears tried to edge their way into her mind, but she shoved them aside. Not now. Not this time. There was no room for doubt, and yet . . . what if?

What if the celibacy thing was real, and Alaric lost all of his power? How long would it take for him to hate her? What if the emotion that had caught them up with the force of a whirlwind was driven by excitement and danger, and now that she was no longer a rebel leader, their lives would become ordinary and boring? What if they wound up stuck together for a very long time, maybe even hating each other?

But she looked at him—really looked at him—and she realized she didn't believe any of the doubts or fears. She *couldn't* believe them. She'd seen inside of this man, this proud, dangerous, terrifyingly courageous man, and she *knew* him. Knew his heart; knew his spirit. He'd never stop loving her—even though he hadn't yet said the words, she knew he did—and sometimes, life was worth a leap of faith.

"Yes," she said, finally, simply, staring into his incredibly green eyes. "Yes, I accept you. Um, I thought the soul-meld had to be—"

"No. It can take place platonically," he said, but then he flashed a breathtakingly wicked smile at her. "But it won't be nearly as pleasurable, I imagine."

He crossed the room in three quick strides and took her hands, but she shook her head, placing a hand on his chest to stop him. "Not here. There's no magic here. Downstairs, with the art. If we can't create beauty with our bodies while we do this, let's at least be surrounded by it."

He led the way down the stairs, and the weight of what they intended to do—and the knowledge of what it might mean for Atlantis's survival—echoed in each footstep. She glanced around the room and almost immediately settled on the perfect spot in front of the windows, as the sun set in a blaze of glorious golden light. She turned and held out a hand to Alaric, swallowing any nervousness when she saw him walking toward her, walking into the spotlight of sunshine, his strength and passion outlined in every line and angle of his strong, beautiful face.

He would be *hers*—for as long as she survived—and the knowledge was a gift she held close to her heart.

"The painting you admired," he said, gesturing to the canvas. "What better symbol for our union than hope?"

She nodded, unable to trust her voice, as Alaric took her hands in his and solemnly looked at her.

"Are you sure?"

She smiled up at him, and realized she truly was sure. No matter where she went in the future, Alaric was a man who could and would stand by her side. Fight by her side. Love her. Always.

"Yes," she said, and her voice rang out clear and strong, like a bell chiming the way to her future.

"Close your eyes."

She did, and he leaned his forehead against hers. "Now open your mind and heart and soul to me, *mi amara*, as I do to you."

She took a deep breath, tightened her grip on his hands, and threw her emotional shields wide open. Then she fell to her knees as pure power, of a scope she couldn't have even begun to imagine, poured into her. She realized Alaric had dropped down to kneel, too, still holding her hands, and she cried out as more and more and more energy rushed through her body.

"I can't," she said. "It's too much. I'm only human."

"You're far more than human, Quinn. This is part of the soul-meld for a high priest of Atlantis."

She thought he said something else, but she couldn't hear it, couldn't hear anything, couldn't *feel* anything except the inferno of magical energy threatening to swamp her mind and incinerate her nerve endings. She found herself balancing on the edge of a towering and terrible knowledge, and as it poured into her and filled her, she suddenly *knew* things.

Knew things she couldn't have known, saw things she couldn't have seen.

Flashes of brilliant blue-green light scorched through her mind and illuminated scenes of Alaric's life, careening from image to image like some insane Ghost of Atlanteans Past, and all she could do was try to hold on for the ride.

Alaric as a child, running and playing with the other boys. Carefree and happy; but, even then, there was a certain reserve to him. He stood apart, and she felt the loneliness that never quite left him.

Alaric as a young man, riding a horse at a breakneck pace across green fields, with Conlan chasing after him, both of them laughing.

The two of them, carousing in what looked like a tavern, surrounded by admiring young women.

Quinn cried out again as an especially intense surge of power or magic or whatever Alaric must carry around inside of him *all of the time* spiked into her brain and she lost her senses for a few moments. When she climbed back up out of the dark to conscious thought, the images showed her an older, harder Alaric.

He shouted at Conlan that he didn't want to be high priest. He didn't want the duty or the responsibility. "What happened to our plans to travel around the surface for a few dozen years, doing nothing but eating, drinking, and wenching?"

But the Conlan in the vision only shook his head, sadness on his face, and the insane tour continued, with Quinn soon floating on the edge of a dark, dark room.

"The darkness of the Rite of Oblivion is only equal to the darkness in your own soul," a voice was saying, but the voice's owner was hooded and robed, so Quinn couldn't see his face. She could see Alaric clearly enough, though, wearing nothing but a loose pair of pants, struggling as three robed figures pushed him toward a hole in the floor. Alaric's clenched jaw, and the corded muscle starkly outlined beneath his skin as he tried to resist, told her that whatever waited for him underground was something that would terrify anyone with less courage.

"If the oubliette accepts you, it will give you back to us. If it does not, it will take you a very long time to die," the sadistic bastard said, and then the three of them shoved Alaric into the hole.

Quinn screamed, but she couldn't protect Alaric from his past any more than he could protect her from hers, and the merciless barrage continued.

Alaric, rising from the oubliette, noticeably thinner, his eyes sunken and wild, and the robed figures kneeling to him as one of them draped a robe over Alaric's shoulders.

"All bow to Poseidon's new high priest, long may he rule over our holy temple," they chanted.

She wanted to kill them all, steal Alaric away and comfort and feed him, but the visions sped past, and soon she was watching him grow stronger, harder, and colder. More and more alone. He learned to wield the Trident, which was plenty powerful enough without its gems, and he learned to hunt and fight and kill vampires.

She watched him battle rogue shape-shifters and nests of

murderous vamps. She watched him save and protect and rescue, over and over and over. So many deaths on his conscience, so much blood on his hands, all in service of protecting his prince, his people, and humankind.

After what felt like centuries of images buffeting her mind, she saw Alaric watch Conlan with Riley and felt how conflicted he'd been when he'd realized his prince loved this *human*, and then a blast of intense emotion nearly knocked her on her ass, but this wasn't *her* emotion, not this time.

It was *his*.

She was watching him heal her, Quinn, from that bullet wound when they first met. She watched him as he fell back, blasted into shock by the force of his own feelings. She listened to him confess how much danger he believed himself to be in, simply from touching her.

"You want to know what happened?*" With two steps, he was right up in Conlan's face.*

"I'll tell you what happened, *my prince," Alaric continued, rasping out the words. "What happened was I sent my healing energy inside Quinn. Inside that* human. *And she grabbed hold of me."*

He shoved a hand through his hair and laughed a little wildly, eyes flaring green and hot.

Savage.

"She dug her mental claws into my balls, *is what happened. I healed her, and she destroyed something in me. Shredded it."*

"What—" Conlan never got the question out.

"My control," Alaric snarled. "The absolutely rock-hard control that I've spent centuries perfecting. Your little girl-friend's sister reached out with her emotions, or her witchy empath nature, or what the hell ever, and all I wanted to do was fuck *her."*

Conlan stepped back half a step at the ferocity in the priest's voice and dropped his hands to his dagger handles. For an instant, icy death menaced the air between them.

Alaric laughed, bitter again. "Oh, you don't need your blades. In spite of the fact that I wanted her more than I've wanted anything in my life, I won't touch her. Although, even now, my mind tortures me with images of pounding into her body, right there on the ground in the mess of her own blood, fucking and fucking her until I drive myself into her soul." Alaric viciously kicked at a tree and shards of bark flew into the air, then disintegrated in the green energy bolts he shot at them.

This was new and dangerous territory, and Conlan attempted to proceed with caution. "Alaric, you must—"

"Yes. I must. I must never succumb to any lusts, or my power is ended. Certainly, I would be of no further use to you or to Atlantis. No use to the jealous bastard of a sea god whom I serve," the priest said flatly, his voice suddenly devoid of the rage and passion that had infused it moments before.

"I must get away from her," he continued. "Now. From this place. I am ruined for this day, in any event. This . . . this energy drain has voided any hope I had of re-scrying for the Trident until I recover. I will meet you back at Ven's safe house tonight."

Conlan grasped his friend's shoulders, shaken by the blasphemy he'd never heard from him before. "Alaric, know that your use to me and to Atlantis goes far beyond the powers you gained from Poseidon. Your wise counsel has served me well for centuries, and I will need you when I ascend to the throne."

Alaric stared over Conlan's shoulder toward Riley and her sister. "These empaths. They signal a treacherous difference in our ways, Conlan. I can sense it. Change is coming. Peril that comes from within our very souls."

Quinn shuddered as the most powerful wave of magic yet seared through her body, and she realized it was tinged with a dark, disturbing emotion.

It was tainted with shame.

Alaric must have seen what she was seeing; discovered that she had learned how he'd reacted to her that very first time.

"It was the same for me, you must know that," she cried out, not knowing if he could hear her, or if her voice was trapped in the vision with her. "I was terrified of you and of the feelings you evoked in me. You can't be ashamed of how you feel about me. Please, no."

But the horrific visions kept coming, showing her what he had endured since she first met him; the impossible decisions he was forced to make on a daily basis; and, most of all, the bleak, icy loneliness he endured.

He was a man doomed to be alone by the very god he served, and not only for the space of a normal lifetime. Tears streamed down her face as the pressure crushing his heart and soul, increasing exponentially over the centuries, grew so much worse when, one by one, his friends and companions all found true love and the soul-meld.

He, of all of them, still alone. Always alone, with only the dream of Quinn to sustain him on so many long, dark nights.

"Never again," she vowed, her heart full to bursting with her determination to protect him—even from Poseidon—to never let him be alone again. As the final vision, of Alaric standing on the roof of the palace in Atlantis, grim and solitary, faded, and the room around her came into view again, she reached another realization. Alaric's magic *hadn't* stopped funneling into her with all the speed and fury of that tornado in Japan.

Instead, she had somehow become able to control it. She didn't know how, or why, but somehow she'd gained the capacity to contain every ounce of the power he was thrusting into her in a metaphysical reflection of a far more primal act. All she could do was hang on for the ride, but at least she *could* hang on, with no more worries that the magic would incinerate her brain. With that realization came another, even more basic.

Even more *important*. One that he needed to know.

"I love you," she told him. Without qualification; without hesitation. Never again would she doubt it.

His entire body shuddered, as if he'd been terrified of a far different reaction, and he opened his mouth to speak, but then his eyes glowed even hotter, and tiny blue flames danced in his pupils. He tightened his grip on her hands and said,

"Quinn," and then he was gone, probably lost to his own visions, and all she could do was hold on and pray that he still wanted her after he'd seen the blackest regions of her own soul.

～～～～

Alaric didn't even have a chance to apologize to Quinn. He'd had no idea that the soul-meld would subject her to the blasts of his magic, or he never would have asked her to do it. Hells, he never would have *allowed* it. He'd tried to release her when the surge of power intensified beyond human endurance, but the ancient ritual refused to be interrupted once begun, and its magic was far too strong for him to break.

He'd feared that she'd banish him from her presence, cast him aside, and even ridicule him once she learned the darkest secrets of his being, but instead—miraculously—she'd *smiled*. She'd told him she loved him. And now—now the soul-meld took him, and the time for reflection was gone.

Alaric watched, trapped on a crazy whirlwind like an insane version of a child's carousel, as Quinn's life spun in front of him in terrifying flashes. Losing her parents, joining the rebels, and lying to her sister. Constantly being forced to deceive the few friends she'd ever made; growing more and more alone and isolated. Choosing the harder path at every fork in the road, and offering herself up like a sacrificial lamb for the most dangerous missions and most suicidal battles.

He watched, his own composure rocked to its foundation, as she lost her faith in the very people she was fighting to protect, when the rebels were forced to fight against other humans. The collaborators were the worst. She *despised* them. Her hatred was so strong it smashed the walls of his mind as he watched her argue with a human who had killed other humans, again and again, for the chance to become a vampire.

"I'll live forever," the man had told her, smirking.

"Better luck next time," she'd said, and then she shot him in the head. She stood over the man, impassive, as he died, and then she dropped to the ground and cried. She'd been fighting for several years by then, but it was the first time she'd been forced to kill another human, and something inside her had shattered, irrevocably broken.

Her innocence, perhaps.

He felt her emotions ice over, and her mental shields grow ever stronger, as she used her gift of emotional empathy to ferret out traitors among the rebel forces. He watched as she climbed through the ranks; as her clear head and fearlessness made her a natural leader.

He felt her cautious hope and then joy, when she met a tiger shifter who made a big impression, and a part of Alaric that he hadn't realized was still afraid relaxed, as he experienced her love for Jack. A sister's love for a brother—a warrior's love for her comrade—but never a romantic love.

He swore to himself that when all this was over, he'd find a way to heal Jack and return him to himself. Surely in the combined knowledge of all of the libraries of Atlantis, there must be a way.

The soul-meld dragged him relentlessly on and on, forcing him to see the vicious attack when the vampire captured Quinn and killed her companions. Her terror and pain, hidden so well while she pretended to be her captor's willing slave, nearly drove him mad. His throat ached, and he realized that perhaps the voice he heard roaring in rage and fear was his own.

But the visions kept coming.

The cascade of images was oblivious to his pain and rage, and unfeeling in the face of her darkest memories. They pushed him past the first time he'd met her, showing him her shock and terror at her reaction to him, letting him feel the powerful emotion that swept through her whenever she saw him or even allowed herself to think of him.

He felt the despair she'd known on that rooftop in D.C. when she'd told him she was ruined. He saw inside her heart when they'd first kissed, and now he knew that the searing heat of passion between them wasn't only one-sided. She'd felt it, too.

Her amusement, gratitude, and resentment pulsed from

her when, time after time and often in spite of her protests, he'd healed her from minor and major injuries alike.

Finally, *finally*, the visions showed him the dank space underground to which Ptolemy had stolen away with her, and her terror when Anubisa arrived. His stomach roiled with fury at Anubisa's demands, and he felt Quinn's anger and compassion for the girl who'd also been held captive.

The hotel. Quinn's shock when she saw the wall of photos of herself; her relief when Alaric came for her. Her love for him.

Most of all, her love for him. It shone forth like a beacon, and his shriveled heart flourished in its warmth and light.

The visions faded, and he could finally see her again. His woman had the heart of an Atlantean lion and the soul of a fierce warrior, and yet was filled with the capacity to love so fully, so deeply, and without fear of whatever new crisis the future would bring them.

A thousand warriors combined could never match her courage.

"I never told you I loved you," he said abruptly, and Quinn's smile started to fade.

He pulled her hands up to his lips and kissed them, one and then the other. "I knew I wanted you, and I knew I *needed* you, but I wasn't sure how to love, or even if it was possible for me. You showed me how very wrong I was."

She started to speak, but he continued, needing to get the words out with some small measure of eloquence. "*Mi amara*, I will tell you now and every day for the rest of my life that I love you. You are the center of my existence, and you are the heart that beats in my chest. I would kill for you, and I would die for you, and I will spend all of eternity doing my best to make you smile."

She was crying and she was laughing, somehow both at once in the peculiar manner of females. She launched herself into his arms, knocking him backward, and then she was kissing him, and his world was right with the universe.

Or it was, at least until he started glowing.

"Quinn?"

Her shock was plain to see—she didn't know what was happening, either—and he could see light reflected in her eyes. He looked down and realized his entire body was glowing. *Worse* than glowing. He was shining like a lighthouse beacon, and the reason soon became painfully clear. His mind exploded outward as power rushed in—more than he'd ever channeled. More power than he'd ever *dreamed* of wielding, even in his darkest dreams of magic.

"You're *shining*," Quinn said, awestruck. "You're *beautiful*. Doesn't that *hurt*?"

He flew up into the air in the center of the loft and spun around, shedding light and magic like a whirling fountain. He floated back down, laughing out loud, as dawn broke and touched pale fingers to the brick-and-glass face of the building across from their windows.

"The sun is rising," Quinn said wonderingly. "We were trapped in those visions all night long. Who needs the sun, though, with you in the room? This is amazing, Alaric."

"Keely was right. The soul-meld has actually increased my power by at least tenfold."

She flashed him a wicked smile. "Maybe she was right about the sex, too."

He couldn't bear not to be touching her, so he pulled her into the air with him and kissed her until she couldn't breathe.

"Now all we have to do is defeat the bad guys," she said when she caught her breath, and he grinned at her like a fool because she was just so damn beautiful, and she was *his*.

Always his. *Forever* his.

"Mine," he said happily, and she started laughing.

"Yes. Yours. Now let's go save the world."

Christophe suddenly broke through with a mental blast that had an edge of panic:

Alaric, wherever you are, I need to reach you now!

Alaric realized that the soul-meld must have blocked all else.

I am here, he sent back.

Finally. We have less time than we thought. Ptolemy must be using the tourmaline, because the Trident started going

*crazy again, and water is now seeping into Atlantis. You have
to hurry and find that stone.*

Alaric nodded and sent the good news back.

*The soul-meld was successful. I will immediately strengthen
my connection to Atlantis to help contain the Trident and shore
up the dome's defenses.*

He focused his new torrent of energy and did exactly that,
and he could hear Christophe's whoop of joy in his mind.

You did it! Hey, did you and Quinn—

Alaric cut the connection, but he was smiling. He relayed
the message to Quinn, who stood up, her eyes flashing.

"Right. Now I have to go back to Ptolemy and get him to
give me that rock."

Chapter 24

It took nearly an hour of argument, during which they'd raided the refrigerator and eaten a cobbled-together breakfast, and Quinn had to pull out the "we're soul-melded, you should trust me" card, but Alaric finally agreed to let her approach Ptolemy, so long as Alaric was within one hundred feet of her at all times. Rescuing distance, in other words.

Once an overprotective high priest, always an overprotective high priest.

He planned to travel as mist, because even if Ptolemy really did have an Atlantean mother, that wasn't enough for him to be able to sense Poseidon's high priest when he didn't want to be discovered, Alaric said. Of course, he hadn't seen the extent of Ptolemy's power, but Quinn decided not to mention that. Alaric was already about an inch away from trying to lock her in a closet somewhere, rebel leader or no, and so she decided not to press her luck.

Another hour and a call to an associate yielded her sympathy she didn't want and a nonmetallic, poly-fiber combat boot knife she did. She didn't want to be at the mercy of Ptolemy's metal-melting skills again. Alaric had leaned against the doorway like an unreasonably gorgeous body-guard the entire time she'd spoken with the man, making both of them nervous.

"How to find him is the issue," Alaric said. "You thought he'd returned to his demon realm?"

Quinn shuddered, remembering the burst of dark energy that had pressed against her in a suffocating wave. "Yes. But if he's back, I figure a glory hound like Ptolemy will be making his presence known again."

Sure enough, when she switched on the TV, his face filled the screen on both the local and national news channels, broadcasting live from the Statue of Liberty in the bright early-morning sun.

When the camera turned to the reporter, she showed no trace of the typical newscaster smile. Instead, strain drew lines around her mouth and nose as she faced the camera, her shoulders hunched over, one hand wrapped around her waist.

Quinn frowned and reached for the remote control, to toggle off the mute button. "Okay, a reporter who isn't cheer-ful or perky is odd—"

Screams interrupted her as the volume switched on. The camera panned out, wide, and showed them a scene of un-controlled chaos. Men, women, and children ran in all direc-tions, with only one thing in common—they were running *away* from the reporter and her camera. As they watched, a group of three young guys knocked over an elderly woman in their panicked flight, but two of them immediately stopped to lift her bodily off the ground and then carried her with them.

"I suspect we have found Ptolemy," Alaric said grimly.

Before Quinn could reply, the camera zeroed back in on the reporter. She visibly swallowed and then spoke, gripping her microphone with a white-knuckled hand.

"To repeat, Ptolemy Reborn, the king of Atlantis, is very unhappy with the person who stole his future bride, and he plans to kill a tourist every hour until she—"

They heard a voice in the background, and the reporter froze, and then resumed, her voice shaking as wildly as her hands. "I misspoke. He will kill *many* tourists, and *as often as he feels like it*," she corrected, as the first tears broke free and ran down her perfectly made-up cheeks.

Quinn's hands curled into fists. "He's going down."

"I'm going to kill him," Alaric said, simultaneously.

They didn't waste another second on talk or preparation. Quinn grabbed a few things she thought might be helpful from Lauren's tools and then they headed out for the Statue of Liberty. She locked up the loft carefully, and Alaric took her in his arms and leapt into the air.

In spite of the danger they were soon to face, and the desperate consequences if they failed, Quinn couldn't help but be mesmerized by the beauty and stark elegance of the city as they flew over it. New York bustled through the morning like an artist's dream of gritty realism painted with a kaleidoscopic palette. But the fanciful imaginings faded from her mind as they flew across the water toward Liberty Island and their target.

Instead, the theme music from *Underdog* starting playing in its place.

When they reached the familiar landmark, all manner of police boats and helicopters encircled it. Alaric turned up the speed, and they moved through the obstacle course of official vehicles so fast that nobody had a chance to stop them. Quinn wished her hands were free to cover her ears and block the cacophony of bullhorns and loudspeakers.

"He must be there. Put me down behind the base of the statue, where he won't see you," she said, as they approached, flying low so that the statue itself blocked them from view. "And let me say it pisses me off that he's using America's best-known symbol of freedom in his twisted game."

"Not so much a game, if he succeeds in opening a gateway to a demonic dimension," Alaric said as they landed.

"I know. That's why you're going to trust me, and stay out of this for a little while, so I can figure out how to get Poseidon's Pride without Ptolemy leaving Earth—and us—behind. You are the bravest and most powerful man I've ever met, but all that courage doesn't do us any good if we can't get to Ptolemy," she said, for the thousandth or so time.

Alaric's eyes glowed hot, and he clenched his jaw, probably to keep from telling her she was an idiot.

"You have five minutes, and then I'm coming after you," he said firmly. "Five minutes, and only because the fate of all of Atlantis is on the line. Not one second longer."

She kissed him, hard, refusing to wonder if it would be for the last time, and before she could lose her nerve, she ran around the corner of the statue and toward the monster who wanted her to have his demon babies.

She didn't know whether to cry or laugh at the shocked expression on Ptolemy's face. He and Alaric had something in common, then. They both thought she was an idiot. She was starting to agree with them.

She resorted to her old standby: being a smart-ass.

"Hey, did you miss me?"

Ptolemy glared at her. He wore the same business suit, but it was immaculate. Maybe he owned a dozen of them. "Where have you been? Who took you?"

"One of the fake Atlanteans, but he only wanted information, and when I told him I didn't really know anything, he let me go." She shrugged, the picture of nonchalance. Or so she hoped.

She slowed her pace and stopped about six feet away from him, and she tried to distract him before he could wonder how she'd gotten to the island. Or with whom.

"Like you're going to do for the nice tourists, right? Let them go?"

He gestured as if at an annoying bug. "I don't care about these vermin. They can go."

As the people began to run away, Quinn had to resist the urge to run with them, because suddenly Ptolemy was turning the full weight of his undisguised alien eyes on her, and he didn't look happy to see her. Not one bit.

"You just escaped, is this what I am to believe?"

"You come from an alien demon dimension, and you just

happen to speak English perfectly, is this what I am to believe?" she said, mocking him.

"I have studied your world for hundreds of years," he said, raising his chin like an offended schoolgirl.

All *righty*, then. Maybe she *could* get to him through his vanity.

"Fine. Good. So you know all about Lady Liberty? The French actually sent her to us, you know? There's even a hideous song they made us sing in grade school, based on the inscription on the base, 'Give us your tired, your poor, your huddled masses—' "

"I have no interest in these things," he said. "We're leaving. However, speaking of huddled masses, I need to prove that I will carry out my threats, or they won't have any teeth, will they?"

Before Quinn could blink, Ptolemy pointed his finger at an old man in a wheelchair and the equally elderly woman pushing him. They were following the escaping crowd as quickly as they could move, but it wasn't fast enough, Quinn realized.

Not anywhere *near* fast enough.

"No!" Quinn screamed, but it was too late. An arrow of orange light shot across the sidewalk and incinerated the two, completely obliterating them, until only bones and the twisted steel of the chair remained.

"I'll kill you for that," she said, not caring that tears streamed down her face as she reeled in shock from the realization that—however indirectly—she'd caused him to kill those people. He'd wanted to prove a point to *her*, because she'd been acting like a smart-ass.

She looked up and saw Alaric speeding toward Ptolemy, who was clearly unaware of the Atlantean vengeance approaching, because he smiled, a slow smile, hideous in its triumph.

"Is this our first spat, my darling?"

Before she could answer—before Alaric could reach them—Ptolemy ripped open a jagged tear in reality and shoved her into his profane version of the Atlantean portal.

She screamed Alaric's name and heard him roaring behind her, but it was too late. The opening closed behind Ptolemy and sent the two of them spinning away from Alaric, New York, and probably even Earth itself.

Despair swallowed her whole and spat her back out, after another nausea-inducing trip, into a pretty good approximation of hell.

Sulfuric fumes assaulted her nose and mouth, making it difficult to breathe. Nothing in sight lived: no trees or plants, animals or birds. For miles and miles, she could only see desert and rock and the rubble of a collapsed civilization. The sky was the worst, though. Three low-hanging moons shone a sullen orange over a blasted apocalyptic landscape.

"Where are we?" she demanded, but she was afraid she knew, and terror rose up in her, flailing around like a gibbering creature strung up in a noose. Her heart pounded so hard that she was sure Ptolemy must be able to hear it.

"We're in my dimension now, Quinn, where you can't play games with me, because here there are no rules but mine." He grabbed her arm with one newly claw-tipped hand and started dragging her down a narrow path between two tumbled stone columns. "Isn't it just what you imagined, when you dreamed of a house with a white picket fence?"

He leered at her and started laughing, but his teeth were changing and growing sharper, and his face was contorting right there in front of her. If she'd ever doubted his claim to be demon kin, she didn't any longer.

"You know nothing about my dreams, buddy." She reached deep inside herself to where the light of Alaric's magic and the battered but unbroken foundation of her own courage still burned. She'd pretended to go along with one despicable monster before. She could do it again, until she'd achieved her goal. She'd be so convincing that she'd deserve an Academy Freaking Award.

"You have no idea what a joyous day this is about to become," Ptolemy said, dragging her along. His laughter grew more and more shrill, until it didn't sound anything close to human, but that wasn't the worst part of it. Not at all. The worst part was the twisted, grayish-orange creatures that had started crawling up out of the rubble and following them. They didn't have any recognizable limbs or appendages at all. Mostly, all they had was teeth. Lots and lots of teeth.

∽⁓⁓⁓⁓

Hours or minutes later—Quinn couldn't be sure which, since time seemed to run sideways here—they reached their destination. The building, built in a twisted approximation of a Greek—or maybe Atlantean—temple, was at least partially still standing. Ptolemy dragged her inside an open stone doorway and then finally released his grip on her arm.

She rubbed her wrist and looked around warily, mostly to avoid looking at him. He'd become more and more bestial as they marched across the hideous terrain of his world, until now he was almost impossible to look at without flinching. There was something simply *wrong* about him. Dark and hideously twisted; just like his magic. She cast a glance back over her shoulder to see if the grotesque creatures following them were anywhere near the building, but the doorway remained empty.

The room they'd entered, though—the room was incredible. She couldn't believe what she was seeing. It was as beautifully ornate as any of the rooms she'd seen in the Atlantean palace. Vividly blue marble mosaics lined the walls, which were decorated with images of ocean waves, fish, mermaids, and fantastical flowers portrayed by ancient craftspeople with amazing artistic sensibility. The floor was cool tile in jade green—or maybe it really was jade—and it, too, was beautifully designed.

"Well," Ptolemy said, his voice gravelly, as though his tongue no longer worked quite right. "What do you think?"

"It's magnificent," she said honestly.

He whirled around and snarled at her, and she took a prudent step back.

"You mock me?"

"No. Trust me, when I'm mocking you, you'll know

it," she said bitterly. "Like 'Hey, troll face, nice teeth.' Or 'Hey, way to show your courage by *murdering helpless old people.*'"

A flash of an indefinable emotion crossed his face, and if he'd been anyone else, she'd almost have said it was shame.

"It was my mother's room," he finally said, turning away from her.

He jerked his head at one corner of the room.

She walked over to where he'd indicated, and found a portrait hidden in a niche. It looked incredibly old, but somehow the colors were still as fresh and vibrant as if newly painted. The subject was a woman, clearly Atlantean—she could have been Serai's sister—holding a baby.

"She's beautiful," Quinn said, feeling an unwanted flash of compassion for the monster beside her. Beauty had borne the Beast. How much must that have hurt them both?

Ptolemy must have been able to read Quinn's sincerity, because his hunched posture relaxed, and his features resumed somewhat of their human cast, at least enough so she could bear to look at him.

"Yes, she was. She was also one of the *aknasha'an*, like you."

Quinn whirled to look at him. "Is that why? You—"

"My kind is unable to bear children without a female who can read emotions. Whether by reason of an ancient curse none of us remember, or simply because of a cruel twist of fate, we must steal women from other dimensions in order to procreate," he said. "You became known to me when I was studying your world, and I would have taken you simply for your abilities alone, but your exploits as rebel leader fascinated me until I became obsessed. Your strength and courage. Your leadership skills. These are qualities I want for my heirs."

His sincerity made her teeth hurt, so she told herself she was simply dealing with a man with serious mommy issues. "You do realize that you can't just go around stealing women to use as breeders, right?"

He smiled at her with teeth that were still far too sharp, and quite possibly serrated, from the look of them. She repressed a shudder.

"But that is exactly what I have done, my dear *wife*."

"*Don't* call me that." She thought longingly of the knife in her boot and forced herself to change the subject when he leered at her again. "What happened here?"

He paced around the room slowly. "The same thing that always happens with warlike creatures. We destroyed each other and our dimension. We've had to roam farther and farther afield for mates, and many of our people never return to this blasted wasteland of a realm, for obvious reasons."

"Why did you? What is there here for you?" She pointed at the landscape through a crumbling window frame, its glass, if it had ever had any, long gone.

"Why, my brothers are here," he said, and then he threw back his head and made a long, ululating whistling noise that she was sure would make her ears bleed.

She clamped her hands over them and almost missed what he said next.

"When you and I rule Atlantis and then the rest of your world, they will serve as my most trusted advisors and staff."

Her mouth fell open. He was bat-shit crazy.

"I don't think Anubisa is going to go along with that plan."

He sneered. "Anubisa is a mad relic of a time long gone. I will have no trouble with her, as you've seen. I plan to rule her vampires, too, or destroy them. It matters little to me."

She didn't have time to form a response to that, before his brothers started arriving. And if she'd thought Ptolemy was hideous, she'd sorely underestimated the meaning of the word. He was Prince Charming compared to his family.

She gritted her teeth and fought really, really hard not to scream.

Chapter 25

Alaric's first instinct was to shatter the Statue of Liberty into crumbling dust, and everyone still on the island with it. The berserker rage climbed up inside him again, and with the recently increased capacity of his power, he was likely to destroy the entire state of New York.

Only one thing stopped him from doing so: he could still sense Quinn. Somewhere, either so far away he had no idea of how to reach her, or else nearby with her presence blocked by the pretender, but he could still feel her. The soul-meld had given him that much. She was alive and unharmed, at least for now, and he *would* find her.

Now that the demon had gone, the police and other officials were closing in, fast, and it was time for him to disappear. He transformed into mist and soared up until he rematerialized on top of Lady Liberty's torch and balanced on the edge. The view was spectacular, had he cared about such things.

Below him, police and rescue workers scurried about, assisting the remaining people and searching for evidence of Ptolemy, no doubt. Alaric felt a moment's compassion for the human police, who'd had to adapt to so much when the vampires and other paranormal creatures made themselves known. Regular handcuffs didn't do much to restrain a wolf shifter in a full-on rage; he couldn't imagine that any of their weapons would have had any effect on a demon.

Quinn was definitely correct in that—Ptolemy was undoubtedly some kind of demon. The taint of his magic was so different from any that Alaric had previously encountered that he was beginning to believe the tale of a different dimension, too. If the monster had taken Quinn to a different dimension, Alaric might never be able to find her.

Therefore, it could not be so. He would not allow it.

He glanced down at his hands, unsurprised to find them glowing again, and forced his fingers to relax before he inadvertently destroyed the Statue of Liberty, thereby insulting both the United States and France before Atlantis had even had a chance to make diplomatic overtures. He almost smiled at the thought of Conlan trying to explain *that* one. Instead, he took a deep breath and called out to Christophe.

Status?

Yeah, hello to you, too, Alaric.

Christophe sounded weary, and little wonder. The brunt of maintaining the Trident and the dome had fallen to him.

Alaric focused his intensity and sent a greater measure of his magic soaring toward Atlantis, to reinforce the dome. The metaphysics of the connection were beyond him; the distance should have made the link impossible. He was Atlantis's high priest, however, and the bond between them was forged of unbreakable steel.

Christophe replied immediately:

Whatever you just did, that helped, man. The pain in my head lifted a lot, and Serai says the same.

Serai entered the mental communication:

You must succeed quickly, Alaric. Christophe and I, even with the aid of all of your acolytes and Myrken, can hold this for only one more day. Two days would be our very outer limit.

Alaric couldn't tell them what had happened. If they knew

Ptolemy had disappeared with Poseidon's Pride, they might lose hope. Instead, he told them he was nearly there, and disconnected the communication.

He needed help, and he was willing to admit it. He sent his senses winging out over the city, until he located a certain son of the god of war. Faust probably could help him find that abandoned subway station he'd seen in his vision of Quinn during the soul-meld. There was a chance that Ptolemy had returned there to plan and plot. He certainly wouldn't have returned to that hotel.

It didn't take long before he sensed the youngling, although a police helicopter found Alaric standing on the torch at the same time. Before the annoying loudspeaker commands could begin again, Alaric leapt into the air. He hovered for a moment next to the surprised officer hanging out of the side.

"We are on the same side, human. I will find and destroy the demon Ptolemy for you, this I swear on my oath as the high priest of Poseidon."

With that, he transformed to mist and, leaving one very surprised policeman behind him, headed for the location where he could feel Faust's presence burning like a flame in the heart of the city.

Only to discover that Faust was inside a police station.

Alaric groaned as he walked out from behind the truck where he'd transformed so as not to cause a disturbance. The boy was solidifying Alaric's belief that children were far more trouble than they were worth. Although a child with Quinn . . . His steps slowed as he visualized Quinn's flat belly rounding with his baby, and he almost walked into a police car as it pulled into a parking space.

Time for mental daydreams later.

But thinking of Quinn and his future child was like gasoline to the flame of his fury. It took every ounce of self-control he possessed to keep from blasting a hole in the side of the building and snatching the boy, but somehow he managed it.

Barely.

After a quick check to make sure that he wasn't glowing

again—he had a feeling he'd find that hard to explain to the police—he strode into the building as if he owned the place. A quick scan revealed Faust arguing with a female police officer in front of the desk, so Alaric approached respectfully, so as not to appear hostile or aggressive. Especially since his face had certainly been on television while he destroyed City Hall. The humans tended not to appreciate that sort of thing.

Luckily, there was no sign of recognition on the policewoman's face. Lots of frustration, but no recognition.

"I apologize for my son, officer," he said. "Is there restitution to be made?"

Faust started to protest, but Alaric shot him a stern look. "You're in enough trouble, young man."

The officer shook her head. "No restitution, but he can't keep hiding street kids from the authorities. I'll let him go this time, since he was clearly trying to help those children, but you'd better straighten him out before he gets in real trouble."

Alaric took a firm grip on Faust's arm and started walking, thanking the officer as he left. It was always better to cooperate with law enforcement, a lesson the boy at his side had yet to learn, from the sound of the tirade he was spewing as they left. Something about bureaucratic idiocy, but Alaric didn't care and he definitely didn't have the time.

When they reached a corner alley several streets away from the police building, on a street lined with small shops and eateries, Alaric finally let go of the youngling.

"Silence," he commanded, and Faust stopped speaking, mid-sentence, and changed course.

"Um, are you going to kill me?"

"Why would I bother to remove you from police custody, if that were the case? I could have killed you there far more easily, and without having to listen to your incessant babble," Alaric pointed out reasonably.

For some reason, Faust did not seem to be reassured by his words. Stupid human.

"I told you I'd take care of you and your friends," he told the boy. "You can all move to Atlantis and live happily ever after, once I retrieve the tourmaline, and save the dome, so Atlantis can rise. But for now, I need your help."

Faust backed away a little. "You're completely off your rocker, aren't you? Atlantis?"

"You've seen the sea god in action, and you doubt Atlantis? You're not particularly intelligent, are you?"

He started to turn away in disgust, since he would clearly receive no useful help here, but a stray thought stopped him. "How is the child?"

Faust grinned at the reminder of his tiny friend, and his shoulders relaxed. "She's fine, thanks to you. Perfectly healthy and doesn't even remember what happened."

"She had no need to remember the trauma, so I removed it from her memory."

The boy looked up at him with a new measure of respect. "Really? You can do that? Well, thanks."

Alaric considered the boy. "How old are you?"

"I'm eighteen."

Alaric said nothing, simply waited.

"Okay, I'm sixteen, or at least I will be next month," Faust finally admitted. "But my ID says I'm eighteen, and I've been taking care of myself and the kids for almost two years."

"Admirable."

The boy visibly puffed up a little, probably surprised to hear approval instead of condemnation from an adult, even one he considered to be *off his rocker*.

"If you would thank me, do so by helping me find an abandoned subway station," Alaric said, making a sudden decision to trust the boy.

Faust backed up as a group of women walked by, chattering about lunch plans. He waited for them to pass before he shook his head.

"For reals? Those places are seriously scary, and that's before you get into the new players like this Ptolemy guy. I'm talking gang hangouts, rats, drug dens, rats, shorted-out electrical wires, and rats."

Alaric raised an eyebrow. "You're afraid of rats?"

"Heck yeah, I'm afraid of rats. They carry all kinds of freaky germs, like the next bubonic plague, probably."

"You may be right. I will destroy the rats. Now, can we go?"

Faust sighed, and then brightened. "I'll do it for a hundred bucks. I can feed the rest of the kids for a week on that, if I'm careful."

"I don't have any of your currency."

"Man, that sucks."

Alaric felt the new magic boiling up in him, wanting to destroy, and he forced it down again. "I will obtain some, or give you gold in the equivalent of five thousand of your dollars, to do this for me. Now. We're running out of time, and I'm running out of patience."

~~~~~

Nearly three hours later, Alaric admitted defeat. They'd searched every tunnel and hole that Faust could find, but there was no trace of Quinn. Finally, they'd come to a room that he was sure was the one from the vision, even down to the shabby sofa, but there was no trace of Quinn or Ptolemy, except perhaps for a faint trace of her scent.

Frustration borne of helpless despair rose up in him, and he blasted the couch into tiny shreds.

"This isn't working," he said, all but snarling at the boy, the room, and the situation.

Faust stared at the black hole in the concrete where the couch used to be. "I don't know, that seemed to work fine."

The boy flicked his finger like a gun and shot a thin finger of flame across the room to incinerate a pile of newspapers.

"Why would you fear rats, when you have that power?"

Faust shrugged his thin shoulders. "I don't really know how to control it. My mom kicked me out when it showed up and I started fires in the house," he said, staring down at his hands as if they belonged to someone else. "Maybe you could, you know, take me on as an apprentice when this is over."

"I won't be taking on any more acolytes, ever. I told Poseidon that I'm done with him."

The boy's shoulders slumped, but then he grinned. "You really told Poseidon—*the* Poseidon—that he could take his job and shove it?"

"Shove it where?" Strange human.

Faust laughed. "Never mind. Old saying. It was a song, I think."

"I don't care about songs or old sayings. If we don't find Quinn soon, my entire civilization will be destroyed," Alaric said, and then he raced out of the room and out of the tunnels, until he reached fresh air, or at least as fresh as it got in New York.

Dusk had settled its shadowy cloak around the city, and Alaric was no closer to finding Quinn. Faust arrived, slightly out of breath, and Alaric realized he had no idea what to do next. He sent his senses searching for Quinn, but only the faintest murmur of her existence echoed back to him.

Random searching was worse than useless.

He had failed. Atlantis and Quinn were doomed, and it was entirely his fault.

"What we need is some food," the boy said.

Before Alaric could answer, that damnable voice was speaking to him again, and he whirled around to find the portal forming behind him.

"You have *need*?"

"No," Alaric shouted, but yet again it was too late, and the portal took him. He and Faust fell tumbling through the vortex and into Atlantis.

"Take me back, now. I must find Quinn and Poseidon's Pride," Alaric roared, but the portal blinked out of existence.

A solid minute of calling it yielded nothing but a hoarse voice.

"Somehow, sometime, I will find a way to choke you to death," Alaric told the spirit of the portal, which apparently either wasn't listening or chose not to respond to the death threat any more than it had listened to his calls to return.

Gathering the tattered shreds of his calm, Alaric turned to find Faust slowly turning in a circle, trying to see everything at once.

"Oh this is *wicked cool*," the boy yelled, gazing open-mouthed up at the dome, as Marcus and the portal guards stared at the two of them in surprise.

"You *would* think so," Alaric said. "Don't start any fires. Marcus, please ask one of your men to take the youngling to the kitchens and see that he's fed. I'm going to find Conlan and Christophe and Serai and see what's happening before I completely lose my mind."

"You know that you're glowing, right?" Marcus's face was impassive as he posed the question, as if it were a regular occurrence for Poseidon's high priest to light up like a bonfire.

"Yes. It's a new development," Alaric said tersely. "I'll explain later, if we survive this."

It was a very big *if*.

When he reached the palace, it was to find Conlan attempting to destroy the throne room, using his royal sword to smash his throne into shards of wood, gems, and precious metals, while Ven tried in vain to stop him. Conlan's shirt was loose, and his back was wet with the sweat of exertion, so he'd been at it for some time. The high prince whirled to face Alaric.

"Alaric? Do you have the stone?" Conlan pointed the sword at him. "Where is it? We need to get out of here and find Riley and Aidan and the others. Did you hear from them?"

"We need to find them, *now*," Ven said, his eyes wild.

"And I thought I was the only one going mad," Alaric said, calmly enough for a man who'd managed to lose the woman with whom he'd soul-melded. Even as he thought it, he realized Conlan and Ven were in the exact same situation.

"We will find them again," he told them. "Healthy and whole. I swear it."

Or he would destroy the entire world.

But they need not know he held on to sanity by only the slenderest of threads.

"We need—" Ven began again, and then the godsdamned

portal decided to materialize in the middle of the throne room.

"You have *need*?"

And it dumped out a precious cargo, indeed: Keely and Eleni walked out, followed by Erin, and then Riley holding Aidan.

As Conlan dropped the sword and ran to embrace his family, and Ven did the same with Erin, Alaric watched the portal, hoping without cause for one final traveler, but it again vanished before he could reach it.

"You're defective," Keely shouted after it, and he noticed that, oddly enough, her nose was sunburned. Her entire face, actually.

"Where were you?"

Riley looked a little embarrassed, but she held up Aidan for everyone to see, which was tough since Conlan was holding his family so close. When she finally managed to squirm free, Alaric saw that the baby was wearing a shirt that said ALOHA.

"You were in Hawaii?" Ven swung Erin around and then put her down. "Hawaii? While we were here going out of our minds?"

"Like we had a choice. What? You think we were surfing?" she snapped. "We were going crazy wondering what was happening back here. Is it fixed?"

"Not hardly," Conlan announced grimly. "In fact, the Trident is worse."

"So why did it bring them back? So we can all die together?" Ven tightened his hold on Erin. "We were better off before."

"Nobody is going to die today," Alaric said. "I'm going to the temple now, to determine how I can help reinforce the Trident's containment, and then I will find Quinn if I have to blow up the portal to do it."

He ignored their barrage of questions, left the palace, and raced for the temple, traveling as mist, sparing a thought for what Marcus and the others would make of Faust. Hopefully the boy hadn't set anybody on fire. Alaric flew up the temple steps and transformed back into his body as he reached the Trident's room, where Myrken and several of the acolytes slumped outside the doorway, their faces white with strain and exhaustion.

"We're still holding it, my lord," Myrken said. "It's just easier to do while sitting down. Lord Christophe is inspecting the dome for further damage, but he still lends his support, as does Lady Serai."

"I'm here, at least for now. Go get some sleep. You all look like you need it, and you certainly deserve it."

Alaric headed for the door, preparing his magic for the barrage he was sure he'd find inside. He wasn't disappointed. The Trident was putting on quite a show, bucking and twisting in its protective barrier like a wild animal trying to escape— almost like it sensed its final gem was missing.

Could this be due to Poseidon's Pride leaving for a demonic dimension outside the Trident's range?

"I, too, want to find that gem for you," he told it.

He realized he was wasting time talking to an inanimate object. He called to his new, more powerful magic, and found that its force had intensified by a hundredfold now that he was in Atlantis. He funneled quite a bit of it into stabilizing the Trident and the dome, until slowly, bit by bit, the Trident slowed its gyrations and floated down to its cushion and lay still.

At least temporarily.

Myrken staggered into the room, holding his head. "My lord? Was that you? I have never felt such power—"

"I'll explain later," Alaric said, yet again.

Then he tried one more time to reach the portal.

"I call to you, spirit of the portal who has taken Gailea's place," Alaric said, as respectfully as he could manage. "I have *need*. Come and get me. Now."

But, yet again, the damned portal didn't seem inclined to answer.

He probably shouldn't have threatened to choke it to death.

Chapter 26

Big Cypress National Panther Preserve headquarters, Florida

The portal spirit, who up until just a few days previously, when a killer wave had lived up to its name, had been a surfing champion named Danny, was a little drunk on his new power and self-righteously determined to carry out Poseidon's instructions. After all, the sea god had saved him from a broken neck and subsequent drowning and transported him to this new, *awesome* reality. Dude was wicked amped, for a mythological divinity and all. Said he needed *new blood* in the portal, now that Atlantis was rising.

Atlantis. How massively bitchin' is that?

The spirit concentrated on Florida, specifically the panther headquarters, and flashed his lovely new oval shape into existence in the center of the room, where a meeting had been taking place.

The room's occupants, who included two panther shifters and one Atlantean warrior, all stared at the portal with varying degrees of surprise.

"Expecting company?" the warrior called Bastien asked the male shifter, Ethan.

The portal spirit stretched its dimensions a bit; after all,

Bastien was nearly seven feet tall with very broadly muscled shoulders. He might not fit in so easily.

Ethan stood up eagerly. "No, but Marie doesn't always let me know when she's coming."

He looked disappointed when his mate Marie, whom the spirit knew to be Bastien's sister, didn't appear. This was sad, but the spirit knew it would be soon resolved.

The woman shifter, Kat, Bastien's mate, looked puzzled. "Is it here for you?"

The Atlantean shook his head. "No, I didn't call it, and nobody seems to be coming through. I wonder—"

"You have *need*," the portal spirit said happily, and sucked them all into its vortex and off to Atlantis, chortling to itself. A shape-shifter had never before set foot in Atlantis. This was going to be interesting.

❧～～✦

Somewhere in the wilds of Montana, at a secret rebel training facility

The portal spirit watched as Atlantean warrior Alexios and his mate, Grace, descendant of the moon goddess Diana, who was also known as Artemis, sparred in a demonstration bout. She was quite obviously pregnant, but it didn't hamper her in any way, although Alexios was careful that his practice sword never came anywhere near her. They were fluid in all of their movements; a study in perfect symmetry and deadly intent. When they finished their demonstration, they simultaneously turned in neat half circles and bowed, and then gestured to their students to pair off and spar.

It was lovely and so exciting to watch, but the portal spirit had no time for frivolous distractions. It had a mission to perform. Materializing in the middle of the sparring ring, it spoke its mantra:

"You have *need*."

Then it swept Grace and Alexios off to Atlantis.

❧～～✦

The Fae lands, home to the princess Maeve

The portal spirit had to work much harder to open his new magic inside the Summerlands, but he was determined, and he had the power of right and *need* on his side. He found the crystal clear pool he'd been seeking, and the Atlantean warrior sitting half in and half out of the water, with a naked Fae princess on his lap.

The portal spirit cheered up considerably at the sight of her, but she and the Atlantean warrior, Denal, looked rather sad.

"I'm sorry but it's time for me to go," Denal said. "I've enjoyed these three years, perhaps more than any other three in my life, but I don't know how much time has passed outside of your enchanted lands, and my people might need me."

"They take advantage of you," the princess said, with real regret. "But since I cannot convince you to stay, I will allow you to leave, so we do not lose our friendship in a less than amicable parting."

"You are as wise as you are lovely, Maeve," Denal said.

"You have *need*," the portal spirit said, and it took Denal, and only Denal, to Atlantis.

～～～◈

Boston, inside the offices of a major newspaper

The portal spirit watched Atlantean warrior Brennan as he laughed with his mate while they opened cartons and prepared to eat some really awesome-looking Chinese food. The spirit missed food, but in an abstract kind of way. He'd always loved egg rolls.

He knew the history here, just like he'd absorbed everybody else's story when Poseidon turned him into a magic doorway. After a terrible curse had forced Brennan to live for thousands of years with no emotion, he'd found his one true love and broken the curse by her death.

Tiernan didn't look any the worse for wear, luckily, even though she'd been the one who died. Big win for CPR.

"You have *need*," the portal spirit told them, before taking them and their food to Atlantis.

~~~~~~

Paris, France, in the penthouse suite of a very luxurious hotel

Lady Serai, who was smoking hot for an honest-to-goodness Atlantean princess from eleven *thousand* years ago, sat slumped in a fancy chair while the vampire she loved massaged her feet. Dudes seriously did *not* stay in any Motel 6.

"You can't keep this up," Daniel said, frowning. "The power drain is killing you. Do you have any update on what's happening now?"

"Alaric just arrived, and he brought some enormous source of new power with him," she said, her eyes wide. "It's as if his magical abilities have quadrupled or even more. We might have a chance to save Atlantis. I need to be there, Daniel."

"You have *need*," the portal spirit agreed, and it carried them gently to Atlantis. Lady Serai was royalty, after all.

Chapter 27

Somewhere inside a demonic dimension

Quinn cautiously moved behind Ptolemy, considering him the lesser of many, many evils, as she watched his "brothers" caper and tumble around on the ancient mosaic tile. Its beauty compared to their hideousness created a sickening juxtaposition that her brain kept trying to reject. Apparently the mind shut down when reality took such a horrible left turn. Her stomach also contributed to her general misery, since it roiled at each new assault to the senses.

Ptolemy's family wasn't just a *visual* tragedy.

Oh, *no*.

They *stank*, too. They reeked with a stench like rotting sewage and sulfuric acid, which led her to wonder anew if she really had landed in her dimension's version of hell. It certainly smelled bad enough.

She finally ventured a question, when Ptolemy and his brothers ended a conversation that had consisted of squeaks, grunts, and shrill whistling noises. "What do they want?"

"They want you," he said, sounding amused. "*They* don't have mates, either."

"Oh, *hell* no," she blurted out.

He turned to her and smiled that hideous smile full of teeth. "Possibly they only want to eat you, though. Suddenly I look better to you?"

She wanted to disagree, but in comparison to this bunch, he was at least mostly human-looking. She'd be damned if she'd be signing up for either option, though.

The din built up to a dull roar again, and Ptolemy turned to give his family his full attention. Probably safest. Quinn watched with growing interest as he drew a familiar small wooden box out of his pocket. She didn't know what he'd done with the scepter.

"I have retrieved the crown jewel of Atlantis!" He withdrew the tourmaline, placed the box on a ledge, and flourished the gem about. The chattering and squeaks rose to a nearly unbearable level, and then a hush fell on the room as Ptolemy prepared to do . . . nothing.

He waved Poseidon's Pride about in a high arc over his head, and absolutely nothing at all happened.

"Maybe it doesn't work here?" Quinn held out her hand. "Want me to take a look?"

"It's not a faulty handgun, you moron," Ptolemy snarled at her. "What possible use would you, a mere non-magical human, be?"

She held up her hands, palms out, in surrender. She didn't have any desire to be his next victim. "Hey, I was just offering to help. Shutting up now."

One of the bolder brothers—cousins? uncles? Quinn had no idea and didn't really want to think about it—started to lurch closer, chittering loudly, until Ptolemy leapt forward and smashed it in the face with one clawed hand. Sensing weakness, the others swarmed the fallen one and tore it to shreds before moving back and giving Ptolemy and Quinn a little space.

She'd been in enough battles to realize that the temporary retreat wouldn't last. This was pretty clearly an "eat what you kill" kind of society, cousin or not, and she was starting to worry that she would be the one who got eaten. Or worse. Her mind stuttered away from the alternatives.

"It must be useless in my dimension," Ptolemy finally said, and Quinn rolled her eyes.

"Gee, I wish I'd thought of that." She sniped, and Ptolemy casually backhanded her so hard she flew backward and cracked her head against the wall before falling in a heap to the floor.

Maybe there really *was* a time to quit being a smart-ass, and captive in a demonic dimension was a good place to start. Her skull rang with pretty little bells for a few long minutes, as she blinked and tried to focus. She was fairly sure he'd torn open her lip, too, but she didn't care enough to take her hands away from her poor, aching head, until she noticed one of the smaller atrocities staring at her like she was catnip and he was a very hungry kitten. Then she started to worry. More.

"Wipe your face," Ptolemy said, throwing a piece of cloth at her. She looked at it and realized he'd torn it from his shirt.

"Human blood is a delicacy to them," he said nonchalantly, but she noticed his gaze was fixed a little bit too intently on her chin.

"Only to *them*?" She wiped the blood away and then rolled up the cloth and threw it as far as she could from where she still sat on the floor. Several of the creatures hurled themselves into a biting, snapping frenzy over the cloth, which she didn't find reassuring in the least.

"If I can't get this to work, we might have to run for it," Ptolemy said, continuing the hit parade of *not reassuring*. He shoved the gem into his jacket pocket and scowled as he scanned the room.

"Can't you just call your portal and get us out of here?"

"Not without taking some of them with me. Do you think your world is ready for them?"

She looked around at the mass of monsters inching bit by bit closer, many of them actively drooling long, glistening ropes of slime as they watched her with, generally, more than two eyes each.

"No, my world is definitely not ready for them," she agreed. She put a hand on her knife hilt and prepared to kill as many of them as she could before they killed her.

She just hoped Alaric found a way to be happy, one day. The thought of Alaric reminded her of the shell he'd given her and bolstered her courage, in spite of the pain still ringing in her skull, and she climbed to her feet, the better to fight off the atrocities.

"I'm not asking this to be a smart-ass, but why did we come here again?"

"I wanted you to see why I must escape this place, so you would better understand me when we are mated," he said sadly. "Instead, I have caused you to become even more horrified by me."

For one brief moment, she almost felt sorry for him. She thought *she'd* had sibling rivalry problems, when she and Riley hit puberty together, and there were two emotional empaths in the same house. At least neither of them had tried to kill and eat the other one's boyfriend.

Of course, neither she nor her sister was a murderous kidnapper who wanted to take over somebody else's world, either.

She squared her shoulders and tried to put a tiny bit of empathy in her voice as she forced herself to lean forward and hug him. "I actually do kind of understand, and I'm sorry for what you've endured, but kidnapping me and forcing me to have your kids, plus conquering my world, isn't the way to my heart."

He looked surprised, and then he laughed. "I don't care about your heart. It's another organ entirely that I need."

Leering, he patted her stomach, and any shred of sympathy she'd had for his plight vanished in the wave of revulsion that punched her in the gut as hard as he'd punched her in the face.

"For now, though, you have to go," he said as, at some unknown signal, his family started to swarm the spot where they stood. "I'll hold them off and then make it back to you later. You'll be safe enough."

He picked Quinn up and threw her at the wall as hard as he could, over the gaping, shark-toothed maws and grasping, claw-handed reach of the atrocities who were leaping for her.

She braced for impact and wondered if she could survive a shattered skull, but the wall dissolved into the garish orange light of his portal, and she fell through it. The last thing she saw of his dimension was one of his relatives stabbing its swordlike appendage into Ptolemy's back so hard that the tip of it came out the front of his chest, exactly where his heart would have been if he'd been human.

Ptolemy opened his mouth to scream, and a blackish-green oily liquid gushed out. Surely that had killed him. *Surely*. In spite of the nausea-making vortex, she smiled fiercely—both with triumph and because she had a wonderful secret. Those creatures were trapped on their side of the vortex; none of them seemed to be smart enough to figure out the portal.

And, even better, Quinn's past had come to her rescue. One of her mentors in her early days of rebel training had been a champion pickpocket. Quinn had forced herself to embrace Ptolemy for a very, very good reason. She put her hand inside the front waistband of her borrowed pants and double-checked that the leather pouch she'd borrowed from Lauren's things was still secure.

And that Poseidon's Pride was secure inside it.

She'd known she was quite likely to die from daring to touch the gem, but she'd had to try, and apparently Alaric's magic, which he'd shared with her, was powerful enough to protect her. Or else it was gearing up to incinerate her, but she was frankly too tired to care which, especially if this never-ending trip through the demon portal didn't end soon.

As if on command, it dumped her—out of the portal and into the frying pan, so to speak—and she landed in the same hotel room where Ptolemy had held her hostage before. The windows Alaric had blown out were in the process of being replaced, and seven thugs pointed seven guns at her.

She raised her hands in surrender and sank slowly into a velvet chair. "Hey, as long as I'm here, can we order room service again? I'm kind of hungry."

"You don't get food, bitch," one of the uglier ones said. These were all humans, though, so ugly was relative compared to what she'd seen back in Ptolemy's homeworld.

Ha. Ugly was *relative* compared to his *relatives*. She'd made another funny. Either that or relief was making her giddy. She laughed out loud.

Big, bad, and comparatively ugly raised his hand, as if to hit her, and suddenly the other six guns were trained on him.

"Ptolemy said not to touch her. Not to lay a single finger on her in any way, or he disembowels all of us," a very serious-looking man dressed in all black said firmly. "I like my intestines where they are."

"She laughed at me," the first one complained, and the man in black shot him in the head.

Quinn quit laughing, fast.

Brain spatters on your clothes tended to do that to a person.

She lost the battle, after all. She leaned over and threw up all over one of the thugs' shoes. Then she sat there, huddled into a ball in the chair, with her eyes shut tightly as she tried to contact Alaric. She could still feel him through the soul-meld link, and even more strongly than when she'd been in the same room with him, which made her wonder if her own terror or the presence of the tourmaline was causing that.

She didn't care which it was, ultimately, so long as it worked.

After a little while, she decided to conserve her energy for another try later. She opened her eyes and looked for the man in black. The brain shooter.

"I need to go to the bathroom, please," she said politely.

He nodded, and she walked straight to the bathroom, closed the door, and cleaned up the best she could. She washed the blood and brains off her face and hands and clothes and realized that very few people could say that about themselves, that they'd washed brains off their clothes.

Then she realized that her racing thoughts, breathing, and heart rate meant that she was slipping into a state of shock, which made sense, given the events of the past several days. She had to sit down on the edge of the tub, put her head between her knees, and take deep breaths.

A knock sounded at the door, and it opened before she could answer.

"Are you all right, ma'am?" It was the man in black again. He must be in charge.

She raised her head and considered him for a moment. "Would you be?"

Something shifted in his icy blue gaze, but he simply nodded. "Fair enough."

He retreated and closed the door, and she sat alone in the bathroom, on the cold edge of the tub, for a very long time. When she thought she had the strength to try to call Alaric again, she powered up and fired out the loudest mental blast she could manage.

Alaric, I need you right now.

This time, he answered.

I'm on my way.

Quinn smiled again, doing little more than baring her teeth. The guy with his brains on the floor might be the lucky one of the bunch.

Chapter 28

Atlantis

Alaric walked out of the temple to a scene of mass confusion. Dozens of people seemed to be milling about; a few were laughing and talking, but mostly they conversed in quiet and serious tones. On closer inspection, he realized they weren't random people. They were the Warriors of Poseidon, and they were all back in Atlantis.

The Seven were together again, for the first time in far too long. Even Denal, who seemed to have aged years in the months he'd been in the Fae lands. Unfortunately, that was a risk that anyone who entered the Summerlands had to expect. He was hugging Riley, who was laughing and crying at the same time.

Apparently a family trait.

Alaric's mouth suddenly fell open, and he had to clamp it shut. A *family* trait. One she shared with her sister. Now that he and Quinn had reached the soul-meld, did that make him brother-in-law to the high prince and princess? He shook his head at the irrelevance of the question, given the current situation, but he couldn't help but flinch at the idea. Riley was the type to expect regular family dinners, no doubt.

Given the circumstances, if they even survived long enough to have family dinners, Alaric resolved to appreciate them.

"Alaric," Daniel called out from where he was talking to Bastien and his mate, Kat Fiero, and Alaric nearly did a double-take at the sight. He scanned the area and, sure enough, there was Ethan, another panther, sweeping Bastien's sister Marie into a passionate embrace.

"There are shape-shifters in Atlantis," Alaric said wonderingly, and Conlan, who'd suddenly appeared from the gods only knew where, clapped him on the back.

"Who would have thought we'd see the day?" the prince said. "I'm glad the old taboos have fallen, but I could have wished they'd picked a better day to visit."

"They're visiting?"

"No, it was a poor attempt at a jest," Conlan said grimly. "The portal abducted them all and brought them here. Everybody's story is the same. They suddenly heard 'you have need,' saw a flash of light, and the portal whisked them here. Everybody except Denal showed up with the person or persons who'd been with them. Even Grace and Alexios brought a very surprised rebel training class."

Conlan pointed at the group of mostly young humans standing off to one side gaping at everything.

"Denal?"

"He left Maeve behind, but he'd planned to do so, anyway, he says, so he's not in the least upset." Conlan scowled at the youngling. "I see he's already hugging my wife again."

Alaric started to reply, but a mental blast cut through the noise and the chatter and all but stripped the gears in his brain.

Alaric, I need you right now, Quinn mentally shouted at him.

I'm on my way, he sent back, and then he clapped Conlan on the shoulder so hard he nearly knocked the prince off the temple steps.

"She's back. She's back, and I know just where she is," he crowed. "That hotel must enjoy replacing windows, though."

"What do you need?" Conlan asked, instantly grasping the situation.

Alaric yelled for Justice, who was standing near Alexios. "Bring me a sword."

If his magic misfired around the demon, he wanted a backup option. To Conlan he said, "What do I *need*? Interesting question."

"Hey, portal," he shouted. "Come listen to what I *need*, or I'll let Atlantis be crushed under five and a half miles of water."

"Nice touch," Conlan murmured. "I'm guessing portals don't understand about bluffing."

Alaric shot him a look. "Who says I'm bluffing?"

Conlan's smile faded, but then the portal appeared, surprising both of them.

"If these people and my baby die because you kidnapped them and dumped them here, I'll make it my mission in life to exterminate you, you egotistic, pathetic excuse for an elevator," Riley said, marching up to the portal with a sleeping baby in her arms.

Aidan didn't even open an eye. Perhaps he was used to his mother's fierce personality and was comforted by it. It occurred to Alaric with the force of a spear to the chest that perhaps he and Quinn would one day have a child a lot like Aidan. He suddenly found it hard to breathe.

"Get in before it disappears," Conlan said. "Hurry up, Alaric, we need that stone."

Alaric jumped into the portal. "Take me to Quinn."

As he traveled through the vortex, the strangest thing happened. Alaric thought he heard the portal say, "Duuude."

Before he could analyze *that* bit of oddity, it dumped him in the middle of a room filled with a gang of armed men, a dead man, and one human female who glowed—at least to *his* senses—with the intensity of a miniature sun. The sight of the Atlantean energy gave Alaric hope he hadn't dared to feel, which surged up inside him, dancing with his joy and relief from Quinn's presence.

She was alive and safe. Thank all the gods.

But then Quinn turned her head toward him, and he saw that the side of her face was one massive bruise, and her lip was split and swollen.

A blinding rage swept through him, and he attacked the men with the sword and with his power, driving ice spears through their throats one by one. Distantly, he heard her yelling at him to stop, but a primal fury had crushed his reason and destroyed his logic. He sensed that Poseidon's Pride was enhancing and increasing his power, but he had no intention of trying to stop.

They'd hurt her, so they had to die.

There was only one left alive—a man dressed in all black who'd tried to shoot Alaric until he'd frozen the man's gun to his hand in an impenetrable block of ice. Alaric raised his sword again, but then Quinn stepped between him and his target.

"No," she shouted, waving her arms. "This one protected me from the others, and even more important, he might know more about Ptolemy's plans."

Alaric slowly lowered the sword as her words penetrated his raging mind. "He hurt you. I see your face."

"No, that was Ptolemy. I'll tell you everything, but it wasn't this man. He protected me." She stepped closer and put her arm around Alaric's waist, careful not to block his sword arm.

"This one protected you," he repeated, still not believing it.

She nodded. "He shot the dead one for trying to hurt me."

"And yet he held you captive at gunpoint," Alaric said, his outward calm back in place. "He will die for that alone."

"I can't tell you anything if I'm dead," the man said, finally speaking up. He must have had ice in his veins, since he wasn't shaking or begging or crying.

"Do you know anything to tell?" Alaric placed the tip of his sword against the man's throat and pushed, just hard enough to cut the skin. Blood dripped down the man's neck.

Quinn nudged Alaric to the side a little. "What's your name, and what did Ptolemy tell you?"

"I'm Westbury. He didn't tell me much, unfortunately," the man said. "His plan once he arrived was to head to the Bermuda Triangle, if that makes any sense at all."

Alaric exchanged a grim glance with Quinn. It told them far too much.

"It's a measure of your integrity that you admit you know little," Alaric said. "And yet you have no loyalty, to admit so much."

"He doesn't deserve my loyalty," Westbury said, holding up his ice-encumbered right hand with his left. "He took my sister and promised to give her back to my family in exchange for my services. Now I may never see her again."

Quinn's eyes widened. "What does she look like?"

"I have a picture, but . . ." The man glanced pointedly down at his frozen arm.

Quinn looked at Alaric. He considered, then nodded. Made the ice vanish.

Westbury showed her a photograph on his telephone, and Quinn smiled.

"I met this girl. She's fine, or at least she was mostly fine when I last saw her. Bruised but mostly unharmed," Quinn said. "I don't know—"

The man's phone rang at that moment, and a different photograph of the same girl flashed on the screen. Westbury answered it, spoke briefly but with unmistakable emotion, and then closed the phone.

"She's in the emergency room. She said that you saved her, and I was . . . I can never make this up to you," he said hoarsely to Quinn, and Alaric watched as she made another conquest right before his eyes.

"Go. She needs you," Quinn said, brushing Westbury's gratitude aside.

She was embarrassed when they did this, the thankfulness. The devotion. Alaric knew her well enough to understand this.

Westbury was wise enough to look to Alaric, though, before moving. "Either kill me or let me go to my sister."

Suddenly, Alaric wanted nothing more than to be alone with Quinn . He came to a decision.

"Go. Your actions were somewhat offset by your motives," he said abruptly. "But never let me see you again."

Westbury nodded before taking a card out of his pocket and handing it to Quinn. "Any time, any place. Just call me, and I'll be there."

As soon as the man left the room, Alaric called to the portal, which again appeared almost instantly. He wrapped his arms around Quinn, and together they stepped into the portal.

"Back to Atlantis, now," he commanded.

"I had to sacrifice the shell you gave me. I needed the weight for the switch," she told him.

"I'll find you another," he promised.

"I have it," Quinn whispered. "Poseidon's Pride."

"I know," he said, and then he healed her lip and face before kissing her senseless. He sank into her emotions with the first touch of her lips, and he claimed her mouth with every ounce of possession and need he felt for this miracle of a woman.

His woman.

His for all of eternity.

He was still kissing her, with her enthusiastic participation, when they arrived in Atlantis. Suddenly the air rang with applause, and Alaric realized they were the center of attention.

"Oh, no," Quinn said, pushing away from him. "Put me down right now."

He did as she asked and then held out his hand. She withdrew Poseidon's Pride from her pocket and handed it over, and in the exact moment when both of their hands were touching the gem, a thunderclap sounded *inside the dome*, and a lightning strike of power sizzled through Alaric's body. Quinn cried out in shock, so she must have experienced it, too, but then someone started screaming that Atlantis was collapsing.

"Not on our watch," Quinn said, but it would have sounded

better if she hadn't been having such a hard time catching her breath.

A part of Alaric wanted nothing more than to return to the kissing, especially now that every nerve ending in his body was on fire with the gem's magic, but the current emergency outweighed all else. So instead he took Quinn's hand and headed into the temple. At least twenty people followed them.

~~~~~

Quinn couldn't believe she'd been caught kissing Alaric in the middle of Atlantis, during the worst crisis in the history of the continent, but after what they'd been through, she kind of didn't care. When she passed Riley and Aidan on the way to the temple, Riley gave her a thumbs-up.

"Way to go, sis."

Alaric growled and walked faster, and Quinn had an insane urge to laugh. Family dinners were going to be interesting.

Alaric stopped outside the door to the Trident's room, where a half dozen exhausted men and women, plus Myrken, sat against the wall. Five more were asleep or unconscious on the floor a little farther down the hall.

"Stay here," Alaric commanded. "I do not know how bad this will get."

She nodded but said nothing, not even *"Have you met me?"* As soon as he went inside the room, she looked at her old pal, Myrken.

"Got any rope? I've got an idea."

He jumped up before the words were out of her mouth. Not bad for someone who looked as though the Trident had drained all the life out of his body. She headed for the stairs and on the way explained the exact place she was seeking. When they arrived at the vantage point she'd been hoping for, she explained her plan and watched Myrken turn seventeen shades of pale.

"If I get you killed, Lord Alaric will kill me next."

She shook her head. "I won't let him kill you, and anyway, I won't die. So pull that panel off the wall, so I can find out if I can squeeze into that vent."

She managed to fit, just barely, but it was tight, and her newly discovered claustrophobia came screaming back. She didn't have time for phobias, though, and so she powered through, all of her mental focus on what was going on in that room beneath her. When she pushed through to the end of the vent and edged out onto the narrow niche, she looked down and flinched.

Alaric was leaning forward, clearly straining to control the Trident, which appeared to be trying to beat him to death. Or else it was trying to reunite with the tourmaline and being really aggressive about it. Either way. Alaric was in trouble, and he'd closed or sealed the door to the room, so nobody else was there to help.

Quinn to the rescue. She didn't stop to wonder whether or not being able to touch Poseidon's Pride meant she would be able to touch the Trident. She didn't stop to think she might be plunging to her death on a rope that wasn't strong enough to hold her.

All she cared about was Alaric. He needed her. She double-checked her grip on the rope, made sure that Myrken and his pals had a good hold on the other end, and she leapt. Down through the air, aiming straight for the Trident. She caught it in midair as she fell, and pure, unadulterated power flamed through her, setting her on fire from the inside out. She screamed because it felt like her blood was literally boiling in her veins, and the pain was beyond any torture she'd ever endured. She realized she was coming down too far and too fast, and she prayed for a quick death, but she didn't let go.

She did not let go.

She screamed again, just before Alaric's strong arms caught her and he was there, holding her and snatching the Trident from her miraculously unblackened hand. He kissed her face, kissed the tears running down her cheeks, and held the Trident at arm's length from her, all while swearing a blue streak in Atlantean.

Or at least she thought it was Atlantean. Now that she wasn't being roasted from the inside out by the weapon of an angry god, relief made her almost giddy.

"You need to teach me to cuss in Atlantean," she said, and he actually growled at her before he put her down, shoved the tourmaline in the Trident's empty slot with an audible click, and slapped the whole thing down on the cushion on its pedestal.

Then they both stepped back and stared at the thing, which seemed content now to lie there peacefully, glowing softly, like a colicky baby that has finally exhausted itself.

"If you don't drive me to drink or madness within the year, I will count myself exceedingly lucky," Alaric said slowly, and she realized he was clutching his head as if he were in pain.

"You know, I could say the same thing about you, Mr. I Must Do the Dangerous Stuff Alone," she shot back at him. "Also, feel free to heal my head, because I think Ptolemy gave me a concussion in addition to this split lip, and playing *Mission: Impossible* didn't help any."

His aggravation instantly turned to concern, and he sent healing magic through her face and head, and then through her entire body for good measure, and she suddenly felt as if she could take on the world all over again.

"I will kill him," Alaric said, and although she had her pick of contestants, it was a safe bet he was talking about Ptolemy.

"There's one you can check off your list." She told him about the atrocities and the sight of Ptolemy being stabbed through the chest.

"It might not have been his heart," she added, considering the demons' questionable anatomy. "But even so, they didn't seem like the type to help a guy when he was down. He's probably lunch."

"None deserved it more," Alaric said flatly. "I only regret I was not able to kill him myself. You have an annoying habit of getting yourself out of trouble."

She grinned. "Rebel leader, remember? Although, not anymore. Maybe we can have a nap and then decide what to do with the rest of our lives."

The clamor and pounding at the door grew louder. Alaric waved a hand, and the door burst inward under the weight of half a dozen warriors and many other people, both men and women.

"What's happening?" Conlan said, pushing to the front. "Alaric, I'm going to kick your ass if you ever do that to me again."

"As you see," Alaric began, except then, naturally, something *did* start to happen.

"You don't have some kind of ritual?" Quinn asked nobody in particular, but she forgot her question as the Trident levitated into the air and rotated until it was standing on its base, with its three prongs pointing up. An arrow of light shot out of each of its tines, and the three streams joined together to form a shining column of pure white light that was headed straight for the ceiling.

Quinn immediately saw a potential problem. "Um, is there a skylight?"

"No," Alaric said, and she prepared to jump out of the way of falling stone, but just as everyone started moving toward the door, the ceiling of the temple opened like the petals of a flower. The tower of light shot up and up, straight past the top of the temple and up to what must be the ceiling of the dome.

"Oh, boy," Quinn said. "If that blasts through the dome, when we're underwater . . ."

This time it was Myrken who answered her. "No, my lady, this is exactly what the ancient scrolls say is supposed to happen. We should go outside for this."

They all raced outside, and the ground gave a jarring lurch right underneath their feet, like an earthquake. Quinn grabbed for Alaric's hand.

"Look," he said, pointing.

She looked, and saw the most spectacular sight. Atlantis was *rising*. The water movement outside the dome, and the way they lifted up and passed first a whale and then a school of lighted fish, proved beyond a shadow of a doubt that Atlantis was, in fact, actually rising.

A huge cheer rang out, and everyone started hugging and laughing. Quinn was too practical and far too skeptical for that.

"Will the fractured dome survive the pressure changes as it rises, or are we in for a massive continental case of the bends?"

Alaric smiled, and it was a *real* smile, the one that felt like a gift to her heart.

"I can only guess what this 'bends' means, but the Trident's power is far more than enough to accomplish this ascension. The rest of us can relax now."

She threw her arms around Alaric and kissed him, right there on the temple steps, in front of the gods and everyone.

"We did it," she said. "We actually did it!"

"I couldn't have done it without you," he said, and his saying so was another gift, the best present ever.

"How long will it take? Do we need to help it along?"

Alaric smiled. "I think you've done enough, my fierce one. It will be at least ten hours before we reach the surface. Right now, I suggest we find something to eat and get some rest."

"And a shower," she added.

He groaned. "I'm not sure I can take any more of imagining you in the shower."

She grinned at him. "Who said you have to imagine it?"

They raced each other to his rooms.

Chapter 29

Alaric slammed the door to his rooms shut behind them and sealed them with the most powerful ward he knew how to create. Nobody was getting in that door. He thought about it for a moment and then added soundproofing.

Quinn stripped out of her borrowed shirt and pants on the way to the bathroom and then turned around and smiled at him, standing there in nothing but a few strategically placed scraps of lace. He almost swallowed his tongue.

She bit her lip and then grinned. "Didn't take me for a girly underwear kind of woman, did you?"

He couldn't answer her, because his brain and his vocal cords had both quit working. In fact, nothing on his body seemed to be functioning, since he was literally frozen in place, or at least so he thought, until his pants started pressing into his crotch.

Ah.

She bit her lip again. "Are we really going to do this? Remember the Elders."

"The Elders can go fuck themselves," he growled, and she started laughing.

"I have given Poseidon my resignation from the office of high priest. If, in fact, giving up my celibacy means that I have given up my magic, I will mourn it for a fraction of a second, and then I will roll over and kiss every inch of your body again."

She smiled at him but still didn't move. "What will you do with your life if you can't be a magical warrior?"

"I'll raise peacocks and roses in the palace garden," he said, trying to jest, forcing himself not to move, when every fiber of his being cried out for him to leap across the room. "I've always thought I'd look good in one of those floppy hats."

"I hope that's all you've got that's floppy," she said, and then she unfastened her bra and dropped it to the floor, right before she stepped out of her lace bottoms.

Alaric lost all ability to focus on anything else, and he stalked her to the bathroom, stripping off his own clothes as he went.

She stepped into the shower and started adjusting dials, and clouds of steam billowed out into the room.

"This is a wonderful shower, I hope you know that."

Words. She was making words, when she was naked. And she had that body. And those small, firm breasts. And an ass that made his mouth water. All naked, too.

"Want," he said. "Need. Now."

She took his hand and pulled him into the shower with her. "Okay, Tarzan. I want you, too."

Just before he kissed her, he confessed to a horrible truth. "Quinn, this isn't going to last long. It has been a really, really long time."

She smiled and put her arms around him, and all he could do was feel the glory of her body against his. It wasn't a mirage, or an illusion, or a fantasy created by his lonely mind during a long, dark night. She was really here, in his arms.

Quinn.

His body touched hers, and the feel of her was a miracle and a promise and a blessing. Skin to skin, heartbeat to heartbeat. He wanted, and he *needed*, but just for this moment, the simple touch of her silken skin calmed the beast he'd become when he thought he'd lost her.

He stroked her arms, her back, and the smooth curve of her hip, while kissing the softness of her cheek and the graceful length of her neck and pulling her closer to him. Always closer. She put her hands in his hair and pulled his head back from her shoulder so she could kiss him, and he slanted his head to take her mouth. He drove his tongue into her mouth like he wanted to drive his cock into her body, balancing on the edge of losing control, and she gasped, a tiny, hiccupping sound that inflamed him to the point of madness.

Control shattered and restraint vanished. Alaric dropped his head to her perfect, perfect breasts and sucked the rosy tip of one into his mouth. Quinn cried out and he was fiercely glad—fiercely triumphant—this perfect woman wanted *him*, too, and everything was absolutely and completely right with his world.

He lifted her up and set her lovely ass on the ledge that surrounded the shower, which clearly had been built with her in mind, since it put her at exactly the right height for him to bend down and take her other breast into his mouth in its turn. He had an instant of perfect clarity, where he thought that nothing in his life would ever be better than this, and it lasted until she took his hand and put it between her legs, while still kissing him.

When she moaned, he nearly came right then and there.

"I cannot wait much longer, Quinn."

Her laugh turned into a gasp as his fingers found the secrets of her body. "Who wants you to?"

❧

Quinn thought she might help things along, because Alaric was obviously trying to go slow and make everything wonderful for her, but he was naked in the steamy shower with her and all those hard muscles in his shoulders, chest, legs, and everywhere else on his body, glistening with water droplets, were enough to make any woman lose her mind and beg for satisfaction.

Every nerve ending was tingling; her nipples were hot and swollen from his kisses, and her body pulsed with want that was centered between her thighs. Wonder, relief, and triumph combined in a heady mix inside her until she thought her heart might pound its way out of her chest. She loved him— this crazy, courageous warrior. But now, all she needed was for him to be deep inside her *that very minute* or she might explode, and she was too shy to say that, so she tried some show-and-tell.

He stroked the cleft between her legs and looked at her in wonder. "You're so hot and wet and slippery," he said, probably not even realizing he was talking a little dirty, and the combination of sensation and stimulation sent her body rocketing up the arousal zone until she nearly came in his hand.

"Yes," she said instead, crying out a little as his clever, clever fingers found delightful places. "More."

He stroked her and she let her head fall, helpless against the pull of sensation. She was swimming through sensuality, drowning in desire. She wanted him.

She *needed* him.

Now.

She drew in a shaky breath and gathered her courage, and then she put her hand on his erection. It was his turn to cry out, and he bucked against her and pulled away.

"Quinn, no, I'll go off like a youngling in your hand," he said, and the anguish on his face might have been funny if she didn't feel exactly the same way, so she decided to take charge this first time, and she pulled him closer, wrapped her legs around his waist, and positioned herself just right.

"I'm going to make love to *you* now," she whispered, suddenly shy at being so brazen, but she ignored the heat in her face because the expression of total awe and love on his face was all she needed to see. She lowered herself onto his thick, hard shaft, suddenly wondering if he'd even fit, but there was a will, so she'd definitely find a way. Slowly, slowly, she fit herself around him, and the tight filling sensation drove her crazy, so she pushed down a little faster than she'd meant to, and he groaned.

She froze. "Am I hurting you?"

His wolfish grin was all the answer she needed, and in fact her warrior priest was a quick study, because he grabbed her butt in those big hands and started thrusting into her so hard and so fast that she started coming immediately—it had been so *long*, so very long, and she'd wanted Alaric for what seemed like forever—and as she cried out and her body shattered apart around him, he thrust one final time, deeper than before, and then he roared out as he came inside her.

A prism of color and light flared around them, sparkling fireworks of magic spinning through the water of the forgotten shower, and Quinn leaned against Alaric as she tried to relearn how to breathe.

"Oh, *mi amara*," he said, over and over and over, still standing locked inside her. "You have given me the greatest gift of all."

"Oh, it gets better," she said, when she could manage to speak again, and he grinned down at her.

"I meant your love, but now I'm ready for you to show me *better*."

"Right now? My, you Atlanteans are quick to recover," she said, running her hands down the hard muscles of his glorious chest. "I'm not sure I'll survive it if we try for more. Now? Really?"

"Yes, now," he said, getting that intent look on his face again as he reached for crystal bottles of what looked like soap and bath oils. "I want to make you scream again."

And so he did.

❧──────↦

Alaric stared up at the ceiling, sated and a little dazed from his third climax, and Quinn's fifth or sixth, and he wondered how and why he'd ever thought anything in the world was worth giving up *this*. Quinn lay curled up next to him, her arm over his chest and one leg across his, and he thought he had never been so perfectly content simply to be still—present in the moment—in his entire life.

But then he thought that he wanted to try to make her come with just his mouth and hands.

He turned his head to look at her, and she shook her head. "Oh, no. Not again. Alaric, you're insane. I'm not Atlantean, and I don't have your magical powers of recuperation. If you don't let me get some rest, I won't even be able to walk to-morrow."

"I'm happy to heal you. With my mouth," he said, flashing his most wicked smile. "I'll even let you rest. Simply lie still, and I'll do everything."

"Oh, this can't be— Oh. Oh, boy," she murmured, as his lips closed around one taut pink nipple. "You don't . . . ah, oh. Oh."

"You're a little incoherent," he informed her, just before he moved down in the bed, pushed her thighs apart, and put his mouth on her. He did as he'd promised and sent a pulse of healing power through her, to soothe any small abrasions he'd caused with his . . . exuberance, and she moaned and arched her body into the air as she came, yet again.

He raised his head and aimed a fierce smile at her. "You can come, as you have just proved. Now you will do so, again."

"You're giving me orders, Alaric. Even in bed, you're—" She cried out and jumped, clutching at the bedsheets with one hand and his hair with the other. "You can't, we— Oh. Oh, oh, oh, ohhhhh," she moaned, as he licked and sucked at the pink bud that brought her such pleasure.

He knew the anatomy, of course, but he had never done such a thing, even back in the brief period before his service to Poseidon. He'd had no idea that the act could bring a woman so much satisfaction, but now that he did, he decided to experiment, and he slid two of his fingers inside her while he stroked her with his tongue, and she bucked underneath him again, arching her back, and then she came so hard she screamed his name.

"I have decided to spend the rest of my life giving you orgasms in various beautiful settings, all over the world," he announced, feeling quite pleased with himself as he realized that her eyes were glazed and she probably hadn't heard a single word.

"Mine," he said, kissing his way up her body and then lifting her to lie on top of him, enjoying the blissful expression on her face and the almost-boneless feel of her body, which was limp with pleasure and satisfaction.

"Mine."

⁓⁓⁓

When Quinn floated back down to the bed from wherever that latest earth-shattering orgasm had sent her, she found Alaric leaning over her with a glass of water in one hand and a towel in the other.

She took both, but she decided a trip to the shower again was in order, if she could only get her shaky legs to carry her there. When she told him her dilemma, Alaric carried her into the shower and washed every bit of her, which led to him soaping her breasts more carefully and thoroughly than he'd even done a few hours earlier, which ended up with her leaning against the wall, hands on the shower ledge, while he took her from behind. She came again, helplessly, endlessly, and he thrust into her with so much power and passion that the sheer eroticism of his joy in making love to her sent her over the edge once again. He roared—a primal sound filled with so much purely male satisfaction that it made her laugh—and then he came again, hard, and leaned down to pull her back against his chest and embrace her.

But even that simple hug turned into something more, when his fingers couldn't seem to resist her nipples, and he started to caress her breasts again. She moaned a little, almost in spite of herself, but she grabbed his hand when it started to move down her belly.

"I can't keep this up," she said, but she bucked back against him helplessly when he ignored her restraining hand and stroked her again.

"I seem to be able to keep this *up* quite well," he said, so proudly—so absolutely, positively *male*—that she started laughing.

She carefully moved forward and then turned around on suddenly very shaky legs. She stumbled and would have fallen if he hadn't swept her up into his arms and carried her back out of the shower, dried her off, and helped her to bed.

"I have to sleep now, or I might die of too much wonderful sex," she informed him.

"Lovemaking," he said firmly. "We have been making love, not merely having sex. Do not forget it."

"Yes, sir," she said, smiling sleepily and raising two fingers in a mock salute, and then he climbed into bed with her and wrapped his arms around her. She knew nothing but blissful warmth and lovely sleep, until sometime in the middle of the night, when she woke to find him stroking her nipples with his long, sensitive fingers.

She retaliated by scooting down in the bed and taking his penis into her mouth, and he yelled something in Atlantean and his entire body stiffened and went rigid. He dug into the sheets with both hands and continued speaking in a low tone, saying something that sounded beautifully lyrical—either an oath or a promise—and she licked the entire length of his shaft, smiling as whatever it was he was saying grew increasingly more fervent.

"You cannot—"

"Oh, I can," she interrupted. "Don't move. This is my turn."

She took her time with it, driving him to the edge of madness and beyond, as she cupped his firm balls in her hand and sucked on the sensitive tip of his penis with varying pressures, until she found exactly what he liked and exactly what made him lose all vestiges of control.

He cried out again, and she heard her name, and *mi amara*, and something that sounded a lot like *oh, holy shit*, and then his entire body went rigid, his penis hardened even further and swelled, and then he came in her mouth.

When she sat up, he looked both extremely blissful and so

comically surprised that she fell over sideways on the bed laughing.

"You . . . Oh, by all the gods . . . you . . . But I have never lost control like that," he finally said, and she kept laughing until he rolled her over and started tickling her, which led to kissing, which led to him lifting her over his body and lowering her to straddle him again, and this time they both cried out when he found his way home.

She was so deliciously sensitive after the marathon of lovemaking that she was right on the edge of sore, and he knew it, of course, since they'd long since opened the barriers between their emotions. He held her tightly, although he moved in long, slow strokes, claiming her as his at the same time he was so careful with her. When pleasure threatened to pass over the line to pain, he reached down between their bodies and gently pinched her between two fingers, and the added pressure sent her off like a rocket. She collapsed on his chest as he came inside her, yet again, and she had a moment to wonder how she'd ever survive the sheer pleasure between them, before unconsciousness claimed her.

When she woke up again, he wasn't touching any part of her body, which was so different that it startled her into wakefulness. She sat up and scanned the room, only to discover that Alaric wasn't there. He'd probably gone to find them something to eat, or at least the growling in her stomach hoped so, but hunger pains faded into insignificance as she stared at the new addition to the room.

For some reason, Alaric had brought an amazing light sculpture into the room while she was asleep. It was unbelievably beautiful. Similar to Art Deco in its lines and curves, it also possessed an inner light source that was almost magical and took the piece from simply art to *Art*, with a capital A. She was quite literally transfixed by it.

Until the light sculpture turned to her and started talking.

"We have a small problem," it said in Alaric's voice.

Chapter 30

"If this is how you try to impress a girl, I would have been okay with pancakes and bacon." Quinn sat up in bed and wrapped the blankets around herself, staring at Alaric the human light sculpture the entire time. "Well. What's this about? You couldn't bear to go without a crisis for ten whole hours?"

"I have no idea what this is about." His voice was deepened and magnified by the magic, and it touched places deep inside her that a voice had no business touching. She shivered and then shook it off.

"Yes, you do. It's the Nereus thing. Where having great sex, combined with the soul-meld, turns you into an Atlantean super-magician human lightbulb."

"I don't think Keely said anything about the quality of the sex," he said doubtfully, but she couldn't really read his expression while he was the Atlantean equivalent of the Human Torch.

She blinked. "Are you saying it *wasn't* great sex?"

"It was undoubtedly the most spectacular sex in the history of the planet, but I think we have other things to discuss right now." He raised his arms in the air and actual sparks flew off his skin in an arc of iridescent shimmer.

She whistled, long and low. "That's actually really freaking cool, but I'm guessing you don't want to hear that right now?"

"You guess right," he said.

"Maybe we should ask for help?"

"Who would we ask?" He shrugged and more sparks flew. "People generally come to *me* with magical problems."

He stood up and walked toward her, and she stared at him, utterly fascinated in spite of everything. It really was Alaric, but he was incandescent with pure, shining light. He reached out as if to touch her, but she backed away from him.

"No way, buddy. Don't touch me until we figure this out. You might electrocute me, which would totally ruin my day. Or, worse, it would send some kind of energy beam through me like when you, um, healed me earlier, and I'm not going to try making love to a glowing light stick just yet."

He laughed, and the resonant sensuality of it sent shivers down her spine.

"Speaking of glowing light sticks," he said, gesturing.

She couldn't believe it. He was naked, a fact she'd tried to overlook, what with the glowing, and his very erect penis was glowing, too. It was actually kind of cool, as far as magic went, and she suddenly threw caution to the Atlantean winds, leaned forward, and licked the tip of his jutting erection, just for the fun of watching his response.

He arched his back and groaned, and then he quickly stepped away. "The sensation is far too intense like this. I don't think I could bear it," he said.

Naturally, that was like laying down a challenge, so she jumped out of bed, knelt at his feet, and took as much as she could of his erection into her mouth. He yelled hoarsely and then pulled away from her, and a stream of shining semen arced through the air.

"Now that," she said, pointing, "is kind of astonishing. Those sparkly vampires in the kids' movies have nothing on you."

He closed his eyes and took deep breaths, and Quinn was fascinated by the swirls and galaxies of lights dancing over his skin. It was as if constellations had decided to take up residence on his body. She'd never seen anything like it, ever.

When he finally opened his eyes, she was astonished to see that the constellations of stars had spread to his eyes, which glowed hot emerald green and silver.

"I don't know about movies, *mi amara*, but what effect might this have on our children?"

She sat down so abruptly that she missed the bed and landed on the cold floor, on her naked butt. Scrambling up, she ran to the bathroom and closed and locked the door, and then wrapped herself in a towel and sat on yet another edge of yet another tub. The parallels to her situation the day before didn't escape her.

So. Here she was. Ex–rebel leader, current soul-melded girlfriend to the high priest of Atlantis, and possibly pregnant with a sparkling half-Atlantean baby. She suddenly wanted to throw up again, which made her think of morning sickness, which made it worse.

"You can't be pregnant now, Quinn," Alaric said from the other side of the door. "We must petition Poseidon to allow us to have children."

She glared at the door. "What about free will?"

"I think the light effect is fading, but the magical high is not," he said, ignoring her question. "I do not wish to create a distraction when Atlantis breaks the surface of the waves."

"What time is it? Shouldn't we be near the surface by now?" She pulled on a robe and flung open the door. "Did I sleep through the whole thing?"

Alaric was still glowing but not as much. Or maybe that was simply wishful thinking. The first radiance of magically created dawn was beginning to shine through his windows, and a quick glance out showed her that the tower of light from the temple was still going strong.

"We are still rising," Alaric said. "I can feel it."

She took a deep breath and walked over to him, wanting to

put her arms around him—her glowing darling—but not quite ready to be incinerated. "We'll figure it out. Hey, we can always work it into our new job plans. Give the Naked Cowboy a run for his money. You can be the Glowing Gardener."

He glared at her, or at least she thought he did, since magical sparks shot out of his eyes like lasers.

She started laughing. "You know, this is actually really cool. You're going to be quite a hit with fourteen-year-old boys who love video games."

"You are having far too much fun with this, when I am concerned I may actually explode from an excess of power flooding through my body." He swung around and touched her with a single finger, as if to test the connection.

She screamed, and he leapt away from her.

"Quinn, I'm so sorry, where are you hurt?"

She couldn't help it. She started laughing. "Sorry. I thought somebody needed to break the tension."

His mouth actually fell open a little. She'd succeeded in fooling the most powerful man in Atlantis. The small success made her grin, at least until he raised one hand and pointed a finger at her. A ribbon of glowing silver-blue light arrowed out from his finger and sped across the room toward her, swirled around her until it wrapped her up tight, and then inexorably, inch by inch, pulled her toward him.

"Oh, I am going to make you pay for this," she warned him.

Judging by the insufferably smug grin on his glowing face, he wasn't very concerned. "You deserve it," he told her, and then he released the energy, pulled her into his arms, and kissed the breath out of her. The energy flooding his body added an extra punch to the sensation, increasing the sensual power of his kisses until she was sure she'd drown in a wave of heat and passion.

"Stop right now," she finally managed to say, and he reluctantly released her. "We need to figure this out."

She walked over to an ornately carved wooden table and poured him a glass of water from the blue-and-white porcelain pitcher. "Drink this and think mundane, non-magical thoughts."

He raised an eyebrow at her high-handedness, but he drank the water. Either that or the non-magical thinking must have worked, because he started to dim, little by little, until he was almost back to his normal self, only glowing a little around the edges. He promptly grabbed her and kissed her again, and this time when she finally pulled away, breathless again, he pointed silently at her hands.

Which were also glowing.

"Oh, boy."

"Human lightbulb," he said, and it took her a minute to realize he was actually joking about job opportunities.

He started laughing, and she shook her head.

"Wow. Sex must be really, *really* good for you. Have I ever heard you tell a joke? *Ever?*"

"Tour guides equipped with our own flashlights for all the midnight ghost tours," he replied, and she nearly fell over. Two jokes in one century? From *Alaric*?

"Hey, nobody but me gets to touch your flashlight, buddy," she quipped and was rewarded with another easy smile, almost as if he were at all used to smiling. It was kind of like a minor miracle.

She had to grin at the idea of Alaric giving a guided ghost tour, though, but then she thought better of it when an awful truth hit her. "Ghosts? Are there ghosts, too?"

"You've seen vampires, shape-shifting giant monkeys, and demon kin from another dimension, and you're going to quibble over ghosts?" As he talked, he pulled on fresh clothes from his apparently limitless selection of black shirts and black pants, and she spared a moment to mourn the loss of the view.

All that lovely, muscular, naked man. And all hers. She felt like purring.

"Ghosts?" he repeated, probably wondering why she was staring at him like a lovesick cow.

"It's just that ghosts are dead people, and quite honestly I've seen enough dead people to last me a million lifetimes."

Alaric took her in his arms and held her tightly. "Never

again. We'll be ordinary and boring together. No battles, no dead people, no flying monkeys."

She laughed a little. "Let's go see this thing. How often do you get to watch the most famous lost continent in the history of the world actually rise?"

Alaric's smile faded.

"Hopefully, rise without being destroyed," he said grimly.

"I could have lived without thinking about that."

Alaric and Quinn walked into the palace gardens, and he was amazed to see that while the two of them had been . . . resting, the whole of Atlantis had been transforming the gardens into a giant banquet facility. Tables were everywhere, spread with snowy white linens and set with what looked like every dish and cup on the Seven Isles. Baskets of hot bread and fresh fruit, and heaping platters of eggs, meats, potatoes, and fish promised enough for a hearty feast.

As they looked around for a place to sit, Conlan noticed them and waved them over. He hugged Quinn and grinned at Alaric, but he didn't say a word about where they might have disappeared to.

I appreciate your discretion, Alaric sent to Conlan.

Conlan grinned even harder. *Did you know your ears are glowing?*

Quinn murmured an excuse and hurried away to find Riley, and Conlan grabbed Alaric and pulled him into a fierce hug, with much back pounding.

"You did it," the prince said.

"We all did it. It took more than just me. Christophe, Myrken and the acolytes, Serai—so many gave so much for this to be accomplished."

Conlan threw his head back and laughed. "I was talking about you finally taking Quinn to your bed. Sounds like it was awfully crowded in there."

None too gently, Alaric elbowed his friend, the high prince soon to be king, and together they went to find their women. Their *family*.

"Hey," Conlan said, throwing a companionable arm around Alaric's shoulders. "Guess what I just realized? We're going to be brothers-in-law."

"You can imagine my joy," Alaric said dryly, but Conlan just laughed and proceeded to introduce Alaric to everyone they met as his new brother-in-law. This confused most of the Atlanteans, who knew full well that Alaric was Poseidon's high priest, but it made the warriors laugh really, really hard.

Conlan looked out into the sea of faces. His family. His friends. His subjects, no matter how uncomfortable he was with the demands of kingship. He knew he had to say something to mark the momentous occasion, but he was drawing a blank.

"How about, one small step for Aidan, one giant leap for Atlantis?" Riley offered the suggestion as she watched their son like a hawk while he charmed everyone in sight, being passed from lap to lap to lap.

"That has a certain ring to it."

She started laughing. "No, no, no, you can't use that, I was kidding. It's already been used."

Conlan reached for his dagger. "Who else is giving speeches about our child?"

As she walked away, still laughing, he realized he never would fully understand the human woman who had won his heart. He glanced across the table at Quinn and Alaric, and he knew that it was okay. Complete and total understanding would make life dull, and the gods themselves knew that neither he, nor Alaric, nor any of his warriors would ever have to settle for that. He scanned the long table of laughing people and named them, these men and women who had forever had his back and would forever inhabit his heart:

Ven, brother and protector. Jokester and deadly warrior. Paired with Erin, his gem-singer witch, he was happier than he'd ever been.

Bastien, who had undervalued himself for so long. The panther shifter Kat Fiero had opened his mind and his heart.

Marie, first maiden of the Nereid Temple. She had given so much of her long life to aiding in the childbirth of others. She deserved the happiness she'd found with the panther alpha Ethan.

Justice, only recently discovered to be Conlan and Ven's half brother. Deadly and always forced to walk the balance between his dual natures. If he hadn't found his archaeologist and object-reader love, Keely, they would have lost him to his darker impulses. Together they and their adopted child, Eleni, formed one bridge to Atlantis's future.

Brennan, so long burdened with the curse that none of them thought he'd had a prayer of recovering his emotions, until he met and nearly lost Tiernan, whose own truth-teller gift had helped Brennan find his way.

Alexios, so fierce with his scarred face, rock star hair, and killer instincts. Only another warrior would do for him. Grace, with her archer's bow and deadly aim, had never stood a chance against him. And soon, their daughter would add her own guidance to Atlantis's future.

Christophe, their problem child. All attitude and arrogance until he met the infamous cat burglar, the Scarlet Ninja, otherwise known to only a select few as Lady Fiona, famous children's book author and illustrator. Fiona and her little brother had curbed some of the wildness in Christophe. Not all, Conlan amended, remembering that he had heard about more exploits of the Scarlet Ninja only last month when he'd gone to London. Just enough.

And Serai, ancient Atlantean princess, held in stasis for so long that she'd nearly died trapped in a crystal box. Daniel, her eleven-thousand-year-old vampire consort. They'd met before Atlantis had ever sunk beneath the waves, and only found each other again recently, after so many millennia of each believing the other dead.

Now, finally, Alaric. Conlan's best friend for nearly five hundred years had met his true mate. The soul-meld had caught them both, and Conlan truly believed they would be the better for it, as he and his own *aknasha* had discovered.

Then he considered the idea of baby Alarics running

around and didn't know whether to laugh or flee, but he finally knew exactly what to say.

He stood up at the head of the table, with the magical crystal arrangement in front of him that would carry his voice to every table in the garden and every home in the land, and he reached down to pull Riley and Aidan up to join them.

"Today marks the day we have anticipated for thousands of years. Atlantis will finally rise and take its place in the world again. We are here to celebrate that amazing accomplishment and honor those who made it possible. But I am also here to acknowledge the strides we have already made in joining the wider world."

He gestured. "You see at the table here to my right that today we have our first-ever shape-shifter guests in Atlantis. More than that, both of them are soul-melded to Atlanteans, so we consider them part of the family."

Everyone cheered and Kat waved, but Ethan stood up and bowed. "You can be part of my panther pride, too, anytime, Your Highness. I've seen you Atlanteans in a fight!"

Another cheer.

"After eleven thousand years, one of our own, a Nightwalker Guild mage, returned to Atlantis to claim the princess he'd loved and lost. A vampire sits at the table to my left, soul-melded to an ancient Atlantean princess. He, too, is part of our family."

More cheering, but then Serai stood up as gracefully as she did everything. "If you call me *ancient* one more time, Prince Conlan, I will challenge you to a duel," she said, smiling. "And I get to pick the form."

For a brief moment, Serai disappeared and a saber-toothed tiger stood in her place. The crowd went wild, cheering and stomping their feet, and then the very elegant princess reappeared and took her seat. Conlan bowed deeply in her direction, grinning at Daniel as he did so. He had a feeling that the princess kept her vampire very busy.

"We were once a very great civilization, when Atlantis rode the surface of the waves. Today we will rejoin the world, and the eyes of every country and every people will be upon us."

He looked around at the faces of those he loved so much. "We will continue as our ancestors began, more than eleven thousand years ago. Atlantis will become a productive member of the world economy, a valuable participant in international strategy, and—most important of all—we will continue the work that my warriors still perform today, so many millennia after Poseidon first assigned us the task."

He gestured with his hand and every one of the Seven, every warrior in training, and every warrior assigned to every segment of the Seven Isles, stood.

"Because now, finally, our prophecy is fulfilled and we will protect humanity no matter what is to come. Warriors, to me," he shouted, and the warriors all streamed up to stand near him, and turned and faced the crowd and recited the oath with him.

> *We will wait. And watch. And protect.*
> *And serve as first warning on the eve of humanity's*
>   *destruction.*
> *Then, and only then, Atlantis will rise.*
> *For we are the Warriors of Poseidon, and the mark of the*
>   *Trident we bear serves as witness to our sacred duty to*
>   *safeguard mankind.*

"We have waited, and watched, and protected," Conlan said. "And now, Atlantis will rise!"

As if on cue, a booming noise sounded and the whole of Atlantis jerked sideways, as if buffeted by a huge wave or an immovable object. Everyone looked up, and for the first time in more generations than anyone could count, they could see real sunlight over the dome of Atlantis. With a mighty heave, the dome broke through the waves and kept rising and rising, until the Seven Isles floated on the ocean's surface once more.

Everyone waited, seemingly afraid to breathe, and for a moment even Conlan feared that the dome was too damaged to open, but then the top and sides unfolded like the petals of a giant crystalline flower, and Atlantis showed her face to the world.

And the world was there to greet them. Conlan shot up into the air in mist shape and viewed the sea in all directions, and he realized there were hundreds of ships, helicopters, and airplanes, and even a hang glider carrying a homemade banner that said WELCOME TO THE WORLD, ATLANTIS on it in bright blue letters.

Conlan floated back down to report, and his people started cheering again, as the first helicopters flew overhead and called down on loudspeakers for permission to land and greet them.

"We made it," Riley said, holding Aidan tight.

"We did," Conlan agreed, putting his arms around them both. "Are you ready to go be High Princess Riley for a little while?"

"Let me get my glass slippers," she said, and together they walked forward to face the future.

Chapter 31

Quinn walked around for hours, exploring Atlantis, enjoying the celebratory spirit of the people, and loving the feel of the ocean breeze on her face and the dispersal of her slight feeling of claustrophobia. Alaric was busy; Riley was busy; everyone had tasks to do and people to meet, except for her, and she was perfectly fine with that. She needed time to process what had happened with her life and her career.

She also needed time to absorb the fact that she was now soul-melded to a magical Atlantean high priest—who was definitely a wizard in bed. Her cheeks heated up at the thought, and she deliberately ignored the slight soreness between her legs. After so many years of famine, she and Alaric had definitely had a feast, and she was feeling the aftereffects a little. Mostly, though, she just wandered around, smiling blissfully like a schoolgirl with her first crush, which was not only uncharacteristic for her, but also kind of embarrassing.

The day was sunny and clear—perfect weather for a lost continent to suddenly reappear. Quinn continued to walk, in no particular direction, content simply to observe. The Atlanteans were so delighted to be free of their long captivity under the waves that everywhere she looked, people were laughing and hugging and, in a few memorable cases, breaking into song. Everything was absolutely wonderful, and Quinn felt a little like singing herself, which made her laugh.

A cold breeze swept over her, chilling her flesh and carrying a dark sensation of impending danger that only an emotional empath should have been able to sense, but as she watched, the people nearest her shuddered and drew closer to one another, looking around themselves in mild alarm.

The first pings of unease snaked down her spine, and she opened her emotional shields to see what she could pick up. At first it was only the expected—the ordinary. People were excited and curious about the outside world. Most of them had already brushed off that ill wind as an unaccountably cold ocean breeze, which, after all, most of them had never felt in their lifetimes.

Sure. That *must* be all it had been. Except . . . *no*.

Quinn had seen far too much to discount her instincts at this stage of the game. Her skin kept trying to crawl off her arms, and her fingers were itching to go for the guns she wasn't carrying. Her muscles tensed involuntarily, steeling for a blow, and she was suddenly absolutely, one thousand percent sure that something—somewhere very near—was preparing to go spectacularly wrong.

Alaric. We have a serious problem.

She broadcast the message as loudly as she could, in the same manner as she'd called to him before, and she counted on the powerful connection the soul-meld had forged between them to carry it to him.

What is it?

Not a single word of question or doubt; she could feel his belief in her, and his confidence bolstered her own.

I don't know, but it's bad. Could it be Anubisa? Can she travel here in daylight?

I do not think so, but we have never known the full extent of her powers. Let me finish this and find you.

He left her with an impression of a meeting with Conlan,

Riley, and a roomful of dignitaries and ambassador types, but also with the sure knowledge that he was on his way to her.

The chill wind brushed by her again, carrying its haunting message of dread and despair, and she knew it couldn't be fast enough.

It took them quite a while to pass through the crowds on the way to each other, even though she could feel his exact location in her mind, like she was suddenly a human GPS system, due to the soul-meld. It was simply a matter of working their way through all the people, both Atlanteans and guests. Everyone wanted to meet the Atlanteans and see the mythological lost continent, and no matter how his impatience raged—and Quinn could feel every bit of it—she sternly ordered him not to blast them all out of his way with "just a small windstorm."

She hadn't been able to understand how everyone had been on hand to see Atlantis, but Riley had explained that Conlan had been preparing for the event for a couple of years now, and he'd arranged some kind of notification system so that when Atlantis did begin to rise, the magical community of the human world would recognize what was happening and convey the news to everyone else.

Which was wonderful for international relations, but Quinn's dark feeling of premonition grew stronger and stronger as each minute passed. When several Atlantean children rushed by, shouting about a party and staying up late, she realized that the sun was suddenly sinking in the horizon, which meant that dusk was coming. When night fell, for the first time in millennia, Atlantis would be fully unprotected from outside supernatural forces.

In the ocean, in the dark, with no protection.

Quinn started running.

Vampires. Conlan had talked about Daniel, but they'd forgotten about the more prevalent kind of vampire. The murderous kind. And Anubisa was out there, boiling with rage and madness, and no longer with Ptolemy to run interference.

Quinn pushed her pace to run even faster. She started calling out to Alaric on the mental pathway between them, and she finally found him and filled him in on her new suspicions. He listened and instantly understood, and he grabbed her hand and headed for the palace.

"Conlan is meeting with foreign dignitaries," he said. "We have to find him, now. If you're right, it's going to be a very bad night."

"Why does Anubisa hate your royal family so much?"

His face hardened. "It's a long, complicated saga. Basically she once wanted an Atlantean prince who chose an Atlantean woman over a vampire, and all Anubisa has done ever since is plot and carry out revenge against Conlan's family and his ancestors before him. She murdered his mother quite brutally."

Quinn pointed to the sky. "Alaric, does sunset come early in the Bermuda Triangle this time of year?"

"We have to move, *now*," he said, and they started running.

───◦───

Alaric burst into the throne room, startling Conlan and scaring a foreign ambassador who was wearing a top hat, of all improbable things.

"Conlan, crisis. Now," Alaric snapped out, and the prince immediately excused himself and strode across the room at top speed.

"Quinn has a bad feeling," Alaric said, and Quinn felt like a fool.

"I have an *Anubisa* feeling," she corrected, and Conlan's jaw tightened.

She filled him in on Anubisa's interaction with Ptolemy and the vampire goddess's evil plans, and Conlan grew angrier by the second.

"You thought you would keep this from me—*why*?" he demanded, but Alaric stepped between them.

"Do you forget what she did for us? Can you blame her for forgetting details in the exhaustion of the moment? If you would blame anyone, blame me. I should have known that evil bitch goddess would use our welcome as an excuse to attack. We are unprotected for the first time in millennia."

"But it's so far. How would she get any of her minions and thugs here? It's not as if the navies of any of those countries will transport her. They all hate her," Quinn pointed out.

Conlan slowly nodded. "You may be right. If the gods be benevolent, you will be right. But we must plan as if for attack. I will discuss the issue with our new allies and see what resources they will be able to offer."

"I will inform the warriors," Alaric announced, and he and Quinn headed out to gather the forces. "At least for once they're all here."

"I bet that will be an interesting story. Why the portal suddenly went around collecting everyone. Noriko can probably explain some of that," Quinn said, all but jogging to keep up with Alaric's long legs.

Alaric stopped suddenly. "I want you to know that after this crisis is over, we will return to Japan and do whatever we can to help Jack. I pledge you this."

She hugged him, speechless for once, and the soul-meld flared hot between them. "You are amazing."

"I know," he said smugly. "You had nine orgasms."

He started walking again, leaving her standing there in shock, face flaming hot, scanning the area for anyone who might have heard. Nobody seemed to be openly mocking her, so she ran after him and punched him in the arm, hard.

"That's the kind of thing you don't talk about in public," she whispered.

"Why not? It was the best night of my life. Had I the time, I would hire the youngling with the gliding apparatus to paint a sign extolling your virtues and fly it over Atlantis," he said solemnly, but the edge of his mouth quirked up, and she realized he was teasing her. Trying to take the edge off her worry.

That, alone, was enough to make her nearly fall over.

Sex, playfulness, teasing, and jokes. From High Priest Warrior Man. It would be the best day of her life if the vampires didn't attack.

Please, please, please, don't let the vampires attack.

Alaric paused to speak to several warriors, but Quinn saw Riley strolling around the garden fountain, carrying Aidan, and she ran across the grass toward her and started talking before she even reached her sister. "Riley! We've got to get you somewhere safe. It may be nothing, but we're a little worried—"

Quinn's words fell off into a horrible gurgle when the sharp edge of a very shiny sword suddenly appeared between Riley's breasts, barely missing the baby who lay sleeping against her shoulder. Quinn's sister's eyes opened very, very wide and she held Aidan out to Quinn.

"Take him. Love him. Raise him," she whispered, and then she fell to the ground.

"I think not. I'll take that baby," Anubisa said, appearing as if by magic from where she was hiding behind Riley. The vampire snatched the child from Quinn's hands with preternatural speed and flew up into the air.

Alaric screamed vengeance from behind Quinn, but he couldn't attack without risking Anubisa harming the baby.

"Now you will see what my wrath costs, Quinn Dawson," Anubisa said, and, terrifyingly, she didn't sound the slightest bit crazy.

"What did you do?" Quinn asked, falling to her feet next to her sister. "What did you do? I'll kill you!"

"I think not. I played the poor madwoman for your Ptolemy, in order to assess the extent of his power, but he's disappeared from this dimension, hasn't he? Would you care to tell me what happened to him?" Anubisa floated just out of Quinn's reach, holding the baby in front of her, wearing a long white dress that looked like a shroud and would prove to be prophetic, if Quinn had anything to do with it.

Quinn rocked back and forth on the ground, devastated with grief, as she dimly heard people running toward her.

"Your Atlanteans are mine now," Anubisa cackled. "I could kill you, but I think it will hurt you much more if I leave you alive to watch."

"You have *need*," whispered a familiar deep voice behind Quinn, and when she frantically nodded, the portal appeared—in the sky over the top of Anubisa's head, and a familiar shape came soaring out. A quarter ton of tiger, with a small Japanese woman riding on his back, flew through the air and crashed into Anubisa, who dropped the baby. Quinn sprinted for Aidan and caught him on the way down in a perfect football hold. The baby blinked up at her and then started screaming for his mother, and Quinn wanted to scream, too.

Anubisa, currently on the ground, lying flat on her face underneath the enormous tiger, screamed, too.

The only ones who didn't scream were Alaric and Noriko, who both bent down to examine Riley. Their gazes met over her body.

"You're too late," Anubisa hissed, and then she vanished, and Jack fell over with a thump.

"I am never too late," Noriko said, placing her hands in the air about an inch above Riley's chest. Alaric added his supercharged new magic to hers, and together they formed a blue-green shield above and around Riley's body. Long seconds passed, and then Riley coughed and sat up, looking around like she'd just woken up from a very bad dream.

"She was still alive, only hanging on by a thread, but her *kami*—her spirit—is very strong," Noriko said, rising to her feet and holding out a hand to Riley.

"*Konbanwa*, Riley-san," Noriko said. "You will need to rest."

Riley stared up at the ex–portal spirit/Japanese woman combo as Quinn stared at them both, tears running down her face. "And you are?"

"It's complicated," Quinn broke in. "For now, let's get you and the baby to a safe place before Conlan finds out about this."

But they were far too late for that. Conlan hit them at top speed, nearly bowling over Alaric, about two seconds later.

"What in the nine hells happened to my wife?" he roared.

Quinn made a face at Riley, faking a nonchalance she was worlds away from feeling.

"Your Atlantean is overprotective, too? This is going to be a very long night."

Riley blinked, dazed, and touched her shirt, and her fingers came away soaked with blood. "What happened?"

"We will tell you on the way," Alaric said. "Now move."

Chapter 32

Quinn knew that Alaric wanted nothing more than to sweep her up and deposit her someplace safe, but he could feel from the soul-meld, burning brightly between them, that she'd try to kill him if he even attempted it. Not to mention that she was currently wrapping her arms around an enormous tiger.

"Jack, you came. You came," she repeated.

The tiger licked the side of her head in one giant slurp, and Alaric glared at them.

Please tell Jack that I will punch him in the head as soon as I am able to make him human again.

"You can punch anybody you want, as soon as we defeat the vampires," Quinn said.

Jack turned his enormous shaggy head toward Alaric, and she could have sworn that the beast was laughing at him.

"Now, Quinn," Alaric said. "We need to get Riley to safety, and I think if you would stay with your sister and the child, you could—"

Quinn stood, one hand still on Jack's head, and glared at him. "This is what I *do*, Alaric, and you know that about me. I fight."

"Fight later, if you please, but now we should run," Noriko said, bowing to both of them.

"Alaric," Conlan shouted, as he swept his wife and child into his arms and started running.

"Already doing it," Alaric replied, before briefly closing his eyes.

Before he'd even opened them again, an overpowering wave of fear buffeted Quinn. The people all around them blasted her with the powerful emotion as they turned to look at Alaric, either nod or bow to him, and then began herding their children toward the nearest available buildings.

"I sent out a warning," Alaric said. "They will arm themselves and protect their families. My concern is that, other than ceremonial pieces and the odd family heirloom, none but the warriors keep weapons."

Quinn dodged to get out of the way of a woman running with one child by the hand and a baby in her other arm. The woman's emotions were a mixture of fear and determination. She'd fight hard for her children—of that Quinn had no doubt.

"Well, they haven't had to protect themselves for a long time," Quinn said. "But they'll do their best. Are we on the way to find weapons for ourselves?"

Alaric simply nodded and sped up his pace, until they were practically running.

"Wherever Anubisa disappeared to, I have a bad feeling she didn't go far," Quinn said, shivering as goose bumps rose on her arms.

"Evil is never far enough away," Noriko said, keeping pace next to Quinn. The former portal spirit glanced at Alaric. "So you did find a measure of peace, and the soul-meld. I am pleased for you."

Jack, who was padding along between them, snarled, and Quinn rolled her eyes.

"*Arigato*," Quinn said. "I don't want to know how you know that, though. And you? Have you found peace? Also, would you have any idea what the current portal spirit is up to? He has been kidnapping people left and right and sending them wherever he feels like sending them."

"He?" Noriko shook her head. "No, I have no idea. But Poseidon has much control over our actions. It is he who released me from my bond."

"And Jack?"

Jack's ears flicked back, but he didn't look at Quinn.

"Nothing has changed, unfortunately," Noriko said, but she did briefly touch Jack's head.

"We don't have time for this now," Conlan said, pointing up. "That doesn't look like anything good."

They all looked up to find swarms of darkness covering the twilit sky. A blinding burst of pure, primal terror flooded Quinn, and she couldn't breathe for a moment, until she realized most of it was coming from the Atlanteans who were still outdoors. Of course they wouldn't have seen vampires before. Their fear tasted like acid in Quinn's mouth—there was nothing more primal than the loathing and terror of creatures who wanted to drain your blood, and these were attacking in such masses as to block out the first sunset the Atlanteans had seen in eleven millennia.

"She's back, and she has reinforcements," Quinn shouted, slamming shut her emotional shields so she could survive the massive amount of terror pounding her brain. "Run!"

Seconds later, the swarm of vampires hit Atlantis like a plague of locusts, attacking everyone in sight. Alaric turned and walked backward, hurling energy spheres as he moved. Wherever one of his deadly little balls landed, vampires screamed and died.

But most of the screaming and dying was happening to the Atlanteans and their guests. Quinn flinched as three of the bloodsuckers attacked a man and ripped him apart.

The palace finally rose up in front of them and she raced Jack indoors. Once inside the palace, Conlan stopped running and let Riley walk on her own.

"I'm taking her to the safest place in the palace," Conlan said. "Our rooms are warded and defensible."

"Take Noriko," Quinn advised. "She has a killer force field. She can help protect Riley and the baby."

Conlan nodded, and they sped away. Quinn headed down a corridor after Alaric.

"The armory is this way. How are you with a sword?"

She rolled her eyes. "Not all that great. I don't have much practice with boiling oil or cannonballs, either."

Ven met up with them and caught the gist of what she was saying. "Stick with me, kid. We non-magic types have to work to our strengths."

He opened a locked door just past the larger doors to the palace armory, which was swarming with warriors gearing up before running back outside to protect their people. Ven threw open the cabinet to display an impressive range of all the best tech for the serious gun enthusiast. Quinn chose a Glock similar to the one Ptolemy had melted, another just like it, a selection of throwing knives and stabbing knives, and then she slung a mini-Uzi over her shoulder.

She looked down at Jack. "Want an Uzi?"

He snarled and lifted one massive paw, tipped with very sharp claws. She nodded. "Still not coming back, huh? Well, now is a great time to be a tiger."

Ven was arming himself with enough weaponry to single-handedly assault a small country.

Quinn loaded her pockets with extra ammo. "Silver?"

Ven nodded. "Best kind."

Alaric's patience, what little there was of it, had evidently reached its end. He backed her into the wall and got right in her face. "If you are outnumbered, you *run*. If you find yourself in an indefensible position, you run. If—"

She stood on her tiptoes and kissed him. "I love you, too. Now, let's go save the day."

Ven's mouth fell open, and then he whistled. "Nobody is going to believe this. The terrifying Alaric brought to his knees by *luuurve*."

Alaric bristled and took a step toward Ven, but Quinn spoke up.

"Oh, yes, Erin dear. Can I rub your back, Erin darling? Should we watch that chick flick again, Erin dearest?"

Ven flushed a dull red and muttered something, and Alaric grinned at her before they all settled down to the deadly earnest job of defending Atlantis.

Marcus ran down the hall, damn fast for his age. "My lords, Anubisa is on the roof of the palace, and she has the princess and the baby trapped. Conlan ordered me to find you and Lord Justice."

"I'm going to *kill* that bitch," Quinn shouted, and Marcus nodded.

"If I don't get a chance first," he said grimly.

"Go find Justice. We'll take it from here," Alaric said, and he, Ven, and Quinn ran up the stairs toward the roof and the vampire goddess who had taken so much from so many of them.

Quinn checked her weapons as she ran, although she privately doubted any of them would suffice to kill a vampire so old that she claimed to be a goddess. She hoped Alaric and his new magic could help with a knockout punch—even Quinn could behead an unconscious vamp.

"If she has hurt Riley again, or the baby—" Quinn couldn't finish the sentence. Couldn't even think the unthinkable. She'd get there in time to prevent it.

She had no choice.

When they reached the roof, they stopped to assess the situation. Night had fallen hard, and only the moon and a few scattered torches illuminated the scene. A clearly terrified Riley stood just out of reach of at least fifty vampires, and Noriko was unconscious—or dead—on the ground near her. Conlan stood between the vamps and his wife and child, armed with nothing but a single sword. Anubisa, leading her contingent of bloodsuckers, walked up to the prince, only stopping when she was almost close enough to reach out and touch him.

"Oh, my princeling," the vampire goddess said happily, clapping her hands like a gleeful child. "It's so wonderful to see you again, after we made so many lovely memories together."

Jack snarled, and the vampires nearest to him edged nervously away, but Anubisa and Conlan didn't notice any of it, since they were so intensely focused on each other.

"I will take your head for a trophy, if you don't leave immediately," Conlan said from between clenched teeth. "You have already harmed my wife and threatened my child, so you deserve the most hideous of deaths, but I will offer you this one chance, and one chance only, to leave us in peace and take your filthy swarms with you."

As bluffs went, it had no teeth, since the prince was overwhelmingly outnumbered, even now that the three of them had arrived. Quinn sent a wave of emotional reassurance to her sister, only to discover that Riley was like a mama wolf, and much tougher than she looked. She was prepared to kill anything and anyone who came near Aidan—with her teeth and bare hands, if that's what it took.

Anubisa glanced back at Quinn, Alaric, and Ven, and she laughed at them all. "The weak, the stupid, and the human. What a pathetic group you make."

"Well, you'd know all about *pathetic*," a new voice drawled from the other side of the roof, a voice coming from the warrior strategically positioned behind Anubisa's vampires.

Justice stepped into view, his braid hanging over one shoulder and his massive sword held casually at the ready. Quinn estimated that it probably weighed more than she did. She was quite happy with her Glocks and Uzi.

Anubisa shrieked, practically vibrating with rage. Quinn knew she'd hated Justice with a particular passion ever since he'd pretended to be attracted to her in order to save Ven and Erin.

"You!" the vampire screamed. She turned to her bloodsuckers. "I want him *dead*!"

Her minions obediently attacked, but in her rage she'd forgotten to give explicit directions, so they *all* headed for Justice, leaving Anubisa's army undefended from behind. Alaric took advantage of the situation to blast them with an intense surge of white-hot magic, destroying at least ten of them in one blow.

Alaric threw back his head and roared out a command that was so powerful, Quinn was surprised the air itself didn't catch on fire.

"Poseidon! Trident, tool of the sea god! To me! Lend me your power to destroy this monster," he shouted, and this time, the glowing didn't happen gradually.

This time, Alaric *blazed*.

He blazed like a beacon—like a signal fire. He blazed like the hope of Atlantis made flesh.

And then he waded into the masses of vampires that rushed him, at Anubisa's command, and they all began to die horrible, flaming deaths.

"What in the nine hells?" Ven shouted, but then he shrugged and started forward.

Quinn used him as cover and ran through the vampires and toward Anubisa, with no thought but to protect her sister. Jack leapt into the fray, ripping and shredding vampires like a crazed kitten playing with a catnip-infused toy.

Quinn aimed and fired steadily as she ran, but Anubisa batted the bullets out of her way as if they were pesky flies. Conlan used her distraction to advance on Anubisa from behind, and Ven tore into the fight near Alaric, with a gun in one hand and a silver stake in the other.

Conlan let out a yell of pure berserker rage, and Anubisa hurled a bolt of black and foul-feeling energy that smashed into him and knocked him back, but he jumped up and came at her again.

The hideous cacophony of vampire shrieks, tiger roars, and Atlantean battle cries pounded against Quinn's skull. She ran toward Riley and Aidan, but Anubisa shifted to block her path.

"I don't think so, little rebel leader," the so-called goddess said, sneering. "I have other plans for you."

But within another few moments, Alaric, Conlan, Ven, Justice, and Jack had destroyed the goddess's blood pride, or at least the faction that was on the roof with her, and the three brothers and Alaric surrounded Anubisa while Jack ran over to Noriko and sniffed the fallen woman's head, nudging her gently as if to wake her up.

"It's okay, Anubisa, you're going to die," Riley said in a singsong voice.

Quinn realized that her sister was going into shock. Not surprising, considering the amount of blood Riley had lost earlier while lying on the ground watching an insane vampire toss her son around in the air. Magical healing always made a person tired, and in need of food, too, so that probably didn't help.

"I'll get you out of here, and we'll make you some tea," she called out to Riley, feeling like an idiot for talking about tea in the middle of such danger, but trying to be reassuring.

But Quinn wasn't feeling particularly reassuring, because she noticed something that snaked a chill of ice down her spine. Although Anubisa stood alone on the roof, surrounded by enemies, she didn't seem afraid or worried in the least. In fact, she was smiling.

"No wonder you always lose. You're all moronic buffoons," the vampire said, slowly turning in a circle to try to watch all of the Atlanteans surrounding her. "Do you think I swore an oath five thousand years ago to destroy you, just to have it end like this?"

"Really? Is that all you've had to occupy yourself for five thousand years?" Quinn laughed as scornfully as she could manage. "You need a hobby, chick. Get your nails done. Watch *Survivor: Vampire*. Do *something*. You're a one-note wonder, and everybody here is bored."

If success was measured as "the screaming vampire nearly took off my head just from the sound of her screeching," then Quinn figured her taunt was a rousing success. The part where she collapsed to the ground with her ears bleeding? Not so much.

"Enough," Alaric said, shining so brightly with barely restrained magic that Quinn had to shade her eyes to look at him. "Now you die."

"I think not, priest," Anubisa said, laughing. And then she

screamed and flung her hands out and down, as if opening something.

Something like a *portal*.

Quinn's skin tried to crawl off her bones again, and she only had time to think, *oh no, oh no, oh no*, before the empty air near Anubisa opened onto a toxic orange landscape, and Ptolemy leapt through, leading a horde of the atrocities he called family. Anubisa, laughing, transformed into a cloud of oily black smoke and disappeared.

The demons poured forth, more and more and more, racing in all directions to attack, and Riley screamed, high and wild. Quinn started shooting, but a wave of hopeless, helpless revulsion and despair threatened to shake the foundations of her courage like never before.

Alaric hurled an enormous energy sphere straight at Ptolemy's head, but the demon almost casually deflected it, and it smashed into one of the crystal spires of the palace and shattered it.

Justice and Conlan fought like madmen to defeat or even contain the horde of demons, and Ven, like Quinn, fired shot after shot into the swarming masses.

"Now that is *butt* ugly," Ven yelled, stomping on a foot-high creature that was all teeth and elbows as it tried to bite him, but Quinn only heard him with a fraction of her attention, because all of her focus was on the monster she'd seen being impaled back in his own dimension.

"Hello, honey," Ptolemy said, his face and body shape monstrously distorted. He flashed a giant, shark-toothed smile. "I'm ho-ome."

Chapter 33

Alaric's rage exploded outward in a storm of lightning bolts at the sight of the monster who had abducted Quinn not once, but twice. The demon who'd forced her to kill an innocent man.

Alaric had gotten his wish. Ptolemy had come back from the dead, just so Alaric could kill him again. Slowly and painfully.

From across the roof, Jack's roar sounded over the noise of battle.

Ptolemy glanced back at the tiger, and then he started laughing. "Oh, the gang's all here. Even my beloved's kitty-cat friend."

"You die tonight," Alaric said, and he started toward Ptolemy, striding over dead vampires and striking down any not yet dead ones that got in his way.

"How does the interdimensional demon speak perfect English, even down to American slang?" Ven called out.

"We'll discuss later," Quinn said, and then she shot Ptolemy in the head.

Or at least she tried to. Apparently the demon's head was

made of bullet-deflecting materials. She screamed in frustration as the bullet bounced off Ptolemy, but Alaric steered its path so that it ricocheted right into the ass of one of the atrocities and the entire creature exploded. Then it was Ptolemy's turn to scream in rage, and Alaric smiled the smile that had made fully trained warriors fall to their knees.

"Hey, guess your baby brother won't be looking for any emotional empath mates," Quinn said, taunting.

"I will hurt you for that," Ptolemy snarled. "I will make you bleed and beg when I fuck you."

"I think not," Alaric said, and when Justice finally turned from the four vampires he'd been slaying, he saw Alaric and gasped.

"What in the nine hells?" Justice was so busy staring at Alaric that he almost missed the atrocity getting ready to jump on his leg, teeth first.

Quinn shot it for him. "Two," she called out, and Ptolemy gnashed his teeth, tearing strips of skin off his face as his features grew even more bestial in form.

"Quinn, to Riley," Alaric commanded, forgetting that Quinn didn't take commands very well.

Naturally, she took a step toward Ptolemy, pointing her gun again. Another creature rushed her, and Alaric incinerated it with another lightning bolt.

"Isn't lightning somebody else's gig?" Quinn said. "What's Poseidon going to say about that?"

"That is no longer my concern. The impending death of this demon, however, is," Alaric said calmly. He circled his hand in the air—once, twice—and a miniature tornado formed at the edge of his fingertips and shot across the roof toward Ptolemy.

The demon didn't even see it, though, because all of his attention was on Quinn. As he stalked toward her, Ptolemy's shape enlarged and contorted, until he was nearly unrecognizable as the suave politician they'd first seen on TV.

"You took it, didn't you, you sneaky thief?" Ptolemy took another step, and the tornado, which had grown to at least ten feet tall, crashed into him, whipped him up off the roof, and smashed him into the stone wall of the palace, hard. The demon screamed, and Alaric's eardrums reverberated with the echo of Ptolemy's rage.

He scanned the rooftop. Conlan, Ven, Justice, Jack, and Quinn were destroying the rest of the creatures who'd rushed through the portal, and Riley, holding Aidan, was crouching down near Noriko, who was awake now and holding a force field around the three of them.

In the chaos, Anubisa had vanished. Again. But one glance at the night sky, spectacularly lit up by the stars, the moon, and Alaric himself, showed a new problem. A black swarm was advancing on Atlantis over the open sea.

"It's the fucking apocalypse," Justice said, his face hard. His deadly sword slashed and sliced, decapitating demons in a vicious whirlwind of death. "I have to go to Keely. Now."

"How is that possible? Vampires can't travel over the ocean," Ven said, staring at the sky. "They're terrified of water. It messes with their powers."

"They're more afraid of Anubisa. If she tells them to stick stakes in their own hearts while munching on garlic and wearing crosses, they'll do it," Quinn said grimly. "And maybe they hijacked one of those ships. All it would take is for Anubisa to have rolled one captain with her eyes, and the ship would be hers."

"Don't ignore me," Ptolemy screamed, picking himself up off the ground. "Where is it? Where is my gem?"

"Not too worried about your family, are you?" Quinn taunted him, as she shot another of the creatures.

Ptolemy screamed with rage again.

"Poseidon's Pride wasn't yours, and it never will be. Nor will Quinn," Alaric told the demon, launching himself across the rooftop toward the demon and blasting him with his new and more powerful energy spheres. He got a direct hit, and the demon screamed and bled, but then Ptolemy called up his own power and formed a spear made of hideous orange-red light, which he hurled at Alaric with every ounce of his demonic strength.

The spear was only inches away from Alaric's chest when

he destroyed it with an energy sphere. He hadn't expected that kind of speed from a monster who'd become as bulky and grotesque as Ptolemy's new shape.

He wouldn't make that mistake again.

Alaric called to his new, vastly increased power and drew a shining sword from thin air. The sword's edge burned with the pure white energy of magic, and Ptolemy flinched before it. Alaric himself blazed ever brighter, until the remaining monsters cowered at the sight of him.

He hurled more energy spheres at Ptolemy with his left hand and then—realizing his hands were not needed—he simply stalked forward, surrounded by spheres that formed and attacked the demon just because Alaric willed them to do so.

He was on fire—he was the most powerful high priest Poseidon had ever known—he was a *god*.

Quinn's laughter sounded in his mind.

Don't get carried away, there, god-boy.

Her warmth and humor snapped Alaric out of the power's seductive grip and back into himself, just in time to crush Ptolemy's sneak attack with what appeared to be a magically created battle-axe.

The two of them battled with everything in their respective arsenals, seemingly equally matched, until Alaric balanced on the edge of utter fatigue and a potentially fatal case of magical exhaustion. He'd been carrying Atlantis's safety and the stability of the Trident for too long, and it had drained him. Ptolemy, sensing weakness, laughed and threw a dagger at Alaric, who sent a pulse of magic to deflect it.

Except it wasn't a magical dagger. It was ordinary steel, and the magic had no effect on it. Alaric realized it just as it pierced his side, and he felt the hot, wet gush of blood running down his ribs almost before he felt the pain of the stab wound.

"Not as good as you think you are," Ptolemy sneered. "You don't deserve Quinn, and I'll remind her of that every day when you're dead and she's pregnant with my heir."

Something vital snapped in Alaric, and any restraint or

caution he might have felt toward accepting the full promise of his new powers vanished. He flew up into the air, trailing actual flames, and then he dove toward Ptolemy with the strength and speed of a raptor seeking its prey.

The demon never had a chance.

Ptolemy's magical shields and weapons blew apart like tissue paper in a windstorm in front of Alaric's towering fury. Alaric hurled the demon back, farther away from Quinn, and smashed him back to the rooftop every time Ptolemy tried to get up.

A primal rage thundered through Alaric with hurricane force. "Nobody touches my woman, do you understand me?"

But Ptolemy was beyond words. The demon shrieked unintelligible, garbled sounds of hate and frustration, and gathered his strength for one final rush at Alaric, who let him do it. When Ptolemy had almost reached him, hands outstretched for Alaric's throat, Alaric threw open all of his shields and channeled the power.

All of the power.

Endless oceans of power poured into him and filled him and burned to be set free. Alaric roared out his triumph and his mastery over the magic, and it obeyed his mental command and formed into a lightning bolt of pure energy that shone as brightly as Alaric himself now did.

"Now you will die," he told Ptolemy, and then he plunged the lightning bolt down and through the top of the demon's skull. The magic cut through bone like butter, and Ptolemy shrieked with all the anguish of the nine hells, and then his body split in two, right down the middle, and the two halves fell to the ground, already dissolving.

Alaric watched, breathing hard, as the demon melted. And then he smiled.

The creatures who'd been trying to sneak up behind him shrieked and ran away at the sight of him, but it was too late. Alaric threw a rapid-fire burst of energy spheres at them and incinerated them all.

They'd tried to hurt his woman. They died. Nothing could be simpler.

His gaze arrowed toward Quinn, who was standing, a gun in each hand, in front of Noriko and Riley and the baby, and he laughed.

I see you have rescued yourself again.

She smiled at him across the fallen bodies of their enemies.

Not bad yourself.

~———~

Quinn was fiercely, overwhelmingly glad that Ptolemy was dead.

"What happened to Alaric? Why is he all Johnny Torch?" Ven shouted, but Quinn shook her head. No time.

She pulled out the Uzi and swept the roof clear of the few remaining of Ptolemy's brethren, and she cheered at the sight until her voice was hoarse.

Threaten to "mate" with her, would they, the little monsters? Now they wouldn't be mating with anybody.

Quinn, my love, leave me something to kill.

She waved at Alaric and blew him a kiss.

I think you've done enough.

A brief flare of pain alerted her to Alaric's injury. He was still shining, but not quite as much as he had been.

Hey, you're hurt. You need to heal that right now.

It is nothing, he replied.

She started toward him. "Tell me that again, and I'll shoot you myself. Let me see it."

She pulled his shirt up and her heart jumped into her throat at the sight of the wound. "That's not nothing. Fix it. Now."

Instead, he pulled her closer and kissed her so deeply that her knees buckled. His magic poured into her like a high-voltage current, and for a minute she was afraid she was going to have an orgasm right there on the roof surrounded by the Atlantean royal family and a whole lot of dead demons.

"Now I will heal it," Alaric said, when he finally released her.

She blinked up at him, dazed, and he smiled that completely male, entirely self-satisfied smile again. It made her want to hit him.

It made her want to kiss him again.

She settled for neither. "You did slay an interdimensional demon for me, so I guess I'll let you get away with this one."

His smile faded. "But Atlantis is not safe yet. Where is Anubisa?"

As if on cue, Atlantis rocked like an earthquake had shattered its foundation, and Quinn fell against a stone pedestal and knocked off a marble statuette of a porpoise.

With her head.

"Ow," she complained. "Why is it always my head?"

"Hardest part on you?" Ven suggested, and she groaned.

"Anubisa," Alaric said, staring into the far distance at something only he could see. "By all the gods, Anubisa is going after the Trident."

Conlan, who was comforting Riley and Aidan, froze. "Alaric—"

"I know," Alaric said grimly, as he started running for the stairs. "If it falls into her hands, all of Atlantis is doomed."

Jack snarled, and Quinn wanted to do the same.

Ven groaned. "Why can't we ever catch a damn break?" He took off after Quinn and Alaric, and Justice and Jack followed close behind, silent and deadly.

"We need to end this, once and for all," Conlan said, matching pace with Alaric.

Alaric nodded, the movement all the more striking since he was glowing again and tiny sparks arced from his motion. "I agree. Tonight we discover how to kill a goddess."

Chapter 34

Alaric hit the stairs running and shot through the palace like an arrow loosed from Artemis's bow, wondering if even his newly increased power would be sufficient to defeat a vampire goddess.

His heart ached at the idea of losing Quinn before he'd had a chance to live his life with her, but nothing mattered more than defeating Anubisa. If she managed to kill him—and the odds were against him—she'd use the Trident to destroy Atlantis and everyone in it.

Quinn *could not* die. She would not die. If it took his life to save her, he'd gladly sacrifice it. But that was not the optimal choice.

Dying was, as Ven would say, Plan B.

He stopped twenty paces from the Trident's chamber, caught Quinn's arm, and used her momentum to swing her into an empty room.

"You will stay here," he commanded her.

Before she could argue, he took her face in his hands and kissed her with every ounce of his longing and his love. His entire body shook with his passion, and he felt her tremble against his body.

"If you are safe, I can survive this, I think, *mi amara*," he said. "Please, just this one time, stay back."

Quinn's eyes flashed and he could see on her very expressive face the internal battle she waged.

"Fine." She lifted her chin. "Fine. Go fight your magical battle, but you'd better remember that all you need to do is call me, and I'll be there to back you up."

"I can never deserve you," he said roughly, his muscles tensing up at the thought that he might not live to see her again.

She grinned her perfect, irrepressible grin. "Killing Anubisa would go a long way toward changing *that*."

He laughed and headed for the most deadly, dangerous fight of his life.

Conlan, Ven, Justice, and Jack caught up to him as he reached the door to the Trident's chamber.

"Jack, please stay back with Quinn and protect her," Alaric asked, one warrior to another. "If I cannot . . . If I do not survive this, I will go to the afterlife knowing that you will be at her side."

Jack roared and ran back toward the doorway where Quinn stood, watching Alaric, her eyes enormous but dry.

"Now?" Conlan asked.

"Now," Alaric agreed.

They entered the chamber together, Justice and Ven right behind them. Alaric's shoulders relaxed a fraction at the sight of Anubisa levitating near the Trident's pedestal, where it still rested on its cushion. She hadn't been able to take it, yet.

"You cannot touch the tool of the sea god, you foul creature," he told her contemptuously.

"I kind of hope she tries," Ven said, as the princes fanned out to flank him. "I'm looking forward to watching it melt her hands off."

Anubisa shrieked with laughter, and Alaric saw Conlan's face harden at the sound. The dark memories of torture that must be contained in her laughter for Conlan made Alaric all the more determined to kill her, once and for all.

"You cannot stop me, even with your new abilities, O priest of light," she sneered. "Poseidon has abandoned his children while he plays power games with other pantheons, and I am delighted to step into the breach and finally, finally, murder every last one of the hideous Atlantean royal family."

She turned her horrible red gaze to Conlan, and she cupped her breasts with her hands. "Shall I nurse your fat baby with milk from my breasts, princeling? Shall I tell him bedtime stories of how his daddy bled and screamed at my whim for seven long years?"

"You will never touch my son," Conlan roared, and he ran toward her, raising his sword.

"No, Conlan," Alaric shouted, but it was too late.

Anubisa threw a spear formed of oily black smoke at Conlan. It smashed into his thigh and took him down. The spear disappeared, but the gaping wound in the prince's leg pulsed blood.

Ven ran to his brother and applied pressure to the wound, but when Alaric tried to go to Conlan, Anubisa laughed again.

"I think not. I like Conlan best when he is bleeding on the floor," she crooned, and she shot a barrage of magical arrows at Alaric that forced him to dodge and twist out of the way while blocking them with his own magic.

Alaric hurled a series of energy spheres at Anubisa, but she shattered them with ease, all the while keeping up her perusal of the Trident and continuing to shoot her deadly black spears and arrows at Conlan, Ven, and Alaric.

Justice, who had been quietly edging around the room, leapt at Anubisa from behind, but she waved a hand in the air, and he slammed backward against the wall so hard, headfirst, that he collapsed, either unconscious or dead, on the floor.

"I've wanted to kill that one for a while," she said, doing a little pirouette.

She reached out a hand—so close, almost touching the

Trident—and Alaric took advantage of her distraction to hurl a spear of his own at her. She twisted away at the last second, but the weapon, formed from pure, glowing, silvery blue light, sliced through her side, and she screamed as a flow of inky black blood stained her dress.

"I will kill you even more slowly for that," she shouted, levitating higher and higher into the air, until she floated above them.

Drops of her blood fell from her side, dripping steadily, but she appeared no weaker for the injury.

Alaric called to his new power and created a magical shield between Anubisa and Conlan, and he ran to the prince and sent a pulse of healing power through the leg wound. Conlan nodded his thanks, and he and Ven stood up and ran to the side just as Anubisa hurled a blast of power at them, destroying Alaric's shield.

"You cannot escape me, fools," she said, twirling around in midair. "I am all powerful. I am the goddess of Chaos and of Night. I am—"

"You are an ugly, twisted, sadistic, old *hag*, and my entire family has had enough of you," Conlan said, moving to stand side by side with Alaric.

Anubisa snapped to attention at his words, and her howl of outrage nearly shattered Alaric's eardrums. From the way the princes flinched, he could tell they'd felt it, too.

"Hag? Did you call me an ugly *hag*? I'm the most beautiful woman any of you have ever seen," she shrieked, floating down nearer to them either by intent or through sheer rage.

Ven took his place on Alaric's other side, quickly catching on. "Have you ever seen a vamp blood junkie? All strung out and filthy, hasn't bathed in weeks? Most of them are better-looking than you, you ugly, washed-up, *old woman*."

She howled again and began firing her dark spears, but Alaric blocked and destroyed every one of them. He glanced at Justice, wondered briefly what was even possible with his new powers, and decided that nothing ventured . . .

He threw a burst of healing energy across the entire chamber toward Justice, still lying on the floor behind Anubisa, and Justice sat up and grinned and gave Alaric the two-thumbs-up signal.

Anubisa never noticed a thing, because she was still shrieking with rage and throwing energy bolts at them with manic, deadly intent.

Justice, using the stealth he'd gained during centuries as one of the most lethal warriors in Atlantis, ran up behind Anubisa, raising his sword, and swung it with every ounce of his strength at her neck.

At the last possible second, some primal instinct warned the vampire, and she ducked, but the blade caught her in the shoulder and sliced her arm from her body. She screamed so long and so loud that Alaric was sure his skull would explode, but he ignored the pain and ran toward her, gathering every ounce of his magic as he ran.

This is it, Quinn, my beloved, my life, he sent to her. *If I survive this, I will never leave you again.*

She sent back no words, but simply a wave of courage and reassurance and warmth—she enveloped him in her love, and it gave him the courage to do what he almost certainly would not survive.

He put his hands around the throat of a goddess.

"You dare to touch me! I will kill you all," Anubisa screamed in his face, and a blast of such twisted, black, and powerful magic smashed into him that he very nearly lost his grip on her as she hissed, clawed, and fought him.

She regenerated her arm with little effort and swung out at the princes, but Conlan easily ducked her spear this time.

"Good-bye, Anubisa," Conlan said. "You are done. This is for my mother, and for seven long, wasted years."

With that, Conlan pushed Alaric to the side and plunged his sword into Anubisa's heart.

"This is for *my* mother, and for the lifetime I missed with my brothers," Justice said, and he plunged his sword into her neck.

"This is for all of our family over the last five thousand years who suffered because you didn't know how to take rejection," Ven said, and he shoved his dagger into her gut.

Her black, black blood spattered across the marble floor like macabre patterns of evil traced on a pristine scroll, and she screamed and screamed, calling so much dark power to her that Alaric knew she'd be able to heal her wounds and escape them before long.

He had only a single recourse available to him, and he had no way to know if he'd survive it.

He must use the Trident.

He leapt into the air, shot over to the pedestal, and dared to borrow the greatest power object of the sea god to whom he had once, so long ago, sworn his life.

"I call upon you for assistance, in the name of Poseidon, and in the name of Atlantis," he told the Trident, making the words both plea and command.

And, by all the gods, the Trident heard and responded.

It leapt into his hand, and Alaric whirled around and plunged its tip into Anubisa's body. The Trident blazed up with a corona of pure, silver-blue energy—power that nearly seared Alaric's skin off the bones of his hand where he held it. Power that no mere mortal was meant to wield rushed through him, and he shouted as the vampire screamed.

The room lit up with the glow of the Trident's magic, and Alaric was sure he would either explode or die from trying to channel it, because there was too much—far, far too much. It was pure, ocean-based life force—it rang with the song of the whales; it danced with the joy of the dolphins. It soared with the majesty of all sea creatures in Poseidon's dominion, and Alaric's body shook with the power of its mystery and majesty.

It was *life force*, and as such, it was anathema to a vampire, especially one who claimed to be a goddess of death.

Anubisa glowed a bright, terrifying blue, and light streamed from her eyes and nose and mouth and ears, and then she screamed and begged as the Trident stripped her magic, her powers, and, finally, her beauty from her, leaving her a shriveled, wasted creature lying on the ground.

They stood in a loose circle around Alaric and Anubisa—Conlan, Ven, and Justice—impassive, weapons ready, and they watched the monster who had tortured the Atlantean royal family for millennia as she died.

Alaric yanked the Trident from her skeleton and replaced it on its pedestal after cleansing it with a burst of purifying water magic, which took the very last ounce of his energy. Channeling the power of the Trident had exhausted him, and he had no idea when—or if—his magic would replenish, but he decided that must be a worry for another time.

"Atlantis is safe, and I have you to thank for it," Conlan said to Alaric, reaching out an arm to clasp his friend's.

"Thanks for the help," Justice told Alaric. "We were afraid we were done for."

Together, the four of them walked around Anubisa's body to stare at the Trident, now resting silently on its cushion but still glowing with barely contained power.

Ven whistled. "I can't believe you used that thing without getting blown up."

"Nor can I," Alaric confessed.

"Do you think Poseidon even knows Atlantis has risen?" Conlan asked.

A tiny sound alerted them to movement far too late for any of them to do anything about it, and the bolt of black magic smashed them all to the floor, face-first.

"He won't know until you are all dead," Anubisa shrieked.

Alaric raised his head to see a creature from a nightmare— all bones and melted flesh—hovering behind them, prepared to fire a death blow of magic, and Alaric called to magic that would not answer.

He'd burned out his powers wielding the Trident, and now his mistake would cost them all their lives.

No. Not Quinn. He reached deep inside himself for a reserve that he couldn't have guessed he had, and he came up swinging a sword of pure silver light. From seemingly out of nowhere, a small form came running across the floor toward Anubisa at the exact same time, firing bullet after bullet into the vampire.

"I think *not*," Quinn shouted.

When Anubisa whipped her head toward Quinn, Alaric's

blade sliced in an arc of flashing silver fire, and the vampire goddess's head flew through the air.

Anubisa's body, separated from her head, melted into a spiral of oily black smoke and then disappeared.

Alaric strode over to Quinn, who dropped the gun on the floor in a clatter of metal on marble.

"Your excellent distraction saved our lives," Alaric said, and then he lifted her into his arms and kissed the very breath out of her.

"I think it was your magic that saved our lives, and all of Atlantis," she replied, when she could talk again.

"We all did it," Alaric said, looking around the room. "Together."

Conlan walked over to Anubisa's head, which was slowly disintegrating against the wall. "If I were one of my ancestors, I'd display this on a pike on the castle walls."

"She'd deserve it," Justice snarled.

"But who wants to look at her ugly mug?" Ven said. "I'm going to go find my woman, if we're done fighting demons and vampires and any freaking other thing that might want a piece of us."

"Your woman?" Erin said, entering the room. "Really? We've been looking for you for half an hour." She looked around the room. "Why are you here? Taking a break?"

"They killed a vampire," Riley said, walking into the room holding Aidan.

"To be fair, it was *the* vampire. Anubisa is finally dead. And we killed a demon and all his brothers, too," Ven said, pulling Erin into his arms.

Keely ran into the room and headed straight for Justice. "Don't you ever, ever do that again."

"Do what?"

"Nearly die. I could *feel* it," she said, before kissing him.

"It wasn't on purpose. But now we feel like we can sleep without tainted dreams again," Justice told Keely. "We can't believe she's finally dead."

"Who's cleaning this up?" Erin wanted to know, gesturing

to the two oily black stains on the floor, which were all that was left of Anubisa's head and body.

"Since when is Alaric super-light-up man?" Keely asked.

"Later," Quinn promised. "Do we still have more vampires to kill?"

Keely shook her head, her red hair flying. "Nope. Anubisa must have been controlling them, because just about the time you must have been killing her, the rest of them melted and vanished. All of them. The only live vampire left on Atlantis is Daniel, and trust me, he killed his share of Anubisa's minions."

"He, too, has a special reason to hate her," Alaric said.

"Past tense," Quinn pointed out. "He *had* a special reason, because the wicked vampire goddess is dead!"

Alaric caught her when she leapt into his arms, and he turned and headed out.

"Don't call me, and don't knock on our door for at least twenty-four hours," he called back over his shoulder.

"You said 'our' door," Quinn said, smiling.

"You don't think you're getting away from me now, do you? After I saw you with that sword? I'm thinking hedge trimmer for a new job. You'd be great in a floppy hat," Alaric said, laughing down at her.

As they left the palace and he launched himself into the air, heading for the window of his rooms in the temple, she considered what he'd said.

"I don't really like floppy hats. I'm more fashionable than that."

"No, you're not."

"Yes, I am."

"Quinn, you are the most beautiful woman in the world to me, and I love you, but you look like you find your clothing in a homeless person's trash can."

"I guess you don't want me to buy a red bra and panties, then," she said, lowering her eyelashes and peeking up at him through them. "Am I seducing you yet?"

He groaned and flew faster. "I should have told them not to disturb us for forty-eight hours. Or three weeks."

"You have to bring me food this time," she said, practical to the last. "I'll need my energy to keep up with you."

Power flooded back into him as his magic recharged under the welcome sight of the moon over Atlantis, shining brightly on his people after so many thousands of years. His body began to glow again, and she smiled.

"You're lighting up. Does that mean my feminine wiles are working? If I even have feminine wiles," she said, laughing. "I think they got rusty over the past decade."

"Your wiles are more than sufficient to make me want to drive my cock inside you and never stop until you scream," he said sincerely, bending down to fasten his lips around her nipple right through her shirt. The power surged through him and into her body, and she moaned.

"Can't you go any faster?"

He flew through the window, tossed her on his bed, and ripped her clothes from her lovely, perfect body, while she frantically tore at his pants, finally succeeding in pulling them off.

"Please, please, *please*," she said, and she wrapped her hand around his erection.

It was his turn to moan.

He was thrusting into her body within seconds. She was screaming his name soon after.

He was going to be the happiest damn gardener in the history of the world.

Chapter 35

It wasn't twenty-four hours, after all. It was more like three days. Every time Alaric touched Quinn, his mind rebelled at the idea of letting the outside world anywhere near them just yet.

When he kissed her, she tasted like hope. Hope for a future that didn't involve swords or death. Hope for happiness and love.

He pulled her closer to him and stroked the curve of her hip, marveling anew at the texture of her skin. It was pale luminescence in the moonlight, softer than the finest Atlantean silk. Warm and delicate; tantalizing him with delight. His fingers traced the tip of her breast, and she shivered in response.

That had been a wondrous surprise to him—that his fierce rebel warrior woman would be so sensual in his bed. He lowered his head to kiss her nipple, and she gasped a little.

"Tell me you want me," he demanded, raising his head to look into her eyes, his voice low and rough. He needed to hear the words, even though her body showed him the evidence. "Tell me again and again."

"I do want you, you know I do," she said, her eyes darkening. "I want you more than I ever knew was possible."

She bit the curve of his neck, and need swamped him. Need and white-hot desire. He touched her cheek and wondered that this complex, enticing, incredible woman could truly be his.

He was *home*. Forever.

~~~~~

Quinn laughed a little as Alaric's eyes began to glow a hot emerald green. She'd never have to wonder if he wanted her. He broadcast his passion as strongly as his other emotions. She wanted him again and again and always. He was refuge and respite and release. He was love.

She opened her lips and her body to him and kissed him, tasting his mouth and tongue, and teasing him by nibbling at his bottom lip gently. His hard body shook in her arms, and she gloried in the feel of knowing he was losing control, even as she herself began to tremble.

Any remaining barriers between them dissolved as the magic of the soul-meld and the simpler, far older magic of love swirled around and through them, adding an edge of fierce intensity to their touch. She caressed the muscular line of his shoulder and then his chest, and he caught his breath when she traced her tongue over one flat nipple.

"I cannot get enough of your touch," he said. "Never. I might not ever let you leave my bed."

She laughed a little, but then she allowed her hand to roam lower until she grasped the hard length of his erection. "I may never let *you* leave. Did you ever consider that, my bossy Atlantean?"

His body tensed, and he pulled her even closer. "You have an hour to stop touching me like that," he said, grinning that deliciously wicked grin.

"I never knew it could be like this," she blurted out, honesty making her clumsy. "I never knew."

"Nor did I," he said, and then he kissed her until she

couldn't think, couldn't breathe, couldn't feel anything but the whirlwind of passion between them.

"But if I had known, I would have come after you a lot sooner," he said firmly.

Her laughter faded as he rolled over and settled his body over her.

"I find that I need to be inside you now. Do you agree?"

She wrapped her legs around him and guided him to her, sighing as he slowly entered her, inch by glorious inch. "I agree."

He thrust ever so slowly in and out of her, over and over, until she thought she'd go mad with frustrated desire.

"More," she urged, digging her fingers into his lovely, firm butt.

He grinned down at her, but the strain of maintaining control was showing on his face. "More what? I'm a simple warrior. You'll have to tell me what you want. Explicitly."

She felt her cheeks flame hot, but she was a rebel leader. A fighter. A strong woman. She could surely be a little brazen. She whispered in his ear exactly what she wanted him to do, and she made sure to use the words "hard" and "strong" and "deep."

Alaric lost all restraint, and he almost lost his mind. To hear such delightfully raunchy talk from his beautiful mate was an unexpected gift. He drove into her, harder and harder, claiming her in the most basic and primal way possible.

"I love you. You are mine, and you will never, ever leave me," he told her, desperate to make sure she understood.

"I love you, too, and you will never leave me, either," she replied, gasping, her beautiful face rosy with passion, and then she cried out as she crested, her body pulsing and clenching around his cock.

He couldn't resist the force of her climax; it took him over the edge to his own, and he raised his head and roared out her name while he came inside her.

"Mine. Forever," he whispered, as he kissed her cheeks and nose and forehead and lips, over and over and over. His mind was frantic to make sure she understood, even as his body was sated and replete.

"Forever won't be long enough," she murmured, nestling closer to him, and the final barrier inside his heart. that had been terrified of a future without her, finally fell to the realization that she loved him.

She loved him. Forever. He held her close as she fell asleep, smiling as he noticed that, this time, they were both glowing.

Quinn had never in her life spent three solid days doing nothing but engaging in utter hedonism. She felt drunk on pleasure. Anytime she wanted him, he was ready, and he always wanted her, so they spent most of their time making love and talking.

Making love and laughing together.

Making love and making plans.

She actually wanted to travel to every corner of the world just because she wanted to see the sights, not because she had to hunt and kill something there.

"London at Christmas," she said, writing it down on a tablet that was resting on Alaric's naked back. "Also, does even your back have to be buff? It seems a bit like showing off."

He laughed. "I don't know how to do swordplay exercises without using my back, but I can try."

She licked a path down his spine, distracted from the conversation and her list by his muscular perfection, and they forgot about the paper and pen for a few hours.

Another time, his housekeeper brought them dinner, and there was chocolate ice cream, and he decided to paint her body with it and discover if the contrast between the icy chocolate and his hot mouth could entice her into any further heights of pleasure.

Turns out that it could.

It took her nearly half an hour to learn how to breathe again after the ice cream.

They dressed up in formal robes he had in his closet and

danced to the music wafting in from the window when the Atlantean symphony played. But dancing involved touching, and they were too new to touching to be able to dance and not explore. The robes fell away, and soon his mouth was on her breast and her hands were on his butt, and then they were dancing in a whole different style on the silk coverlets on the bed.

He told her things he'd never shared with anyone, not even Conlan, and she told him of the terrors she'd faced as a rebel. She cried when he told her about the long days in the oubliette, and he tensed and gritted his teeth when she described the time the wolf shifter had caged her for three days, saving her for a snack, before she'd finally escaped.

"It was actually the best I ate that whole year," she said, laughing in retrospect at the experience, which had been terrifying at the time. "He kept feeding me roasted chicken to fatten me up, and I love roasted chicken. He would have been better off to eat the chicken himself and let me go. I was a lot of trouble, and I stole his wallet on the way out."

"How old were you?"

"Maybe seventeen," she said casually, and he winced inside at the thought of her teenage self going through such a horrible ordeal, but he tried not to let her see it.

The soul-meld didn't let them hide from each other, though, and she smiled. "You can't save me from my past, remember? You can only protect me in the future."

"We can protect each other. We are a good team," he said, and she rewarded him with a kiss, and then they didn't say much other than *yes*, and *please*, and *more*, for a little while.

On the third day, he brought up the scariest topics of all. Marriage and children.

"You do realize I want a little girl who looks just like you," he said, and she choked on her glass of wine.

"Do you really see me as mother material?"

He considered her question seriously. "You've been taking care of an entire rebel army for several years. Do you think a child would be more difficult than that?"

"Yes. I can't shoot my daughter if she annoys me."

He laughed, but she wasn't entirely sure she'd been kidding.

"Why don't we just spend more time with Aidan and see what we think?"

"Fine. For now," he said. "Also, do you want a church or an Elvis?"

This time she fell off the bed. When he leaned over, she stared up at him, not moving. "Do you even know what that means?"

"Yes, it means we will marry in the human way, and you will buy a horrible dress that looks like a cake, and also there will be real cake to eat, and Ven will take me to a bar in which a half-dressed woman will jump out of a very large cake."

He reached down and pulled her back on the bed. "What is this human obsession with cake?"

By the end of the third day, both of them were willing, if not exactly ready, to join the rest of the world again.

"Thank you for this," she told him. "This wonderful respite from anything dark or unpleasant in the world. I have never enjoyed any time more in my adult life."

"I, too, have not wanted this time to end. Perhaps we could make this a regular occurrence," he suggested. "Not only here, but in places around the world, as we travel for pleasure, as you said, and not for fighting or missions."

"I would love that," she admitted. "And I love you. I only hope that real life doesn't intrude and pull us apart."

"Never. In any event, we have a tiger shifter to cure."

Quinn and Alaric had dressed slowly, neither of them in a hurry to leave their refuge, but when they finally rejoined the rest of Atlantis, it was to find that only good things had been happening for the formerly lost continent, almost a reflection of their own path over the previous three days, so they could add guilt-free to the list of superlatives about their time together. Quinn headed off in search of her sister and nephew, feeling lighter than she had in many years.

A baby? Her? No.

Well, maybe.

She put her hands in her pockets and whistled as she walked, and she almost didn't notice and certainly didn't mind when many of those she passed smiled indulgently. A life of leisure. She could get used to it.

Maybe.

"About time he unchained you from the bed," said a voice she'd been afraid she'd never hear again. She whirled around to find Jack, in human form, grinning at her like a big loon.

She ran at him and threw herself into his arms, and he hugged her a little too tightly, for a little too long, before he put her down, but they both pretended not to notice.

"So, are you happy?" His voice was rough and almost hoarse, as if spending so much time in tiger shape had damaged it, or maybe the hoarseness was from the emotion she could feel circling around in him.

Regret and resignation were there, true, but also the glimmerings of something that felt a little bit like peace.

"I've never been happier," she was able to tell him honestly. "But what happened? How did you finally change back? I thought you'd be a tiger forever."

"It wasn't easy," he said, his expression strained. "Part of me—the biggest part of me—never wanted to come back. I've seen too much, Quinn. Done too much, in the name of the rebellion. I think that when my body was injured so badly, my spirit decided it was time to retreat."

"But you came back," she said, fiercely glad it was true. "You were still a tiger when you arrived, but now—"

Jack started walking, and she matched her pace to his long strides as they roamed together through the gardens. "Now I'm human again. Mostly. I came back because the portal arrived and told us you were in danger."

He left it at that, and she let that part of it go. She would have done the same for him. She needed to know the rest, though.

"When did you decide to shift? How? I tried so hard in

Japan to help you find your way back. I'm sorry I failed." She walked a little faster, determined not to let him see the tears forming in her eyes.

"You did help," he said gently, touching her arm. "But this was something I needed to do on my own. I think it was the aftermath of the battle, here in Atlantis, realizing that if an eleven-thousand-year-old lost continent could find its way, then so could a relatively young tiger shifter."

He fell quiet, and when she realized he wouldn't say anything else about it, their talk continued to less personal subjects. They walked in the gardens, circling under and around the fantastical trees and fountains, engrossed in catching up and content with the familiar pleasure of spending time together. All the while, however, Quinn had the bittersweet feeling that the conversation was a prelude to good-bye.

"I'm ready to move on and do something else," Jack finally said, when their talk of Atlantis and the world had died down. "The next group of rebel leaders has already stepped into our shoes, and I don't want to go back to that life anyway. I think this time I'll try seeing the world without the need to take charge and save the day. I have an uncle in Florida I've been meaning to visit for a few years. He lives in a town named Dead End, can you believe it?"

Quinn laughed. "Sounds interesting."

"Probably not, but that's what I'm looking for right now. Someplace *not* interesting." He plucked a flower off an absurdly round purple bush and handed it to her.

"You'll always be a hero, Jack," she said. "No matter where you go. That's who you are, and you can't change that."

His eyes darkened, and just for a moment, it was the tiger looking out at her, and not the man. "I don't know if that's still true, Quinn. I need time to learn who I am without the battles and the blood and the killing."

"I'm always here if you need me," she said. "You know that, right?"

He hugged her, hard, and then let go, and she felt a moment of deep sadness, as if he'd already gone.

"Quinn, I . . . If you ever need me—"

"I know," she said, brushing the tears off her face with the back of her hand. "I know. Same goes."

She reached out, one final time, to try to sense his emotions as she told him she loved him and she wished him well, and they both promised to keep in touch.

She felt it in him, as in her own heart, that they both doubted they would.

They didn't say good-bye this time. Once had been enough.

She watched him walk away, down toward the shore where he'd said a friend with a boat was waiting, and she finally let the tears fall freely.

"Good luck, Jack. I love you, too."

Alaric walked up behind her and pulled her into his arms. She rested her head on the hard muscles of his chest and watched Jack disappear into the noise and chaos of the people renovating the Atlantean port, so long unused.

"He deserves someone who loves him the way I love you," she said through her tears.

"He will find her," Alaric said. "I have a very strong feeling about that tiger. He's going to have an interesting life."

"Oh, boy. I'm not sure that's a good prediction," Quinn said, laughing a little. "Our lives have been far too interesting already."

"It's an Atlantean curse, you know. May you live in interesting times," Alaric said. "And so true of the Atlantean family who adopted Faust. When I saw him earlier today, he'd just set the archery targets on fire. All of them."

Quinn started laughing and turned around to look at him. "He's a good kid. He'll do well. But anyway, I thought that saying was Chinese."

Alaric raised one silken eyebrow, and she started laughing. "Yeah, yeah, I know. You guys were here first. Well, my interesting Atlantean, let's go to the palace. Riley is making me try on some ridiculous fancy dress for her coronation."

"The queen's sister cannot wear rags," Alaric said. "However, you could wear those red silk undergarments, so I can think of taking them off you with my teeth—"

"While you're crowning Conlan and Riley king and

queen? I think not." She pretended to be horrified by the suggestion, but then she stood on tiptoe and whispered a very, very naughty suggestion of what he could think about instead, and when he groaned and yanked her against him, she kissed him, right there in the middle of everything, for a very long time.

Chapter 36

The palace throne room, Atlantis, a week later

"In the name of Poseidon, I crown you King Conlan of Atlantis. Long may you reign!" Alaric placed the gem-encrusted crown that he knew Conlan would probably never wear again on his friend's bowed head, and an overwhelming feeling of peace swept through him, as the crowd of Atlanteans and visiting dignitaries roared their approval with thunderous applause.

Finally, *finally*, the prince was crowned king, and the Atlantean ruling succession was secure. Now it was Conlan's turn. Alaric swept his ceremonial cloak, rich velvet in Conlan's colors of cerulean blue and silver, to one side, bowed low to his friend the king, and then handed him a second, smaller crown.

The king turned to his wife, the princess Riley, and smiled. Both of them wore shining silver, edged in the same deep ocean blue as Alaric's clothing, and baby Aidan, safe in his mother's arms, shone like a tiny beacon in matching blue and silver. Ven, Erin, Justice, and Keely stood on either side of the throne, dressed in similar finery, presenting a united front of the Atlantean royal family to all of Atlantis and, through the miracle of modern media, to the entire world.

Quinn, standing next to her sister, wore a simple blue gown edged in silver, and Alaric almost could not bear to look at her for fear he'd forget every word of the coronation ceremony and simply whisk her off to his rooms and ravish her.

Again.

The rehearsal had gone badly for that very reason.

Stand down, boy, she sent to him, laughter infusing her thoughts. *Let's get them crowned, and we can escape the party early.*

Conlan gently placed the crown upon his wife's head, and then turned to the assembled crowd. "Behold my wife, Queen Riley. Long may she reign!"

When the applause died down, Conlan took his son and hugged him, and then he addressed the crowd.

"We have endured much in our millennia of isolation from the world, but it has made us stronger as a people. Today, Riley and I stand before you, your representatives to the international community, and we promise to do everything in our power to bring Atlantis into the world as a strong, vibrant country whose people believe in peace, justice, and freedom. Long live Atlantis!"

The crowd picked up the chant. "Long live Atlantis! Long live Atlantis!"

The cheers were deafening and lasted a long time, but Alaric, always tuned in to the undercurrents, noticed a few small pockets of resentment. A human queen of Atlantis, when there had always been many women willing and ready to step up to the job of being Conlan's wife—well, that was certainly a reason for discord. Politics and maneuvering, usually at the forefront of any royal court but relatively unknown in Atlantis, were beginning to surface after thousands of years of relative peace.

An Atlantis beneath the waves was a far different proposition than an Atlantis above the waves. Outside forces would be a factor—shifting alliances and constant betrayals—

"Why the frown, Alaric?" Conlan said, clapping him on the back. "Can you not find a smile at my coronation?"

Alaric's forebodings dissipated, and he grinned. "I'm sorry, Your Majesty. May I bring you some chilled grapes, Your Majesty?"

Conlan winced. "Don't even joke about that. I've already had to deal with an increase in bowing and curtseying from a lot of people on my palace staff who should know better."

Ven pounded his brother on the back. "No worries. Just wander on down to the warrior training grounds and I'll kick your ass in a sparring match."

Justice grinned. "We will knock that kingly arrogance out of you in no time, brother."

The queen took her husband's arm and pretended to glare at them all. "You can knock each other's heads together later, boys. We have a coronation party to attend."

She, Conlan, and the baby made their way through the room, chatting and laughing and making each person in their conversational orbit feel special.

"It's a gift," Quinn said, slipping her hand into Alaric's and indicating her sister. "They make the royalty thing look easy, don't they?"

"Long may they reign," he replied. "Conlan suggested I might want to sit at the high table at dinner and serve in an ambassadorial capacity."

She burst out laughing. "Has he *met* you?"

"I wondered the same thing," Alaric said dryly. "I'm not exactly the most tactful or political person."

"Suck it up, buttercup," she whispered, still laughing, as the first of many of the Atlanteans and foreign guests came up to talk to them, barring them from escaping for a very long time.

~~~

Quinn escaped to a dark corner of the corridor that led to the banquet hall, and she sat down on a bench and immediately removed her shoes, sighing in blissful gratitude and relief. An icy breeze caressed her bare legs, and she smiled.

"I can fight battles on little sleep, march for hours on little food, and survive beatings and worse, but I have to admit I've met my match in these instruments of torture Riley made me wear," she said to the seemingly empty corridor.

Alaric immediately materialized, his eyes glowing hot emerald green. "You sensed my presence."

"I will always be able to sense your presence, especially now that we're soul-melded," she said, trying not to pounce on him. He was just so unbearably gorgeous in his ceremonial attire, and she had the privilege of knowing what he looked like underneath the silk and velvet. "So you can quit trying to sneak up on me."

"I never sneak," he said, joining her on the bench with his usual fluid grace. "I was merely trying to escape the party with some measure of subtlety, rather than tossing energy spheres at the Chinese ambassador when he spoke rudely to his wife."

"You understand Chinese?"

He raised an eyebrow. "I speak all languages. It is one of the gifts that comes with the duties of Poseidon's high priest."

"About that," Quinn began, hesitantly. "If you've changed your mind and want to keep your job—"

He lifted her chin with one finger and proceeded to devour her mouth with searing kisses that tasted like wine and spice and Alaric. She leaned into him and put her arms around his neck, not even caring that somebody could walk down the hall at any minute.

"I want to say I'll race you to our rooms, but my feet hurt too much," she admitted, when she finally pulled away.

He promptly lifted her feet into his lap and massaged them, adding tiny bursts of healing energy, so she was soon moaning in pleasure and relief.

"I'll give you five minutes to cut that out," she said, leaning her head back against the wall.

"I have a better idea," he said. He scooped her up into his arms and strode off down the corridor, in the direction opposite to the banquet hall.

"My shoes," she protested. "You left my shoes."

"You hate the shoes, why would you care?" Alaric sounded honestly puzzled. "Is this to be like the cake conversation?"

"What cake conversation . . . Oh. That cake conversation. No, I gave up on that one after the Elvis bit," she said, laughing in spite of herself.

"That," he said decisively, "is entirely too bad."

He turned into an open doorway, still carrying Quinn, and she was shocked to see that the room was full.

"Put me down," she hissed at him, but he ignored her and strode to the front of the room, still carrying her, while everyone watched and grinned at them. Quinn's face burned so hot she probably could have lit up all of Atlantis.

"Where are they?" Alaric called out, and just then a door opened in the near wall and Conlan and Riley stepped through into the room.

"We're here," Conlan said. "Are you ready?"

Alaric finally released Quinn so she could stand on her own two—bare—feet, and she blinked. "Ready for what?"

He took her hands. "We could not find an Elvis, but Queen Riley has informed us that the king of Atlantis has the legal power to perform a wedding."

Quinn's mouth fell open. "A wedding? Now?"

Alaric knelt gracefully before her. "Quinn Dawson, *mi amara*, heart of my heart and soul of my soul, will you wed me, bear my children, and remain by my side for all of eternity?"

Quinn blinked really hard, but several tears escaped as she stared at the most powerful man she had ever known, who knelt before her asking for her hand.

"I can never deserve you," she whispered, taking his hands and pulling him to his feet.

"Wearing those red silk undergarments would go a long way toward changing *that*," he said, flashing his most wickedly seductive grin.

"Alaric," she said, flushing a hot red all over again.

But the laughter that surrounded them floated on waves of emotion that were warm, encouraging, and kind. She turned to see that the people in the room were in fact only the Warriors of Poseidon and their mates, and every single one of them felt like family.

Family.

"I believe I have waited more than long enough for your response," Alaric said, his face beginning to show the strain of doubt.

"You knew my answer before you ever asked, my warrior priest," she said, throwing her arms around his neck. "Yes, and yes, and yes. Forever and ever."

She kissed him, and only the repeated sound of royal throat clearing brought her out of it.

When Alaric put an arm around her and nudged her to turn toward Conlan, she realized that everyone in the room was paired up and also facing their new king and queen.

Conlan turned to each couple in turn, and before continuing, he waited for each to respond with their assent to the question, "Do you each take the other as beloved mate, husband and wife, for now and until the waters of the ocean run dry?"

He stood before them. "Alaric and Quinn."

Even as Quinn said a fervent *yes*, Alaric took her hand and placed a silver ring, set with a beautiful sapphire, on her finger.

"Yes," he said, looking into her eyes with his beautiful emerald gaze. "For always and eternity."

Conlan and Riley smiled at them, and Riley sniffled a little, before they turned to the next couple. Quinn listened to the words, almost in a daze, as she stared at Alaric.

"Ven and Erin."

"Justice and Keely."

"Bastien and Kat."

"Alexios and Grace."

"Marie and Ethan."

"Brennan and Tiernan."

"Christophe and Fiona."

"Serai and Daniel."

When each of them had responded with a heartfelt assent,

Conlan flung open and held wide his arms. "Then, without further ado, and by the authority vested in me as king of Atlantis, I now pronounce you husbands and wives," he said, smiling. "And long may you live and love, standing by our side and ushering the next generation of Atlanteans into the world."

A little cheering, a lot of kissing, and many tears and hugs later, Quinn and Alaric had congratulated and been congratulated by everyone in the room. Riley had hugged her tightly for a long time, saying over and over again how happy she was, and happily planning family dinners, but then Alaric and Ven walked to the door next to the one through which Conlan and Riley had arrived, and Ven shouted for quiet.

"We have a little surprise, boys and girls," Ven said, grinning like a fool.

He and Alaric flung open the door and led the group into a courtyard garden that had been transformed into a private wedding reception just for the newly wedded couples and a few close friends.

"Hit it, Marcus," Ven called out, and Quinn was surprised to see the very relaxed head of the palace guard leaning down to an enormous array of musical equipment.

The silken tone of Elvis Presley's voice soared over the room, and Quinn didn't know whether to laugh or cry when the familiar lyrics began. "You got Elvis, after all."

"I couldn't help falling in love with you, either," Alaric told her solemnly. "I tried to fight it; I never believed I could deserve you. But love had different plans for me than a lifetime of solitude and loneliness."

A blast of salt-drenched sea air blew Quinn from Alaric's arms, and it was their only warning before Poseidon appeared in the center of the room, next to the enormous seven-tiered cake.

AND YET YOU DID NOT ASK ME ABOUT MY PLANS FOR YOUR LIFETIME, ALTHOUGH YOU ARE HIGH PRIEST OF MY TEMPLE.

When Poseidon's voice roared through the room, the speakers exploded in pops of electrical sparks and smoke.

"I resign," Alaric said, crossing to Quinn and taking her hand. "Find someone else to do the job."

Poseidon, who'd decided to appear in the guise of a ten-foot-tall Atlantean warrior, sneered at Alaric but then appeared to be distracted by the cake. He lifted the entire top tier and put it in his mouth, and a blissful smile spread across his face.

I DO NOT UNDERSTAND THIS HUMAN FASCINATION WITH CAKE, BUT I APPROVE.

"You can't—" Quinn began, but he pointed one giant finger at her, and she found she couldn't speak.

DO NOT TELL ME WHAT I CANNOT DO, HUMAN. YOU HAVE ALREADY RUINED THE MOST POWERFUL HIGH PRIEST IN ATLANTEAN HISTORY WITH YOUR SEDUCTIVE WAYS.

Quinn didn't know whether to be appalled or amused at "seductive ways."

Alaric stepped between them, powering up his magic until he shone as bright as the noon sun. He waved a hand at Quinn, and Poseidon's hold on her broke.

"She ruined nothing," Alaric told Poseidon, his voice icy calm. "My power increased a thousandfold during the soul-meld."

WILL YOU DEFY ME FOR HER?

Poseidon roared, and suddenly the Trident flew through the air and into his grasp. He pointed it at Alaric, and Quinn ran to put her body in front of her new husband's.

"No," she shouted. "No. Don't even think about hurting him. He has been yours for hundreds of years. It's my turn now."

Alaric tried to push her behind him again, but she planted her feet and wouldn't move. Poseidon glared at her, and everyone in the garden seemed to take a deep breath at once, undoubtedly waiting for him to blast her to pieces for her insolence.

Instead, the sea god started laughing. Quinn and Alaric stared at each other as Poseidon laughed, long and hard, louder and louder, until finally he slapped one hand on his enormous thigh and subsided.

I THINK THIS ONE WILL MAKE STRONG BABIES, ALARIC. IT'S ABOUT TIME YOU FOUND YOUR BALLS AND STOOD UP TO ME. YOU HAVE MY BLESSING. WHERE IS THE ALE?

With that, Poseidon turned to the fountain, pointed the Trident at it, and turned the bubbling water into ale. He snatched a punch bowl off the nearest table, dumped its contents on the grass, and scooped himself up a couple of gallons of ale, which he proceeded to down in one thirsty gulp.

KING CONLAN. YOU WILL TELL ME YOUR PLANS FOR MY ATLANTIS NOW THAT THE THREAT OF WAR BETWEEN THE GODS HAS PASSED.

As Conlan and Riley walked over to the sea god, Quinn finally let out the breath she'd been holding.

"Do you think we're going to be okay?"

Alaric nodded, a smile playing at the edges of his lips. "I think we're going to be better than okay. We're going to be terrific."

An hour or so later, after Poseidon had vanished, and they'd said their good-byes to Riley and Conlan and everyone else—with many promises to return soon—and Alaric had invested Myrken with the title of interim high priest of Poseidon, which had left the man nearly reeling with shock, they made their way to a quiet corner of the garden and Alaric called to the portal.

"Where do you want to go first?" he asked her, pulling her into his arms and kissing her forehead, nose, and cheeks, before capturing her lips.

The portal chose that moment to appear, and a familiar voice sounded from its center. "Dude, let's hit it."

"Do not *ever* call me dude," Alaric growled.

"Rio, I think," Quinn said, laughing and pulling Alaric's head down for another long, leisurely kiss. "I want to see if Alaric knows how to dance to something spicy."

As they entered the portal and spun through the vortex

toward their future, Alaric could have sworn he heard the portal laughing. He chose to ignore it.

"I am very good at naked dancing, as I have proven many times," he murmured in her ear.

She blushed as he continued describing all the things he claimed to be very good at doing naked. Her arrogant, amazing Atlantean warrior priest.

"I will love you for the rest of my life," she said fiercely, interrupting his naughty recitation.

As they stepped out of the portal into the hot, fragrant air of late afternoon in Rio, he flashed her one of those purely male smiles that melted her bones and made her body heat up in all the most delicious places. "And I will love you for all of eternity, *mi amara*, my heart."

"That's totally awesome, dudes," the portal called out to them before it vanished.

Alaric narrowed his eyes. "We have *got* to find another way to travel," he grumbled.

She started laughing and took his hand, and they walked forward into their future.

Together. Forever.

And she wouldn't have it any other way.

Epilogue

Château des Loups, in the Swiss Alps, six months later

Quinn sipped the fine cognac and sighed with pleasure. "This is the best trip we've taken yet."

"You said that about Paris," Alaric said, smiling at her over his ale. He was sure she became more beautiful every day, especially now that she actually ate on a regular basis. "Also Rio, Alaska, Fiji, London, China—am I forgetting any?"

"They were *all* the best trips ever," she said happily. "Nobody needs me to tell them what to do, or figure out how to feed fifty new recruits with a budget that doesn't stretch past macaroni and cheese, or shoot any vampires, or rescue any skunk shifters—"

"Really?" He grimaced. "Skunk shifters?"

"In the Smoky Mountains," she said. "You wouldn't believe—"

"I don't want to know," he said firmly. "Some stories are better left untold."

She grinned. "I didn't know you were squeamish, tough guy."

"I simply have discriminating taste," he said haughtily. "And skunks don't taste good."

They both laughed.

She bit her lip, always a sign of nerves with her. "So you don't ever get, I don't know, maybe a little bored?"

He wondered how to avoid any hidden reefs in this conversation. "Well," he said cautiously, "there are times when I wonder if I could be of use for more than vacation and leisure."

Her eyes lit up. "Exactly! Not that we want to go back to the way things were, but maybe we could do something to help someone once in a while. You know, not officially but on a kind of pro bono basis."

He grinned at her and leaned back in his chair. "Yes. I think I'd like that. Only if you would, of course. I'm perfectly content to spend all day every day licking that place on your—"

"Alaric!" Her cheeks turned scarlet, as they always did when he teased her, and he marveled anew that his wanton wife was so shy in so many ways.

A commotion at the front of the lodge caught their attention, and a man and woman clutching each other ran in, shouting and crying.

"Our son, please, somebody help us, they took our son," the man shouted.

His wife, for clearly they were a couple, just sobbed, unable even to speak.

"We were on the trail behind the lodge, and they came out of nowhere, like giant hairy ghosts," the man said, his eyes wild. "We've never seen such monsters! You must believe me, we would never make this up. They were gray, with red eyes, and at least eight feet tall—"

The old man nursing a whiskey at the bar interrupted him. "We've got a feral pack of shape-shifting yetis around here. They like to take kids, young and juicy. Let 'em sit around for a couple of days before they kill 'em, so you still have a chance if you go now."

The woman's eyes rolled back in her head and she dropped like a stone—fainted dead away. Her husband caught her on the way down, but then he burst into tears. "Who will help me?"

Quinn put her hand on Alaric's. "Oh, honey, isn't it a lovely day for a hike?"

"It's freezing outside."

She stroked her lips with one finger and then lightly licked her lips and finger, both, while she watched her husband's eyes glaze over.

"Brisk, is what I meant to say," he amended. "Great day for a brisk walk."

Quinn stood up and walked over to the couple sitting on the floor. "Don't worry. We'll find him for you."

"Yetis," Alaric said, coming up behind her with her coat. "It had to be yetis."

"Better than skunks," she reminded him. "Our life together will never be boring."

"Thank the gods for that," he murmured, before he helped her into her coat and walked out onto the frozen mountain-side to hunt for shape-shifting yetis.

In the very back of the bar, a large man with eyes that constantly shifted from blue to green to blue again watched them go.

AND HE CALLED ME A DERANGED FOOL, Poseidon thought, smiling fondly. *I'LL HAVE HIM BACK YET. ESPECIALLY WHEN THEY FIND OUT THEIR FIRST DAUGHTER IS ON THE WAY. THEY SHOULD NAME HER AFTER ME.*

POSEIDONA, I THINK.

Still smiling, the sea god dropped a gold coin on the table and vanished. He had the next generation of Atlanteans to worry about now. That Prince Aidan was going to be a handful . . .